THE DUST OF DEATH

An Inspector Starrett Mystery

Paul Charles was born and raised in Magherafelt in the north of Ireland and is one of Europe's best-known music promoters and agents. He is the author of eight Inspector Christy Kennedy novels, the most recent of which, *Sweetwater*, was published by Brandon in 2006.

PAUL CHARLES
THE DUST OF DEATH
An Inspector Starrett Mystery

First published in 2007 by Brandon
an imprint of Mount Eagle Publications
Dingle, Co. Kerry, Ireland, and
Unit 3, Olympia Trading Estate, Coburg Road, London N22 6TZ, England

www.brandonbooks.com

2 4 6 8 10 9 7 5 3

ISBN 978-086322-369-3

Mount Eagle Publications/Sliabh an Fhiolair Teoranta receives support from
the Arts Council/An Chomhairle Ealaíon.

Cover design: www.designsuite.ie
Typesetting by Red Barn Publishing, Skeagh, Skibbereen
Printed in the UK

Dedication and thanks

To John McIvor for his company, wit and humour on the
hundreds of hours of driving around the length and breadth of
the county introducing me to his Donegal. Further thanks are
due and offered to Steve and the fab Brandon team for their
invaluable energy and support; to Terry Fitzgerald for her
eagle eye; to Andy and Cora for a lifetime's energy and to
Catherine for the sense of adventure that has taken us down
many a lane in County Donegal.

Chapter One

I T HAD EVERYTHING to do with light, which itself has everything to do with darkness.

As Garda Inspector Starrett wandered around the space, he couldn't help but think that this crime wouldn't have been half as effective on a dark winter's morning as it was on the first Friday of summer.

No, he thought, for this crime to enjoy the utmost impact, it needed the power of the early-morning summer sunlight that was shining through the stained-glass window. The coloured light gave it the illusion of being itself a biblical scene cut in a stained-glass window.

In his twelve-year career as a member of Ireland's national police service, An Garda Síochána, the inspector had found that if he focused on this kind of thinking he could pick his way better through the minefield of the crime scenes he came across. One slight trip and he might stumble into the area of "How could humans possibly do this to each other?" and he would be of absolutely no use to the poor unfortunates before him. Not that catching the perpetrator, or perpetrators, was ever going to be of any real use to the deceased. It could, however, act as some kind of closure for the relatives and loved ones left behind.

Starrett walked slowly towards the remains of what had once been a human body.

The body would have been visible to any man, woman or child who might have entered the Second Federation Church on Church Street in Ramelton, County Donegal, that morning. Geographically speaking, Donegal is in northern Ireland, although politically it's part of the Republic of Ireland, or, as it is now popularly known, southern Ireland. The church had been started in Dallas, Texas, in 1908 by a Donegal man, William O'Donnell, and the premises the gardaí were cautiously starting to search was their only church outside of the USA.

"My God, my God, why hast thou forsaken me?" Starrett murmured. When Jesus called out that verse from Psalm 22, was he pointing the finger of accusation at his Father, or merely accepting his fate? Starrett's mind wandered down through the rest of the psalm to, "My throat is dried up like baked clay; and my tongue cleaveth to my jaws; and thou hast brought me into the dust of death."

Starrett wondered what the last words of the victim before him might have been. Who did this poor unfortunate in front of him accuse in *his* final moments? Because, just like Jesus, the victim had been pinned to a cross. But unlike Jesus, he had been crucified inside a house of worship.

Chapter Two

"OUR BOYO HASN'T just been nailed to the cross," Starrett said, as much to himself as to Garda Sergeant Garvey, who, as usual, was by Starrett's side. "No, Packie, he looks like he's suffered the indignity of a copy of the full crucifixion."

Inspector Starrett, a forty-five-year-old local, spoke in a slow, considered drawl, punctuated with many pauses, which sometimes gave the impression that he was voicing thoughts that had just occurred to him.

Sergeant Garvey, thirty years old, from Galway and a hurling champion, tended to let his superior do most of the talking—and most of the thinking. However, Packie, as he was known on and off the field, wasn't scared of rolling up his sleeves and getting stuck in to less cerebral police work. It wasn't exactly that he didn't need directing (on or off the field); he positively thrived on it.

Starrett and Garvey considered the victim in silence.

The victim was male, Caucasian and probably in his early forties. He was roughly five feet ten inches tall and approximately 140 pounds in weight. Aside from a chamois loincloth, he was naked. What must have been dark brown hair was severely matted and almost black from the blood which had wept from the lesions his barbed-wire crown of thorns had caused. His head hung slightly to the left and at about a ninety-degree angle to his chest.

A stainless-steel nail had been driven through each wrist, fixing one to each end of the horizontal beam of the cross. The right foot was placed over the left, and another six-inch stainless-steel nail pinned them both to the lower part of the stipes of the cross. There was an inch-wide stab wound six or so inches beneath the heart.

His lifeblood had dripped from his many wounds, and the red and blue patterned floor was distorted with what looked like the outline of a great red-black landmass, similar in shape to North America—with Australia grafted on to the east coast for good measure.

"Who discovered the body?" Starrett asked.

"The caretaker, Thomas Black," Packie replied, not for a single moment taking his eyes off the cross. "He came in here as usual at about 8.40 this morning to clean up after yesterday's service."

"How many services do they have?" Starrett enquired.

"Every weekday at 7 p.m., and then there's three services on Sunday: eight o'clock in the morning, noon and seven in the evening," Packie replied. "They work on accommodating the farmers: eight in the morning's just after milking time; noon's just before lunch time; and seven comes after second milking."

"Was the church locked up?"

"No. It's the Second Federation Church's policy to leave its doors open at all times as a safe haven for those in need. Apparently in America, at least according to Thomas Black, they leave bread and water as well."

"If they tried to do that around here, people would start using the church as a café," Starrett said, walking towards the body, carefully skirting the blood.

The rough, weathered pine cross had been attached crudely by rope to the front of the high pulpit, into which Starrett cautiously climbed. From his new vantage point, he could see—just—that the victim's upper torso around the shoulders and on the sides was a crazy maze of congealed bloody welts.

As Starrett turned to descend the nine steps, he noticed that local Garda Francis Casey and Bean Gharda Nuala Gibson had entered the church and were standing by the door, four eyes transfixed by the cross.

"Make sure no one else comes in here," Starrett ordered before continuing his journey around the congealed blood shape. But once again the elegantly carved antique oak pulpit obscured his full view of both the victim's back and the front of the cross.

Starrett turned towards Packie. "Did Thomas Black say whether or not he generally had a lot of cleaning up to do after their services?"

Starrett could see that the blood had drained from the usually rosy-cheeked sergeant's face. Years had been added to the deceptively youthful looks of his sergeant; neither he nor new arrivals, Gibson and Casey, could drag their eyes away from the horrific scene.

Starrett clapped his hands three times, the sound echoing around the church loudly, snapping them out of their trances.

"OK?" Starrett said loudly. "Let's get stuck into our work here, please."

"Sorry," Packie replied. "Ahm, yes, the caretaker said that it was mostly sweetie papers and tissues."

"And was there any such mess this morning?" Starrett interrupted.

"Well, Thomas Black did say that when he first arrived he didn't immediately notice the addition to the altar, and he worked his way through the pews cleaning up. It wasn't until he'd made it up as far as the elders' front pew that he registered our friend here."

"You're joking!" Starrett said.

"I know, I know. I said the same thing to him, and he said he was so preoccupied by his own thoughts. He said that when he did see it though—when he'd reached the front pews—the shock was so powerful it literally took the legs out from under him. More so because he'd been in the victim's presence for so long without realising it."

"And the sweepings?" Starrett pushed.

"Still beside the front pew."

Starrett heard a slight commotion at the door and turned towards it.

"Sorry, sir, you can't come in just now," Gibson was saying, stepping into the path of a stout, five-foot-five ball of energy.

"Whatdoya mean, trying to deny me entry to my father's house?" came the reply from a fine oratorical voice, one you would never have placed inside its owner's body.

There was a little pantomime scuffle as both Gibson and Casey tried to restrain the intruder, who, when he saw the cross and the body nailed to it, dropped to his knees, clasped his hands in front of the most southern of his chins and recited: "My God, my God, why hast thou forsaken me?"

"Hello, Ivan," Starrett said as he made his way back towards the entrance. "I've been expecting you."

"First Minister, please," the wee man said as he awkwardly rose from his knees, using Gibson and Casey as human crutches. "What exactly is this travesty, Inspector?"

Starrett offered his hand in friendship. It was ignored. "Sorry, First Minister Morrison, pray forgive me. It's just that I'm not used to seeing you without your cassock. Let's you and me leave the professionals here to examine the scene, though I'm not sure how much good it will do. I've always thought that if a murderer is stupid enough to leave any incriminating evidence, he might as well leave us a note, and most murderers in my experience are anything but stupid. My sergeant here, on the other hand, believes in getting out the proverbial fine-toothcomb. Tell me, First Minister, have you ever seen a fine-toothcomb?"

Moving his ignored hand to Morrison's back, Starrett applied a gentle force to turn the First Minister of Ramelton's Second Federation Church back in the direction of the early-morning light.

Chapter Three

INSPECTOR STARRETT AND First Minster Morrison stood on the steps of the church. Starrett, his hands buried deep in the pockets of his black polished trousers, swayed backwards and forwards on to the toes of his well-polished, black leather shoes. The pink collar and cuffs of his shirt stuck out from under his blue woollen jumper, and his protection against the legendary and lethal Donegal winds and frequent showers was a black, American-style, zip-up windcheater.

Morrison was dressed straight off the peg in a yellow and black patterned three-piece suit and a mismatched light blue paisley shirt. The sandals without socks and the uneven buttoning of his shirt were further testimony that he'd dressed in a hurry.

"Look at that, would you?" Starrett said, nodding in the general direction of Rathmullan. They could see in the distance—over the rooftops of Ramelton—Lough Swilly and beyond Buncrana to Slieve Main, Slieve Snaght and the other mountain ranges of the Inishowen Peninsula in all their majestic and colourful glory. "I can never figure out, when we have all this incredible natural beauty on our doorstep, how anyone could ever be inspired to create a man-made scene of such darkness as the one we've just witnessed inside."

"It appears that we humans find more inspiration looking within ourselves than we do looking outwards," Morrison replied smugly.

"Too deep for me, First Minister," Starrett said, and they both fell into silence. The inspector continued to be captivated by the views while Morrison turned around to gawk at the several crows on the roof of the church playing a precarious game of leapfrog on the ridge of the Bangor Blue slated roof of the church.

"Have you figured out yet who played the part of Pontius Pilate in our indoor drama?" asked Morrison

"Bugger Pontius Pilate; I still haven't figured out the identity of the boyo pinned to the cross," Starrett admitted.

"Oh, that part's easy. That's James Moore; he's a local carpenter."

"One of your flock?" Starrett asked, thinking that the great thing about clergy, no matter their denomination, was that you just needed to give them a wee push and they were off. Wind and push.

"No, no, we're not divine enough for the likes of him," Morrison admitted, looking as if he were trying to act uncharacteristically chummy. "Some people really do need to see that you're able to walk on water before they'll join your flock these days. Now, at the Second Federation, we do believe that there is a practical explanation for the majority of miracles."

"And that particular one?" Starrett asked.

"Well, when you take into consideration that Jesus' father was in fact a carpenter, it's easy. What we'd say was that he built a platform half an inch beneath the water level and, *voilà*!"

"Ah now, come on, First Minister Morrison, you're kidding."

"I'm not kidding. I never kid," Morrison snapped indignantly. "In this world, and in today's society, more than any other, all religions boil down to is a simple ability for mankind to coexist. The rest is all window dressing. So, you give people an odd trick or two, let them see that there is something more to life than just themselves; a man walking on water is really just a political spin: 'Hey, vote for Jesus of Nazareth. He can walk on water; he can come back from the dead; he can feed thousands with five loaves and two fishes.' And they follow in their droves. Why, do you think, are congregations called flocks? It's because they act like sheep."

"Well, I'd thank you to keep your voice down a bit. The majority of my team are members of somebody's flock, and I'll tell you that after today's job they're certainly going to need something they can look up to."

"I agree," Morrison replied, dropping to a conspiratorial whisper. "I've certainly never knocked any other religion or denomination. Our view at the Second Federation Church is that men by themselves are weak, but men bonded together by a shared goal or ideal are strong. They can become a very potent force, in fact."

Starrett was half tempted to inquire why, if the Second Federation Church was such a potent force, it had only one church in the whole of Ireland.

"What can you tell me about James Moore?" he asked instead.

"Not a lot really," Morrison replied, turning to face Starrett and attempting to ape the Inspector's hands-in-pockets stance. Either the First Minister's short arms or else his large stomach made such a gesture impossible, so he chose to rub his hands together instead.

"At this stage in the investigation, a few choice crumbs will suffice," Starrett offered in encouragement.

"Well, I know him only because we had to replace all the bookshelves in the library at the Manse a few months ago," Morrison said, a shower of spittle ejecting from his mouth as he spoke. "We couldn't find a master craftsman amongst our own flock, so my wife, Mrs Morrison, sourced James."

'Do you know how she found him?"

"I do, as it happens. Mr Moore had done some similar work for her best friend," the First Minister replied.

"OK, so where does our Mr James Moore live?"

"A cottage over in Downings."

"Do you know exactly where?" Starrett asked, beginning to grow impatient at having to drag every morsel of information from Morrison.

"Oh, up on the hill somewhere. Mrs Morrison will have his exact address. She took care of all the business end of the transaction."

"And how long did the job take?"

"Around four months. You know what tradesmen are like," Morrison said.

"So when exactly was this?" asked Starrett.

The reply was interrupted by the arrival of the forensic team, including the local pathologist, Samantha Aljoe. Starrett was surprised that Morrison hardly acknowledged her presence, even when he went to the trouble of introducing the beautiful young lady.

Fuss over, Starrett and Morrison resumed their conversation.

"I already told you that James Moore did the work a few months ago. Why ask the same question twice?" Morrison responded defensively.

"Well," Starrett said, his ice-blue eyes bearing down on the First Minister, "as you'd told me he worked for you for four months, I just wanted to pin you down to when he completed his work for you."

"Oh right, I see," Morrison replied, with all the innocence of a child. "He concluded the work two months ago. He started work on the project in January and completed it for us on the last day of April."

"And were you pleased with the standard of Mr Moore's work?"

"Well, the shelves are still standing," Morrison offered, less charitably than one would expect from a member of the clergy, particularly when the person under discussion was pinned to a cross not more than thirty yards from where they stood. "Mrs Morrison seemed extremely happy with his work, so much so that she recommended Mr Moore to another of her friends, who was in need of some cabinets for her kitchen."

"Could I trouble you for the names of both of her friends, please?"

"Yes, let me see, now . . . Mrs Eileen McLaughlin and Mrs Betsy Bell."

"And in that order?" Starrett continued.

"No, actually it was the other way round."

"OK," Starrett continued, raising his right hand to his face. His index finger was permanently bent in a less than acute V, which fitted perfectly around his chin. Starrett was always joking that his forefinger was so shaped for giving directions around the hilly winding roads of Donegal.

"What?" Morrison said impatiently.

"Sorry, I was just thinking. When James Moore was working for you, did you ever spend any time chatting to him?"

Morrison looked at Starrett as if he'd just asked him if he ever stepped in cow clap in his bare feet whilst walking in the nearby hilly fields.

"I may have passed the time of day with him on a couple of occasions, and I wrote the cheques," Morrison replied.

"So, you can't tell me anything else about him?"

"I'm afraid not."

"When did you first see him this morning?" Starrett asked, hoping to pull a rabbit and not a turkey from his invisible magic hat.

"Why, just now . . ." Morrison started slightly flustered.

"I don't think so, Ivan."

"I'll thank you not to use that tone of familiarity with me, please, Inspector."

"OK, First Minister, I'll apologise, if you will."

"Sorry?"

"Well, I'd respectfully suggest that when you entered the church a few minutes ago and fell to your knees in prayer, you were too far away to recognise exactly who the victim was, particularly with his head bowed and his features obscured by his hair."

"Look, Inspector," Morrison tutted, "do you really think that my caretaker was going to report this to the gardaí before he reported it to me? Guardians of the Peace you may be, but at the end of the day, I pay his wages."

"At the very end of the day, First Minister, the church pays both your wages," Starrett replied quickly, "and I'm sure it doesn't pay those wages just so you can waste my time. So, what I'd really like to know is, why did you go through that whole charade, pretending you hadn't seen James Moore's body crucified on that cross before?"

"Shock," Morrison offered quickly, without any apparent degree of remorse. "I'm afraid I can put it down to nothing more than shock."

"Ahm," Starrett said, stretching the word until he could find what he wanted to say, "I can't see how it would have advantaged you to behave in that way."

"Exactly, Inspector," Morrison replied, looking slightly relieved but still transmitting an air of superiority. "Trouble yourself no further, as I can assure you there was no advantage. And I'm afraid I can't swear to that on a Bible. We don't have a Bible in the Second Federation Church, although we do work to a version of the Ten Commandments, only we have twelve and they are infinitely more practical."

"If you haven't succumbed to the Bible, how come you dropped to your knees in prayer and quoted from it when you first entered the church?"

"I didn't claim I was perfect, and in times of stress, I find myself reverting to my childhood instructions and beliefs. What you were witnessing was purely a knee-jerk reaction."

"Right then," Starrett said. "Is Mrs Morrison in the Manse at the moment? I'd just like to ask her a few questions about James Moore."

"Ach, no . . . Mrs Morrison is not currently in residence," Morrison replied, looking somewhat uncomfortable.

"Oh, and when do you expect her back?"

"That's the problem," Morrison said, refusing to meet Starrett's stare. "I'm afraid I have to report that I know not where she is, nor do I know when she will return."

Chapter Four

STARRETT WATCHED AS Morrison departed the church steps and waddled off to roam alone in his spacious rectory. For a husband who said he didn't know the whereabouts of his wife, the first minister seemed remarkably unconcerned. For a minister who had just witnessed the desecration of his church, he seemed positively blasé. For a human being who had just observed the grotesquely tortured body of a fellow mortal, he seemed more preoccupied by everyday concerns.

By contrast, the young members of Starrett's team were plainly traumatised by the scene and openly respectful of the remains of James Moore as they lowered the cross to the floor. After the photographer had been allowed several minutes to snap the victim from every possible angle, under the careful supervision of Dr Samantha Aljoe, the steel nails were painstakingly removed.

Starrett watched from the distance of the doorway as his team went efficiently about its work. That they were all young—probably the youngest team in the entire service—wasn't entirely accidental. Starrett had no time for old-timers with their arrogance and their airs of superiority. He liked to recruit members into his team soon after they joined the gardaí, before they'd had a chance to learn any of the many bad habits and the shortcuts evident in the work of the old-timers. Starrett preferred his team to be made up of youngsters, ambitious in the art of detection and, as in the case of Sergeant Packie Garvey, not afraid of a bit of strenuous legwork.

Thinking of legwork, Starrett thought as he focused on Dr Aljoe, she was a fine figure of a woman in anyone's eyes. She was based in Letterkenny, the largest town in County Donegal. Letterkenny was being forced to grow too quickly, robbing it—at least Starrett believed—of the opportunity ever to become a magnificent or even a soulful city. Starrett reckoned Letterkenny was a bit like his young guards in that they both needed to be nurtured and cared for in order to give them a chance of achieving their goals. He knew that there was a good chance Letterkenny had missed its opportunity; he was infinitely more hopeful about the members of his team.

Strictly speaking, Dr Aljoe wasn't a part of his team. She was attached to Letterkenny General Hospital, and whenever the Dublin pathologist was already on a case, Dr Aljoe could be on call for the whole of County Donegal. Starrett's domain covered the county north of a line from Ramelton through Kilmacrenan, on across the Derryveagh Mountains to Gweedore and on to the west coast at Bunbeg. Obviously, most of the bigger towns like Milford, Rathmullan, Dunfanaghy, Falcarragh and Carrigart had their own garda stations, but they all fell under the umbrella of the area covered by Starrett's Serious Crime Squad. And umbrellas were always a necessary accessory when in the hills of Donegal.

"What can you tell me?" Starrett asked Dr Aljoe, who was busy examining the body, her long blond hair pulled back out of her way in a ponytail.

"I can tell you Liverpool beat Chelsea last night, I can tell you that Gay Byrne no longer hosts the *Late Late Show*, and I can tell you that my car's not going to last the summer," Samantha Aljoe said, as she examined the corpse and, in particular, the numerous and still moist welts on his back.

"I was thinking more along the lines of what you could tell me about our victim here, Mr James Moore."

"Oh, you've discovered his name then. That means you must be a detective, Detective. Or was he just one of your drinking buddies?"

"I know nothing about him apart from his name and the fact that he was a carpenter," Starrett continued, pleased that the doctor wasn't in the slightest in awe of him, which meant—in his eyes at least—that he was in with a chance with her.

"You're forgetting the other obvious fact," Aljoe said, "that he's dead."

Starrett, amused at her wit, discreetly observed Packie Garvey and Nuala Gibson breaking into their first, albeit reluctant, smiles of the morning.

"You say he was a carpenter?" the doctor continued as she removed with a pair of tweezers something invisible to Starrett's naked eyes, and bagged it.

"Yes."

"It's all a bit unimaginative, isn't it? 'Oh, he's a carpenter,' says the murderer, 'so we'll have to crucify him then, won't we?'"

"Fair play to your imagination there, Dr Aljoe, but you're making too many assumptions. At least two, in fact."

"Oh, and pray tell me exactly what am I assuming, Inspector?" she said, rising from her hunkers as agilely as any athlete. She turned to face him.

She was close enough for Starrett to smell her breath and her unique blend of scents. He always thought that people's aromas were as unique as their fingerprints. He'd never in his life met two women who smelled the same, and he would also admit that this particular piece of information came from a long exhaustive investigation. Samantha Aljoe, even in a shapeless, transparent, disposable blue body-suit, moved with the agility and grace of the slim, shapely and extremely sensual woman she was. She held his stare. Starrett thought that, even considering the circumstances they continued to meet under, she was probably aware of the effect she had on him.

"And?" she prompted, winking at Starrett, obviously enjoying herself.

"OK; although his earthly father, Joseph, was a carpenter, Jesus actually wasn't."

"I'll bow to your obvious superior knowledge on that one."

"It's a common misconception," Starrett offered as an olive branch.

"Why, thank you," she smiled and offered him a curtsy, "and my other assumption?"

"Well, with the use of the word 'they', you're suggesting that there was more than one perpetrator," Starrett said, trying to recall if she'd ever winked at him before.

"Surely it would have taken more than one man to carry out this charade?"

"And there you go making another assumption," Starrett replied as he and Garvey helped roll the corpse over on to its bloodied back.

"You're not suggesting it might have been a woman who did this to the poor man, are you?"

"Why on earth not?" Starrett replied, shocked and surprised that Aljoe would have been the kind of woman to have supported the "women are the weaker sex" theory.

"Well, Starrett, for heaven's sake, only a man would ever put this on another man," she said, pointing to the loincloth. "I mean, please . . ."

Nuala Gibson was now openly giggling and just about able to contain it to a respectful chuckle.

"OK," Dr Aljoe said, sounding more businesslike. "Mr Moore here could have died from any one of his wounds. Our murderer seems to have gone to a lot more trouble than was necessary. From all the bleeding, I can tell you that he definitely died on the cross. The nails were driven into him when he was still alive. I can't figure out why they were put though the wrists and not the palms of the hands, though."

"If you put nails into the palms of the hands they would tear out of the flesh between the fingers once the weight of the body was pulling against them. The Romans sussed that if you drove the nails between the small bones on the wrist, the body would hang on the cross for as long as they needed."

"Of course," Aljoe said. "I suppose I was biased by the numerous religious paintings I've seen; obviously they exploit the effect of blood-stained palms."

"Correct," Starrett muttered.

"Both of his legs are broken," the doctor proclaimed. "Was that another Roman refinement?"

"Correct," Starrett said. "When the legs were broken, the poor souls couldn't use them to take any strain or pain away from their arms or upper torso."

"The pain this poor man endured would have been excruciating. Are you suggesting that maybe our James Moore was made to suffer the exact same death as Jesus Christ?"

"Well, not exactly," Starrett sighed. "Surprisingly, Jesus Christ's legs were not broken, although those of the two thieves who were crucified with him were."

Chapter Five

S TARRETT SAW DR Aljoe to her car, a pink Volkswagen VW130 shaped like a tent. He took great pleasure in helping her out of her plastic overalls and felt even greater pleasure when the doctor removed her hair-band and her strawberry blond mane tumbled free. Underneath the hospital-issue one-piece, forensic-safe, disposal romper-suit, she wore a more stylish black trouser suit and a snow-white man's shirt, buttoned the whole way up to the top. She undid the top three buttons and exchanged her work slip-ons for a pair of black high heels, unrolling the bottoms of her trousers to accommodate them while Starrett stood back and admired the metamorphosis.

Although she offered to phone him later with the results of the autopsy, he said he'd prefer to receive them in person, and as he was due to visit Letterkenny towards the end of the day (a fabrication), perhaps they could discuss it then? Maybe even over a drink?

They arranged to meet at her office in Letterkenny General Hospital at 6.30.

Ten minutes later, Starrett—accompanied by Sergeant Packie Garvey, Bean Gharda Nuala Gibson and Garda Francis Casey—was sitting at the corner table in Steve's Café on the corner of Church and Bridge streets. Starrett was a regular, and most days he'd eat his breakfast there. There were three reasons for this: first, the food was second to none; second, the staff were friendly and helpful; and finally, and most importantly, he figured you could get a better sense of Ramelton village life by sitting (obviously minus the uniformed gardaí now accompanying him) in Steve's for an hour than you could patrolling for a week the twenty-five streets which made up the village's nucleus.

As Starrett studied a family of six eating at a nearby table, Packie Garvey asked, "Has Ivan Morrison really no idea at all where his wife is?"

"The first minister claims not," Starrett replied, still distracted by the family table.

"Have we talked to anyone who knows the victim?" Gibson asked.

"So far just the first minister," Starrett replied. "We need to talk to Betsy Bell and Eileen McLaughlin though. Betsy recommended James Moore to Mrs Morrison, and she in turn recommended him to Eileen. So I suppose after breckie they should be our first call. Packie and myself will visit both of them while youse two go through the records and see if you can't get any other information out of that clapped-out television with typewriter attached they call our computer."

"I keep telling you, Inspector," Packie protested as their breakfasts arrived, "it's not a computer problem."

"Oh yes, that's right," Starrett replied; "we need a bigger motorway to get the information highway into Ramelton, is that it?"

"Not exactly, Inspector," Packie smiled. "It's called broadband, not a motorway."

"Right, I've got it, and tell me this, Packie, how many lanes does this broadband have?"

"Say twenty or so."

"And how many lanes does our current system have?"

"No more than one."

"So, we're at the end of a country lane in more ways than one," Starrett said. "Ah well, no bother, less competition for this amazing grub."

"It's all a wee bit too much of the comfort food, you know, Inspector," Gibson offered, as she accepted delivery of her tea and toast.

"Nothing wrong with comfort, Nuala," Starrett replied, eyeing his baked beans and sticking a serviette into the V of his blue jumper. "And I would have thought that with your title 'Bean Gharda', you'd have at least a few mouthfuls of these little balls of energy on that lonely looking toast of yours."

"Yes, Inspector," Francis Casey said as he squared up to his sausage, bacon, eggs, potato cakes and tomatoes, "even if it's pronounced 'bean' and not 'ban'."

Nuala Gibson shot Casey a "he-knows-already" glance, trying hard to conceal her annoyance at Casey for coming so unnecessarily to her aid.

"That's not to mention the fact that the service officially dropped the term years ago," Casey continued unperturbed. "We're one of the few teams I know who still use it."

"Respect," Starrett said. "It's just a mark of respect."

Of course, Starrett knew the Irish language as well as he knew English, but he felt that a touch of banter around the table, particularly after what they'd just witnessed, might clear their heads and better set them up for the busy days ahead. As he looked around the plates, he noted that, aside from Gibson's, the scene up in the Second Federation Church certainly hadn't dented their appetites. He'd also clocked from Gibson's and Casey's exchanged look that there was definitely something going on there. They made an unlikely couple in that Francis was quite a bit shorter than Nuala. He added to his height with a thick head of dark brown hair in what could only be described as a Caucasian version of a polite Afro-cut. Casey wasn't what you'd call handsome, but neither was he what you'd call ugly. He was well-mannered and ambitious, maybe just a wee bit too ambitious. Starrett felt that there was only so much he could teach his team, and he knew that the majority of their successes would come from their working from their own instincts, and that was something that took time to nurture. Starrett had the feeling that perhaps Francis Casey's true vocation lay more in administration and research than on the front line.

Nuala was a little heavier and, overall, bigger than Casey, but in an attractive way. While in uniform she never wore make-up, but she scrubbed up well once off duty.

At this stage, the café was packed and abuzz with numerous conversations. At one table, Starrett noted a regular, Dermot Dunne, who was, as ever, bending some unsuspecting single farmer's ear about how great a time he'd had in England. Dermot had been in London for most of the 1980s and 1990s and had had a newspaper stall outside Camden Town tube station for most of that time. He was always keen to enthuse to all who would listen, and even a few who wouldn't, about how wonderful it had been "across the water" and how great the people were and how Alan Bennett, Julian Clary, Christy Kennedy, Sean Connery, Barbara Windsor, Boy George and Gerry Rafferty had all been regulars of his. Starrett often wondered if, during his twenty-odd years in London, Dermot had spent his time over there telling everyone who'd listen how great it all was over in Donegal, and how, as a barber, he'd cut the heads of Daniel O'Donnell, Pat Kenny, Charlie Haughey, Jackie Charlton and Phil Coulter. Maybe an acute case of the other man's grass always being greener, particularly, Starrett acknowledged, when the man in question resided in County Donegal.

Gibson and Garvey were deep in conversation about the whys and wherefores of crucifixions and theories as to why someone would want to kill a victim in such a way. Moore may have been married. There was a paler ring of skin on his wedding finger where a wedding band might have been recently removed. They wondered how his wife would take the news when they eventually tracked her down. Garda Casey looked to Starrett as if he were slightly uncomfortable being excluded from Gibson and Garvey's conversation, so the inspector turned to him and, in a discreet whisper, said, "What can you tell me about that family at the table by the door?"

Francis washed down a generous mouthful of eggs and toast with a draft of coffee, dabbed around his mouth with his serviette and said, "Well, for one thing, they've never been in here before. They're probably tourists."

"Good; how can you tell?" Starrett asked. He encouraged his team to examine every situation they encountered in the greatest detail. He wanted them, both on and off duty, to be on the look-out for information others might miss. For instance, it wouldn't have been enough for Casey to justify his strangers' claim by saying that he'd never seen them before.

"Well, they sat nearest the door. It's probably the worst table in the café, but it would have been the most inviting one to them as they came in."

"Anything else?" Starrett asked. Gibson had stopped talking midsentence, now showing interest in Starrett and Casey's conversation and the objects of their attention.

"Well, the adults keep looking around the walls at the posters and stuff, and none of the locals who've come in have spoken to them," Casey offered.

"Yep, good, good, and?"

Casey seemed stumped, and this time it was Gibson who spoke up.

"There's something contradictory about the man and woman's open fondness for each other. You'd think that after four children the novelty might have worn off."

"Not necessarily," Casey protested.

"No, Nuala's got a good point," Starrett said. "The couple may be married, but not in fact to each other."

Now Packie Garvey was trying to steal discreet glances at the table under investigation. "How can you tell that?

"Well, the two boys call her 'mammy', but they call him by some name I can't make out. The two girls call him 'daddy', but they call her Patricia, and none of the children are bickering with or teasing each other, which in a family of six would be an absolute impossibility."

"What else have you picked up, Inspector?" Nuala Gibson asked, genuinely impressed.

"Well, I'd say they're moving here or hereabouts. He, like our Mr James Moore, is a carpenter, and at least the man and the two girls are from Sligo."

"Sorry?" Gibson said, shaking her head in disbelief.

"OK," Starrett said, thoroughly enjoying himself. "Their Volvo estate car is parked over on the corner of Castle Street, the number plate is 01 SO 461, telling me their car is a 2001 model and they are from Sligo. There is a serious amount of luggage packed in the back, which points to them moving house. They couldn't have driven from Sligo this morning, so they must have spent the night somewhere close by. They wouldn't have stopped off here, great and all as Steve's is, if they weren't close to, or at, their actual destination. Then there's a toolbox and various saws and other larger tools visible in the back."

"And how do you know it's his car?" Packie asked.

"It's badly parked," Starrett replied. "As in, it's disgracefully parked, and a woman would never ever park a car that poorly for fear people would think badly of her."

"Right then," Starrett announced after a pause. "Breakfast's on me, and I'll see you down in the station in a few minutes. Packie, you and I will head over and see Betsy Bell and then Eileen McLaughlin."

Starrett paid the bill, made his way over to the family by the door and introduced himself.

"Hello, I'm Ivor Gallagher and this is Patricia," the man said, rising and taking Starrett's offered hand. "This is Paddy and Jack and Roisín and Dolores."

"You folks new to town, or are you just passing through?" Starrett enquired as he pulled up a seat and sat down beside them.

"We've just moved here," Patricia said smiling, and smiling even more when she added: "*This* morning, in fact."

"Well, welcome to Ramelton," Starrett said, returning the smile. "You fixed up with a place to stay?"

"Yes, we bought the wee house down Castle Street on the right-hand side," Declan said. "Our furniture doesn't arrive until this afternoon."

"Right, would that be the teacher's house with the original boot scraper by the front door?" Starrett asked.

"Aye, that's us," Ivor replied proudly.

"Congratulations, good health to you all," Starrett said. "I don't mean to be nosy or anything, but I noticed that you're a carpenter and, well, there's always lots of work around here for good tradesmen."

"Thanks, I'm all fixed up. My uncle has plenty of building work in Letterkenny, and he wants me to get started as soon as I can."

"Ach, yes, the Boom Town," Starrett sighed. "The Klondyke had nothing on the Letterkenny boyos; but instead of prospectors, Letterkenny is infested with developers. You'll be fine then. It's going to be a great time until the gold runs out up there. Look, I just wanted to welcome you here; I know the first few days in a new town can be stressful. You will be fine here, though. Ramelton is a nice wee town, the people are warm, and you'll be made welcome. Here's my number. If you ever need anything, just give me a shout. I'm based at Tower House, the big building in Gamble's Square at the foot of Bridge Street. It's on the right, just by the river. You can't miss it."

"Why, thank you," Patricia said, visibly moved at Starrett's welcome.

Chapter Six

TEN MINUTES LATER, Starrett and Garvey were rattling over the noisy manhole covers that marked the road towards Rathmullan.

"Handy enough, those loose covers," Starrett said. "They're loud enough to wake even the back-section passenger of a hearse."

Starrett loved driving out on this road. His car was a black BMW, which sounded grander than it actually was. Tommy Adams at the Bridge Garage had souped up the engine so that it passed everything bar a petrol station, and Starrett's number plate—00 DL 7—was well known about the county. For most of the short journey from Ramelton to Rathmullan, one had sight of the glory of Lough Swilly. In Starrett's case, this could prove to be an extremely dangerous distraction on what was a tricky road to navigate at the best of times. Even after all these years, he never tired of the natural beauty of the lough and the various mountain ranges that surrounded it. Garvey found it easier to close his eyes and keep his fingers crossed rather than endure the usual white-knuckle ride.

"I hope her ladyship is receiving visitors," Starrett announced as they pulled up outside a light-blue 1970s-style dormer bungalow, roughly four miles from Ramelton.

Betsy Bell didn't quite have a lough view—not unless she was prepared to balance on the tip of the aerial attached to her chimney stack. She did, however, have a busy, well-stocked garden, packed with nooks and crannies. For a fifty-three-year-old widow's garden, it was remarkably well taken care of. Betsy herself was also remarkably well-preserved, if a tad inappropriately dressed.

She greeted Starrett and Garvey dressed in a light blue, waisted jacket and short matching skirt. Starrett firmly believed that nobody should ever wear any item of clothing that wasn't pleasant to the touch. The material in Widow Bell's suit looked about as agreeable in this regard as an industrial carpet. He could never work out what motivated women in their choice of style. Was it their priority to look great, or simply to appear different? Betsy Bell certainly looked different. People around Donegal rarely experienced the sun for long enough to take their jackets off, let along cultivate a tan; but Betsy's canned colouring, it's worth noting, favoured more of a farmer's weather-beaten look than a glow achieved on the French Riviera.

For all that, she had great dignity and poise, and Starrett was convinced that were she asked to walk from here to Ramelton with a stack of telephone directories on her head, she could easily have accomplished the task.

Greetings and salutations over, the inspector said, "Betsy, I wonder if we could have a chat with you about a gentleman who did some work for you, a Mr James Moore?"

"Why, yes, Inspector, come on in . . . Why don't both of you come on in?" she said in a pitch high enough to hit the highest notes required of a choir. Her accent sounded as if she'd started life in County Derry but had spent much of the intervening years travelling the world.

Her home was too cluttered and a bit too old-fashioned for Starrett's taste, but it was spotless. He wondered if the fussy décor and furnishings had anything at all to do with the fact that she lived alone.

Betsy Bell led them to the back of the house, through the kitchen, to a small but perfectly formed conservatory. Here the two policemen settled into comfortable wickerwork armchairs arranged around a glass coffee table, which displayed a coffee pot and a lone cup and saucer.

"I was just about to have my elevenses," said Betsy over her shoulder, as she nipped back into the kitchen. She returned a heartbeat later with two additional cups and saucers. "Coffee OK?"

"Perfect," Starrett said. Betsy played mammy and poured a cup of coffee for them all.

Starrett took a sip. "I understand you had James Moore in here to do some carpentry work for you?"

"Why, yes," Betsy said, sitting down and offering them each a Jacob's Mikado. "My bespoke kitchen is James' handiwork."

Starrett was trying to find his way out of this Miss Marple moment.

"Look, Betsy, I think I'd better tell you . . . James, well, he was found dead this morning . . ."

The Miss Marple instantly disappeared as Betsy Bell let out an almighty scream and dropped her coffee cup and contents all over her skirt.

"Dead?" she eventually uttered, a look of total shock on her face.

"I'm afraid so."

"An accident?"

"I'm afraid not."

"Not an accident?" Betsy whispered, regaining some of her composure as she dashed back into the kitchen, presumably to mop down her sopping skirt, and yelled, "What on earth happened? Heart attack? Stroke?"

"Betsy, all I can tell you at this time is that he died in mysterious circumstances."

"Is that garda-speak for he was murdered?"

"Betsy," Starrett said, choosing to ignore Betsy's previous question, "we don't know anything about Mr Moore, and First Minister Morrison told us you'd recommended him to Mrs Morrison."

"Yes, yes, of course, they wanted to re-shelve their study," she answered. "But I don't see how . . ."

"Well," Starrett continued, "for a start, do you have his address and telephone number?"

"Why, yes, of course," she replied, still looking like someone about to submit to the dentist. "He lives . . . lived . . . in the wee house next to the Downings Bay Hotel."

Again she darted back into her kitchen, and they could hear her go up the back staircase, and walk across the room above them. She returned calling out a telephone number, which Packie dutifully recorded in his notebook.

Once she'd returned to the room, Starrett asked, "And what about a family?"

"A family?" Betsy said, looking noticeably more twitchy.

"Yes," Starrett said quickly. "What can you tell us about his family?"

"Ahm, let's see . . . he had a wife and, I believe, three children."

"And do you have a number for them?"

"Yes, well, I mean, I've got Jimmy's number, too. I'll get you that."

"How long did it take him to complete your kitchen?" Packie asked. Starrett was pleased: that was going to be his next question.

"Let's see now; I'd say he was here on and off for about four months or so. I mean, you know what builders are like; they keep disappearing to finish other jobs. There's always a great first week, and you start to think it's going to take less time and less upheaval than you expected, but all they're doing is lulling you into a false sense of security. Even so, at the end, when all the work is done, you look back on it and realise it was worth all the grief. Anyway, I'd say the whole job took four months max."

"Are you and Mrs Morrison good friends?" Starrett asked, changing direction and, he hoped, gear.

"Oh," she laughed, "Mandy and I go way back. I went to Queen's University with her older sister."

"Do you see much of each other?"

"Oh yes, Mandy and Eileen, that's Eileen McLaughlin—she lives in Ramelton, too—we meet up a lot. If Eileen and I ever manage to get Mandy interested in golf, we might as well all move in together. Tell me, Inspector, what did Jimmy die of?"

"Sorry, Betsy. I'm afraid we can't release that information yet."

"Surely you can tell me if he would have suffered in the end," she continued. Starrett felt as if she were trying to get him to reassure her.

"Ah, Betsy, no demise is entirely pleasurable," Starrett replied with a sigh. "But mmm, look, when Mr Moore was here working for you, did he ever talk about himself, about his life?"

"Well, Inspector, Jimmy was a great listener, but he never really said much about himself."

"Betsy, help me here, please," Starrett pleaded. "The man was here for four months; he worked for you and your best friends for possibly another eight months between them . . . I'm just guessing here, but if we take that as a minimum, that means he was in your life for at least a year. Now if Packie here and myself and say another of our mates had a woman working in our lives for that time, we'd be rabbiting on and on about whatever bits of information we had picked up on her."

Betsy smiled, showing off her green eyes properly for the first time since they had arrived. She flicked her eyelashes a few times before replying coyly, "Boys will be boys, but girls *never ever* tell."

"None the less," Starrett laughed, "the reason for my asking is not a search for gossip, but rather to gather information for a murder investigation."

"Oh my goodness, Jimmy was murdered," Betsy exclaimed, the cent finally dropping.

"Yes, Betsy, and we desperately need your help. At the minute, you're the only person we've spoken to who had any contact with him."

Betsy took another couple of sips of her coffee, fluttered her eyelids a few more times, looked to the floor, glanced up to the sky. For all the world she looked like a contestant on *Mastermind*, faced with a particularly thorny question. Eventually, eyes glued to her stained pine floor, she answered, "I think you'll find that Mandy Morrison knew him a little better than Eileen and I did."

Chapter Seven

"SHOULD WE HEAD over to Downings?" Garvey asked, once he and his boss were back in the car.

"Yes, we should," Starrett agreed, not particularly relishing his duty at the other end of the journey. The radio speaker erupted in a loud crackling noise. "Ah, the tide's going out down at Portsalon," Starrett laughed, disengaging the gearstick. "Either that or the station house is trying to get us on the two-way. Jeez, Packie, all this modern technology and we still have to use radio gear left over from Michael Collins' days."

He rang into the garda station on his own mobile. There were two messages for him. The first was from his boss, Major Newton Cunningham, who, hardly surprisingly, wanted to see him as soon as possible, and the second was from Maggie Keane.

"Did you take her call yourself?" Starrett asked the station operator.

"Yes, Inspector Starrett."

"And what did she say?"

"She said she wanted you to ring her."

"OK," Starrett replied, "but can you tell me exactly what she said?"

"She said, well, first she asked to speak to you and then, when I told her you were out, she said, 'Could you have him ring me?' and then she said, 'Tell him it's kind of urgent.' Then she said, 'No, don't tell him that; just tell him that I'd like him to ring me.' "

"Did she sound like she was . . . OK? Worried? Stressed?"

"Inspector Starrett, my switchboard is lighting up like a Christmas tree. Maggie Keane would like you to ring her, maybe sooner rather than later, OK? Can I go now?"

"Yes, yes, of course . . . sorry," Starrett said, breaking off the call. Excusing himself to Garvey, he turned off the engine, got out of the car, and dialled the number the operator has passed on.

"Starrett?" a voice said at the other end.

"Maggie, are you OK?"

"I'm fine, Starrett. I need a favour please."

"Name it, Maggie."

"It's my mother; she's in a right state."

"What's happened to her?"

"OK, there were these men working at the house next door to her, and one day one of them, a well-dressed man who had an official-looking pass, came to her and claimed that the people next door, you know the McGraths, were going to great expense to have a gas line brought up to their house from the new gas main. Anyway, this man—who was dressed in clean blue overalls each time my mam met him—said that sometimes, behind the gas board's back, they took a gas feed off the main line to service older people's houses . . ."

"Such as your mother's," Starrett prompted, fearful of where this might be going.

"'Such as my mother's," Maggie agreed, before continuing. "They said for €895—which was the cost (and not a cent more) of the raw materials and for digging the ditch—my mam could enjoy a lifetime supply of gas. He also assured my mother that her neighbours wouldn't suffer in any way. The only condition was that she tell no one."

"Maggie!" Starrett said in exasperation down the telephone line.

"She's seventy-seven years old, Starrett, and €895 is less than her annual oil bill."

"So she paid the money and never saw them again?" Starrett said, now trying to sound sympathetic.

"No, actually they dug a deep ditch and spent a day laying a pipe. Then they connected up the pipe to my mam's cooker and boiler, and the bootleg supply actually worked."

"Wow!"

"A week later, the gas supply ran down."

"Ach!"

"The problem was that they had disconnected my mam's normal supply of oil, so she was without her cooker for a few days before she plucked up the courage to go up to the neighbours' house. It transpired that it wasn't a gas supply her neighbours were having fitted, it was a new sewage tank, and the bogus team was only using the legit team's work as a smoke screen. Eventually my mam had to swallow her pride and call out the council. They dug up the ditch and found the new gas line connected to nothing other than a Calor Gas cylinder."

"And it had run empty?" Starrett asked, wondering what he could do.

"I know this is not your usual area, Starrett," Maggie continued, "but my mam was out for a drive this morning, and she thinks she saw the same team at work."

"That's very unusual; these boyos don't usually work the same patch."

"No, not around here. My mam drove down to the Glebe Gallery in Churchill. She just loves Derek Hill's work and goes down there at least once a year for the tour. Anyway, just outside Glendowan, she passed a van she recognised. She doubled back, and eventually she saw the man with the clean blue overalls again."

"Where's she now?"

"She's back in the tea room at the Glebe Gallery."

"OK, Maggie, have her wait there. I'll have someone pick her up in about ten minutes, and she can show them where the lads are."

"Hey, thanks, Starrett."

"Thank you, Maggie, and thanks to your mam. These scam merchants are usually long gone before they're reported to us. With a bit of luck, we'll catch them in the act this time."

"How are you, Starrett?"

"I'm fine, Maggie. Look, I really do need to go and get a few of the locals set up . . ."

"Sorry, sorry, and thanks again Starrett . . ." And she disconnected before the inspector even had a chance to say goodbye properly.

"Right, Packie," Starrett said as he climbed back into his car and started the engine, "let's mosey on over to Downings and see James Moore's family."

Chapter Eight

THIRTY MINUTES LATER, Starrett and Garvey were knocking on the door of James Moore's home over in Downings, the holiday-home heaven—or hell (depending on your point of view)—of Donegal.

Still preoccupied by his conversation with Maggie Keane, whom he'd not heard from in nearly two decades, Starrett was startled when a woman who looked old enough to have been James Moore's mother opened the door. In fact—in response to the presentation of their ID cards—she introduced herself as Nora, his wife. She then wiped her hands on a tea towel for what seemed like ages before offering a hand to Starrett and Garvey in turn.

Nora Moore honoured one of Donegal's golden rules—"Never keep the gardaí standing on your doorstep"—by immediately inviting the two members of the Guardians of the Peace into her house.

The Moores' home was single storey and over a hundred years old, and Starrett assumed that it had been James Moore who had lovingly restored it to its former glory and beyond. Starrett, who loved houses, particularly old ones, knew that during the restoration process, many owners opted for the stripped-wood look which would have indicated a shortage of funds on the part of the original builder or owner. Back then, the majority of people would have ensured that all surfaces were covered by paint (if not wallpaper) to brighten it up a bit and also to protect the surfaces for as long as possible, even if it meant going as far as mixing the remains of numerous tins of varying colours of paint. The owners of this particular cottage had shown a preference for natural National Trust colours and varnishes. The result was a particularly warm and cosy feel, coupled with a lived-in family look.

Nora Moore led them through to the kitchen-dining-sitting-room space, which Starrett presumed James Moore had knocked through into one room. The walls were absolutely packed to overflowing with family photographs, paintings and posters—one of Rathmullan House and one a Guinness advertisement. If the ageing of the paper was anything to go by and this was an original poster, Starrett reckoned it was worth at least €1,000. He was saddened to see photographs of Nora and the man he had seen on a cross a matter of a few hours ago together with, if he wasn't mistaken, two sons and a younger daughter, the children Betsy Bell had mentioned.

"What can I do for you, Inspector?" Nora asked, continuing to wipe her hands nervously.

Starrett walked over and put his hand across Nora's shoulders. Before she, clearly embarrassed, had a chance to shake free of him, he felt through her dark brown cardigan that there wasn't much more to her than skin and bone. She couldn't have had an ounce above seven stone, he thought, on her five-foot-five frame. To Starrett, she looked more like a worrier than someone with an eating disorder. She was dressed in what were generally referred to as "clothes suitable only for the house". Her mismatch of browns and greys—apron, cardigan, skirt, tights and faded canvas shoes—fitted in so well with her persona that they looked like a second skin. Her grey hair was unkempt but clean, and she didn't wear a trace of make-up.

"Nora," Starrett began, as Garvey looked on self-consciously, "come over and sit down beside me here at your grand table."

In that split second, the look in her eyes changed, and she semi-stumbled in the direction of the table, still not allowing Starrett any physical contact. She leaned against the table, both her hands spreading out in an arc from her body. Her fingers busily found the table's numerous scars, and she read them like braille: a deeply engraved set of initials, CM; a four-inch straight line where a sharp bread knife had obviously missed its target; a sector of wood, like a generous portion of an apple tart, where her husband had expertly replaced the original antique timber after a few too many knocks; hot-saucepan stains;

teacup stains; puttied nailless holes; a couple of places where knots of wood had simply dropped out, creating one-inch-diameter holes. There were even several depressions marked by blacked stains on the wood where cigarette butts had been left unattended for a few seconds too many. Perhaps the offender had just nipped off to the toilet. Hey, perhaps they'd even gone to answer the door to be confronted by two members of the gardaí who had also arrived out of the blue with news. Well, in truth, Starrett knew that no one had ever delivered news such as he was about to give Mrs Nora Moore.

As Nora's fingers ran out of distractions, she sank deeply into a chair and whispered, "It's Jimmy, isn't it?"

Starrett crunched his chin into its socket.

When confronted with potentially devastating news, survivors of the recently departed never realise how much of a gift they are giving the unfortunate messenger when they offer such a question.

"Yes."

"Ach, no," Nora cried out loudly. "Ach no, no, not poor Jimmy."

Starrett moved closer to her and placed his hand back on her shoulder. His bent forefinger formed a bizarre hanging hook on her back.

This time she did not recoil from his offer of comfort. Instead she fell limp and wailed like a banshee.

Starrett feared she would fall off her chair. He turned her tearstained face to him and pulled her towards his own chest. She recoiled slightly and pumped her fists against his chest.

He knew her anger was not directed at him but at a fate which had cheated her of the man who had persuaded her to put her life on hold in deference to her children, and at a society which had robbed her of all of her dreams and made her scrimp and slave and save for a better life for her, her husband and her family; a world that had promised that eventually, just down the line, maybe right around the corner, things would get better. Now, as she hammered away for all her might on Starrett's chest, she knew that her life would never get better ever again. She knew that just as sure as she knew that her husband was dead. She knew that she had, in effect, died as well. The main difference between her and her husband was that she'd have to remain in this state of purgatory for another five, ten, twenty, maybe even—if God really hated her—another thirty years.

But even in all of her despair, her punches couldn't injure Starrett because, as had been proved to be the case with everything else in her life, God hadn't equipped her properly to achieve her goal.

Starrett told Garvey to phone for a doctor. He arrived and sedated Mrs Nora Moore, offering a brief release from her pain and desolation.

As he did so, members of the local gardaí visited three separate schools and brought fifteen-year-old Chris Moore, fourteen-year-old Claudia Moore and ten-year-old Brian Moore back to the family home to hear the heartbreaking news, and to comfort their mother and each other.

Chapter Nine

ALTHOUGH STARRETT HAD waited at the Moore house until all the children arrived home, he'd fully intended to leave them alone together and visit them later that day or early the following morning. It would be at least twenty-four hours before he would be able to have any conversation with Nora Moore.

But Chris Moore, the eldest of the three and the first to arrive home, proved to be a remarkable young man. As Chris was told the news about his father, Starrett thought he could see him physically grow in stature as he automatically and immediately fell into the role of family leader. He excused himself from Starrett and went to see his mother. When his brother Brian, followed a few minutes later by Claudia, arrived home, he took them to one side, broke the news and immediately set them tasks: Claudia to take care of their mother and Brian to finish off their mother's chores.

"How can I help you, Inspector?" Chris finally asked.

The inspector studied the teenager. He looked so much like his father he could have been a younger brother. He had short brown hair, brown eyes and an inquisitive face. Nora Moore had definitely turned her children out well. They were all clean as buttons and dressed in proper school uniform.

"Well, Chris," Starrett began cautiously, "the more I can learn about your father, the better the chance we have of finding out who was responsible. That's my priority, but I can accept it may not be your priority at this stage."

"I can see that," Chris replied, sounding very earnest, "and I *would* really like to try to help you."

"OK, good," Starrett said. "Let's you and me go for a wee walk on the beach, and we'll have a chat about your dad."

Three minutes later, they were walking north along the shoreline with the holiday-home camp banked up on their right. Chris Moore seemed content just to walk along in silence, deep in his own thoughts. Starrett wondered why everyone was so attracted to the sea, and he wondered how many times James Moore had walked this beach, either by himself or with members of his family. His workshop, at the back of their house, afforded him a great view of the beach, and Starrett pondered whether he'd done much of his thinking, wishing, dreaming and planning while looking out on the Atlantic Ocean. The inspector wondered whether every wood shaving James had planed from a piece of timber and every nail he had driven felt like it had brought him a few micro-metres closer to achieving his goals. What were his goals?

Relatively speaking, Starrett was enjoying his walk with Chris Moore, who remained silent. What had it felt like to be James Moore? What had driven him? Starrett imagined him in his workshop, working away, perhaps with one of his children keeping him company and asking questions. Was he ambitious? Did he take pride in his work, or was it a means to an end? A way he knew he could make money to support his family?

And what of Nora Moore? What had happened that had made him available to Mrs Amanda Morrison?

"My mam hasn't always been like this, you know," Chris said, breaking their silence.

"Aye," Starrett said, "it's not easy bringing up a family these days."

"Have you any children?" the young Moore asked.

"I'm not married, Chris," Starrett replied, looking off into the distance.

"Have you ever been?"

"Ah, nope."

"Ever wanted to be?"

"I'd have to say, yes, there was a time when I wanted to be married."

"Just the once?" the boy continued, starting to sound like Gay Byrne's natural successor.

"Yes, Chris, just the once."

"A long time ago?"

"Aye, a long time ago," Starrett sighed. He was now distracted from his own questioning, thinking instead of that very long time ago.

"What happened?"

"Well now, I was young and I felt there was something else I had to do, and by the time I realised that I'd nothing else I really needed to do, I'd ruined what I had . . . if you get my drift."

"I think I do, but you've still got a great career," Chris offered.

"Well, not the same career actually. The garda work came later, and I really do enjoy what I do, so I guess one out of two isn't a bad batting average."

"Fifty per cent success rate," Chris Moore offered.

"Bejeepers," Starrett said, snapping out of his mindset. "When you put it that way, it's not really a result to be boasting about. Tell me, Chris, do you have a girlfriend?"

Instead of the customary embarrassed teenage reply, Chris said, "Well, I have a great friend, yes, and obviously we're too young, but we're both hoping it will develop into something. It's kind of difficult though, you know, when you're good friends and you feel something for somebody, but inside you're very scared in case you grow apart through no fault of your own. We talk a lot about it, though, so you never know."

Chris Moore appeared to remember suddenly exactly why he was out walking on the beach, and the smile that had started to move across his sharp features faded into a frown.

"Well, Chris, all I can tell you, and the *only* thing I have learned in my life, is that you should never ever put anything before your relationships, and I'm not talking just about romantic relationships."

"I agree, Inspector, and if anything, the older society gets, the more important human relationships should become," Chris said, appearing hopeful, but then adding: "But sadly, that's not proving to be the case, is it?"

"Oh, I don't know, I've got a lot of young people working in my team, and I can tell you, I'm mightily impressed by their human commitment."

"Ach, good," the lad replied. "My dad and my mam always taught us to look after each other. My dad was always saying how easy it is to have enough money, but how difficult it is to have enough friends. My dad thought that 'enough money' was when you had sufficient to clothe, feed and house your family. My mam . . ."—and here he sighed in the same way an older man might—". . . was much more ambitious. I think it was her ambitions and the conflict they created between the two of them that finally did her nervous system in."

They were getting close to the water's edge. Starrett steered them further up the beach.

"Look, Inspector, I didn't mean that my mam and dad were always fighting; they weren't in fact. It's just that they were both coming from totally different points of view. My father was preoccupied with where the sun rose and how that fact impacted on our house, whereas my mam was desperate to get beautiful material for curtains."

"How long were they married?"

"Fourteen years," Chris replied immediately. Starrett did the maths, which put Nora in her mid-thirties at best. If Starrett had been asked to guess her age, he would have sprung for early to mid-fifties.

"Do you know how they met?" Starrett continued. He knew that the best chance he had of accumulating important information was not by asking important questions, but by asking questions, which unconsciously released vital details.

"They met at a party my Aunt Peggy—she's my mam's elder sister—was giving over in Portrush where she was on holidays. My dad is from Coleraine and my mam is from Cranford, but she always loved Downings when she was growing up and always dreamed of living here. It is beautiful," Chris said, turning around 360 degrees, yet still keeping pace with Starrett. "But outside of the summer, not a lot happens here. Do you like music, Inspector?"

"Yes, I do. At least, I think I do."

"You think you do?" Chris Moore repeated, scrunching up his eyebrows.

"Let me explain . . . I have a colleague who positively loves music, she absolutely lives for it, so when you ask me do I like music, I'm tempted to compare my interest in music to hers and . . . well, quite frankly, I have to admit, it's really that I can take it or leave it."

"And when you can take it, who do you like to listen to?"

"Well, I've got a confession to make to you here, Chris," Starrett began, "I don't even have a CD player. I've never bought a CD in my life. I'm still a vinyl man myself, so that pretty much dictates whom I listen to. For me, the governor is Neil Diamond. I don't mind Frank Sinatra either. I used to go and see Rory Gallagher's band, Taste, live; he never really got it down on record, but in concert he was something else—a Donegal man, you know?"

"Really?"

"Yeah, Ballyshannon," Starrett replied, offering up the answer to the only pub quiz pop question he was capable of answering. "And yourself, what's your taste in music?"

"I like Killers and Damian Rice, big time. But anyway, what I meant to say back then was that there is not really a lot to do around here, apart from listening to music."

"Did your dad listen to much music?" Starrett asked

"He's a bunch of Planxty, and Simon and Garfunkel CDs, but he rarely listens to anything other than traditional music. My mam has stuff like Dexy's Midnight Runners and Soft Cell. I'm not sure she really likes it, though, because she never plays any of her cassettes. Anyway, my parents met at Aunty Peggy's party. My dad was doing some work for an ex of Peggy's, and he tagged along with a workmate. Dad and Mam spent the whole evening walking the North Strand in Portrush—and talking. My dad was a bit of a hippie in those days. My mam liked him immediately. They used to joke that it was she who pursued him. When I was younger, they'd rib each other about it, but from what I can gather, it was my mother who caught my father."

"The other side of that is that some people are just waiting around to be caught, if you know what I mean," Starrett suggested.

"Well, whatever way it worked, my dad proposed. They were married a few months later, and six months after that I was born. We lived with my mother's parents for the first two years of my life. Both my parents were out working all the time, but they still managed to have Claudia a year after I was born. My dad was a self-employed handyman and had all the work he could handle. We moved out of my grandparents' house and moved into the house back there. My dad spent a lot of time refurbishing it over the years, room by room. I was five years old and Claudia was four when Brian was born.

"My dad finished work on the house about four years ago, and then converted the outhouse into his workshop. He began to be much more selective over what work he accepted, and then he put his prices up. He wasn't really comfortable doing it, but eventually he saw the sense and started making more money. My mam, God bless her, fell ill with a terrible flu about three years ago, and she's never been the same since. The four of us try to help her as much as she'll let us, but she's terribly sensitive. I tell her she's clinically depressed and she should do something about it, but she just laughs it off, saying she's much too busy to be clinically depressed. She thinks that clinical depression is for rich folks."

"Does your dad have many friends?" Starrett asked.

"A few, ahm . . . Colm Donovan, they used to work on jobs together; and then there's Daniel McGuinness. Dan is probably his oldest friend; they used to work together. He's the mate my dad would go to things with; Dan's a *big* man. He's always around here. Then there's my uncle Dolphie, Dolphie Cowan, Aunty Peggy's husband. My dad and Dolphie get on like a house on fire at family do's." Chris Moore stopped talking and stopped walking at the exact same moment.

He stood frozen to the spot for a few moments as tears gently trickled down his cheeks. Starrett stretched out a hand, rested it on the boy's shoulder and gently patted it a few times.

Chris Moore broke the stalemate, walking and talking at exactly the same moment. Starrett's hand fell unobtrusively back to his side.

"Inspector Starrett, can you tell me why anyone would want to kill my father?"

"We don't have an idea, Chris. That's what I have to find out."

"But," said Chris, sighing a long sigh. "I mean . . . it's my dad we're talking about here. He was a hippie; he'd never hurt anyone; he'd never steal money; he'd never be involved in a hit and run; he'd never be a member of an illegal organisation; he'd never get drunk and fall down; he'd never even illegally park his car; he paid his taxes; he never did cash jobs, it was always on the books. He was always telling me and my brother and sister, 'Never ever do anything that results in your having to look over your shoulder all the time.' He'd say that it just wasn't worth taking the risk to make an extra few euros. You're wasting your life and your energy. And, of course, he was right, but then you have to say, look where it got him. Inspector, what do you think happened?"

"You know, Chris, maybe he was just in the wrong place at the wrong time," Starrett offered, using the suggestion as fuel for his next question: "Do you know what work he was doing recently?"

"I'll show you," Chris replied enthusiastically, quickening his step and leading them back towards his house. When they were about a hundred yards away, he said quietly, "Inspector Starrett, I'd appreciate it if you'd not mention my blubbering on the beach just then. I need to be strong for the others."

"Hey, you know what, Chris, there's a pretty strong wind out there, and sometimes I've been known to catch a grain of sand in the eye myself."

Chapter Ten

As CHRIS MOORE led Starrett into his father's workshop, the incredibly rich aromas, a blend of various woods, glue, paint, varnish, and James Moore's own sweat, all combined to hit the inspector smack in his nostrils the minute he stepped through the door. The room was much larger than the detective had imagined, but as Starrett had correctly assumed, it had an amazing view of the beach through a large picture window. To the right of this was James Moore's workbench, with two vices and a very tidy rack of tools collected on the wall above it. On the opposite side of the room was a stash of wood of varying sizes and types, and against the entrance wall was the carpenter's current work-in-progress: a project he was destined never to finish.

Starrett spent a few moments studying what looked like a broad, upside-down bath—either that, or an extremely ornate boat minus one end. After a few seconds, during which Starrett had mentally stood the piece up on its end, he realised that it was a grand pulpit of some kind. The construction, with all its intricate carvings and inlays, was a fine testament to a master carpenter.

"Bejeepers," Starrett said in wide-eyed amazement. "This is certainly a beautiful piece of work."

"Yes," Chris Moore replied, the pride evident in his voice. "He was very proud of it."

"Do you know who commissioned it?"

"I think it was for that Second Federation Church over in Ramelton. He's been doing some work for them recently. You know, for that American-styled religion that won't let people into the church unless they're kitted out in their Sunday best. No sports gear in there, I can tell you."

"Do you know anything else about them? Was your father a member?"

"My father didn't subscribe to any religion, unlike my mam who worships at the local church. My father said we kids should worship there until we were old enough to make up our own minds. I don't know anything about the Second Federation, apart from their clothes rule, and once my dad told me that he thought they believed that their power came from sticking together. Do you know much about them yourself, Inspector?"

"No, not a lot," Starrett sighed. "But I'm beginning to feel it's about time I did a bit of research in their general direction. Tell me, Chris, when did you last see your dad?"

"At dinner last night. Then he went out. I knew he didn't go out to the workshop because I checked, but I assumed he was out working and he'd left for work before I got up this morning."

"Do you remember what your father was wearing when he left home yesterday evening?"

"He always dressed the same: denim jeans, a blue denim shirt and a T-shirt and a pair of yellow steel-capped Timberland boots. Unless it was very cold, he'd always wear the denim shirt open over his trousers."

"Anything else you can tell me about what he was wearing, you know, anything really distinctive?" Starrett asked.

"Erm, well, my brother and sister and I bought him two shirts just alike. They had little brass buttons with the letters 'Levi' embossed on them."

"Good, anything else?" Starrett pushed.

"Not really," Chris said slowly, "unless maybe his belt?"

"Yes?"

"Well, he really loved his belt," Chris said. "It was a genuine US marshal's belt. It had this big buckle. It was, let's see, about two inches deep and four inches wide. It wasn't like a usual buckle in that you didn't put a pin through a hole. The front of the buckle was solid and it had a smaller hooked pin on the back so that you just threaded it into the hole. The front was very decorative, with two Colt 45s crossed at the barrels and a steer head and horns, with the words 'US Marshal' across the top."

"And did your father wear any kind of cap?"

"Nope," Chris announced. "Rain or shine, my father never needed anything on his head."

Chapter Eleven

"RIGHT, THEN, LET'S see how far Betsy has been able to spread the news," Starrett said as they hopped back in the BMW and set their sights for just the other side of Rathmullan. He knew that the Eircom phone lines would be red hot by now with Betsy and her mates gossiping about the demise of a certain James Moore.

Starrett also knew that no matter how much the gossips speculated, they'd never ever be able to guess the path this poor unfortunate carpenter had taken to meet his maker. Not unless they had helped him on his way, that is, and Starrett doubted if that was the case. He wondered how long it would be before the murder and its method of execution became household knowledge in the area.

Once the news of the crucifixion surfaced, Ramelton would be a madhouse, with the world's media descending on the town like the proverbial flock of vultures. "RTÉ were making tapes, taking breaks and throwing shapes," as Christy Moore once famously sang. What with the world now as small as it was, thanks to the likes of Sky News and CNN, Ramelton could even expect representatives of the Vatican's *L'Osservatore Romano* breathing down the gardaí's collective necks by sundown.

But for all of that, and mindful of the grief he knew was surely around the corner, Starrett knew that the only way to deal with the investigation was to proceed at his, and his team's, natural pace. Otherwise there was a danger they'd join the mass of people destined to run around the town like headless chickens. He did resolve, as he pulled into Miss McLaughlin's gravel driveway, to have as much of Ramelton cordoned off from outsider parking as was safely possible. At least if the media circus were going to arrive, he didn't want to make it easy for them. And neither did he want long lines of locals on the doorsteps of Tower House complaining about not being able to cross the Lennon Bridge to the town's favourite watering hole, the near-legendary Bridge Bar, on the other side.

Eileen McLaughlin was another bottle-blonde. Starrett and Garvey found her wandering around her garden talking to her dog, a shifty-looking cocker spaniel bitch who licked her lips every time she circled Garvey's ankles. Eileen was slimmer and taller than Betsy, although the illusion of height may have been helped somewhat by her puffed-up hairstyle. Even in the morning's gentle breeze, Starrett couldn't spot a single strand of hair out of place. Eileen looked as if she'd never forgiven God for giving the looks she felt were reserved for her to Michelle Pfeiffer. Mrs McLaughlin was dressed in a yellow tracksuit top, green tracksuit bottom, with the essential additional Donegal layering—an orange woollen scarf around the neck—to protect the throat, at least on the outside, from the perennial damp air. She was topped and toed with a Ferrari baseball cap and a pair of purple Dunlop pumps, which all but covered a pair of two-tone blue socks. She looked like a straightened-out human rainbow as she strolled through her garden, and Starrett speculated that she could lose herself amongst her beds of multicoloured tulips.

"Good morning, gentlemen," Eileen said. "Beautiful morning, isn't it?"

"Yes," Starrett replied, dragging the word out as though he had only just realised the fact himself. "As a matter of a fact, it is. You know, this garden is a real credit to you, Eileen."

"Why, thank you, Starrett. That's very kind of you. There's no short-cut to gardening; you quite simply just have to put in the hours. I was just saying to Betsy the other day, 'Betsy,' I said, 'there are just not enough hours in the day to attend to all the plants and flowers and trees and lawns in my garden.' Well, at least that is what Seamus, my gardener, tells me once a month when he hands me his invoice."

"For something as beautiful as this, Eileen, you'd have to say that every cent was well spent. Sure, with the high skies, all these magnificent trees and the Swilly just across the road," Starrett said, turning slowly a full 360 degrees, "you've got your own little corner of paradise here."

"Yes, but I'll tell you what, talking about a rude intruder in paradise, that car of yours does makes a bit of a racket, doesn't it, Packie?" Eileen continued in her best Donegal lilt: "Madonna and I were just saying that it sounded like a Sherman tank coming up the lane. Weren't we, Madonna?" Having said that, she bent over and ruffled her dog's ears, which were big enough for her to be able to grab a playful handful. The dog pretty much ignored her, choosing instead to eye up Garvey's extremely appetising ankles.

"Sorry about that," Starrett muttered, barely audibly. "Sergeant Garvey, remind me to take another pool car next time we're out."

Eileen chose to ignore Starrett's little charade. Straightening her back, she seemed to experience, if the look in her eyes were anything to go by, a considerable degree of pain as she asked, "What's this I hear about our poor carpenter being killed earlier today? Sure, that's a terrible thing altogether, isn't it?"

"Aye, you're not wrong, Eileen," Starrett conceded, mindful that he'd lost the element of surprise. "Tell me, how long had you known him?"

"Well, now, let's see, only really a few months," she replied, simultaneously shooing a couple of bees away from her blood-red tulips. "Yes, about three months."

"He'd been doing some work for you, I believe?" Packie Garvey asked, taking out his notebook.

"You can put that away for a start, Sergeant Garvey," Eileen tut-tutted in her singsong voice. "No, no, no, we'll have none of that auld 'and the Widow McLaughlin *said*' nonsense."

"Ach now, Eileen, don't go mistaking Sergeant Garvey here for a journalist," Starrett said, breaking into a smile.

"Journalists, the gardaí, what's the difference?" Eileen said, now aping Daniel O'Donnell's accent perfectly. "They both try and get you to commit a statement to paper and then throw the same words back at you to hang you."

Starrett nodded to Garvey to put away his notebook and pen.

"Sorry, Eileen," he said, "you were just about to tell us about how Mr James Moore came to be doing some work for you."

"Well, look now, Inspector, I'll tell you the truth and I'll tell you no lie," Eileen started, looking around her garden in a conspiratorial manner. Seemingly happy that she'd spotted nobody lurking in her bushes, she continued, "Amanda, that's Amanda Morrison, Betsy's and my best friend, well, she persuaded me to give Jimmy some work."

"She was impressed with his work then?" Starrett offered.

"Some might say," Eileen replied coyly. Just then Madonna finally made her play for Garvey's right ankle, and Eileen turned gently on the beast: "Oh, careful pet, young Packie Garvey needs his ankles in perfect working condition this weekend, when he plays against Armagh in the semis, isn't that right, Sergeant?"

"Aye, well, you know," Garvey replied, in effect saying really nothing at all.

"Pay no attention to Madonna, she's harmless. Her bark is worse than her bite, and all she's doing is trying to get attention."

"Aye, a bit like her namesake across the water," Starrett replied, trying to draw a line under the doggy conversation

"Oh, if the stories I hear are correct, it's not the men's *ankles* the other one would be after," Eileen said, nodding knowingly. She looked around the garden again before continuing in not much more than a whisper, "I've heard there wasn't much acting going on in that movie she was in, the one with the s-e-x. Not much need for *acting*, if you get my drift."

Starrett, although exasperated, decided that now that Eileen McLaughlin was in a gossipy mood he might be able to lure her into giving something away about Amanda Morrison—if, in fact, there was something to give away. Starrett knew that the deal with gossips was that they traded in gossip: once you gave some, you stood to get a morsel in return.

"Yes, well, I can well believe that," Starrett said, before offering, "Of course, you know Lola Cashman?"

"The woman with U2's hat and glasses?" Eileen said gleefully.

"Well, apparently that case wasn't so much about Bono's hat and glasses," Starrett said, recalling a story he'd heard in the Bridge Bar.

"Really? Oh my goodness, you mean the whole case was all about other stuff she has."

"Apparently."

"What other stuff, Starrett? Photos? Videos?"

"I don't rightly know, might even just be a rattle, Eileen," Starrett offered, flicking his bent forefinger past the end of his nose a couple of times. "But you know what they say."

Eileen nodded positively, and Starrett wondered who she thought "they" were. "Ah," he continued slowly and quietly, "weren't you going to tell us something about Amanda and James Moore?"

For a moment, Eileen looked to be lost more in her just-suppose about what a certain dresser had been up to, than in giving up the dirt on her best friend. However, without missing a beat, she offered: "Well, Starrett, the thing is that Mandy had fallen big time for Jimmy, and she'd run out of things for him to do around the Manse, so she had me employ him here to fix up my kitchen just so she would, well you know, have . . . erm, well I suppose you'd have to say, *access*, yes that's it, just so that she had access to him."

Eileen smiled in the devilment of sharing this news, particularly with a member of the Garda Síochána, but her smile froze in a pathetic grin as she realised that one of the subjects of her gossip was dead. Her jaw dropped in shock, and she raised her left hand to her mouth as if trying to return the offending words.

"Oh my goodness, poor Amanda," she said in a rush. "Poor Jimmy, what exactly happened to him?"

"We're still investigating the details, Eileen," Starrett replied, far from a lie, but then again, even further from the truth. "What can you tell me about him?"

"About Jimmy?" she replied, looking surprised.

"Erm, yes . . ." Starrett said, slightly taken aback by her reaction, but trying hard not to show it.

"He was a great worker, no matter how much Mandy wanted to continue their . . . well whatever it was they had. He always insisted on doing a full day's work. I mean, he was a very quiet man, not really the kind you'd dream would have an affair. But then, you know what they say, don't you, Starrett? They say that every man will stray if he can find a woman who catches his eye and is willing to play, but only a certain type of woman will dander away."

"Did, erm . . ." Starrett began vaguely. "Did ah . . . First Minister Morrison know about the relationship?"

"Oh," Eileen replied, laughing the exclamation out into three syllables, "Ivan knew nothing about anything; I always thought he considered the dammed thing was for stirring your tea with."

"Sorry?" Packie Garvey said, his eyebrows shooting up.

"Well, Starrett, tell me this, you're a man of the world . . ." Eileen began. "Why would a man, in full possession of his faculties, marry an absolute goddess like Mandy and not want to ravage her every single time he set eyes on her? Eh, Starrett, tell me that. I mean, even Daniel O'D would have a charge at Mandy, wouldn't he?"

"Well, Eileen," Starrett began, "you have to realise that not every man is so inclined."

"Oh Starrett, you fool, of course I know that, and God bless them all so disinclined; the most of them want to run our country, or our ministry, for us. But my point would be that if I bought a Ferrari and only drove it to Whoriskey's once a week at 30 miles an hour to pick up the messages, well, wouldn't that just be a sin? Yes, it might even constitute criminal negligence. So, I'm not going to buy a Ferrari unless I'm prepared to give it a hammering every now and then on a nice long trip to Dublin or Galway or even Belfast, for heaven's sake. So, why would Ivan think he could get away with marrying Mandy—and believe you me, she was every bit as expensive as a Ferrari—and not . . . and not, well . . . cover your ears now, Packie, if you need to . . . give her a damn good seeing to every now and again?"

"Yes, we do get your point, Eileen," said Starrett.

"But the thing you don't know, Starrett, is that Mandy was a very needy woman," Eileen said, coughing in fake embarrassment before continuing: "I've been known to have a moment or two myself, you know, but Mandy, well . . . when God created her, he should have issued her with a health warning."

"Did Amanda have many extra-marital relationships, then?" Starrett asked in a moving-swiftly-along tone.

"Surprisingly few, really," Eileen replied, sounding a little sad. "She genuinely believed in the whole trip of a woman, a man, falling in love, marrying and living happily ever after—the fool!"

"But come on, Eileen, First Minister Ivan Morrison, for all his virtues, and God knows he has some, is hardly someone you'd compare to George Clooney, so why did the beautiful Amanda end up with him?"

"Aye, if that's not the eighth wonder of the world, Starrett. Both myself and Betsy counselled against it, but then I suppose we all have to realise and accept that women do have needs other than the physical."

"Financial, for instance?"

"Financial, for instance," the Widow McLaughlin agreed.

"But what was in it for First Minister Morrison? A trophy wife?" Starrett asked.

"Exactly!" Eileen replied, emphasising the three syllables.

Chapter Twelve

MAJOR NEWTON CUNNINGHAM was waiting on the steps of Tower House for Starrett when he returned to the garda station.

The major was deep in conversation with local publican and raconteur James McDaid, and, for a short time, Starrett thought he was going to be able to stray under his superior officer's radar.

"Ah, Inspector," the major's clipped tones boomed out over Gamble Square. "I'm due to leave for a course shortly, and I need you to brief me immediately on the ahm, Second . . . ahm . . ." He turned to McDaid and said, "Sorry, forgive my manners, James. Could you excuse me? Duty calls and all of that. I'll see you on the sixth for a spot of lunch then?"

James McDaid put his hands in his back pockets, Bette Davis style, and walked away whistling "Ballad of a Thin Man".

"Yes, sir," Starrett replied, wondering which of the major's regularly frequented golf courses he was off to. "How much do you know?"

"Well, Starrett, not a lot, to be truthful," Newton Cunningham said. "Aside from there's a bleeding crucifixion on my patch and my lead detective has gone AWOL."

"Now, Major, sure wasn't it you who taught me to get on the trail before it gets cold? And that's what I'm doing, sir, following your standard procedure."

"I'd say without the slightest fear of contradiction, that the *only* procedure you are involved in right now is blowing smoke up your superior's . . ."

"Oh, Major, don't forget the Bean Gharda, will you,"

"Where, where?" the major asked, rising up from his customary seat on the ancient railings which bordered the tricky stone steps up to the station house. The major needed to rest his back. He couldn't stand unassisted for long periods of time, so he had his regular series of props around the station house and Ramelton where he could support himself without actually being seen sitting down: radiators, backs of chairs, sides of desks, walls, steps and staircases were all called into operation. If there was ridge with a minimum three-inch ledge, the major incorporated it into his circuit.

His wiry frame was always clothed in a checked shirt, Royal Ulster Rifles regimental tie, and white and brown brogues, which after twelve years were only starting to wear in and shine up properly. On the golf course, where he seemed to spend the majority of his week, he changed out of his usual tan chinos into a pair of plus-fours, which were in matching Donegal tweed to his jacket. His other concession to the course was that he exchanged his ferruled ash for a golf club. He was permanently slightly stooped, lowering his true height of six feet one inch to five foot ten-and-a-half inches. Members of his team claimed that this was so he no longer had to stoop while crossing under the low doorways of Tower House. Starrett, however, knew that it was the result of a war wound. The major's back was gone, his liver had all but packed up, his heart was dickey, his hearing was suspect; but he still had the eyes of a hawk, a nose primed for clues and a full head of flowing grey hair. Whereas the nickname Tarzan usually applied to a man much more junior than the major's seventy-two years, it also implied that in his younger years he must have been a fine specimen. He'd always maintained that he'd retire only into a coffin. He was so feared and revered in Garda circles that Starrett was convinced that the major would see off any and all internal mutinies for at least the next decade. On top of which, he was still great at his job, totally up-to-date with garda politics, and the administrators would ignore his patch at their peril.

That was all that concerned Starrett. He didn't want the chief superintendent's role himself, and he didn't want to have to waste time training up a replacement.

"Right, Starrett," the major said, hobbling down the steps. "Let's wander to the clean Lennon River, so we can enjoy some peace and privacy, shall we?"

"Yes, let's do that," Starrett replied.

A minute later, the major was enthroned on his favourite stone—a stone Starrett was convinced the major had used so much over the years that it had been worn down to an almost perfect fit. The trees on the far bank were in full bloom, and an artist couldn't look for more inspiration than that of the lazy village of Ramelton going about its day, against the backdrop of the rambling river, the majestic trees with their forty shades of green and the blue sky. A Massey Ferguson tractor was crossing the bridge from the Rathmullan side, with behind it a queue of frustrated drivers who, for all their impatience and bravado, couldn't find a way past it. Starrett wondered why they could never realise that it didn't really matter whether they did or didn't pass him: they were going to reach their destination when they were meant to and not a second before. Take James Moore for instance: consider all the tractors and similar vehicles he must have overtaken in his life and look where it had taken him.

"So, what do we know?" the major asked, pulling Starrett away from his thoughts.

"Well, Major, we know that a carpenter, a man called James Moore, was nailed to a cross some time in the early morning, and that the cross was tied to the pulpit in the Second Federation Church with Mr Moore left to die on it."

"He actually died on the cross?"

"Yes. Sam—"

"You mean the delightful Dr Aljoe, of course?" the major interrupted.

"Of course, as I was about to say, Dr Sam-*antha* Aljoe confirmed that he bled to death post crucifixion. And bejeepers, Major, did our boyo bleed. I'd say there must have been at least four pints on the church floor."

"Well, as you appear to have a high level of expertise in that area, Starrett, I'll take your word for it," the major said, before adding: "And what else?"

"James Moore had been doing some carpentry work for Mrs Betsy Bell."

"Oh, my goodness, Betsy Bell," the major said, his ears pricking up so much so he could have auditioned for the part of Spock in *Star Trek*. "Did you talk to her? I will admit there was a time, before I met the current Mrs Newton Cunningham, when I was rather partial to Mrs Bell."

Starrett thought that Betsy Bell could have been only seventeen years old, at the most, when she was the centre of the major's attention. As the major started to reminisce, he turned his dark-green felt hat around in his hand, whilst the finger and thumb of his other hand traced the outline of the wide brim.

"I remember going to choir practice around in the Town Hall in Castle Street just so I could steal a glance at Betsy. Starrett, I can tell you, she was a fine figure of a woman back in those days. I even joined the Dramatic Society and put myself up for several pantomimes just so I could be close to her."

"Anything romantic ever happen, Major?" Starrett asked.

"Well, erm, the current Mrs Newton Cunningham came along and that, well you know, put paid to all of my romantic adventures," the major replied, pulling himself up very short in his story. "So how is she keeping these days?"

"She's in fine fettle, Major, keeping well. Anyway, she employed James Moore to do some work in her house. His carpentry was excellent, so she introduced him to her friend Amanda Morrison . . ."

"Oh, my goodness, Starrett, this is not going to get messy, is it?"

"Well, Major, it would appear that perhaps Amanda and James Moore had a bit of a fling."

"Oh my goodness, there's going to be hell to pay, Starrett; you mark my words . . . hell to pay."

"Perhaps the devil has already collected."

"But surely Ivan Morrison wouldn't crucify someone in his own church?"

"Well, that would be difficult to imagine, Major. The man hasn't seen his own feet for at least twenty years, but stranger things have been known to happen."

"Indeed they have, Starrett, indeed they have."

Starrett knew from the look in the major's eye that he'd lost him at that precise moment. The major rose from his throne and said, "Well,

I'd better leave you to it. Watch out for the press, Starrett. Let's keep them at bay and get this matter cleared up and sent to the courts as soon as possible. I'd hate to be having a messy summer in Ramelton this year. But you say Betsy Bell was looking grand, eh? Perhaps I should mosey on down and interview her myself. I might just pick up on something you missed."

"There's a good chance of that, Major, and I'm sure she'd love to see you again."

"Yes, well, if you insist you need the help, I just might drop in on her on my way down to the course, you know. I'll keep you posted."

"Good idea. See if she knows where Mrs Morrison is," Starrett called after the major as he crossed the road.

Chapter Thirteen

INSPECTOR STARRETT'S NEXT call was to his team, to see how they'd been getting on. Quite a few of them were still out, knocking on doors, house to house, in the surrounding streets of the Second Federation Church. So far, no suspicious sightings had been reported.

Starrett was happy to note that no calls had yet been logged from the press. He was not happy to note that his team had absolutely nothing else to report but sometimes it just worked out that way. You dug and you dug in the hope of finding something. The problem was that you were never even sure you were digging in the right place. The only important thing was that you were digging. His logic decreed simply: no digging, no discovery.

Since Starrett had changed his career, he'd been searching. He'd disappeared to London—he'd had to—and there was a certain amount of shame involved in not achieving what his family had expected from him. There was an even larger degree of shame in not achieving what you had expected of yourself. As was mostly the case in life, the family forgave him a long time before he forgave himself.

London, in the late 1970s and early 1980s was an easy place to hide. Starrett had found, to his surprise, that there was something therapeutic about living in a town where no one, including people living in the same house, knew you or anything about you or your business. This was particularly refreshing to someone like Starrett, who'd come from a small town like Ramelton, where everyone knew absolutely everything about everyone. Yes, he'd been desperately lonely at first, so lonely in fact that if it hadn't been for the situation at home, he'd have been back on the first boat. But London was filled with thousands of kindred spirits, people with their own deeds and thoughts to forget, and the grand city embraced all outcasts as its own. London town, like all great towns and cities, instinctively knows that its new blood is its lifeblood.

One by one, he made friends and acquaintances. A month into his enforced exile, he'd reached the end of one day and realised that not once since he'd woken up had he thought about the folks back home. He hadn't even thought about one person in particular back home.

Starrett had always been a fan of cars, especially classic cars, and so he followed his passion and secured a job at Kensington Classic Cars. Pretty soon—within eighteen months—he was not only their number one salesman, but they'd also allowed him to scout out antique cars in need of care, love, attention. This was the bit he loved most, and pretty soon he was spending most of his time travelling throughout southern England in his endless search for classic cars.

The cars attracted a particular set of people, people fortunately not bigoted against the Irish, which was not always the case for the emigrants of the time. As cosy as Starrett's little scene was, every time the IRA let off a bomb, he could see the look of doubt and even mistrust in some people's eyes as they heard his Donegal accent.

He'd had a few relationships, and few of those had created any lasting impression. He knew the reason for this and tried to avoid thinking about it. He made friends with girls better than he made girlfriends. He enjoyed a pint of Guinness every now and then, which in Starrett's case didn't mean that he had a drink problem, just that he enjoyed sitting around in pubs, chatting, particularly about cars.

The years passed, and the more contacts he made in the car trade, the less he had to search for new cars. But the less he had to search for his cars, the less he enjoyed the work. Soon he realised that it was the thrill of the chase and tracking down leads that put the biggest tick into his job-satisfaction box. He also realised, as he crossed the big three-oh threshold, that he wasn't really living much of a life in London. He was merely treading water, and he wasn't the only one. He could remember sitting in a pub in West Hampstead with a bunch of mates, some of whom were Irish, some not. Not for the first time in his life, he heard an Irishman cry into his beer about the "auld country", and in spite of his natural affinity with a fellow countryman, he heard himself saying, "If it's that brilliant, why don't you just feck off home to the old sod?"

"Well, why don't you just feck off there yourself, Starrett?"

"Bejeepers," Starrett stuttered, as if he'd just been hit by a holy beam of light from a Jaguar Mark II on the dual carriageway to Damascus. "You know what? I think I'll just do that."

And he did.

The following morning, he went home, forsaking the usual ferry, arriving instead at British Airways' infamous cattle pen, officially known as Gate 49, Aldergrove Airport.

His eyes *didn't* drop out when he walked up the street in Ramelton. People *didn't* turn and talk about him and the scandal he'd left behind. Within half an hour, he realised that he was yesterday's news; there was more recent gossip to preoccupy the locals. Starrett was allowed, even encouraged, to blend back into the community as though he never been away.

Even his parents, who hadn't seen him for the entire twelve years he'd spent in the Big Smoke, welcomed him home like the prodigal son. They didn't go as far as killing the fatted calf, but his mam did roast up a chicken for him.

And that was that.

Well, apart from technical and domestic details like flying back to London the following week to put his flat and contents on the market and working out a severance deal with the two principals of the Classic Car Company. At that stage, through his endeavours, Starrett owned 25 per cent of the company. They behaved as total gentlemen, as they always had in their dealings with him. He sold them back 15 per cent for a handsome sum and decided to hold on to 10 per cent so that he'd have something other than money to show for his time in London. Besides, he might want to have some continued involvement, albeit merely as a car scout in Ireland.

It was the best deal he'd ever done in his life.

He was surprised how little he missed London, and even more surprising was how easily he slotted back into the Donegal way of life. In London, everything had gone past in a flash, without his even having a chance to be aware of what he missed. At the Ramelton pace, he really did have time to stop and smell the roses in his father's incredible garden.

A friend of his father's, a certain Major Newton Cunningham, was around for dinner six weeks into Starrett's new life, and after Starrett had told him about how he used to track down the classic cars, the major declared, "With that kind of job experience, it seems to me you'd be great at tracking down some of these petty criminals we come into contact with over at the garda station."

And that was the career taken care of.

Starrett absolutely loved each and every day he worked there.

He did his twenty-two weeks' training at Garda Training Centre in Templemore, County Tipperary; twenty-four weeks at various stations around the countryside; another refresher fourteen weeks at Templemore; thirty-six weeks as probationary garda, and then a final six weeks at Templemore to complete his training and graduate as a garda, returning to the major's patch in Ramelton. The major had found a way around one slightly sticky regulation in the Garda Code of Proceedure, namely a guard not being stationed in his own village, claiming that as Starrett had resided in London for so long, he was no longer a local.

Starrett's subjects had included law, social studies, theory of policing, communications, the Irish language, physical training and technical studies. He could also have covered European languages but couldn't be bothered on the grounds that he'd pretty much decided he wasn't going to travel much, and when on holidays he still had more than 99 per cent of America to discover. This turned out to be a sorry omission, but he wasn't to realise how handy the European languages would have been to him in Ireland within the decade.

Within seven years, he made inspector. He kept thinking that one day someone was going to tap him on the shoulder and say, "The game's up, out you go." But no, he was allowed to make it up as he went along, and he seemed to be making it up with at least some degree of expertise, because the major annually declared their patch to have the best clear-up rate in the country. The major was prouder still when the Templemore boys sent a couple of their superintendents up to Ramelton for several days to monitor Starrett's team and its methods.

What was the key to Starrett's success? The only thing the

Templemore superintendents would report back to their Dublin superiors—who would in turn pass it on to the major, who in turn would pass it on to Starrett—was Starrett's unique ability to read situations and witnesses. According to the Tipperary heads, Starrett seemed to have some sixth sense when it came to assessing the truthfulness of witnesses. When Starrett was told the news, he immediately thought of his mam, who had a kind of healing gift that she spread liberally and freely in the community.

Until the major had quoted the Dubliner's use of the words "sixth sense", he'd never ever considered possible by-products of his mother's genes. But that evening he recalled several incidents from his times in London when he was either very lucky or else charmed in decisions and calls he had made. Like the time he drove a colleague down to Guildford to pick up a car. Starrett refused to allow his workmate to drive the car away until he'd checked the brakes. It turned out that the brake-cable was a micron away from snapping. Like the time he was on a date and they intended to stop off at a favourite watering hole in Soho for a drink on the way to the cinema. On his journey into the West End, Starrett suddenly experienced several disturbing flashes. Later he could recall them only as partial hallucinations of scenes of human carnage blazing through his mind. Starrett detoured to leafy Hampstead instead. Later that night, he saw on the news that a bomb had destroyed the Soho pub he and his date had been planning on visiting. There were several fatalities. Before the superintendent's report, Starrett had put these and similar incidents down to luck.

On his return from London, Starrett had used a modest proportion of his shares income to buy and refurbish a stone barn on the Rathmullan Road with a Swilly view. And over the years he had made it his own hideaway.

He wondered now why James Moore's name had never come up when he'd been looking for skilled and trustworthy local craftsmen. The man he'd eventually used was a master craftsman himself and he'd done Starrett proud, but, he thought, now that Starrett had seen the quality of his work it was odd that no one had even recommended James Moore.

Starrett and Packie headed up the steep hill that was Bridge Street, took a right, enjoyed a quick whiff of the comfort food on offer at

Chapter Fourteen

I T WASN'T SO much that the Manse of the Second Federation Church was ugly, as that it was a contrast to the amazing scenery of the spot where the Lennon River flows into Lough Swilly. The rear overlooked Church Street, and this aspect was unsightly to the degree that every time Starrett walked past the place, he considered what could be done to improve the drab, grey, pipe-infested eyesore. Each time he reached the same conclusion; it could be improved only by a demolitions expert.

A quick trip down Mortimer's Lane, to the right of the Manse, revealed the true front of the house, reached via an ornamental side gate. The grand house's designers had originally intended it to be admired from afar. In recent years, though, the numerous houses springing up around the foothills of the village had restricted the views of and out of the Manse to the extent that it looked hemmed in.

Inside, the house did not betray such imperfections, and it looked as if First Minister Morrison and previous keepers of the keys had gone to considerable trouble to retain each and every one of the Manse's original features in perfect condition. In Morrison's case, the Second Federation Church had paid for the refurbishments, whereas all such similar work would have had to come out of his predecessors' own pockets. From a salvager's point of view, the inside of the house was positively a gold mine in waiting.

For his part, First Minister Ivan Morrison seemed totally oblivious to the worth and beauty of his surroundings. As he led Starrett and

Garvey through the shadowy hallway to the sitting room, he appeared preoccupied. He had changed clothes since they'd last seen him and was now wearing a black morning suit—the type that requires you to throw up your coat-tails before you sit down, which Morrison had mastered with considerable flair.

The sitting room, unlike the hallway, was airy and bright, furnished with antiques that Starrett assumed were acquired when the house was first built. The walls were covered with paintings, prints and photographs from yesteryear. Several vases were filled to overflowing with colourful flower displays, and the pale blue curtains around the large bay window softened the somewhat masculine feeling of the room.

Morrison looked and acted like someone who was visiting his dentist, simultaneously dreading the experience and relieved that he was in the process of putting the horror behind him.

Starrett stood by the fireplace admiring the room as Morrison invited them to take a seat.

"Bejeepers," Starrett half shouted as he sank too deep into the sofa in front of the peat and wood-log fire. "There's a chance you might never get me out of this sofa or this room."

"I'm sure we're both much too busy to be loitering around drawing rooms all afternoon. Can we please get on with this nasty business?"

"I'll tell you, First Minister, I'm parched. Any chance of an auld cup of tea or coffee?"

Morrison gave an "oh, if I must" shrug and rang a bell, which sat on a smallish circular table, conveniently positioned to the right of his leather chair. The table also supported a reading light, a Roberts radio, a copy of *The Irish Times* and several neatly stacked magazines and books. The chair succumbed too easily, and its contours changed too quickly to accommodate Morrison's portly shape, for it to have been his maiden visit there. Starrett guessed it was probably his favourite chair and position, and friends and strangers alike were banned from sampling the comfort it offered.

A few moments later, a dark-haired girl arrived.

"Yes, Agga," Morrison announced, his baritone voice filling the entire room. "Refreshments for our visitors."

"Oh, tea or coffee?" she enquired, her Polish heritage shining through.

"Coffee would be perfect, *please*," Starrett replied. "Thank . . . you . . . very . . . much."

Just as he finished, he realised he himself had been guilty of addressing her as if, just because she was from foreign parts, she couldn't understand English. It reminded him of when he'd visited London first and he'd had to resort to such tactics to make himself, the foreigner in that instance, understood.

Morrison was obviously not ready for the interview to start, because he busied himself with his papers, making notes here and there. Occasionally he looked up to Starrett and Garvey, as if to say, "Are you two still here?"

Agga returned a few minutes later, laden down with a tray precariously crammed with white bone-china cups and saucers, white and patterned pastry plates, a generous milk jug, a deprived sugar bowl, shiny teaspoons, dainty pastry forks, snow-white lace napkins, a scrumptious Victoria sponge cake and an off-white coffee pot. Starrett realised that she was thin as a rake and it had been her dark blue uniform and her blue and white striped pinafore which had created the illusion of a person of greater substance. He rushed over to assist her with her burden, gaining nothing for his trouble bar a roll of Morrison's swinish eyes.

The fact that Starrett and Garvey had not eaten since breakfast and the first minister had his generous girth to support resulted in the better part of the sponge cake being reduced to a sparse scattering of crumbs within a matter of minutes. For his part, Starrett couldn't remember when he had last tasted a cake where the sponge felt so light, the cream so fresh and the jam so much of hand-picked strawberries. "Lofty coffee"—a Second Federation Church version of a high tea— over, the three men finally got down to the business in hand.

They had skirted around the issue of Moore's crucifixion in general terms during refreshments, but now Starrett moved the talk from conversation to interrogation.

"So, Ivan," Starrett said, using a flimsy napkin to dab at either side of his mouth. "You weren't exactly truthful with us this morning, were you?"

"How so?" First Minister Morrison replied.

This wasn't the most passionate denial Starrett had ever heard.

"Well, you didn't tell us that on top of the work James Moore had done for you in the library of the Manse, you'd also commissioned him to build you a pulpit?"

"You didn't ask," Morrison snorted. "I would have thought that by now, Inspector, you would have realised you get nothing in this world if you don't ask for it."

"OK, I'm asking now, Ivan. Was James Moore making a pulpit for you?"

"No," Morrison said. "We've got a perfectly good pulpit as it is. The Texas congregation had it shipped over as a present from our American brothers and sisters."

"We'll come back to that," Starrett said, trying not to show surprise. "Have you heard from Mrs Morrison yet?"

"No, I haven't."

"Aren't you worried?" Starrett asked.

"Oh, Starrett, she's forty-one years of age. She's resourceful; she's well capable of looking after herself."

"Sorry," Starrett said in evident disbelief. "I have to admit to you here, Ivan, you're troubling me. Does Amanda often go missing? Are any of her clothes missing? Has a suitcase been taken? Have you called her friends to check whether they know where she is?"

"Mrs Morrison lives her own life, Inspector. We are not joined at the hip. We have never been one of those pathetic married couples who live in each other's pockets. A wife is not a carbuncle attached to her husband's body. A man can never own a woman, and a woman can never own a man. I can't live Mrs Morrison's life, nor can she mine. She has way too many clothes for me to know whether any of them are missing. I don't know where she keeps any suitcases she may have. All I can tell you is that no doubt they're a matching set and I'll eventually receive the bill for excess baggage. And finally, Inspector, as you well know, a man was found murdered in my church this morning. I've been way too preoccupied with that incident to worry about ringing Mrs Morrison's friends to check on her whereabouts."

"Bejeepers, Ivan, she's your wife. She's missing . . ."

"I'll thank you to address me by my full title. That's First Minister to you, Inspector, and I'd add that until such time as I report my wife missing, her whereabouts are no concern of yours. On top of which, I would have thought, with this morning's mess, your hands would be full enough."

"OK," Starrett said, smiling his way through Morrison's rebuff. "James Moore: how long did he work here?"

"Oh, a few months," Morrison replied dismissively.

"Did the two of you have much to do with each other?"

"I don't have a lot to do with the servants, Inspector."

"For a minister, you don't really seem to have a lot to do with anybody, Reverend Morrison."

"First Minister, Inspector." Morrison said, smiling sweetly. "I don't think it does to become too familiar with hired help."

"I was thinking more of your wife, Vicar," Starrett said, unable to hide a snarl.

"This interview is terminated," Morrison said, fussing this way and that, as he awkwardly squeezed himself out of his chair.

He'd just about made it to a standing position when Starrett jumped up in front of him and shoved him back down into his leather chair. This time the tails of his coat fell awkwardly in trails of several future creases. Starrett's attack could later, if necessary, be interpreted as his having bumped into Morrison.

Starrett spoke next, his tone authoritative and his volume low:

"You're mistaken, First Minister. This interview is most certainly not over. It will be over only as and when the sergeant and I say it's over, and if you have a problem with that, then we'll arrest you here and now and take you down to Tower House and conclude our questioning there. Now, I for one would much prefer to finish the proceedings in these far more salubrious surroundings. What do you think yourself, Packie?"

"I don't know; it would be a close call for me. I mean, with the cells in the garda station being in the basement, below the level of the river, there'd probably be more vermin down there." The sergeant took a long stare at Morrison before continuing, "But then again, maybe not."

"There it is then. All right, Parson?"

Morrison, now beetroot red, looked as if smoke might emerge from his ears any second.

"I'll take that as a yes, then," continued Starrett. "Now, where were we? Oh yes, we were talking about James Moore working in this fine house. Did you see him around much?

"No," Morrison replied indignantly.

"Did you talk to him much?"

"I don't believe I ever did."

"A man worked in your house for several months, a master craftsman in fact, and you're telling me you didn't talk to him even once?"

"I'd no call to; Mrs Morrison took care of all that kind of stuff."

"Then tell me this, Chaplain: what did you think of his work?"

"I assume it was OK. I was concerned only with my valuable books," Morrison said.

"Sorry? I don't understand."

"Well, when he was taking the old shelves down, we had to remove all the books and stack them around the walls in here until the new shelves were ready. I was worried that they might get damaged."

"But none were damaged?"

"No, they were all fine."

"And his work: what do you mean you, 'assumed' it was OK. You don't mean to tell me you haven't examined it yet?"

"I have other priorities, Inspector."

"OK, I accept that, but I'll tell you what, out of respect for the poor unfortunate, let's just go in there now and have a look at his work."

Without waiting for a response, Starrett rose and nodded to Garvey to do the same. Starrett crossed the room to Morrison and offered his hand to help him. The unholy trinity then made their way, led by the first minister, into the library.

It was exactly the same size as the sitting room but windowless, with all four walls packed floor to ceiling with books.

Starrett strode over the royal blue carpet to the opposite wall; he grabbed the edge of one of the upright units between his thumb and forefinger and shook it. What did he expect? That the shelves would collapse around him? The intricate carvings and inlays on the edges of the shelves were similar in texture and design to the decorative finishing he'd seen earlier on the new pulpit. He removed a book at random. The name Seamus Heaney was embossed in gold letters on the brown leather spine. As Morrison looked on nervously, Starrett removed the book from the slipcase and read aloud: "Seamus Heaney, Poems and a Memoir, illustrated by Henry Pearson, the Limited Editions Club."

Starrett carefully flicked through the book.

Morrison took the book and the slipcase firmly from Starrett, with great disdain, flicked to the title page and said, "Look, here, it's signed by Seamus Heaney and the illustrator and someone else. It's a limited edition of 2000, and my edition is number 354."

"Is it a good book, then?" Garvey asked.

"Is it a good book!" Morrison mocked. "It's Seamus Heaney, for heaven's sake!"

"Yes, but have you read it?" Starrett asked.

Morrison laughed to himself as he replaced the book in its slipcase and returned it to the shelf.

"I'll take that as a no, then," Starrett said, winking at Garvey. "What about this one?"

Starrett picked another book at random. This time it had a vibrantly colourful dust jacket.

"Which one is that?" Morrison asked, whilst carefully ensuring that the spine of the Heaney tome was level with those of the neighbouring volumes.

"It's *First of the True Believers* by Theodore Hennessey."

"Oh, that's just airport fodder. It's Mrs Morrison's; it shouldn't even be in here. Just leave it on the table there by the door and I'll have Agga take it up to Mrs Morrison's room."

Garvey, who was also examining the shelves, seemed to have found a book that caught his eye. Morrison now didn't know which way to turn, as Garvey removed a book from the shelves.

"What's that one, Packie?"

Morrison rushed over and relieved Garvey of the large, black leather volume.

"Oh, careful, that one's very rare. That's the *History of the Second Federation Church* by one of our revered first ministers, James Driver from our Las Vegas parish. There were only ever 200 of this particular book printed, and this is the only one outside of the United States of America."

"Is it the history of the church, or your rule book or your Ten Commandments, or something?" Starrett asked.

"A combination of all three in fact. We have no commandments, but we have the Twelve Rules and Thirty-Three Laws of Federation. Bill O'Donnell—" Morrison cleared his throat, perhaps at the over-familiarity of use of the church's founder's name, "—wanted to try to keep our church as basic as possible. His point was that when you tell people that a religion is based on a father sending his son to die, humiliated and nailed to a cross, and then the son ascends in full view up into the heavens . . . well, you have to admit that it does stretch belief somewhat. So the entire foundation of your church is built on quicksand. However, if you say to people, 'Come and join us and we will teach you how to live more successfully with your fellow men and women. We will show you how to make your life easier, not perfect, but just easier.' Well, it's relatively simple for them to take that sort of leap of faith, isn't it?"

"Is it?" Starrett enquired. "Do we not need something bigger and better than ourselves to look up to? Do we not need to believe at least in the possibility of miracles just to help us get through our drab lives?"

"No, no, no," Morrison replied, as if the dentist had just advised him there was nothing needing doing. "That's where the majority of religions fall flat on their collective faces. They assume that their congregations are pathetic and in need of spiritual guidance. What they fail to realise is that, in this day and age, the majority of people believe that when they die that's it: it's over, the end, finito. We become nothing more than worm-food, fertilisation for the soil, so there's not a lot of point in aspiring to, or expecting, anything more. OK now, for the sake of our discussion, let's just, for the moment at least, accept that as fact.

"Then Bill O'Donnell started to consider how we could make our flocks' lives easier. From there it was all very basic and pretty simple. Firstly, if we as humans help each other in our everyday tasks, we increase our level of achievement. Everything literally stems from that. Our Thirty-Three Laws are in reality hints and tips about how we can live together and enjoy a better life by helping each other." Morrison paused and led them back into the sitting room. His precious books would be safer with the two policemen out of the library.

"But all that living together and helping each other is a bit idealistic, isn't it?" Starrett offered, once they were back in their old chairs again.

"We like to think we're more realists than idealists."

"But you're not offering anyone a reason to aspire to greatness," Starrett said. "Take Packie here, for instance . . . now, if you've ever seen him fly up the centre of the hurling field and score, sure it's a sight for bright eyes."

"Yes, but does it physically do anything for the community?" Morrison enquired, with a tone that suggested he'd been down this discussion route numerous times before.

"It inspires them."

"Yes, but it doesn't feed them."

"Man does not live by bread alone," Starrett said and immediately regretted it.

"Ah, that old chestnut," Morrison said smugly. "But let me just say this in conclusion, Starrett: the main difference between the Second Federation Church and every other church is that we do not feel we are superior, nor do we feel a need to convert as many people as possible to our way of life."

"So noted," Starrett replied graciously. "But if you don't mind, I'd like to get back to the subject of James Moore. I'm trying to figure out, if you didn't communicate much with the carpenter, how he took instruction for building the pulpit for you."

"What pulpit?"

"The magnificent pulpit that Chris Moore, James' fifteen-year-old son, showed me just a couple of hours ago," Starrett said. Seeing the bewilderment in Morrison's eyes, he continued, "I'm sorry. I was told he'd made it for you and your church."

"It's the first I've ever heard of it," Morrison replied. "We've no need for one."

Starrett felt that the first minister was telling the truth. He considered his next question carefully, trying it out in his mind a few different ways, but in the end he knew that there was really only one way to ask the question.

"Did you know that your wife was having an affair with James Moore?"

At that precise moment, Agga entered the library, presumably to clear away the tea things. Morrison screamed something at her in a foreign language, which made her turn on a pinhead and run out of the room in tears.

"Right, that's it. The interview is most definitely over, gentlemen. You can see yourselves out," Morrison said, angling himself out of his chair sideways and trotting swiftly out of the room.

Packie made to chase after him, but Starrett shook his head slowly from left to right a couple of times.

"The first minister's going nowhere, Packie," Starrett said, helping himself to the remaining inch wedge of Victoria sponge. "Leave him be for now. Did you know that if you put a few drops of whiskey on the tail of a scorpion, it'll run around in a crazy circle until it kills itself?"

"What, you mean that the first minister is running around in circles now?" Packie asked, clearly confused.

"Nope," Starrett replied as he stood up and winked his left ice-blue eye at Garvey. "What I meant is that it's a sad waste of whiskey."

Chapter Fifteen

As they strolled down Bridge Street, Packie was the first to speak: "So, do you think the first minister knew his wife was having an affair with James Moore?"

"I do, Packie," Starrett replied, hands deep in pockets and feeling and acting twitchy. "That's not the saddest part of their relationship though."

"And what is then?"

"I'll tell you, if I can blag a fag off you."

"Ah, Inspector."

"Ah, don't 'ah' me, Packie," Starrett sighed, more annoyed at himself than his sergeant was. "What time is it?"

"Four-thirty."

"Well, that's great, isn't it? It's only my first ciggy of the day."

Garvey made a fuss about giving Starrett one of the remaining nine Players from the packet he kept in his breast pocket.

"How many left now, Packie?"

"After this one, there'll be eight."

The sergeant carried the packet of Players around for Starrett, who'd been quitting since he returned from London. "This time I'm serious," Starrett had reported to his trusted sergeant. The idea was that the end of this pack was the end of Starrett's smoking life. Secretly the detective was searching for a reason, a bigger reason, to give up the terrible habit, which he enjoyed immensely. In times of desperation, he reasoned with himself, there were worse things you could do to your body. Things like walking around the streets of Letterkenny; if the traffic didn't kill you, the exhaust fumes just might. Things like consuming vast amounts of food filled with additives and preservatives. Things like spending a whole winter in Donegal without taking a break somewhere—anywhere—in the sun. Heck, even a weekend trip down to Belfast might just do the trick.

Starrett grabbed the coffin nail and struck a Lucifer against the brick wall as he passed the derelict hotel. He took a deep drag.

"Ach," he said with a loud sigh of pleasure. "How can something so good be so bad?"

"Weren't you going to enlighten me as to the saddest part of First Minister Morrison and his wife's relationship?" Packie asked.

"Oh yes . . ." Starrett paused and removed a small piece of tobacco that had become embedded between two of his Colgate-white teeth. He felt it was worth the trouble of getting something stuck between your teeth just because it felt so great when you managed to manoeuvre it free with your tongue. Starrett liked the nicotine hit, but he hated the taste tobacco left in his mouth and the sandpaper roughness it left in his throat. Someday he'd give up smoking; some day soon, but not today.

He walked a few more steps before continuing: "Well, I thought the sad thing was not that Morrison *knows* his wife was cheating, but that he doesn't *care* about it. This in turn tends to suggest to me that this is not the first time she has strayed."

"Just because they sleep in separate rooms?"

"Fair play to you, Packie. I wondered if you'd pick up on Morrison's reference to 'her room'." Starrett smiled. They'd just reached the steps of Tower House. "But no, not just that; it was more the look in his eyes. Ivan Morrison doesn't expect anything from life and so he's never disappointed. On top of which, the wee shit is more concerned about how great Amanda looks on the end of his arm than he is about her alleged adultery. Look, Packie, I've got an appointment up in Gomorrah; could you take young Nuala with you and see if you can find those friends of James Moore we heard about? His workmate Colm Donovan, his old friend Daniel McGuinness and Uncle Dolphie, who's not his uncle but his brother-in-law. You know what we're after: literally anything we can find out about James. Oh, yeah, I nearly forgot. On your way back, could you also drop in the Manse and have a a wee chat with Agga by herself. She should have something worthwhile to tell us."

Packie nodded and entered Tower House in search of Garda Nuala Gibson. Starrett remained on the steps, smoking and looking around at the generous scattering of butts at his feet. Starrett spent the final few moments with his dying cigarette trying to guess the identities of the smokers of the butts on the ground from clues such as lipstick smears, butt-lengths and pinch-marks.

He managed to guess only four out of five owners, less than his normal 100 per cent success rate.

Chapter Sixteen

ABOUT FIVE MINUTES after Starrett started out on his ten-minute drive to Letterkenny, Sergeant Packie Garvey and Garda Nuala Gibson, stuck behind a long snake of cars following an ancient Massey Ferguson tractor, were taking the same time to cover half the distance on the same road.

"Just our luck," Packie said as he settled down to accept the eighteen-mile-an-hour journey. "Yer man is blessed in situations like this; or at least he always seems to miss them."

"Yes," Nuala said from the driver's seat. "I've heard he has some kind of sixth sense or something."

She was slightly distracted from her conversation because there was a nutter three cars behind them, who kept pulling out into the oncoming lane for a sniff.

"Ah," Packie said, a hint of a smile creeping over his clean skin face, "the longer you're here, the more you'll see that there is something in all that. But you'll never ever get the inspector to admit it."

"What exactly are we talking about here, Uri Geller or what?"

Garvey sighed in a dismissive way only Galway people can carry off. "Sure *he's* nothing but an auld trickster. No, our man's a bit more special than that."

"Yeah, my mother says that Starrett's mother is blessed with a healing hand."

"There may be a certain amount of truth in that, but I think you'll find she considers herself a helper and not a healer. From the little I know about this area, I'd say it's the ones who make the greatest claims who have the least power."

"Finbar Nolan?"

"Exactly," Garvey replied.

The only comment of note that he'd ever made in Garvey's company was when they'd been to interview a suspect in a hit-and-run incident. The suspect, as it turned out, was (a) a revered pioneer and (b) in his place of work at the time of the incident. However, the same suspect recognised Starrett and invited him upstairs to lay his hands on his sick mother.

Starrett had quietly replied, "That's not part of my gift. I'll bring my mother over later today."

Three weeks later, Packie noticed the pioneer and his mother happily, and apparently healthily, walking down the street in their native Rathmullan.

At that moment, as the nutter pulled out again and was about to try and overtake the line of cars, Nuala pulled out slightly to block him and to let him see the markings of the garda car. The nutter moved closer to her bumper, assuming he was going to get a coat-tail ride through the frustrated traffic. When Nuala pulled out fully into the oncoming traffic lane, the nutter pulled up closer behind them. She braked. It was a dangerous move, but he responded by slowing down. She repeated the process three times until all the traffic had passed them by.

Garvey wound down his window and indicated to the nutter in question to pull in to the side of the road. They charged the berk in the Merc with dangerous driving and advised him that they would recommend that he be banned from driving for at least twelve months. They followed Starrett's standard approach of being so nice and polite to the driver that it drove him totally insane. They left him by the side of the road, incensed but alive.

A few minutes later, Nuala pulled the car into a yard beside a bungalow, just the other side of the Silver Tassie. The yard was tidy and packed with scaffolding frames and poles, planks, a cement mixer, a trailer, a stack of bags of cement, a small town of red brick and a stack of wood under a blue tarpaulin cover. A large white dog came charging towards them, barking his head off.

A man came running out of the back door shouting, "Digger,

Digger, get down!" as he beat the side of his denim-clad leg furiously with his hand. "Sorry about that. Digger's main job a few years ago was to protect the babbies, but now they're all grown he feels redundant unless he gets a good fit of barking in at least once a day."

The man grabbed Digger by the collar and pulled him back towards the house, manhandling him through the back door and slamming it behind him.

Garvey and Gibson gingerly made their way out of the car as the dog-owner came back to greet them.

"We're looking for Colm Donovan," Nuala Gibson said through a large smile.

"Aye, look no further then; I'm your man."

Colm Donovan looked as if he'd just entered his thirties but was reluctant to admit it. He wore his hair short and dyed blond, which kind of worked against his permanently tanned, weather-beaten skin. He wore a snow-white T-shirt with the short sleeves rolled up to his shoulder. A pack of Camel cigarettes was secured in the folds of the left sleeve. The rest of his outfit was the traditional builder's uniform of tight-fitting blue denims and tan Timberland boots with the vital protective toecaps. His boyish looks, charm and easy manner had brought an instant smile to Gibson's face.

Garvey, however, felt that the builder's eyes betrayed something deeper. Or he might just have been trying to read more into the situation than was there because Starrett wasn't with him, he thought.

Donovan was not what you would call stout, but he was built very solidly, Garvey observed, built like a brick shi . . . sorry, he apologised to himself, built like a brick outdoor toilet. Garvey wondered what that saying actually meant.

They introduced themselves. Donovan already knew Packie from the sidelines of hurling matches.

"We believe you were acquainted with James Moore from Downings?" Nuala Gibson enquired.

"Jimmy, aye, yes, of course," Colm Donovan said. "Is he in trouble or something? Look, do you want to come in for a chat?"

Inside, Garvey could still hear the dog barking. He leaned against the garda car and said, "Nah, we'll be fine here. Sadly James Moore was fatally injured and—"

"Noooo," Donovan broke in. "You mean he's dead?"

"I'm afraid so," Gibson said.

"Oh, my God. Oh, my God!" Donovan said, looking unsteady on his feet.

"Are you OK?" Nuala asked, taking a cautious step towards the builder.

"Sorry," Donovan said, looking thoughtful and confused. "No, I mean yes. It's just that I was working with him only last weekend and he seemed fine. It can't have been an accident; he was a very cautious man, very careful. What happened to him?"

"Well, that's what we're trying to find out," Garvey said. "You say you saw him last weekend?"

"Yes, we were working together last Saturday and Sunday."

"Where was this?" Gibson asked.

"Just off the Milford to Kerrykeel road," Donovan said. "A refurbishment for a German gentleman, Herr Karsten Jahnke. He's raising the roof by six foot to get an extra storey, and he wants it done by the time he comes over in July for his summer break. Aye, I'm not one to complain, we both have a couple of jobs on the go, but he might have been better to buy a bigger house in the first place. To be fair to him, though, he does have an amazing view of the water."

"Oh, I know the place, just up past the House of Love," Garvey said, as he mentally drove along the road.

"Yes, just on past that," Donovan agreed.

"Yeah," Garvey continued. "Our goalie, Seamus O'Neill, lives on past there but on the other side of the road."

"So," Nuala Gibson interrupted, wanting to get on with the interview, "what was James Moore's role on that particular job?"

"Aye, right. The builders had cleared off the slates the day before and were protecting the house with plastic sheets. Jimmy and a few of the chippies dismantled the rafters, and me and a couple of my boys threw up the new stonework. Ach, sure you know what it's like. In between the showers, it ended up taking us the entire weekend, but yer man did good by us. He paid us a full week's wages for the two days' work."

"And probably in cash?" Garvey added with a wink.

"Ach now, sure, you know," Donovan replied in a noncommittal tone. "I'll tell you this, though, we all earned our money last weekend."

"OK," Gibson said. "How often did you work with James Moore?"

"Ach now, not a lot," Donovan replied, lifting his right arm into the air and then stretching his hand behind his shoulders to give the area between his shoulder blades a good scratch. "Jimmy's a master carpenter, and he tends to be a bit of a loner. I'm not saying he's a snob or anything like that. It's just that I've never seen a man so content in his own company. You'd work on a site with him for a week, and you'd hardly know he was there. Jimmy's a real artist, you know. You should see the things he could do with a chunk of wood and those chisels of his, ach, my goodness. But he likes to focus on his work. He's not one of those chirpy lads who give a running commentary on everything he does."

"And what about socially?" Gibson interrupted again.

"Well, Jimmy isn't, sorry, of course I mean, *wasn't* really a man for the pub, but you know, there was couple of times when I had to drop up to his house to see if he was available for such and such a job, he'd bring me through to his workshop and we'd talk out there for ages about this and that. I got the feeling that he didn't really have a lot of friends that he could really talk to. So that was probably why he confided in me every now and again. There's nothing beats talking, is there?"

"So they say," Garvey agreed.

"Did he seem unhappy at home?" Gibson pushed.

Donovan shook his head, looking bemused before replying: "Aye, you know what it's like, love. It's a family life and, sure, you just get on with it. He was devoted to his kids, I can tell you that. You see, you have to realise some people, people like myself, who like to work out in the open twelve months of the year, well, the truth is . . ." and here Donovan stopped talking for a few seconds and looked like he was trying to stare through the walls of his bungalow, "and I am speaking for myself now, the truth is, we'd probably be wiser not to put down our roots until we've got the sowing of wild oats out of our system. And Jimmy would never complain about his missus, aye, but jeez she was one right auld bag of nerves. The wains were all growing up great, though, so they must have been doing something right."

Donovan stopped talking and looked towards Nuala Gibson as if he'd overstepped the mark, obviously not used to being candid in female company.

Packie said to Nuala, "Look, could you radio the station and see if Starrett has left any instructions for us about our next call? We're nearly done here, and I can finish up."

Gibson looked first to Packie as if to say, "Are you mad?" But spotting the look of relief on Donovan's face, she said, "Yes, of course." Without bidding goodbye to the builder, she opened the door and steeped into the car.

Donovan and Packie walked slowly across the yard as Nuala slammed the car door, perhaps just a little harder than was necessary. Inside the house, the dog resumed its frantic barking.

"Look, erm, I just need you to know that you need to be candid with me here. We're up against it here on this case, and if we're going to find out what happened to James, we're going to need all the help we can get."

"Aye, I understand, Packie, and you can count on me. I had a lot of time for Jimmy. If he went into a job and they needed a wall-buster, he'd always make sure I got the call. He'd say I could literally walk through walls." Donovan paused and laughed at the memory. He nodded in the direction of the garda car before continuing: "It's always a bit awkward talking about this sorta stuff in front of women. They think the man's always in the wrong, and that's just not always the case."

Again Donovan stared at the walls of his house.

"So, were Mr and Mrs Moore having problems at home?" Packie asked, hoping he wasn't travelling this route too quickly.

Colm Donovan sucked in a mouthful of air, making a "whoa" sound.

"You realise, of course, Packie . . . if Jimmy was still alive I'd never breathe a word of this?"

"I know, I know," Packie said sympathetically.

"Good man," Donovan said, nodding. "Well, you see, Packie, here you have my case in point: Nora Moore. Now, from what Jimmy said, there was never any romance in that relationship. He wasn't slagging her off, you understand; he was just stating fact. You know how it often happens in the country: two people often get together because that's what people are expected to do, have babbies who grow up and do the same and have more babbies. But there's got to be something more, hasn't there, Packie?"

"Ask me one on hurling, Colm," Packie replied, and meant it. "So, Jimmy and Nora, were they about to split up or anything?"

"Well, if they'd lived in the city, they probably would have, but out here in the sticks, we just have to grin and bear it, get on with life. Now listen here, I don't want you to get the impression that Jimmy was moaning about the missus all the time. In fact, if anything, I had to drag it out of him. I'd say something like, 'What are you and Nora up to for the weekend?' and he'd reply something like, 'I've got so-and-so to do and she's doing so-and-so other.' And I'd say, "Don't you ever take a break and go away for a romantic weekend?" And he'd laugh and say, "Don't be stupid." I think their relationship was pretty primitive, phys-ically speaking, if you understand me. Packie, keep this under your hat, but I wouldn't be surprised if the only three times they did have a ride, she got pregnant."

"Oh, come on . . ." Packie protested, "and, ah . . ." he stammered, searching for his question, "so then, ahm, what happened?"

"Well, jeez, didn't the fecking vicar's wife only go and seduce Jimmy."

"Holy shit!"

"Quite possibly, Packie," Donovan laughed, "but as my eldest daughter keeps saying all fecking day long, 'We don't need to go there.'"

"So how did it all start?" Packie asked.

"Well, first off, Packie, answer me this: have you ever seen the woman in question, Mrs Amanda Morrison?"

"I'm sure I have, Colm. I just don't recall."

"Let me assure you, Packie, if you'd seen her, you'd recall. Aye, she's built for speed not for comfort, that one. Oh my goodness, she's an absolute stunner, and she ends up with First Minister Morrison! What's that all about now?" Donovan spat out.

"People have hidden qualities, Colm."

"Aye, no doubt, but then why did she play away from home?" Colm asked. "Mind you, from what Jimmy was saying, some of the times she was even playing at home. In the library he was building for them no less."

"Right, I don't think you need to draw me any pictures," Packie smiled gently. "But to tell you the truth, from the little we've learned about Moore, I'm surprised to hear you say he was boasting about it."

"Aye, I hear you. I was surprised myself, I suppose," Donovan continued in between finding his cigarette packet, extracting one and lighting up. "But he probably needed to tell someone about it, if only to assure himself it was actually happening."

"Tell me, how long had this been going on?"

"Several months. Let see now, yes," Colm said exhaling a large trail of smoke, which was blown away quickly by the wind circulating the yard. "Jimmy was doing one of his bespoke fitted kitchens for Betsy Bell in Rathmullan, and Betsy was all proud of her new kitchen. Anyway, when Jimmy was in there working away, didn't Betsy only go and bring Amanda Morrison in to see the grand work. Now, Jimmy was a modest man. He was more being modest about himself than his work in this instance, but according to Jimmy, Amanda and he got on well right from that first day, socially speaking, of course. If a girl came on to Jimmy, he'd run a mile. Mrs Bell didn't treat him as an employee, if you know what I mean. She treated him like an artisan. Jimmy had to explain to me what that word meant, by the way. It's a grand word, don't you think?"

"It is that," Packie replied.

"They'd shared a couple of cups of coffee with Betsy. Jimmy said it seemed to him as that Amanda Morrison's visits were becoming more and more frequent. He found it as easy talking to her as she seemed to find it easy to talk to him. You see, to Jimmy, who was very much a married man, there was never ever such a thing as a hidden agenda. He was just talking to her as a friend, not trying to get anywhere with her. Well, of course, that was only driving her absolutely mad. The more he ignored her charms, the more she was attracted to him. Pretty soon she started to drop in when Betsy wouldn't be there, and she'd stay and they'd chat away as he worked. Jimmy said she'd do most of the talking and he'd do most of the listening."

"Wasn't Betsy starting to become a little suspicious?" Packie asked. "I mean, if only with how long Jimmy Moore was spending on the job."

"That's, of course, if she wasn't in on it," Colm Donovan said, winking at the sergeant.

"Right, of course," Packie said, nodding to himself.

"Anyway, Betsy's kitchen was nearly finished when Amanda invited Jimmy to quote for replacing the bookshelves in the library of the Manse. Jimmy didn't think twice about it. He quoted fairly, as he always did, and he got the job. That's when Jimmy started to notice that Amanda was dressing a bit more provocatively in front of him, always in the Manse, and always when the first minister was away on some business or other. He says he'd be stealing a glance at her shapely legs or maybe looking at her breasts, and when he worked his way up to her eyes, she'd always be looking at him, with a big smile on her face. And while all of this was going on, they were still having these amazing conversations. She told him about her life. He never gave me the full details, but he said that she was never scared to be totally honest with him. It seemed to me that she knew Jimmy would never ever be the one to make the first move, so she did."

"Right," Packie said.

"Jimmy didn't feel the slightest bit guilty. He hadn't set out to cheat and, in his own words, he figured that if he had been having a full relationship with his wife, the affair would never have started in the first place."

"So it continued for a while, then?"

"Well, I guess so, but he stopped talking to me about her," Donovan replied.

"And, ah, have you any idea if anyone else knew about their relationship? That is, apart from yourself?"

"I'd say there's a very good chance Betsy Bell knew all about it, but if you're referring to the first minister, then, who knows? But sure he's a shifty one all the same, needs a fair bit of watching."

"What about Jimmy's wife, Nora?"

"No chance."

"Tell me, did Jimmy mention Amanda Morrison at all when you saw him last weekend at Herr Jahnke's?" Packie asked.

"Definitely not. You see, we were always around other people."

"How did he seem to you? Troubled?"

"Nah, not really. He seemed reasonably happy to be making an extra bit of money over the weekend, but apart from that, there was still a twinkle in his eye and an inch to his step," Donovan said as he winked to the sergeant.

"Look, Colm, if you can think of anything else, anything else at all, please give me a shout at the garda station in Ramelton."

"No bother," Donovan replied, "no bother at all."

o-O-o

"Right then," Nuala said, the moment Packie was back in the car. "What did you get?"

"The deceased and Amanda Morrison were having an affair," Packie replied, thinking he'd been about to get his ear chewed off by the young garda. "Look, sorry about that, I just felt that, well, you know . . ."

"Of course I know, Sergeant," Gibson said, smiling sweetly as she put the car in gear.

Chapter Seventeen

AT THE SAME time as Garvey and Gibson were making their way back to Ramelton, Starrett was waiting in the Coffee Dock on B-level of Letterkenny General Hospital. Although the Coffee Dock was a pleasant-looking café, with modern steel and wood furniture and soft-coloured walls, it smelled a little too much like the rest of the actual hospital. Right outside the window beside which Starrett had positioned himself, he could see ambulances come and go with frightful regularity.

Since leaving Tower House, he'd replaced his jumper with a dark blue blazer and matching tie. Passing the mirror in the toilet, Starrett had caught himself nervously checking out his reflection before his meeting with Dr Sam Aljoe. Perhaps the agitation he felt was simply founded on the old familiar feeling he experienced each and every time he entered a hospital?

Starrett hated hospitals.

He knew it was an irrational and childish fear, but he didn't care. Starrett had examined his phobia many times during his life, and he'd never managed to come up with a suitable explanation for it other than that, statistically speaking, more people went into hospitals than ever emerged alive.

"Oh my goodness," a gentle voice behind him said. "You're not very happy in hospitals are you?"

"How'd you guess?"

"Your body language is screaming, 'Get me out of here!'"

"I'm that transparent, eh?" Starrett said, smiling and shuffling two tablemats like cards. "I was hoping I could pull it off. I mean, hanging around the ER didn't seem to do George Clooney any harm."

"I'd have cast you in more of a classic Paul Newman role."

"I'll take that as a compliment," Starrett replied, using the air of someone who was happy to send himself up. He noticed with considerable disappointment that the doctor had again gathered her long, wild blond hair back into a ponytail. Otherwise, she was dressed as she had been earlier in the day.

"It was, it was," she protested. "Can you bear to have a cup of coffee here while we go through the autopsy? Apart from anything else, it's by far the best coffee you'll find in Letterkenny."

"Ach, sure, go on then, I'm game for anything," Starrett replied, enjoying the company.

"So I've heard," she said, disappearing in the direction of the counter. She returned with two coffees and two Bakersville cakes.

"OK," she said, "down to business. Mr James Moore was a fine specimen of a man, originally. To me it looked like someone tried to break him, destroy his body. It would appear that whoever crucified him didn't just want him dead; they wanted to . . . well, I have to say that I've never examined a body in such a terrible state." She paused and looked at Starrett, asking, "What?"

"Sorry, nothing." Starrett said sheepishly.

"It *was*, Starrett; it *was* something, I know that look." Dr Aljoe laughed. "You're thinking, that's hardly medical information she's giving me."

Starrett raised his right hand—crocked forefinger and all—in protest.

"In this case, I thought if I merely listed all his injuries for you, it wouldn't fully describe what went on here. It looks to me as if all of the punishment was orchestrated to prolong his suffering during his ordeal. In the end, though, it was his heart that gave out. There are only two points here, beyond the obvious, which may be of help to you. Firstly, both vinegar and sweat were present in his blood stream. By virtue of his punishment, the sweat is not unusual. When his system was collapsing, the sweat glands would have been leaking profusely. But vinegar . . ."

"Maybe his murderer was mocking him," Starrett offered. "Just like when Christ was in his agony and he was offered vinegar to quench his thirst. The same thing could have happened here. And the other point?"

"The contents of his stomach suggest that he ate two full meals in quick succession, neither of which had been digested fully."

"Oh," Starrett said, "that is interesting."

"Yes," she continued. "I found traces of chicken, beef, potatoes, rice, green beans, carrots, red peppers and peas."

"Interesting," Starrett said. "Very interesting."

"Yes, that's what I thought," she replied. "I suppose it might suggest James Moore had one meal somewhere, then had to pretend he hadn't eaten and have another one somewhere else."

"Yes," Starrett said. "Eating two meals suggests to me that he sat down with his family for their main meal. I'd hazard a guess at steak, peas, carrots and potatoes, and then—from what I've learned about him, and this is strictly off the record, Doctor—he went off and had a meal with his mistress. This sounds as if it was something fancier, like chicken with some kind of sauce, rice with vegetables, which would account for the peppers and beans. The second meal was him being sociable; the first was to conceal the prearranged dinner with his mistress. Tell me, Doctor, how long before his death would you say he had eaten?"

"Is that a subtle way of asking if I've determined the exact time of death?"

"Sorry, no," Starrett replied. "No, actually I hadn't reached that point. Right now I'm trying to set up a real-time diary."

"Oh, OK," she said smiling. "I have to work the other way. So, I would say that by the time the body was discovered at 08.40, he'd been dead for nearly three hours. And then we'd have to figure that, due to all his body had been subjected to, his system wouldn't have been working as efficiently as usual in breaking down the food, so I'd say that he probably dined in the 18.00 to 21.00 time frame the previous evening. I'm sure over 90 per cent of families sit down to dinner around that time, so it's not exactly rocket science on my part."

"Quite, but none the less, the fact that he had two meals on Thursday evening: that *is* a very important fact."

"Right," she said, closing her folder with a degree of finality. "Let me return this to my office, freshen up a bit, and then you can take me out to dinner."

"I'm game if you are," Starrett replied with a smile, which she returned. "Tell you what, I could do with a breath of fresh air. Why don't I meet you at the front door?"

"I won't be a mo," she said, practically skipping out of the Coffee Dock.

As he wandered around to the main entrance of the hospital, Starrett thought about the beautiful Dr Aljoe. He'd been aware of her for eight months or so—ever since she'd come over to Letterkenny from her native England, in fact. They'd met on official business several times, but for some reason it had been different that morning in the Second Federation Church. Perhaps he was reading too much into it, as was often the case when it came to Starrett and girls, but she definitely seemed to be more aware of him as a person than on the previous occasions they'd met. Perhaps it was just that while viewing such a horrific death, she preferred to occupy her mind elsewhere, and Starrett had happened to be in her line of view.

Shuffling around outside the hospital entrance, Starrett spied a vision exiting the doors behind him. Samantha Aljoe had changed out of her black trouser suit into a pale blue dress. Starrett was trying to work out the mechanics of how she could have squeezed into such a garment when he noticed that she'd let her hair down again. It was a magnificent mane, to be sure, and for a single split second, he imagined she was out on the prowl and that he was her prey.

She took his hand and said, "Starrett, could you please do me a favour and pick your jaw up off the ground, flattering and all as it may be. I work here, and it could be embarrassing if one of my colleagues were to witness this display of drooling."

"The single negative of being a woman," replied Starrett, "is that she'll never be able to enjoy the vision of a woman the way a man can."

"Tell that to kd lang," Sam Aljoe said, interlocking her arm with his and moving Starrett along from the pavement he appeared frozen to.

"Well, all I can say is that she's very, very lucky."

"Yes, but what about her partner?"

"Now if I'd said that . . ." Starrett started.

Sam giggled wickedly. "Now where's this jalopy of yours?"

Six minutes and an illegal parking of his BMW later, they were sitting at his favourite table under the blue lamp at the Yellow Pepper, Starrett's favourite Letterkenny restaurant, on Main Street.

"So, our first date?" she said, sounding as if she might be teasing him.

"Well, at the very least, we'll enjoy a bit of supper together," Starrett replied, not sure of what else he could say.

And enjoy a bit of supper together they did. Over a couple of glasses of wine, after the plates had been cleared away, they discussed her career: "Something to do that I could do."

Her move to Ireland: "London's tired and full of rude people. I was worried that Dublin might be the same, so I was looking for something in Belfast when I saw the advertisement for the Letterkenny job, and here I am."

She'd taken a few years out to travel around the world, taking in Australia, New Zealand (where she nearly stayed), the USA and Japan.

Starrett asked if she'd been travelling to get away from something.

"You mean a boyfriend, don't you?"

"Perhaps, perhaps not," he replied. "People also go on the run to escape the law."

"Yeah, right, but nothing so exciting in my case. I'm afraid. I was what my father referred to as an 'afterclap'."

"Your father's Irish, then?" Starrett said, "Afterclap is an Irish word, but I'd always thought it referred only to a son who was born much later that the rest of the family."

"Perhaps, but you know what fathers are like with their daughters. Anyway, when I was growing up and becoming a teenager, my brother was twenty-eight and married with two kids, and my sister also married and presented three kids to the family by the time she was twenty-seven. It wasn't that my sister was in an unhappy marriage; it was more that she always felt that her life had been taken away from her. She'd wanted to be a GP and had studied hard for it. She'd just passed all her exams and was fully qualified when she met and married another GP, Joe. Within a year, they had Joseph, and then Christina and Jonathan followed within the next couple of years. My sister had always intended to return to her practice, but there was always something with the kids that prevented her. It wasn't exactly that Joe was a chauvinist who thought that the woman's place was in the home, *but* he did want *his* wife at home bringing up *his* kids." Sam Aljoe paused for a sip of wine.

She continued: "Ahm . . . well, the sad fact was that by the time I was starting to date boys, my sister, who was just about to hit thirty, genuinely felt that her life was over. She felt her only role in life now was bringing up her children. And, well, I swore that I wasn't going to end up the same way, so here I am thirty-three, and fancy free."

Starrett clicked his teeth. He wasn't meaning to dismiss her as a lost cause, but that is exactly how it came across.

"OK, OK, Starrett, time out here," she protested. "Let me just say that, if I'm being perfectly honest, yes it is possible to get married when you are in your late teens and start a family and not feel you've been deprived of your life."

"It's just that you couldn't figure out a way of doing it?" Starrett asked.

"I think," she replied slowly, "for it to work, no matter what age you are, one has to be with the right person."

"So, you don't think your sister . . ."

"No, no, no," she protested violently. "I mean, I think if it were to happen all over again, she'd make all the same decisions."

"Right, so what you are saying is . . ."

"What I'm saying is that there are two types of relationship. There's one where a boy and a girl get together because that's what boys and girls do, and there's the other one where a boy and girl get together because they absolutely were meant to be."

She seemed to grow a little distracted, as if she were considering whether she should say what she wanted to say next.

"I'd like to go now," she said eventually.

"Sure, sure," Starrett said, signalling for the bill.

"Let's go Dutch," she suggested.

"There are no Dutchmen here," Starrett replied, drawing out his wallet. "At least not yet, which means it must still be better over there than it is here."

When he checked his watch, Starrett was surprised to find that it was 10.40 p.m. and that they'd been in the restaurant for over three hours. There was an awkward moment at his car. He didn't know whether to suggest going on for a drink (she'd already said she rarely had more than two glasses of wine), driving her home or driving her back to her car. He was reluctant to let the evening end so he opened the passenger door for her. She climbed in, making herself comfortable with an off-white wrap she'd produced from her handbag.

Starrett was making a fuss putting on his seatbelt to delay the decision, when Samantha broke the awkward silence. "OK, Starrett, you're the native; take me somewhere beautiful."

"Not a bother," he replied, as they departed the illegal parking space at quite possibly an illegal speed.

Twenty minutes, later they were walking in the moonlight on Rathmullan beach.

The vastness and variety of the views, even at night, were truly inspiring. They could see the lights of Buncrana flickering through the haze, as well as the headlights on the far shore coming in and out of view as vehicles passed trees and buildings. The creamy-white moonlight twinkled off the water and a small flotilla of boats bobbing up and down a few metres offshore. An occasional couple passed them, walking in the opposite direction towards the pier, whose base was surrounded by grotesquely ugly stone buildings, which Starrett devoutly hoped were not long for this world, interfering busybodies permitting. The skyline behind them was broken only by house lights spilling out along the ridge.

But Starrett had the best view of all: he could see Dr Samantha Aljoe.

Even the usual salty smells of the beach were softened by the doctor's hypnotic scents.

Starrett and the doctor walked as far as they were able, down to where the beach met the bridge that carried the Portsalon road.

All the time they were chatting about this and that, with Sam doing most of the chatting. When they weren't talking, Starrett tuned into the gentle lapping of the waves on the beach. The occasional crunch of tiny shells beneath their feet acted as an alarm, ensuring that they never drifted too close to the water's edge.

As they turned to walk back, Sam leaned across and kissed him quickly and gently on the lips, saying, "Thanks for a great evening."

She pulled away before he could prolong the kiss, and they

continued walking. This time it was against the wind, which blew the material of her dress tight against her thighs. Somewhere in the distance, the unhealthy chugging of a wan engine echoed across the surface of the water in the darkness.

They hadn't spoken since she'd kissed him.

"The thing I've found out about going out with Irish men is that they either ignore you like they're scared they might break you, or they want to maul you like you're a blow-up doll."

"Are you breakable, then?" he asked.

"Sorry?"

"Well, I know for a fact that you're not a blow-up doll—and I'd also wish it to be taken into consideration in my defence that I've never been involved with a blow-up doll—but I was just checking to see if you were breakable."

She moved towards him, and, this time, their kiss was passionate.

Starrett was surprised by how responsive she was. He was also surprised about how comfortable he was kissing a woman he hardly knew. He'd always considered that kissing was a pretty strange act for human beings to engage in, but Starrett found kissing Samantha Aljoe an extremely pleasant experience.

They walked and talked and kissed until it was just too cold to walk and talk and kiss any more.

"I dug out your file, you know," she said quietly when they were sitting together in the car.

"Oh, feck these computers," he said with good humour. "OK, I'm biting; what did you discover?"

"Oh, I found out that the gardaí wasn't your first career."

"Nor even my second."

"So, what was the first one?

"That type of information is reserved for when we're much better friends. I'm going to need to keep something hidden; otherwise there's a good chance you might go off me too quickly."

"Which is much preferable to my jumping *on* you too quickly?"

He pulled her across the seat for another kiss.

She disengaged.

"We need to slow this down. It's going way too fast, and I need to get to know you better. Now, you can drive me to my car, if you don't mind. It's late and we both have work tomorrow. You need to find a murderer, and I have a whole heap of cadavers to wade through."

"Not literally, I hope," Starrett joked as he drove in the general direction of Ramelton.

After a minute or two, he said, "You were saying you needed to get to know me better. Ask away."

She smiled and said, "I still need to figure out how you got to forty-five and remained single. You've never married?"

"Never did."

"You just never met the right person?"

"Maybe it was more a case of the right person at the wrong time."

"Girlfriends?"

"Aye a few, but then again, as Frank once sang, 'Too few to mention'."

"Were all your girlfriends regrets?"

"Not a single one," he said, closing in on Ramelton and about to pass his own house. "There's my place," he said, slowing down. "Do you want to come in?" The minute the words had left his mouth, he regretted uttering them. They sounded less like the genuine question he'd intended and more like a cheap pick-up line.

"I think I'd better be getting home, Starrett. Apart from which, I never sleep with someone unless I've known them for at least a year. That's an unbreakable rule."

Starrett was rather pleased to hear this.

"OK, fair play," he said. After a brief silence, he added, "This . . . erm . . . year thing . . . can I get something knocked off that for good behaviour?"

"Good behaviour, Starrett? I'll bet you don't even know the meaning of the words," she said.

When they reached the Letterkenny General Hospital car park, he walked her to her car. They had a brief goodnight kiss, and just as he was about to walk off, she wound down her window and said, "Starrett, of course you realise if you wanted to get technical with me, you could claim that you'd already known me for eight-and-a-half months."

Chapter Eighteen

T HE EARLY HOURS of Saturday weren't as clear and bright as the previous morning had been. God and his angels were once again emptying their watering cans over that particular corner of Ireland. Most of the locals, while appreciating His good taste in choosing Donegal, would have been far happier if he'd gone for County Antrim instead.

When he arrived at Tower House at 08.20, Starrett was pleasantly surprised to find that Sergeant Packie Garvey and Garda Nuala Gibson had already left to interview James Moore's brother-in-law, Uncle Dolphie.

Starrett took advantage of the peace and quiet of the lean-to they called his office to write up his crime book. He religiously updated the case-file of a current investigation every day. The thirty or so minutes he stole every morning to undertake the task helped him keep on top of the facts of the case.

As he finished jotting down that day's notes in his extremely legible and beautifully formed handwriting, Starrett focused his attention on Mrs Amanda Morrison.

He read Nuala Gibson's concise report on her and Packie's interview with Colm Donovan the previous evening. Their visit to Agga at the Manse hadn't been as productive. All they had learned was that Agga didn't live in the Manse and she knew nothing about where Morrison's wife was.

Amanda Morrison had to be at the centre of the case, whichever way you looked at it. She wasn't currently at home and no one seemed to know how to get hold of her. Starrett wondered why First Minister Ivan Morrison wasn't at all concerned about his wife's disappearance. Was there something to be learned from that?

Could Ivan Morrison have discovered that his wife was having an affair with Moore and murdered both of them in a fit of anger? If so, what could he have done with her body? Perhaps Starrett should be looking for a search warrant to search the Manse. But if Ivan Morrison was involved in two murders, why should he draw attention to himself by crucifying one of the victims at his own house of worship? Surely he wouldn't be so stupid. Or could it be a double bluff: "It couldn't possibly be the first minister; he'd never have done that on his own doorstep"?

Even if Ivan Morrison was in the frame, how could he have carried out the crucifixion in the first place? He was hardly a fit man, and Starrett recalled that it had taken several soldiers, with the assistance of members of the on-looking mob, to crucify Jesus Christ. If First Minister Ivan Morrison had indeed been the killer and if he had needed assistance, the caretaker, Thomas Black, must be high on the suspected accomplice list. Black by name and dark by nature?

Morrison was a pompous SOB, but was he capable of murder? Harbouring negative thoughts about someone was a long way from actually taking their life. You have to be arrogant to want to murder someone, to take on God's role and decide who should live and who should die. But Starrett wondered if he hadn't focused on Ivan Morrison the previous day simply because Morrison had been the first person he'd met at the murder scene. Could the case have been so simple that he could have solved it half an hour after the body had been discovered?

To have confronted the gardaí in the church first thing would be a pretty brazen act for a murderer. Was Morrison really that cold-blooded? OK, Starrett told himself as he glanced around his packed, yet tidy, office, hold that thought for a second. Could the fact that Amanda was missing mean that Morrison had also murdered his wife? If Morrison really had been that audacious and clever, and if he had murdered James Moore for having an affair with his trophy wife, then surely he wouldn't have needed to murder Amanda as well. Surely his revenge would have been so much sweeter if she had to live with the responsibility for her lover's death?

"Fair play," Starrett said to the four filing cabinets that occupied an entire wall of his office. He stared at the poster above the cabinets; it was of a 1959 green Jaguar Mark II, the same poster which had been a fixture of his office back in London. The classic Jag was pictured driving through lush countryside, and Starrett often used the poster as a trampoline for his thoughts while working on an investigation.

He'd near enough convinced himself that Amanda Morrison was still alive. But where could she possibly be? Betsy Bell had mentioned an older sister, and Starrett wondered where she lived. Sisters may start off their lives at each other's throats, but generally they tend to overcome difficulties and become each other's friend and confidante. Brothers, in Starrett's experience, generally became less close in later years.

Starrett made a list on the next clean page of his notepad:

> Betsy Bell
> Amanda Morrison's sister
> Thomas Black
> Ivan Morrison

He tore off the page, folded it over and slipped it into the pocket of the natty gabardine that hung faithfully on the back of his office door.

Starrett left his office with Amanda Morrison on his mind. He'd known of her as the wife of First Minister Morrison, but he couldn't for the life of him put a face to her name.

o-O-o

Meanwhile, Garvey and Gibson were driving over the Loughsalt Mountains in the direction of Downings. They were so close to the rain clouds, Garvey felt he could slip his hand through the car window and squeeze out some water for himself, not that the clouds around Donegal needed any help with their incessant task of ensuring the greenness of the greenest county in the world.

Packie was preoccupied with making sure he could knock off by 13.00 as he had a 15.00 practice session for the following Sunday's match against Armagh. If push came to shove and he wasn't finished on time, he'd have no guilty conscience about staying on at work. His garda career was his priority, and he knew that there were at least a couple of reserves well capable at taking over his position on the hurling field. Having said that, the gardaí, particularly Major Newton Cunningham, were very supportive of his sports career and bent over backwards in order to accommodate his fixtures. But even that support from on high still couldn't stop Packie from feeling awkward about the rare Saturday matches.

"So, where's the action tonight, Nuala?" he asked, as they drove down into Downings.

"Ach, you know, there might be some craic up at the Mountain Top in Letterkenny, or there's a salsa night over in McDaid's Wine Bar."

"Aye, lock up yer sons; the girls are back in town," Garvey said as they pulled up outside a house set high into the hill overlooking the beach. The house had been built at a time when one cared not a hoot how a house should look, and, Garvey guessed, back then it would have been the only house on the hillside. Now it formed the centre of a small and ever-growing village.

Before they had a chance even to get out of the car, the dark green door of the house opened and the man himself, Uncle Dolphie, strode defiantly out into the street. For someone with a name as nice and friendly as Uncle Dolphie, he looked angry and bad-tempered. Garvey's brain ran through a list of names until he figured out that Dolphie could originally have been Adolph. Possibly pushing his late fifties with long, wild hair, which looked as if it had never seen a comb, Uncle Dolphie had chubby rosy cheeks and a whiskey-red nose. He was dressed for sitting around the house all day long in brown threadbare cords, a thick brown leather belt, a collarless shirt and a sleeveless Fair Isle jumper moulded around a shape pregnant with many a pint of Guinness. A pair of light blue slippers contrasted with the rest of his masculine look.

"Right, lads," he barked as they exited the car. "Oops, sorry, miss, it's so difficult to tell these days. But I want to know, have you caught the bastard who ended Jimmy's life?

"Come on in out of the mizzle; we'll maybe find a bite of breakfast for you. The both of you look like you could do with a bit of meat on your bones. My good God, man, how do they expect wains like yerself to catch murderers? No offence, but it takes a man to catch a murderer."

The less-than-men followed the man into his Spartan abode. It was like stepping back forty years. The only pictures on the walls were religious, and the only furniture was either to sit on or to eat at. The rooms were small but warm, very warm, which might have partly accounted for Dolphie's permanently crimson complexion.

Willie Nelson was singing to the whole of County Donegal about all the girls he'd known, spreading the word via Highland Radio. Uncle Dolphie cut Willie off in his prime by clicking a switch.

The dog under the table was about to make a nuisance of itself, but all it took was one stern, no-nonsense look from his master and he went whimpering meekly away as though a banshee had entered the house.

"The wife is out at work, but I'm sure I can remember how to work the rasher wagon. Take a seat there at the table," Dolphie ordered.

"So, Mr Cowan," Packie said, as the householder threw all manner of food into the frying pan.

"Call me Uncle Dolphie; everyone else does," he said clearly.

"We wanted to talk to you about James."

"Stupid fecking prat," Dolphie said with his back now to the two gardaí. It was really hard to hear over the sizzling. The smells wafting his way made Packie realise just how hungry he was.

"Why do you say that?" Nuala asked.

"Look, you have a man and a woman and they have a few wains. In the Church's eyes that is sacrosanct; no one should ever get in the way of that," Dolphie said, stopping his fussing over the frying pan for a few seconds. He faced Nuala and looked her directly in the eye. "Look, can I be really blunt here, without you getting all upset with me and going off and reporting me to some liberal do-fecking-gooder."

"Yes, of course," Nuala replied. "Please feel free to say what you want."

"OK, good," Dolphie replied, turning back to his masterwork. "OK, as I was saying, in the Church's eyes the family unit comes first and foremost, and everything that needs to be done is done to protect it, right?"

Nuala nodded that she understood what he was saying, but equally had the look of someone who might possibly not share his sentiment.

"Right, so outside of that, if you have an itch to scratch, you scratch it. And no offence, Miss, I'm liberal enough in my ways to know that this privilege should now also be extended to women as well, although in my father's day . . . Anyway, that's got no relevance here. Now I will admit that my wife's sister is not exactly a picture. I've never really known how she managed to snare the quare fella, Jimmy Moore, in the first place. Jimmy's problem was that he always blew with the wind. He'd got the backbone of a jellyfish. At the same time, though, if things got out of hand in the pub, well, you'd not find a better man to stand beside you. But sure Nora and Jimmy made the match, but then doesn't she just go and let herself go to seed. Jeez, for heaven's sake, what does it take to apply a bit of make-up to one's beak, have your hair done a couple of times a year? Eh, answer me that. And why couldn't she have dressed up every now and again, for heaven's sake? I mean, a civil turn-out at the very least for the Christmas turkey would have been a start."

"I can hear what you're saying," Gibson said, clocking Dolphie's hair and dress sense.

"But anyway, Peggy keeps saying that Nora's clinically depressed. I mean, what have any of us got to be happy about? I'll admit from time to time I'm depressed myself, but that's not good enough for Nora; no, she's got to be *clinically* fecking depressed. Now, in Jimmy's defence, he's not the type of bloke who's out chasing skirt every night. And you know what?" Dolphie said as he took two clean plates from a rack in front of him. The statement hung in the air as Dolphie laid out two very appetising breakfasts, complete with toasted soda-breads—the butter, deliciously, melted into them—and two life-invigorating cups of tea.

"Go on?" Packie replied, more than slightly distracted by the sight and smells before him.

"Well, I'll tell you what: I bet you anything you want that he'd never been unfaithful before in his entire life."

"So, tell me," Garvey asked. "What happened to change all of that?"

"Well, Packie, I'll tell you exactly what happened. God created this Jezebel and gave her the perfect body and sent her to the minister of that excuse for a religion. I mean, come on, please! The Second Federation Church; it's no more than a glorified cooperative or a credit union, that's what it is. The only difference is that they don't pay out any interest; they collect it, and not on a plate, mind you, but in a bloody bucket. Anyway, this head-the-ball Ivan Morrison is obviously not what you'd call interested in women. He's only interested in the glory of being a *very* big fish in a small pond. So, what does the devil's temptress do? I'll tell you what she does; she fornicates with every man she meets. Jimmy wasn't the first, nor even the first builder for that matter, but he was quite possibly the most decent soul she met and she had to corrupt him too. As upholders of the law, you know this better than most, but when you go against the order of the universe, you upset some kind of equilibrium, and the ripples this causes tend to have far-reaching effects. That's what happened here."

"Right," Nuala Gibson replied. "And how did you know all of this was going on?"

Dolphie laughed. "Oh, come on, it was obvious. Jimmy was acting like the cat with the proverbial spilt cream, and Mrs Morrison was the only bitch on heat spilling cream around these parts."

"He never spoke to you about it?"

"Never. Come on now, Packie, I hear you're pretty quick around the hurling field, but you need to be a bit quicker on this one. I'm married to his wife's sister. He's never going to talk about this stuff with me. But I've got eyes and ears and I've got a nose. I can suss out what's going on."

"And have you any idea who might have murdered James Moore?"

"Hello! By this time even the village idiot knows who murdered Jimmy Moore?"

"And who would that be?"

"Why the first minister himself, Ivan Morrison," Dolphie said through mock laughter. "It's easy, kids. The man who soiled Morrison's trophy wife had to pay for it with his life. Jeez, I wonder if that Major Newton Cunningham would ever consider giving me a job in the gardaí?"

Chapter Nineteen

MAJOR NEWTON CUNNINGHAM was proving that he still had a bit of a flair for detective work himself.

Once Starrett had finished writing up his crime book, he went off to chat with Thomas Black. He hoped that, among other things, the caretaker might also be able to shed some light on the first minister's sister-in-law.

However, before he could leave Tower House, Starrett happened upon the major, who was making a surprise Saturday-morning visit.

"Ah, Inspector, the very man. I was trying to reach you yesterday evening, but your mobile phone wasn't taking messages," Newton Cunningham said, his rich baritone voice ringing out over the reception area. "I think I might have located your Amanda Morrison."

"Really?" Starrett, replied, not feeling as guilty as he should have about turning off his phone while gallivanting with Dr Aljoe.

"Yes, pretty elementary stuff," the major said in an absentminded kind of way. "After we spoke, I decided that there would be no time like the present to drop in on Betsy Bell. Starrett, she's such an agreeable woman. There was a time I would have attempted to induce her to collaborate on the sin of intimacy. However, these days I'm content just to share a cup of tea with her and admire her from the distance of a few decades. Mum's the word to the current Mrs Newton Cunningham."

"Indeed."

"Anyway, it would appear I caught her unawares."

"Really?"

"No, no, dear boy, nothing as tacky as that, but I believe that just before I'd arrived she'd been enjoying a cup of coffee with a friend."

"How do you know that?"

"Well, there was a spare cup of coffee steaming away when I went in, for one thing. The telltale lipstick around the rim was a bit too vibrant even for most bountiful Donegal women. And there was a distinctive smell of perfume other than that of Mrs Bell in the room. Betsy's always been a stickler for tidiness, and the living room looked like a couple of students had been camping out therein. Hanging on the hallstand was a waisted jacket, much, much too petite for Betsy. No excuses were made, nor did the mystery woman return for her cup of coffee. As far as I'm aware, there's only one person involved in this case who could be termed as missing. Starrett, I do believe if you go down there now, you'll find Mrs Morrison in residence. I did try to be as discreet as possible in my examination of the facts. I pretended I was a doting old fool, not even sure which day it was. I think I play that part quite well. If I were you, though, I'd get down there as quick as lightning. I do believe you'll still be able to surprise them. Ladies of leisure do like to behave leisurely and never, ever commence a journey before they've had their breakfast."

Chapter Twenty

STARRETT, GREEN FELT hat in hand, nabbed the first member of his team he came across, Garda Francis Casey, and soon they were rattling over the noisy manhole covers on the Rathmullan road.

Starrett liked Casey. He was like the poor relation to golden boy Packie Garvey. Not that local hurling champion Garvey took advantage of his boyish looks and high-profile coverage on the sports pages, but even he would have had to admit that he benefited from both. Local boy Francis Casey, on the other hand, was happy, maybe even preferred, to remain in the background and get on with the job in hand: solving crimes. Starrett admired his ability to get to grips with the facts of a case extremely quickly. Casey would talk about the crime in question to Starrett, or any of his other colleagues, until the cows came home, but he seemed somewhat reluctant to socialise with the team. Fair play to you, Starrett thought, as they pulled into Betsy Bell's driveway. Loners tended to be thinkers, and you couldn't have enough of them working on your side on any investigation.

After Starrett had knocked on the front door, he was sure he heard someone whispering inside. Betsy Bell opened the front door and spotted Casey's uniform before her emerald eyes honed in on Starrett, who was unconsciously rolling the wide brim of his green hat through his fingertips.

If Betsy was nervous, she showed no sign of it. She wore a red, floor-length dressing gown, which she had pulled tighter around herself. Truth be told, apart from her fake tan, she looked nearly as good without make-up as she undoubtedly did with it, although her hair was in desperate need of attention.

"Oh my goodness, Starrett," she said, rolling her eyes and trying self-consciously to maul her hair into some sociably acceptable form, "I thought you would have realised by this stage in your life that a gentleman never ever calls on a lady before she's had a chance to put on her face."

"Ah now, Betsy, you'll get no complaints from us on that front," Starrett began, flashing one of his biggest smiles. "It's just that we've a few more questions for you."

"Come on in, then," she said, albeit reluctantly. "See yourselves through to the conservatory. You know the way, Starrett. If you'll just give me a few minutes, I'll be with you presently."

And a few minutes was exactly all she needed to transform herself into her familiar public image.

"So, what's new on the case?" she said, not bothering to hide her impatience.

"Well," Starrett sighed, "I was wondering if you'd spoken to First Minister Morrison since we spoke yesterday?"

"No, why, what's happened?" she asked, rolling her eyes. "For goodness sake, man, this is not downtown Los Angeles, it's Ramelton, so there's no need to try to create an air of mystery that's not there."

"I was just wondering if you'd heard from Mrs Morrison yet?"

"Actually, now you come to mention it, she hasn't telephoned or texted me for a while," Betsy said, smiling sweetly. "So, you're telling me she hasn't turned up yet?"

Starrett ignored her question, "Would you have any idea where she might be?"

"I wouldn't know where to start. Has Ivan no idea?"

"Not so far. What about her older sister, the one you were friends with in university?"

"Oh, you mean Jean? She and her husband and kids moved to Scotland about fifteen years ago. He got a job with a developer finding High Street retailers for shopping malls. It's very American, but it does seem to be the thing. Even Derry has one now."

"Well, you can fly Derry to Glasgow in under an hour, so I suppose it wouldn't be outside the realms of possibility," Starrett said, appearing to go through the process of the journey mentally. "Tell me, would you have Jean's telephone number by any chance?"

"I do, as a matter of a fact," Betsy said, nipping into the main part of the house and returning almost immediately with her handbag.

Starrett never ceased to be amazed by what women carried around in their handbags. It wasn't always an efficient system, because Betsy's bag was overflowing. First she removed her Filofax, placed it on the table in front of her, and then she proceeded to search high and low in her bag for exactly the same vital item of communication and social interfacing. Eventually, just as she was starting to progress into Ulster-speak swear words, she spotted the offending Filofax on the table and tutted as she said, "Oh, silly me, it was here all the time. Now, let's see, Jean . . . and what on earth was the husband's name? Oh yes, Alexander. Jean Alexander—here it is."

Starrett nodded to Casey for him to take down the number.

Betsy looked as if she were bracing herself for the next question.

"So, Betsy, you didn't tell me Mrs Morrison was having an affair with the deceased?"

"I did say that ladies never ever tell, didn't I? Perhaps Eileen McLaughlin has been proving what I've suspected all of these years—that she's no lady."

"Well, I'd prefer to take the more charitable view that she was proving she was a law-abiding citizen, prepared to help us with our enquiries."

"I'd say more likely she was jealous that Mandy got to James first, but that's another story."

"Well, look here, Betsy," Starrett said, rising to his feet, "you obviously don't know where Mrs Morrison is . . . but at least we now have this lead of her sister to check, so we'll be leaving you."

Starrett couldn't tell whether it was Betsy Bell or Garda Francis Casey who was the more surprised. He certainly knew which of the two was the most relieved.

Betsy Bell could hardly contain herself as he said, "It's fine, Betsy, we know our own way out. Thanks for the number."

"Toodaloo then," Betsy said, plucking at her hair in an attempt to make it plump out.

When Starrett reached the door, he quietly slipped back the catch on the Yale lock. Once back in the car, he asked Garda Casey to drive 100 yards down the road and pull into a lay-by.

About three minutes later, Starrett said theatrically, "Oh my goodness, Francis, I've only gone and left my hat in Betsy's conservatory. Hold on here; I'll only be a second."

Just as the sun broke through the clouds for the first time that Saturday morning, Starrett knocked loudly on Betsy Bell's unlocked front door.

"Excuse me, excuse me," he called, pulling open the door and moving slowly inside. "Is anyone at home? Oh hello, Betsy, it's only Starrett. I'm afraid I've forgotten my hat, I believe it's in here . . ."

All the while, he was edging closer and closer to the conservatory.

"Yes, I was sitting over there by the window," Starrett continued, ignoring Betsy who, with coffee cup midway to mouth, was speechless. "Oh, hello, ladies, sorry to disturb you. I won't be a moment. I'm sure it's over here . . . yes, here it is . . . you see . . ." and he pointed to a tag inside the hat, ". . . there's my name: 'Starrett'."

"I bet your mother taught you always to name-tag your clothes," Betsy Bell said, rising to her feet. Her other visitor stood up at the same time.

"Aha," Starrett exclaimed, pantomime style, "and you must be the missing Mrs Amanda Morrison."

"And from the name on your hat tag, you must be Inspector Starrett," the mystery woman said, using a dainty lace handkerchief to dab bloodshot eyes and a running nose.

Chapter Twenty-One

"I'LL TELL YOU what, Betsy, why don't you make a fresh pot of coffee and perhaps root out a few slices of that home-baked wheaten bread you're famous for. Then, when you've done that, perhaps you could take a dander down the road and hook up with Garda Casey and maybe show him the locals sights, as you tell him what's really been happening over the last twenty-four hours."

"Aye, and what did your last servant die of, Starrett?" Betsy asked, before sheepishly making her way out of the conservatory.

"Oh, hadn't you heard?" Starrett mumbled after her. "Why, it was disobedience, of course."

This served to bring the slightest hint of a smile to Mrs Morrison's face, which is exactly what Starrett had being intending. He wanted to see if she was really as beautiful as people had told him, something that has so far been obscured by a permanent frown.

Hearing about someone's alleged beauty before you meet them does tend to prejudice the viewer, Starrett thought. To him, Amanda Morrison's mouth was too wide, her nose too small, and her eyes appeared unsymmetrical, *but* she did have a figure to absolutely die for. Her Jackie Kennedy-style trousers showed off, to great effect, her shapely legs and wonderful bum. Starrett could feel the blood pumping involuntarily through his body to destinations in need. Said locations—due to the excesses of his imagination—were demanding more than his forty-five-year-old body had in reserve.

Her skintight T-shirt made imagination redundant.

Yes, she did have a large mouth; yes, her nose was too small; and yes, her eyes definitely were on a different horizontal plane; but with her expert make-up and Amazonian hairstyle, she was definitely using her given flaws to superlative effect.

And yet beneath it all, there was something very, very vulnerable about the woman. Starrett cautioned himself to keep an open mind and not to start feeling sorry for Amanda Morrison until he'd at least heard her side of the story.

Surprisingly, she seemed happy to talk to him, extremely happy. Perhaps she was just incapable of holding in any longer what had been happening over the previous twenty-four hours.

"Well . . ." she began with a sigh, after a sip of the fresh coffee, which Betsy had delivered with the requested toast. "Where to begin?"

Starrett, halfway through a mouthful of delicious wheaten bread, flamboyantly offered up the palm of his hand in an "it's up to you" gesture.

"OK, from the beginning then; stop me if I'm too boring or anything."

Starrett pondered on the "or anything" for a split second as she struggled to begin.

But the words didn't come immediately. Starrett washed down the remains of his toast with a cup of scalding coffee, burning the roof of his mouth in the process, and said, "Betsy's a good woman, isn't she?"

"Yes," Amanda replied cautiously.

"How long have you known her?"

"Oh, years and years. She was Jean's best friend; Jean is my sister, of course, and we were all at Queen's, at the same time. I was a couple of years behind, and I kinda latched on to them when I started. They were very protective of me. My sister said she wanted to save me from all the hairies, as she called them, yet didn't she only go and marry one herself, Gary Alexander? He was from Scotland, and he was always hanging around the Student Union helping out with concerts. Jean began seeing him just so that we could get free passes for the shows. Anyway, they grew quite serious, and that's when I became better friends with Betsy. I guess I filled the gap in her social life when Jean became attached to her man. Jean and Gary married, and they're still together in northern England."

"Where in England?" Starrett asked.

"Carlisle. He does a lot of travelling in Scotland and northern England."

Carlisle, Starrett thought: at least there was an excuse for Betsy's apparent lie. Many people considered Carlisle to be part of Scotland.

"Betsy and I have remained firm friends ever since. We've both had our ups and downs in the meantime and have had plenty of occasions to need the other's shoulder to cry on."

"What did you do between university and meeting and marrying the first minister?" Starrett asked. He was intrigued by her accent and quirky voice; it was as though they didn't really go together. Starrett pegged it as a cross between Marilyn Monroe's whisper and Juliet Turner's distinctive singing voice.

"Oh, my goodness, how long have you got?"

"As long as it takes."

"OK," Amanda sighed. "Let's see . . . Jean was the first to pair off; she went and married Gary. As I've already told you, they were married and live happily ever after. The rest of us weren't so lucky. Betsy moved to Dublin to work for a charity organisation. She threw herself into that heart and soul. She had an affair with a co-worker. It was one of those bizarre situations where he was in love with someone else who wasn't interested in him; so when he was feeling dejected, he'd take comfort in Betsy's arms. Betsy eventually wised up, but not before he'd married the object of his affections. Men are like that, you know, Inspector. Sometimes they just won't give up. And it's not that we feel that's an attraction. It's more that you tend to feel, 'Well, at least I know how much he wants to be with me, so at the very least it means he'll stay with me.' Betsy then met and married Billy Bell. He was an older man. They found this house together, you know, and lived here happily for years until, about five years ago, he just upped and died. No real reason. He was healthy enough, he hadn't been ailing, but he died. The doctors would say nothing more to her than that his heart gave up on him. Betsy and Billy were relatively happy. I mean he never cheated on her, or anything like that, but he was a quiet wee man, and Betsy loves to be the life and soul of the party. Anyway, she was well provided for in his will, and she's remained single ever since."

Amanda paused, as if in reflection, and Starrett tried to divine where she had drifted off to. Then she continued: "Anyway, when Betsy was off on her adventures, I was still at university. I finished a couple of years after her. I wanted to go into politics. That was until I discovered the politics of going into politics. I tell you, those Hollywood casting couches are nowhere near as busy as the ones at Stormont. Eventually, and I do mean eventually, I got a job with Guinness in their PR department. That was great fun. I had a great boss. He didn't care what hours I worked as long as I worked the hours. He treated me as an equal. I was there for five years, but I have to admit, all that non-stop action just wore me out. I retreated to my parents' house in Strabane to recharge my batteries. Relationships were few and far between, really just a series of one-night stands. When Betsy moved down here with Billy, I started to come down for weekends. At that stage I was working for the Irish Tourist Board, Bord Fáilte. The pay wasn't great, but neither was the work taxing. I met a man called . . . it doesn't really matter what his name was, you probably know him . . . I thought we'd get married, I really did, and then, just when I was starting to worry about not really being in love with him, he dumped me and married his childhood sweetheart who he'd met, he said, at a school reunion. I can't abide all that stuff of looking up old boyfriends and girlfriends just because your current life is a romantic disaster. *Hello*, if it didn't work out back then, you can be sure as hell it didn't work out for a good reason. I had an affair with a married man for three years—another disaster. I was still convinced that I was going to meet Mr Right, just like our Jean had, and settle down and have a family and live happily ever after. Eventually, in order to save my sanity, I gave up on that dream.

"Then Billy Bell introduced me to Ivan Morrison. Billy was a member of the Second Federation Church, and I believe he was one of the elders. Anyway, erm, to cut a long story short, Ivan respected me, treated me as a very special person. I knew he'd never make any demands on me, and, I'll be perfectly blunt with you, I knew he wasn't a poor man and that he'd refuse me nothing. And you know what? I was getting to the age where it was quite pathetic really still to have to be working in order to earn a living. I mean, it's perfectly fine to be working in something worthwhile or interesting to occupy yourself, but it's very depressing if you have to depend on your salary to get by and have to be nice to people to keep your job. I'll tell you something, Inspector, you'd be shocked by the number of men in positions of power who still think it's their God-given right to, at the very least, enjoy a grope from favoured members of staff. I know that I have a figure that attracts that kind of attention, but my husband has never once treated me as a sex object. I'm not sure he even knows what one is."

She paused again and sighed. "But I have to admit, I was naïve; you can't be relatively young and healthy *and* enjoy a sexless marriage. Sorry, sorry, sorry, of course I meant a *loveless* marriage," Amanda said, her voice rising to a pitch of heightened excitement.

Starrett said nothing; he was still reflecting on another part of her statement.

"Sorry, sorry," continued Amanda. "Anyway, by the time I hooked up with Betsy again, she was great mates with Eileen McLaughlin, and after I married we all hung out together. My husband seemed happy for me to do as I liked. He didn't need me to cook or clean the house. He had a cook and a cleaner. He didn't really seem to need me around full stop, so I'd . . . well, Inspector, I'll admit to you that I had my needs. I believe I was respectful of my husband at all times in that I was discreet. Mostly we had girls' weekends and flings in Belfast, Dublin and London, and maybe if you put burning matches under my fingernails, you'd get me to admit that I had one or two relationships around here, but no one seemed aware of them. And then I met Jimmy at Betsy's house, where he was doing some work for her, and it was like 'Hello, where has this man been all my life?' Oh my goodness, yes, I'll also admit that Jimmy awoke feelings in me I thought had been buried for ever!"

"Did Betsy know about you and Jimmy from the start?"

"Well, it was that old cliché where neither James nor I actually saw it creep up on us. First off, I just loved the way he created things out of wood. Yes, yes, of course I thought he was cute. He always kept himself in great shape, but that wasn't important. I was just intrigued by this quiet man who wasn't showing the slightest bit of sexual inter-est in me. He said he wanted to find out about me, and he'd just work away, and I'd sit in a chair nearby talking away with him all the time. He'd get upset when I'd tell him how men had always been taking advantage of me, but you know what, a lot of men used to do that just so they could take advantage of me. But it was like he didn't even consider that as a possibility. I swear to you, it didn't even enter his head.

"We talked about things he'd never discussed with anyone before. It wasn't that he was harbouring all these big secrets; it was more that he just didn't have the kind of relationship with his wife that he could discuss things with her and talk about his dreams and his fears. He was particularly proud of how Chris, his eldest, was turning out, but he felt he couldn't share his joy fully with his wife. Jimmy was incredibly funny, in a subtle way. He wasn't crass; he didn't know how to be.

"I found myself falling deeply in love with him. Really in love, like I'd never been ever before. I was seeing someone at the time, and I broke it off because of my feelings for Jimmy. It was very messy. I figured the only way I could express my love for Jimmy was in a physical way, and I wanted to be free emotionally to pursue that. I knew he'd never make the first move—I doubt if he even fantasised about doing anything about it, so I had to take the lead. To be quite honest, I was afraid I'd scare him off, that he'd run a mile. The only encouragement he ever gave me was to say things like how he couldn't wait to see me again, and that he really loved talking to me. I was so consumed with love for him, though, that I just *had* to be with him. So, I chose a day when my husband was away on a conference. By this time, Jimmy was in the Manse every day, working in the library. I fortified myself with a stiff whiskey, and I walked into the library, in the middle of all of his wood and stuff, and said to him, 'I'm sorry, but I just have to do this.' And I put my arms around him and kissed him."

Amanda Morrison stopped talking and looked deep into Starrett's eyes, holding his gaze for what seemed like an age.

"Inspector Starrett, in telling you this I'm being as honest as I know how to be. I know I'm risking ridicule and shame, but I need you to know exactly how all this happened and what it meant to me. I need you to realise that it wasn't a quick lay, a shag, ride or whatever you'd like to call it. There was nothing cheap about what I experienced with Jimmy, and I hope by telling you this, it will help you discover who took away from me the dearest man I have ever known."

Starrett nodded that he understood.

She smiled.

"We kissed for ages. He said he'd being dying to kiss me since the first time we'd talked. He said kissing was all he needed, that he wasn't looking for anything else. The more he said things like that, the more I was convinced that I had to give myself totally and utterly to him. Jimmy Moore was the only good thing that ever happened in my life. I know it was selfish, but I felt that up to that point in my life I'd never fulfilled my dreams. Do you realise how frustrating that can be? To go through your life, year in and year out, feeling like you've always been cheated, always being treated like dirt. Do you realise how destructive that can be to one's soul? Then suddenly something good had happened in my life. Someone special had come along. It wasn't like he was married and I was married and we were both about to cheat. It was much bigger than that: we'd both felt cheated in the marriage stakes, but that didn't matter because we'd found each other. And I really wanted to fulfil my dream, just once. Once would have been enough. Eventually, I led him upstairs to my room, and I won't embarrass you, Inspector Starrett, by telling you everything that happened, but I can tell you, it just felt like the most natural thing in the world."

Starrett hoped the colour rising in his cheeks wasn't noticeable.

"It was wonderful, but of course that once just *wasn't* enough. So we stole time together whenever we could. But we knew that it wasn't going to be just a torrid affair, so we started to plan a way to have a life together, and then . . ."

She stopped for a moment to compose herself, refusing to break down into tears. It seemed to Starrett that she felt the information she was passing on to him was vital to his investigation.

"The last time . . ." she began, but again faltered. Starrett reached over and rubbed her back awkwardly. "The last time I saw him was on Thursday night. Ivan was at a dinner in Derry, so I had James over. I cooked him a meal. We had a great evening. We made our plans to be together and . . . I kissed him for the last time in the doorway of the Manse."

This time, Amanda couldn't contain her tears, and she began sobbing. Starrett took her in his arms and she responded by holding on to him tightly—so tightly, it seemed as though her life depended on his support.

Through her sobbing she kept repeating, "Why?"

Starrett understood that she had the added burden that her grieving was without the cloak of widowhood that made it socially acceptable.

o-O-o

Starrett had more questions for Amanda Morrison, but he could see that she was in no state to talk about anything, let alone the death of the man she had considered her soulmate.

The inspector took his hat, which was, in fact, a Major Cunningham cast-off, and went in search of Betsy Bell and Garda Francis Casey. They were at the front garden gate, where Betsy was blethering away like she was a schoolgirl on her first date.

"How did you get on?" Betsy asked, walking up the garden path towards him and simultaneously pulling her micro-jumper tightly around her.

"Aye, I think we need to take a break for a while. She's very upset at the moment."

All three stood speechless for a few seconds, taking in the air, lost in their thoughts.

"Look, I have to go back into Ramelton to attend to a few things," Starrett said. "Do you think she'll be OK with you for a while? I'd prefer if no one else knew she was here, not even her doctor, if possible. But if you feel she needs medical . . ."

"No, she'll be OK, Starrett. I've got the very pick-me-up in my medicine cabinet."

"Who else knows she's here?"

"Just you and Francis here, and the major I shouldn't wonder," Betsy replied.

"OK, let's keep it that way for now," Starrett said, setting off towards his car.

"You don't think she's in any kind of danger, do you?" Betsy said behind him, glancing around her pastoral grounds as if there was a chance of imminent danger in the undergrowth.

"At this stage I don't know, but I'd prefer not to take any chances. Best-case scenario, I'd like to spare her from being door-stopped by the press. I noticed a few shifty-looking strangers down on the Mall as we were leaving. I'll be back within the hour. Give us a shout if you need help in the meantime."

"You see, Francis, I told you your mobile number would come in handy," Betsy Bell said, smiling sweetly at Garda Casey. Then the smile disappeared from her face as she thought of her distressed friend inside the house. She hurried inside without uttering another word.

Chapter Twenty-Two

BACK IN CARRIGART, Nuala Gibson and Packie Garvey were busy searching for Daniel McGuinness. Having gone door to door without a definite address to work with, once they'd tracked down their man, they were annoyed to find that he lived in the very first house they'd visited.

It was on the plains, just off the sand dunes on the Carrigart to Downings road, a long, dark, sprawling, single-storey building, fronted by a short driveway, which was dotted with trees and bushes in a vain attempt to shelter it from the cutting winds and rain.

When Gibson and Garvey first called at the house, Dan was still in bed, and none of his children were allowed to tell callers he was in. Dan the Man, half-man, half-mattress, hated leaving slumberland for nosy house-callers, strangers or members of the several local authorities he was trying to avoid. He loved nothing better than to luxuriate in his pit. Well, actually, that wasn't strictly accurate. What he *really* loved more than *anything* else were his several daily meals.

By the time Gibson and Garvey returned from their fruitless search of several locations in Carrigart, Dan the Man had been helped from his sleeping quarters at the back of the house and was positioned on his throne: a two-seater, high-backed sofa, the legs of which had been telescoped an additional fifteen inches by using a log under each leg. The sofa, obviously for his exclusive use, was positioned dangerously close to the blazing fire. Daniel McGuinness sat like a Buddha. His head was of such proportions that it looked as if someone had painted a youngish man's face on to a huge melon. It was impossible to ascertain where the folds of his belly ended and his legs began. Both hands were crossed in front of him and rested on a walking stick, so sturdy that it looked like a telegraph pole-in-waiting. He made his furniture seem as if it had been impounded from a doll's house. The overall effect, with his loose-fitting and expensive-looking black clothes, was quite sinister.

There were several children running around, creating an almighty racket until Dan the Man cracked his stick on the tiled hearth a few times, in the manner of a lion-tamer. Within ten seconds, the room was totally cleared apart from the gardaí and Dan the Man.

"I heard you were looking for me in Carrigart," Dan said, his bass voice gritting objectionably with his North Coast bucolic accent.

"Yeah, we went into Carrigart all right," Garvey replied. "It was closed."

"Hag, hag, hag," Dan the Man chuckled, his throat-tickle sounding like a low foghorn. "Funny line, young Garvey, I like it. I must use that. I need to write these things down in case I forget them," he grunted in a very patronising manner.

Garvey, ignoring Dan's attempt at humour, drew out his notebook and said, "Mr McGuinness, we are here to ask you about your friend, James Moore."

"Yeah, I figured you'd be here sooner or later," the big man grunted. Every word he uttered sounded like a grunt, and a grunt that required a lot of energy at that. He removed his right hand from its perch on the stick and rubbed his upper thigh, or it may have been his lower torso, continuing his slow back-and-forward motion. Garvey felt himself becoming fascinated with it. He wondered if it was the fat man's method of getting at least some circulation going in his body.

"We believe you were a good friend of James Moore?"

"Yeah," he grunted. "We played tennis together every weekend."

Gibson looked as if she were about to say "Really?" when Dan the Man burst into a potentially life-threatening fit of laughter. Garvey really was worried about the man's safety, as he coughed and spluttered dangerously.

"Perhaps you want to write that one down?" Dan chuckled once his laughter and resulting body-ripples had slowed down to a mere wobble.

"I'm one step ahead of you there," Garvey countered.

"Yes, sorry, only kidding," he mumbled. "Yeah, Jimmy was a good mate. Have you figured out what happened yet?"

"We're still looking into it," Gibson said. "How did you know him?"

"Ah," McGuinness replied with a huge sigh, "we used to work together. That was about five years ago, before my accident. I fell from some scaffolding on a refurbishment job we were doing up in Dunfanaghy—a school. Thank goodness it was a school, so I was covered on the insurance. I was hoaking away at a chimneystack on the first floor. I was pulling at this stone, and it came out a lot easier than I thought it was going to, and it came down on top of me and I fell back on to the floorboards. They kind of broke my fall, but they were rotten, and so I went right through and landed on the ground floor. Jimmy clocked this, ran over with a large piece of scaffolding and held it against the collapsing wall until a few other workers were able to pull me out of the way. The scaffolding got jammed on his steel toecap. You should have seen the dint in the toe of his boot. If it hadn't been for Jimmy, the whole flipping wall would have tumbled down on top of me and I'd have been crushed to death."

"Goodness," Gibson said.

"Yes, indeed, both of us could have ended up six feet under that day," Dan said quietly. "I haven't been able to work a day since. Most of my mates have deserted me, but Jimmy was as good as gold—a true friend. He'd often drop in for a chat, and we'd chew the cud and watch the world go by."

"And how long before that had you been mates?" Gibson asked.

"Ah, flip, Miss, we were at school together. We're the same age, you know, both born the same year, just two months apart. I never thought we'd end up in the same neck of the world together. Jimmy was a bit of a dreamer, and I always thought he'd bum his way around the world and stop off in a hippie commune somewhere like San Francisco, but no, he settled down pretty quickly."

"Did he have any regrets?" Gibson asked.

"Show me a man who has no regrets and I'll show you a liar," Dan the Man replied. "Hey, but he hasn't got any regrets now, though, has he?"

"So, what were these regrets of his?" Garvey asked.

"Oh, you know . . . Nora. Now there's a good place to start. She went out and caught him, and after she bagged him and married him, it was as if she gave up on life. But there were a couple of wains by then, and so Jimmy was never going to do the dirty on them, or her for that matter. I'll tell you something you won't believe, but Nora was quite a looker in those days. I mean, a real head-turner. We had a couple of dates way back then. Her sister fixed us up, and I'd go around to her house to see her or take her out, and she was never in. She was always already out somewhere. This happened once too often, so I found pastures new. It transpired that Nora had been two-timing me with a boy whose dad had something important to do with the Rosapenna Hotel. Apparently I was first reserve, in case she didn't get it together with your man. You've heard it before: rich boy turns the head of poor girl by showing her what life on the other side of the tracks is like. Poor girl likes what she sees, and so she rides the boy so that they'll drive off in his Austin Princess into the romantic sunset. Girl falls pregnant. Girl with child isn't exactly a non-stop bundle of fun, so rich boy goes off in search of new blood for more fun, or else a rich girl to settle down with. In the meantime, Nora disappears to 'stay with relatives in England' and returns a couple of weeks later, looking a bit drained and run-down. She made an effort for at least her first couple of months back home, and in those few months she ensnared poor Jimmy. On reflection, I suppose Nora never got over the abortion. It left its mark on her."

"Did James Moore ever complain to you about his wife?" Gibson asked.

"Not his style. He was from the 'I've made my bed, I'll lie in it' school."

"Did he ever cheat on her?" Garvey asked.

"Again, that was never his style."

"What about Nora?" Gibson asked.

"Sorry?" Dan the Man spluttered.

"Did Nora ever cheat on James Moore?" Gibson repeated slowly.

Dan blew a storm through his lips, and his cheeks rippled in sympathy.

"How would I know?" he eventually said dismissively.

"OK," Garvey said, wanting to return McGuinness to a more communicative mood. "Are you sure James never had an affair."

"I know he'd fallen in love with the vicar's wife in Ramelton and that he was very serious about that. It would be wrong to say it was an affair, though. Doesn't affair imply something less substantial than love?"

"I suppose it all depends if you're the husband or the lover," Gibson said.

"We believe James's sole source of income was from his work as a carpenter. Is that the case as far as you know?" Garvey asked.

"Yep," Dan the Man grunted. "But he was a real master carpenter, so he did OK out of it."

"So he never had to borrow money then?" Garvey continued.

"Not as far as I'm aware."

"Do you know of any people he may have had words with?" Garvey asked.

"For instance?"

"Oh, you know, someone he'd fallen out with through his work?" Packie said.

"No, no, there were never ever any gombeens hanging around Jimmy."

"Did he ever speak about anyone threatening him? You know, his house and workshop seem to be on a prime piece of land. Was there ever a developer chasing around after him? Or maybe he saw something on one of his jobs he wasn't meant to?" Garvey asked, searching his mind for possible motives.

"I do remember he told me about a job he was working on; this would have been several months ago. It was a job he had to fit in over the weekend between his other jobs; it involved clearing out a pub. The owner wanted the ornate bar dismantled and removed before the refurbishment commenced. Jimmy took the full two days of the weekend to dismantle the bar. There were a few people hanging around he said he was uncomfortable with. So he got out of there and returned to the bar the Monday morning to tidy up and collect his tools. The place was gone. There was a black smouldering mess on the ground where the pub once stood."

"Where was this?" Garvey asked.

"Over in Creestown. The pub was the called the Fast Trout. Jimmy thought it must have been a torch job because the electricity was already turned off. A few days later, the gaffer on the job called round to Jimmy's house and dropped off all his tools. He said the tools had been discovered in the ruins. But sure, the majority of Jimmy's chisels and hammers and what-have-you had wooden handles, and they were all in a wooden toolbox he'd made for himself, all totally unburnt. So figure that one out."

"And who owned the pub?" Garvey asked.

"I don't remember who the owner of the shebeen was."

"So it was an illegal establishment?"

"No, maybe, possibly. I really don't remember much about it. I think in the early days it had a reputation for being outside the law, but that all changed lately, I believe.

Garvey wondered if McGuinness genuinely couldn't remember, or if he was trying to be discreet. Donegal was rife with rumours of she-beens using their alleged paramilitary connections to ignore the county's building regulations. When in doubt, knocking or torching seemed to be the best way forward. Garvey knew Starrett would definitely be interested in this piece of information. He had a healthy distaste for anyone who thought they were beyond the law and who openly flaunted their outlaw approach, while at the same time retaining a full team of expensive solicitors who knew exactly how to interpret the laws to their clients' full benefit.

"Did James Moore have any suspicions as to who caused the fire?" Garvey asked, picking his words as carefully as he could.

"Do I really look that stupid?" Dan the Man replied, putting on a bit of a show for Nuala Gibson.

"OK, we can understand your reluctance," she responded. "But, Daniel, are there any other people like that you can remember who might have held a grudge against Mr Moore?"

"Apart from the husband of the wife he was having a relationship with?"

"Yes," Garvey replied hopefully.

"Nope, Packie," Dan said. "I mean, Jimmy was so inoffensive that at times it was really offensive that he was so inoffensive, if you get my drift."

Daniel McGuinness started to shift around uncomfortably in his chair.

"Are you OK?" Gibson asked immediately. "Can we get your wife or someone to help?"

"Oh, you're about four-and-a-half years too late on that account. She ran off with a member of a Cork trad band. No, it's just that I always get twitchy around grub time . . . so, ahm . . . if you've nothing else," he said, before shouting, "Food!" in the general direction of the kitchen.

"I suppose that'll do us for now," Garvey replied, checking his watch. It was 13.06.

"Right, I'm going nowhere," McGuinness said. Then he added as an apparent afterthought, "Tell me, Packie, how do you think you'll do against Armagh? Would it be worth my while to get one of the wains to run up to the bookies and put a few euros on you boys?"

"I think you'd be safe on an each-way bet, Dan," Packie said as he and Nuala Gibson left the dark house. They could hear the beginnings of another eruption of laughter as they let themselves out through the front door.

Chapter Twenty-Three

"THAT'S CERTAINLY AN ugly can of worms," Starrett said when Garda Gibson relayed the information about the apparent torching of the possible shebeen in Creestown.

"Yeah, McGuinness was very reluctant to give us any additional information.

"Oh, that's not a problem," Starrett mused. "It'll be easy enough to find out the owner's name. I believe I know exactly who we're talking about here, and if it is him, he's been getting away with this auld carry-on for ten years or so. He thinks he's pretty untouchable, and in fact we've never been able to make any of our charges against him stick. Witnesses tend to disappear. Even the Revenue leaves him alone. Over the past seven years, he's been cleaning up his act. I've heard he's moved into legitimate businesses and surrounded himself with pretty powerful friends."

"How can people like that have friends?" Nuala Gibson asked.

"Money makes friends very easily," Starrett replied. "Tell you what, Nuala, let's go through this by the book. Do me a favour and see who the registered owner of the Fast Trout up in Creestown was at the time of the fire."

Starrett *always* did everything 100 per cent by the book, and he insisted his team do the same. Perhaps there were times when 95 per cent by the book might do, but how far was it from there to work your way down to 70 per cent and 50 per cent and even not by the book at all? While he was having this thought, the earnest Gibson, as

if reading his mind, said, "Packie tells me that you always do everything 100 per cent by the book; that's why I'm so happy to be working with you guys."

Starrett smiled but felt slightly embarrassed.

"Oh shit," she said. "That came out all wrong. I mean, it's not that
I'm unhappy either, but I don't want to sound like a big girl's blouse."

"Right, Nuala, I don't think we need to go there. Why don't
you . . ."

". . . find out the owner of the Fast Trout?" she interrupted.

"Correct!"

"Consider it done," she said, disappearing up the stairs to Tower
House's sole computer.

o-O-o

Starrett took the opportunity to complete another chore.

There had been a series of petty break-ins in the area over the previous few months. No damage had been done, but the gardaí were
intrigued by the offender's resourceful and discreet methods of entry.
However, on the previous evening, the subject in question had been
caught on the premises by the owner, who'd easily overpowered the 16-
year-old Rory De Vieto Junior.

Part of the major's successful tactic with such offenders was to give
them a taste of what life might be like on the other side of bars. A night
in the cells with the local drunks and what have-yous does tend to have
a sobering effect on a young man.

But Rory was a different type. It wasn't that he was cocky, but he
felt that because of his father—a very successful policeman in Boston—
he was untouchable. He more or less admitted to all of the crimes,
which had started around the time he arrived back in Ramelton for his
summer vacation.

"Your father is going to be very disappointed, you know," Starrett
said, once he'd joined the boy in the interview room.

"Whatever," Rory replied, as if he were an extra on *The Simpsons.*

"You know, normally, because of your father, I'd let you off with a
warning," Starrett said, "but you don't seem too remorseful . . ."

Rory shifted uncomfortably in his chair.

". . . so, I think what I'll do is charge you with all of these thefts."

"But I'm only sixteen," he protested.

"Yes, but you *are* sixteen," Starrett said.

"But I didn't take anything last night."

"Only because you didn't get a chance."

"I didn't admit I was responsible for the other B&Es," Rory pleaded.

"Tell you what, boyo, why don't you tell that to the magistrate in Letterkenny on Monday morning? I'm afraid I don't have time to deal with this. You're going to be one of those statistics that slipped through the cracks in our all-too-fallible system."

"But my dad . . ." Rory was close to tears now.

Starrett rose from his chair, closed the file, walked over to Rory and clipped him on the ear. When Rory made to protest, Starrett said, "Just giving you a little sample of what a little rich American boy in prison with a bunch of Irish criminals is going to be in for."

"Oh, look, can you call my father? You can do it collect."

"Sorry, I'm not interested," Starrett said, leaving Rory alone in the interview room.

He told the desk sergeant to leave Rory De Vieto Junior in there for forty minutes and then to release him with an instruction to report to Tower House every morning at 08.30 for the remainder of his stay in Donegal.

Starrett hoped that believing he'd end up in jail would work as effectively for Rory as it had for his father.

o-O-o

"The name of the owner of the Fast Trout Bar and Restaurant at the time of the fire in Creestown was Owen Bonner," Nuala reported five minutes later.

"I figured it might be," Starrett said, looking distracted.

Nuala Gibson hung around the door for a few seconds, awaiting instruction.

"Look, we'll have to leave this until later. Why don't you come down with me to Betsy Bell's again?"

The first minister's wife was in slightly better spirits than she'd been when Starrett had left her an hour and a half previously.

"I'm sorry about . . . before, and you having to return," she said quietly, and then added, "Thank you for being so considerate. Please ask me whatever you like. I'm keen to do all I can do to help catch his killers."

"OK, look, is there any possibility your husband knew you and Mr Moore were having a relationship?"

"Well, it wasn't that we were always covering up our tracks, but we were careful. At the beginning, neither of us knew what it was we were getting involved in, and then, as time passed, we realised we owed it to ourselves to protect the specialness of our relationship by not hurting others, so, yes, we were careful."

"Who knew about the relationship?" Starrett asked, Gibson taking notes.

"Well, Betsy here, and Eileen McLaughlin and my sister, and then Jimmy's mates Colm Donovan and Big Dan McGuinness. I don't believe anyone else knew," Amanda said. "You didn't tell anyone, Betsy, did you?"

"Not that I can think of," Betsy replied, diplomatically but maybe not entirely truthfully. That was a question for a later time and a smaller audience, Starrett decided.

"How many times did you and Mr Moore . . . ? Look, I apologise here if you think I'm being too coarse, but I don't know how to ask this other than: how many times did you and Mr Moore get together in the Manse?"

"Nine times," Amanda replied immediately, without having to give it a millisecond's thought. Starrett realised that, if required, she could probably recall every detail of each encounter.

"Did he ever stay overnight?"

"Not quite," Amanda replied. "Let me explain. I did want him to. To me there is nothing quite so fulfilling as making sweet love to someone you love and then waking up in his arms the following morning. We settled for a 5 a.m. alarm call on the one occasion. He didn't leave until about an hour later." She paused here for a second's consideration. "But it was still dark when he left."

"Had he parked his van in the driveway?"

"No. He'd parked outside Conway's pub, and he even went in and had a drink so that no one would be suspicious. Then he came up Meeting House Lane, Mortimer's Lane and in the Manse's back way. It was all very cloak-and-dagger. We talked about that after-wards—you know, the deceit. I mean, you start off with great inten-tions, but then you end up doing things like that to cover your tracks. That was the first time we discussed that we didn't want to have that type of a relationship, that we wanted to be in a position where we could put things out in the open. Betsy was brilliant to both of us at that point," Amanda said, looking to Betsy for some kind of corrob-oration.

"Well, it's a very difficult situation, isn't it?" Betsy Bell joined in, seemingly happy to take the spotlight away from her friend, if only for a few moments. "The husband is cheating on the wife. On top of which, there were Jimmy's kids to consider. Then Mandy is cheating on her husband, who also happens to be a first minister and a pillar of the community. I told Mandy that if she was as serious about this as she was leading me to believe she was and if she wanted herself and Jimmy to have a future of some kind, then they were going to have to be very careful over what steps they took. There was no point in them being in love but for Jimmy to be miserable for the rest of his life because his kids had disowned him. And Ivan, for all his pomposity, is still human, and he did take in and protect our Mandy at a time when she needed it most. I've always said to her that she didn't blossom as a woman until he took her under his wing as it were."

"Yes, but I never felt like a real woman until Jimmy and I got together," Amanda said.

"Yes, yes, I know, Mandy dear. I wasn't criticising you. I was only explaining to the inspector that I cautioned you both to be careful. Look, in this life, even at the best of times, it's nearly impossible to meet and fall in love with your perfect partner and make it work out. Mandy and Jimmy, through no fault of their own, were beginning from a far from ideal situation. So, my point was, yes, by all means follow your heart, but don't let your heart rule your head to the point that all you're really going to do is ruin your life and at least five other people's lives as well."

"And of course it made perfect sense," Amanda agreed. "We dis-cussed moving away together. But Jimmy loved Donegal so much, and he didn't want to become a stranger to his children. And, I'll be per-fectly frank with you: I'd put in my time with Mr Ivan Morrison. I'd lived up to my part of my deal with him, and I didn't want to be thrown out without a penny. So we'd been discussing the various ways of making this work. The best plan we could come up with was for us to split up with our respective spouses, and then, after a discreet time, we thought just over a year would be about right, we'd find a way—probably with Betsy orchestrating it—to meet and conduct a public courtship. This way, we figured, Jimmy's children and even Nora could become used to us getting together as a couple, rather than suffering some kind of public humiliation. We accepted that divorce was out of the question. Nora would side with her church on that one. But it didn't matter to us. Neither of us was devout anything. I married a member of the Second Federation Church, for heaven's sake. All that mattered between Jimmy and me was that we would be together. That'll never happen now, Betsy."

Starrett was worried he was about to lose Amanda in another emotional breakdown. Amanda rose to her feet, crossed her arms in front of her and walked up and down in the conservatory, backward and forward, backward and forward, on the same journey as before. At times she passed so close to Starrett that he could smell her expensive, heather-infused perfume.

Eventually she said, "I'm fine, Inspector. What's your next question?"

"Good. Can we go back to your husband for a few moments?" Starrett said. "When did he become a minister in the Second Federation Church?"

"I don't know . . ." Amanda started to say, as Betsy Bell interrupted.

"Oh, I can answer that one for you, Inspector. My husband and I have known him for ages. Ivan came back here from Texas in the early 1990s. He was originally from Plumbridge, and he'd gone over to America to seek his fame and fortune with a gospel band in the 1970s. Believe it or not, he plays the piano."

"He plays the piano in the house sometimes," Amanda added. "He has one in his study, and he often records himself playing one of his pieces of music."

"Oh, yes," Betsy chuckled politely. "That's his party piece when anyone goes around to the Manse for dinner. Anyway, he was quite friendly with my husband. Ivan admitted to Billy that when he met up with the Second Federation Church in Texas he couldn't believe it. He said it was the perfect religion for him."

"You see, my husband loved the pomp and ceremony of a real church. He just wasn't fussed about the spiritual responsibility," Amanda said, without making it sound like a criticism of the first minister. "When he discovered that the creator of the Second Federation Church, William O'Donnell, was a Donegal man, he persuaded the elders that they should open a church in O'Donnell's homeland to celebrate the fact. Apparently they'd been thinking of such a move for years, and Ivan just happened along at the right moment."

"Aye, that's Ivan for you," Betsy offered. Looking at her friend, she added. "He has a great gift for just happening along at the right moment."

"How does the Second Federation Church receive its funding? Is it from gifts and collections from its congregations?" Starrett asked.

"I haven't a clue," Amanda replied.

But Betsy broke in: "I believe that is so."

"So, who would the first minister report to?" Starrett asked.

"Well, I believe that would be the elders back in Texas," Betsy replied, but she looked at Amanda for corroboration.

"I suppose so," she replied. "But I think they just let him get on with it."

"And why wouldn't they?" Betsy said. "Ivan has done very well for them. He provided a much-needed alternative for those disgruntled with the effects of 'The Troubles'. For the first time, you had a group of people who, when asked if they were Protestant or Catholic, could stand up and safely say, 'Actually I'm neither. I'm a member of the Second Federation Church.'"

"OK," Starrett said. "Let's consider Mrs Moore, for a while. Is there *any* chance she could have known about you and James?"

"None at all," Amanda replied without a moment's hesitation.

"Why are you so convinced of that?" Starrett asked.

"Because Jimmy told me that, as far as his wife was concerned, nothing had changed. He often worked out in his workshop until the early hours of the morning. Jimmy reckoned that Nora hadn't been out there since he first built it. He told me it wasn't a regular occurrence, but sometimes he'd become so engrossed in his work that he would just be working away and then suddenly it'd be daybreak. He just loved his work, Inspector. He loved the combination of working with wood, creating something special and useful, while at the same time he could let his mind wander. He was always saying that he never considered it work. He would have done it for nothing if he'd had to."

"I need to ask you if you know whether Jimmy was still sleeping with Nora."

"Yes, he slept with her, but that was all they did: sleep," Amanda replied. "Jimmy said they never had had a very active sex life. In the early days of their marriage, Nora made it clear that she thought it was a chore and one she didn't particularly enjoy. Jimmy believed that Nora thought sex was a necessary evil designed only to create children, and that once they'd had their three, she didn't need to endure it any longer. He said he never really missed it because it wasn't something he was preoccupied with. He also said that he didn't think such an attitude was unusual; otherwise why would the pubs be so full most of the time."

Starrett was about to ask another question when Amanda added: "I think it's very important that you understand that Nora and Jimmy didn't have a bad marriage as far as they were concerned. They had their problems and they'd learned to work around them. But it wasn't as if they were fighting all the time either."

"OK," Starrett started slowly. "Are you aware of anyone else involved in James' life who might have had a reason . . . ?"

"What, you mean another woman?" Amanda asked, picking the wrong thread entirely. She stopped her dandering around the conservatory right in front of Starrett and glared down at him defiantly.

"No, I wasn't thinking specifically about another woman," Starrett said slowly, not wanting her to think that it could be ruled out altogether.

"Inspector Starrett, if you think for one moment that there was a possibility James was having a relationship with another woman, then I haven't been very successful in describing our relationship to you. If you are the type of person, Inspector, who thinks that just because Jimmy cheated with me he could cheat with others, I'm very disappointed in you."

"I'm sure Starrett doesn't think that," Betsy said firmly. "However,

Amanda, if he didn't at least consider every possibility, he'd be a pretty poor detective, now, wouldn't he?"

"Mmmm," Amanda said, sounding unconvinced and retaining the look of hurt in her eyes. Slowly at first, she resumed her trek around the conservatory.

"OK," Starrett said with a click of his teeth, "we're assuming that neither Mr Morrison nor Mrs Moore, nor indeed any other women, were involved in James Moore's killing. So, taking that as agreed, is there anyone else you can think of who may have had it in for Jimmy?"

"No," Amanda said. "I'm really very sorry I can't be of more help. Since Jimmy and I didn't really have what you would call a social relationship, I didn't come across his outside acquaintances."

"And in your time together, he didn't confess any worries, any concerns?"

"No, Inspector, he was a very contented, self-contained man," she replied.

"So there's nothing at all you can think of?"

"Well, the only subject I can imagine Jimmy getting into an argument over would be his children. Nothing else in his life would have bothered him as much."

"Had anything been happening in the children's lives?"

"There didn't seem to be. He was very proud of them. He was extremely proud of the way Chris was turning out. He wondered how he and Nora could have produced such a wonderful young man. Oh my goodness, Inspector, you should have seen him when he spoke about Chris. I just couldn't wait to meet him and be part of his life— and Claudia and Brian as well, of course."

"OK, Mrs Morrison, thanks for being so patient with me," Starrett said, taking to his feet. "Please give me a shout if you think of anything else, anything else at all. Betsy, if you don't mind, I'd like Mrs Morrison to remain here."

"Not a bother, Starrett. She's not going anywhere."

"I think I'll send out an unmarked car to keep an eye on the place."

"What? Do you think Mandy could be in some kind of danger?"

"The honest answer is that I just don't know, but I don't intend to take any chances."

Chapter Twenty-Four

"OK, TELL ME this, Nuala, and tell me no more," Starrett said on their return journey to Ramelton.

"Yes?"

"You know how sometimes a girl or a woman will walk around with her arms folded in front of her?"

"Yes?"

"Well, it's just that men don't do that," Starrett said, scratching his chin. "Can you tell me, Nuala, what that's all about?"

"I've always thought it was a form of protection."

"But if you think about it," Starrett said, proving that he had thought about it quite a bit in fact, "it's not really an effective form of protection. By virtue of the fact that the hands are somewhat restrained, you'd have to say that anyone with their arms folded in front of them is more in need of protection than someone with their arms hanging free."

"I can understand that," Nuala said in agreement. "So what do *you* think the folded arms signify?"

"Well, the only thing I've been able to come up with is that it's someone who is sexually vulnerable sending a signal to all around her saying, 'Keep away!'"

"You mean like Mrs Morrison?"

"Exactly like Mrs Morrison, Nuala, exactly like Mrs Morrison."

Chapter Twenty-Five

As STARRETT DROVE over to Letterkenny, he thought of Owen Bonner, current owner of the Fast Trout Bar and Restaurant, and the infamous Bonner family.

Although Bonner was the youngest son of Vincent and Eliza Bonner, he had always seemed destined to take over the family business. Vincey consistently went out of his way, sometimes at the cost of incurring the wrath of his other two sons, Alexander (a.k.a. Milky) and Pádraig, to keep his son out of trouble and in the educational system.

Vincey, himself an only son who, as a fifteen-year-old, had seen his parents turfed off their farm in 1949, had resolved that by hook or by crook, the same would never happen to him. Part of him loved his parents, but another part despised them for being so pathetic and unable to support themselves and consequently him. He hated being poor. It wasn't the lack of clothes or food; what he couldn't bear was the sheer public humiliation of it all. In 1950, Vincey joined the mass exodus to England, landing in Luton in the springtime where he immediately found a job digging drains.

Keeping himself to himself, he shunned the drink. As he saw his workmates drink away their entire wages on a Friday night, he also accepted that the demon alcohol had surely been responsible for his family's problems. He saved every penny he could, staying in work-site huts, and as he always had his wits about him, no one in the hut messed with him. Whenever anyone picked a fight, he never backed down, nor was he ever beaten. He soon was being called on to settle disputes and act as a kind of "security". Vincey didn't like to fight—he felt it was barbaric—and, about two years later and a few steps further up the pecking order, he came up with a scam that ensured he would rarely need to resort to his fists again.

During the week, Vincent Bonner would sell tickets for £1 to raffle off his entire weekly wage of £77. For the first few weeks, he lost money, as he knew he would. But he had good reserves to draw on, and as the news of his enterprise spread, pretty soon he was selling 180 tickets every week. Men from other sites started to subscribe too, and before long he was regularly clearing £300 a week. He would always pay the winner with great flair and in full view of everybody on site.

His next enterprise was supplying teams of men for various jobs around the sites. Not only would the young Vincent Bonner secure work for you; he would also protect you and guarantee your wages, which were always paid on the dot and in cash. He loved cash, folding money—nothing else, including taxes, existed in his world. By then he was as busy as he could be, sometimes working up to twenty hours a day just to keep on top of things. He handpicked four other navvies to work for him full time. Around this time, he first crept across the line of legality. He avoided major crimes because he didn't want to draw attention to himself, but if a building contractor was silly enough to leave money or equipment lying around, well . . . He figured the world owed him, and he was happy to collect.

Vincent Bonner returned to Creestown in 1960 a rich man. He bought a small pub, the Fast Trout. He met and married Eliza (Lizzie), who had produced three sons for him by the mid-1960s. For the next fifteen years, his empire continued to grow. He was involved in the cross-border smuggling of cigarettes, alcohol and cattle. There was talk of robberies, and swindling people out of property and land. As the sons grew older and there was more at stake, he never bothered to call on the gardaí to protect his interests. No, Vincey, Milky and Pádraig and a few trusted soldiers took care of that side of the business, whilst Owen studied his way through university. The Bonners used the dust being blown up by the Northern Ireland "Troubles" as a very effective smokescreen for their core businesses, some of which were being carried out in the name of "the Cause", maybe even with some of it ending up in paramilitary hands.

Fast forward to the early 1990s: Vincey retires and Owen takes over the family business and starts to develop the legitimate front. As Owen perfects the art of window dressing and financing grateful politicians' campaigns, Milky and Pádraig continue with the other, and equally lucrative, side of the business, making their mark—if not their name— by providing stolen cars and motorcycles to a Belgian set-up. By the time Starrett had come face-to-face with Owen Bonner, his father and Lizzie had given up the grey skies of Donegal for the blue skies of Spain, and Milky and Pádraig had publicly—to all intents and purposes— retired after one too many run-ins with the gardaí.

In press coverage, Owen had successfully distanced himself from his two older brothers, but Starrett knew for certain of a couple of instances when the trio had reunited on the wrong side of the law. The bigger the family business grew, the more there was to protect. The more there was to protect, the more they drew the jealous attentions of similarly greedy-minded people. Some of whom, when they became a nuisance, would end up in hospital following serious accidents. Accidents like the brakes on their car malfunctioning. Other less for-tunate people simply disappeared and stayed disappeared. The gardaí investigated, but Owen had learned how to make the law work for him and had managed to perfect this expensive art.

Starrett hoped that patience would prove to be the virtue everyone, including Major Newton Cunningham, claimed it to be.

Chapter Twenty-Six

STARRETT HAD NEVER met Owen Bonner before, and he was in for a few surprises when finally confronted with him. Bonner's large, rambling house was in the area known as the Mountain Top, which overlooked Letterkenny, the hub of his empire.

Bonner was the one member of a lawless family who had successfully managed to find a way, if not above the law, then definitely around it. On the rare occasions the gardaí managed to pin anything on Mr Owen James Bonner, his lawyers would always manage to find some legal loophole to ensure that their client got off scot-free.

Bonner must have had many visitors, because the ground-floor back room, closest to the two-storey garage wing, was decorated and furnished like an upmarket waiting room of a private dentist's or doctor's surgery. There were two matching suites of furniture, black in colour and expensive in feel; two leather bucket chairs; a generous sized antique oak table, which looked as though its legs had been halved to give it a coffee table stature; a high-backed writing desk, complete with white notepaper embossed with the Bonner logo; and a leather cup of black, classy pens, personalised in gold lettering with the legend "Nicked from Owen Bonner". Like numerous previous visitors, Starrett couldn't resist taking one for himself. The coffee table was laden with the most recent copies of *Country Life*, *Antique Cars*, *Autosport*, *The Letterkenny Christmas Annual 2007* and, perhaps to keep the spouses happy, recent editions of *OK* and *Hello*.

A uniformed maid had led Starrett from the front door to the waiting room. She had taken his order for "a coffee and a bickey", but he was delighted when she returned with a cappuccino and a Bakersville muffin. Starrett worked on the American principle that no matter how unhealthy cakes, buns and biscuits were, they were totally acceptable if they contained at least one healthy ingredient, such as brown sugar, ginger or fruit concentrate. Fruit concentrate was Starrett's favourite, because it could cover a multitude of culinary sins. The Bakersville muffin on his plate contained blueberries. Blessed are the blueberries, Starrett thought, for they shall inherit the calories. Pretty soon, that particular Bakersville muffin was a thing of the past, remembered only by a scattering of telltale crumbs, and Starrett concentrated on the objects dotted around the reception room's walls.

Mr Bonner had several paintings adorning his pale blue walls. There was a Derek Hill, enhanced by a picture light, and a Charles McAuley with the paint applied so generously you could almost feel the depth of the scene, not to mention the cost of the piece.

Starrett was trying to make sense of the Derek Hill when a smartly dressed woman entered the waiting room and said, "Hi, I'm Diandra, Mr Bonner's PA. We're sorry for keeping you waiting, but if you'd like to follow me, I'll show you through."

"No problem at all," Starrett replied, noting that it had been "we" who'd been keeping him waiting and not just Owen himself.

Diandra looked to be in her late-twenties, sounded as if she were from the west coast of America, and was dressed like she'd just been released from finishing school, in a sober, dark-blue, pin-striped suit and a crisp white shirt, fastened with a quietly striped tie.

She swaggered her way out of the room with Starrett following dutifully. He was couldn't help wondering—and not for the first time—how women manage to make a chore as simple as walking across an empty room such a sensual, captivating music-less dance.

"We've managed to rejig some meetings in order to find a window for you," she said, leading him out of the room. "But I would be very grateful if you could keep the interview as brief as possible."

Starrett wondered just how grateful she'd be as he followed her through a maze of corridors, rooms and staircases until she eventually let him into a double-aspect room at the front of the house.

This was definitely the room with the view. Starrett realised that the reason the house looked so ungainly from the outside was that it had been built to enjoy the view rather than to be the view itself.

The sophisticated businessman who greeted Starrett was in no way the chancer and thug he'd visualised.

A smartly dressed Bonner was seated, engrossed in a small pile of paperwork in the centre of his tidy, mahogany desk. When Starrett and Diandra walked in, he said, "I'll be right with you," then continued to read and sign papers without giving them a second glance. Diandra stood patiently by Bonner's side and, at the conclusion of his paperwork, passed him the file she held under her arm. He opened it and spent a couple of minutes reading the contents before flipping it shut and dumping it on top of a pile of similar files on the corner of his desk.

He stood up, took the dark-blue linen blazer that had been hanging on the back of his swivel captain's chair and slipped it on in an agile, both-arms-simultaneously-overhead manoeuvre. The jacket, joining a cyan-coloured shirt, red and blue school tie, moleskin trousers and new-looking black leather slip-on shoes completed Bonner's Ralph Lauren, business-yet-casual look.

Bonner was around six foot tall and, Starrett guessed, weighed about 168 pounds. His hair was dark brown and well-groomed, with a parting so sharp you could have struck a match on it. There was not an ounce of surplus fat on the man, and Starrett immediately regretted the muffin he'd just eaten. Bonner's skin was clear, but a hint of darkness around his eyes suggested that he didn't sleep well.

"Inspector Starrett," Bonner said, holding out his hand and breaking into an open smile. "I don't believe we've ever met, but I've heard a lot about you over the years." His voice sounded like the end-product of a good education.

"Aye, and I about you, sir," Starrett replied, reluctantly taking the extended hand.

Starrett sensed the strength and power of the man, cloaked though it was in a gesture of friendship.

"I'll tell you what, Inspector, I've a wee treat for you," Bonner said, dropping Starrett's hand. "Something you'll enjoy seeing. Please follow me."

They left the office via a different door from the one they'd come in through. As they passed them, Starrett mentally logged all the different framed site-plans of building projects Bonner had been involved in or was currently developing. He found himself thinking, *So that was one of yours too. I hadn't realised.*

They took a spiral wooden staircase down to the ground floor and out into the sunlit courtyard.

Bonner took a set of keys from his pocket and opened the door to a large, six-berth, air-conditioned garage. As the sunlight broke in and hit the shiny surfaces of the vehicles inside, he beamed from ear to ear.

"I heard you were a man who loved these old beauties, too. Aren't they just incredible?"

So, that was *my* file he was studying, Starrett thought, as he drank in the visions of perfection before him.

Five incredible cars were neatly lined up in front of him. One was a 1957 Mercedes 300 SL "Gull Wing", one of the sexiest sports saloon cars ever manufactured and probably the first car capable of doing 150 miles an hour. There was also a 1961 E-Type 3.8 fixed-head coupé, the first and definitely the best E-Type; a 1953 Frazer-Nash, a replica of the famous Le Mans GT race car; a 1964 Ferrari 250 GT Lusso; and a 1965 Aston Martin DB5, equally famous both for being the James Bond car and also for being very difficult to drive.

"This is a phenomenal collection of cars, sir."

"Aye, but there's at least one more I'd like to get my hands on," Bonner said, clearly very chuffed that Starrett was impressed with his vehicles.

"Oh, and which one would that be?"

"A Ferrari 250 GTO racing sports car."

"Aye, now that would surely set you back a tidy sum," Starrett said, clicking his teeth. "If you ever managed to find one, that is. There were only fifty-six ever manufactured."

"Yep . . . and about half of them were destroyed or written off during races. Assuming I could ever get my hands on one, it would probably cost me about five or six times the total worth of my entire set here."

Bonner looked wistfully over his collection. "Apparently Nick Mason has one, but then they say he's got one of everything."

"I doubt he'll have a Ferrari P4," Starrett offered. "Only three were ever made: one was destroyed in a fire, another was written off in a race, and the last time one came under the hammer, it fetched twelve million sterling."

"So what would your dream car be?" Bonner asked, appearing reluctant to let the boys-and-their-toys moment pass.

"Oh, that's an easy one: the most beautiful car every made is the Ford GT 40."

"Mmmm, a 1966 model and only forty inches high. What would that set you back these days . . . three quarters of a million euro?"

"In that neighbourhood, and that's a neighbourhood garda inspectors never visit," Starrett replied good-humouredly.

"Here, why don't you sit in this one?" Bonner opened the door of the Mercedes for Starrett and indicated the white leather seat. "They're all in perfect working condition. I've got a burly bearded genius mechanic, Tony Smith, who comes in once a month to service them all. As you can probably see from the tyres and speedometers, these beauts haven't travelled much more than ten miles between them. Oops, maybe that should have been kilometres, in respect of our friends from the Continent who put the breath back in the hibernating Celtic Tiger."

Bonner opened the passenger door of the adjoining vehicle, the Aston Martin, and climbed in. The two men were barely six feet apart.

"I thought you might prefer to have our chat down here. I don't think I'll ever be totally comfortable stuck in an office, but that's what the money men want to see, isn't it? Now, Inspector, what can I do for you?"

"Look," said Starrett, slightly awed by the comfort and extremely expensive smell of the Mercedes, "right now I'm investigating a murder—"

"That of Mr James Moore, I believe," Bonner interrupted, with a tone that suggested he not only knew about the murder but wanted Starrett to know that he knew about it.

"Yes, indeed," Starrett replied. "And I discovered that he worked a while for you in the past."

"Oh, really?" Bonner said, looking away from Starrett and scrunching up his eyelids as if trying to recall such an occasion.

"Yes, apparently he was working on the Fast Trout up in Creestown."

"Of course, that was my father's pub," Bonner said, recognition flashing across his brown eyes. "Tell me, do you have any idea what he was supposed to be doing for me up there? It's a beautiful part of the world, by the way."

"Aye, it is indeed," Starrett said. Apparently James Moore was dismantling an antique bar for you. You see, Mr Moore was a master carpenter." Starrett paused to study Bonner more intently, at the same time trying to keep the chat casual and in the same conversational manner they'd started with. "It would appear that he was moonlighting on the weekend as a favour to someone on your team. Anyway, Mr Moore completed his work late on Sunday, and later that night the Fast Trout was burnt to the ground."

"Oh yes, I do remember something about that, now you come to mention it. I had my site manager carry out an investigation into the cause of that fire, but he couldn't establish what had started it. Of course, Inspector, I realise that out there on the mean streets of Donegal, the great unwashed are probably gossiping away, claiming that it was an insurance job on a listed building or something similar."

"Well, it would appear that this one is nothing as complicated as that, Owen. It seems that it was all quite straightforward."

"What, so straightforward that absolutely no one is gossiping?"

"Aye, no, not exactly," Starrett said through the hint of a smile. "No, from what I can ascertain, by the time Mr Moore had completed his work, he was extremely tired. Reportedly he was a very conscientious worker, and rather than leave the place in a mess, he left his tool box as a sign that he was going to return to finish up."

"OK, I'm still with you," Bonner said.

"But here's where, I'm sure you'll agree, it all gets a little strange. James Moore assumed that all of his tools had been destroyed in the overnight fire. However, a day or so later, one of your boys delivered his tool box, totally intact, to his house."

"Oh yes, I get it; I'm with you now, Starrett," Bonner said. "Yes, I do remember. I've heard all about this one. It was a really beautiful bar-surround this one. I've got to show it to you one day, once we've found a new home for it. It was hand-carved from the wood of the captain's cabin salvaged from the ship *Ubeona*, which ran aground near Ramelton, sometime in the 1870s, I believe. Nine poor souls lost their lives. When my men were removing the pieces of the dismantled bar late on that particular Sunday night, they mistakenly took Mr Moore's toolbox at the same time. Later, when they discovered it wasn't ours, they returned it to its rightful owner."

"Right," Starrett replied. "That would make sense."

"Look, Inspector, here's the thing," Bonner said, sinking back into the plush seat of the Ferrari before continuing. "I realise what people say about me. I accept that. I know I can't control it, and I could drive myself mad trying to. Equally, I know that in the 1950s and 1960s we, as a family, had only ourselves to blame. We were, shall we say, not the most upright members of the community, and, God knows, I've been paying for it ever since. But rest assured, I spent too long at university slaving over business studies to blow it on some stupid petty deal. Why bother to cheat when you can prosper almost as well by being straight. I'd be a complete eejit if I were doing even one per cent of the things being laid at my door. Every time a match is struck, it's, 'Oh goodness, did you hear, Bonner's at his torching again?' Every time a stone falls from a country wall, they'll all shouting, 'Knocker Bonner's at it again, just because he couldn't get planning permission.' Look I rely totally on the planning office for my livelihood. Sure, if they even dreamt there was a possibility that my organisation conducted itself in as shady a manner as people say, they'd be down on me like a ton of Donegal stone."

Bonner paused. He seemed to be studying Starrett's reaction before carrying on: "Oh, come on, Inspector, what else can you expect when you've got a pack of bloodhounds chasing around the country slapping preservation orders on every toilet over ten years old? We do have a few old buildings like the Fast Trout, but from my organisation's point of view, knocking and refurbishing is not where the money is. This is the twenty-first century. The old Celtic Tiger may have been winded, but its generation still wants to party, and I can tell you, they want to party in clean modern buildings with proper plumbing and all the health and safety issues that go with them. You try dealing with these people and telling them you want to connect a modern kitchen—one that caters for a couple of hundred servings a day—on to an old stone building with a prehistoric plumbing system. I prefer to build new on virgin ground from the foundations up. Now, maybe our buildings aren't going to win any design awards, but they're certainly functional, clean and safe. But, for some strange reason, I get a bad press from certain elements in the media and from that Heritage mob, which is probably thanks to the spin fuelled by my competitors. And I suppose it serves to keep the heat off their own backs."

During this entire monologue, Bonner kept an even tone. It was obviously material he'd used before. Starrett thought the developer had climbed off his soapbox, but not so.

"I'm telling you that I'm a businessman, and I'm out to make money. The way I look at it, there is genuine need for all of the projects I'm involved in. If there is demand for a function room of some kind in the middle of the country and I'm the first one to spot that opening, I'll be in there like Flynn. But I'm not interested in uphill struggles, at least not all the time. I'm not going to take on the planners, the taxman, the gardaí or one of these environmental groups if I can help it. I just don't need to. I'm very happy with my business, and besides which, life's too short and I've too much to accomplish."

"Right, so . . ." Starrett said, running his hands around the static steering wheel. "The man who hired James Moore for you—could I please speak to him?"

"Why, of course, you can," Bonner replied, sounding genuinely surprised. "But why on earth would you want to? I've told you exactly what happened."

"Yes, but if your gaffer hired Mr Moore, it means he knew him, so he might be able to give us more background information. I'll admit we know little or nothing about this man Moore, and I need to build a more detailed picture of him for the investigation."

"From what I hear, it's a pretty open-and-shut case, Inspector," Bonner said dismissively.

"What is it you've heard then?"

"Wasn't your man James Moore riding the vicar's wife down there in that sleepy little town of Ramelton?"

"But haven't you just spent ages explaining to me how unreliable all these local rumours can be?"

"Well, Inspector Starrett, I'll tell you this and I'll tell you no more:

there's nothing more dangerous to a man's health than riding another man's wife."

Bonner had not raised his voice for a single moment he'd been talking, but a strange look had appeared in his eyes during his last statement, and the lines in his forehead grew progressively more defined. Finally Bonner, glancing at his watch, jumped out of the car, closed the door very reverentially, and announced, "Right, Inspector, that's it. I'm afraid the window the lovely Diandra opened for you has just closed. I need to be at another meeting or I'll be in big trouble with her, and believe you me, that's another kind of trouble to be avoided at all costs."

Starrett got out of the motionless Mercedes and let Bonner close the door.

The developer held out his hand, saying, "It was good to meet you, Inspector."

"Yep, same here," Starrett replied, this time holding on to Bonner's hand a little longer while using their closeness to stare into his eyes. "Look, ahm, could I trouble you for the details of your gaffer. You know, the one who hired James Moore?"

The other's hand shot away.

"OK, why, yes, of course. Come on back up to the office with me and I'll dig it out for you," Bonner said, his eyes darting away.

Ten minutes later, Starrett was back in the waiting room again. He'd been waiting eight minutes by the time Diandra re-entered.

"We're sorry, Inspector Starrett," she began sweetly in her American singsong voice, "but our project manager on the Creestown job has since left our employment and returned to his native Cork. I'm sorry to have to inform you that he left neither a forwarding address nor a telephone number."

"Oh, bejeepers," was all Starrett could think to say. "Do you have his name, perchance?"

"Well, here's the thing, it's company policy not to give out employees' details without first seeking permission from the employee . . ."

"And as you can't contact the employee in question, you . . ."

"Exactly, Mr Starrett. I'm glad you understand our position."

As they were leaving the waiting room, they were just in time to see Owen Bonner pausing within the frame of his front door. The dark clouds of imminent rain had replaced the blue sky, and Bonner had put on a black overcoat.

In that split second, Starrett saw a different Bonner from the professional PR-conscious, approachable, affable, company chairman who had entertained him. The man standing in the doorframe looked more like Johnny Cash's "Man in Black" personified. Like Cash's alter-ego, the darker character wouldn't always be evident, but you knew it was always lurking somewhere in the shadows.

The shiver that ran down Starrett's spine confirmed his feeling that, for all of Bonner's immaculate dress-sense and erudite manners, he certainly wasn't someone to cross.

Chapter Twenty-Seven

For Starrett, the conclusion of the Owen Bonner interview officially marked the end of day two of his investigation into the crucifixion of James Moore.

The inspector went home, made himself a bite of supper, watched recorded highlights of the day's sports and was considering retiring to bed early when, at the last minute, he grabbed his coat and headed down to the Bridge Bar in Ramelton.

Starrett was bemused by his actions. Ten minutes before, eyes heavy, he'd set his sights on his bed, but then something deep inside him produced a pull stronger than the attraction of sleep. It wasn't that he was a great drinker. In fact, his long-standing record was three pints of Guinness in a night: when you had a beautiful and nutritious liquid such as Guinness, you wanted to enjoy it for as long as possible.

As ever on a Saturday night, the Bridge Bar was packed when Starrett arrived, just as the light was fading at ten o'clock. Henry McCullough was playing in the back corner. Someone said he used to play with the Beatles; someone else, who was wearing an anorak, said, "No, don't be silly, Henry used to play with *someone* who used to play with the Beatles.' Either way, Starrett enjoyed the soulful sound and fine playing of Henry's bearded, denim-clad band.

Starrett sidled up to a group of regulars, and the conversation, shouted above the sound of the band, soon drifted to Donegal's meeting with Armagh the following day. Packie was already "man of the match" as far as the Bridge Bar crowd was concerned. Every now and then, someone would say to Starrett, "Someone here was saying they wanted to see you." Or: "Someone has been asking for you." History had taught him that there was always someone wanting to see the local inspector to settle some dispute or other. The disputes were usually over land or women, or sometimes, in extreme circumstances, both. Starrett's stock reply was always, "I'll be happy to comment, but you have to understand, if I'm here as a member of An Garda Síochána, I'm going to have to ensure that the drinking stops at 23.00 hours on the dot." It was usually at this point that all conversations concerning disputes ceased. The dapper raconteur James McDaid was propping up his usually corner of the bar. McDaid was deep in conversation with local entrepreneur John McIvor over the virtues of the Grateful Dead. They could be discussing how to dismantle an atomic bomb for all the sense it made to Starrett. Even the fact that there was a photograph, taken in this very bar, of McIvor, McDaid and a certain Jerry Garcia, was totally lost on Starrett. Both men broke off from the conversation long enough for McDaid to buy Starrett a pint and to tell him that there had been someone in the bar asking for him.

Starrett had a sudden flash of the images of Milky and Pádraig Bonner. Might they be the ones asking for him? Starrett very much doubted it. The Bonners specialised in not giving people advance notice of their sudden arrival.

The Inspector struggled through the crowd to get a better view of the band, as a voice behind him said, "This band has more crow's feet than the entire flock in Hitchcock's classic."

A few seconds later, the same voice said, "What does a girl have to do around here to get a drink?"

The owner of the voice was so close to him he could feel her breath on the back of his neck. As he was turning towards her, he instantly registered the perfume from his previous night's encounter.

"Bejeepers. Dr Aljoe, I presume?" Starrett said. While he was considering whether to kiss her on the cheek or shake her hand, she made the decision for him, putting her hand gently on the small of his neck, pulling him towards her and kissing him lightly on the lips. They lingered for just a second, but long enough to confirm it was not a kiss of friendship.

"What are you doing in this neck of the woods?" asked Starrett.

She'd done something extreme with her hair since he'd seen her the previous evening. The ringlets were more defined and, he noted with approval, less inclined to the ponytail style. He now noticed most what incredible teeth she had; he had never in his entire life witnessed molars so brilliantly white. It was now her smile, and not her hair, that formed the defining feature of her face. She was dressed in a figure-hugging pair of denims, pink Ralph Lauren shirt—top three buttons open displaying the merest hint of cleavage—and a pair of pink pumps.

Starrett also noticed for the first time that she had a dimple on her chin. She looked just as stunningly attractive as she had the previous night. Starrett found himself so drawn towards Dr Samantha Aljoe that he wondered if it had been this subconscious magnetism that had made him come down to the Bridge Bar and away from the attractions of an early bed.

"I figured it was about time we had our second date," she said, again leaning close to him to make herself heard. Her lips were actually brushing his earlobe as she spoke. The effect of this, together with the allure of her scents, was extremely arousing. "Besides," she continued above the music, "I thought getting out of the house was the quickest way to help ensure that the remaining four months pass quickly."

"And what will you have to drink?" Starrett asked, hoping his puppy-dog devotion wasn't too noticeable.

"Oh, I'll try one of those," she said, nodding at his Guinness.

Starrett disappeared into the crowd, towards the bar. When he returned five minutes later, a rubber man was trying to pour himself all over Dr Aljoe.

"How's about ye?" he slobbered in an Alex Higgins impersonation.

"Excuse me," Starrett said to the intruder, handing the harassed doctor her stout and putting his next pint beside his half-empty glass on the ledge next to two high chairs she'd managed to commandeer.

"It's not an excuse-me, mate; it's my dance. Now would ye ever feck off and leave us alone," the rubber man replied, as he precariously manoeuvred himself into the chair.

Starrett bit his lip and blew some air through the corners of his mouth. The man looked to be in his early thirties. He was dressed expensively but not tastefully and certainly wasn't comfortable in his attire: fawn suit, red shirt, cream tie and tan leather shoes. His head was shaved, his face was red, and he looked as if he were confident he could handle himself. Starrett knew the type too well. They thought their pronounced Belfast accents were all that was required to scare off mere mortals like him.

"I think you'll find the wedding reception is next door in the auld cinema," Starrett said.

"Listen, pal, I'm not going to tell you again," Rubberman began, slurring his words. "If I was you, I'd get a single ticket out of this one-horse town."

Starrett noticed that people around them had stopped their own conversations to eavesdrop on what was fast turning into a potential incident.

"OK," Starrett said with a sigh. "Look, you're not even entertaining, OK? The lady here is with me, and if you don't mind, I'd really just like to get back to our enjoyable evening."

"She's with you, is she? She won't be for long. If you don't clear off, there'll soon be two loud bangs. The first will be me smacking you, and the second will be you hitting the floor." Rubberman then turned his back on Starrett and refocused his attention on Dr Aljoe, who seemed, all things considered, remarkably calm about it all.

Starrett put his hand on Rubberman's shoulder. Rubberman hopped down from his chair and turned towards Starrett, swinging his right hand in the general direction of Starrett's nose.

Starrett saw the fist coming and caught it in his left hand. Rubberman then swung his left, which Starrett caught in his right, his imperfect bent forefinger sending a shock-wave up his arm and across his chest. Starrett secured both fists in his hands and started to squeeze in on them with all his might. At the same time, he used them to pull Rubberman closer to him until their faces were as little as half an inch apart.

He whispered, "Stop your fighting, man, for heaven's sake."

Rubberman was still resisting, so Starrett continued using his own hands as vices, squeezing and squeezing with all his might. He kept whispering, "Stop your fighting. Stop your fighting."

Eventually, tears of pain appeared from the corner of Rubberman's eyes and he collapsed to his knees, apparently in agony. Starrett followed him down, all the time whispering the mantra into his ear. When they were both on the floor, Starrett stared deep into his eyes and said, "You'll never ever swing those fists in anger again without causing yourself horrendous pain. Please believe me, I'm telling you this for your own good."

Starrett then helped Rubberman up from the floor, and sure enough didn't he only go and take another swing at Starrett? This time, although he saw it coming, Starrett just turned slightly so that he took the full force of the blow on his shoulder. As Rubberman's fist connected, it was as if someone had connected his fist into the electric mains supply, and the resultant shock dropped him to the floor, this time in even more agony than before.

"OK," Starrett whispered in Rubberman's ear as he bent down to pick him up. "Now I want you to apologise to this beautiful young lady here and be on your way."

This time the fast-sobering drunk did as he was told.

The whole incident had lasted no more than twenty seconds, and only a few had witnessed it. Among those who had were McDaid and McIvor, who had monitored every move, fearful that they would lose their precious bar seats if it came to coming to Starrett's aid. They tut-tutted, nodded and smiled knowingly, giving the impression that they'd witnessed numerous similar incidents throughout lives rich in worldly experience.

"Now, where were we?" Starrett asked, hopping up on to the stool, which was second-skin close to Aljoe. If anything, he felt in more danger than he had during his encounter with the drunk, but this was the kind of danger he enjoyed.

"I'm impressed, extremely impressed, in fact," Aljoe gushed. "How did you do that? Where did you learn that manoeuvre?"

"It's mind over matter," Starrett said, brushing an imaginary hair from his shoulder.

"Sorry?"

"It doesn't matter if he doesn't mind," Starrett said.

"Yeah, Starrett, you had me going until then," she said, lifting her glass. "I was just about to give you another month off your sentence, but you really do need to work on your punch lines. But maybe not as much as that drunk did," she giggled, her gorgeous full lips disappearing into the creamy-white of the Guinness top.

Chapter Twenty-Eight

FROM SOMEWHERE IN the distance, Starrett heard the sound of gunshots. He could just about discern that they were grouped in threes and that there were infrequent gaps between each set.

Still half asleep, he felt his chest, his abdomen, his legs, his privates. There was no sign of any telltale warm, sticky blood.

Who was being shot? *Bang! Bang! Bang!* There it was again. Unless he was mistaken, they were getting louder. Did this mean that the assailant was getting closer? He was a detective; surely he should know these things.

He slowly came awake and realised that the sound he was hearing was in fact the noise of someone banging on the door.

Starrett found his watch on the bedside table and saw that it was 6.20 a.m. before he dozed off again

Sunday mornings were for lying in. Life-saving Steve's didn't open on the Sabbath, and so Starrett fasted on that one morning. Usually he'd rise around noon, stroll into town, pick up the newspapers at Whoriskey's and stroll back to read them, at the same time playing one of the few albums he owned. Then he'd read his book, currently *Abraham Lincoln: The Prairie Years* by Carl Sandberg.

Starrett reasoned that the person disturbing him wasn't a colleague. No, they'd have rung first, wouldn't they? And his neighbours would have known better than to disturb him on Sunday morning.

Just then he remembered Friday morning's crucifixion of James Moore. He grew confused about the number of days that had elapsed and started to think that maybe he was dreaming that it was a Sunday. He knew that he had been enjoying a twilight moment between dreamland and reality, unless, of course, reading 06.20 on his watch was also part of this dream?

"Holy Shit!" he hissed as he sat bolt upright in his bed in his cosy, tidy, but totally masculine room, "It's . . ."

Starrett hopped out of bed and pulled his heavy curtains to one side, raised the window, and stuck his head out into the crisp cold air to find his hunch visibly confirmed.

He said, "Oh, it's yourself."

"It is, and can I please come in before someone sees me standing out here like a spare rooster at a hens' party?"

As Starrett hurriedly drew on a pair of jeans, a single question and its answer flashed through his mind repeatedly.

The answer to his question: "The person now standing outside his front door."

And the question itself was: "Starrett, who in the world would you most like to have come calling on you?"

Starrett was so excited that he was having trouble breathing as he hopped down the narrow, reclaimed antique staircase. He was so excited that he banged his big toe on the bottom newel as he tried to cut a nanosecond off his time by taking the corner six inches too early. In truth, his big toe was in sheer agony, because he'd given it a right splatter. He would wait until later to deal with the pain.

Starrett could hear his visitor walking impatiently back and forth across his wide York-stone doorstep. He paused, took a very deep breath, counted to three and opened the door. All of his composure immediately dissolved, and in a second he was struggling for breath again.

"I've been banging on your door for ten minutes, Starrett."

Right, yes, he'd say something soon—as soon as he could catch his breath. *This is stupid*, he thought. *I'm a man, have been for some years now, and here I am behaving like a schoolboy.* His mind raced off on one of its tangents, and that disturbing tangent was, "How untidy did I leave the bed?" He wondered why he'd thought that. That was like putting two and two together and getting forty-five, which was his age—and wasn't it about time he started acting it?

"Good morning, Starrett." She was smiling. Maggie wasn't great at smiling; she never had been. She always looked as if she were about to cry. She had jet-black hair and well-defined eyebrows, plus long black eyelashes that cast dark, flickering shadows around her eyes. Starrett had dreamed for a year full of nights about being allowed to kiss those beautiful sad eyelids.

She stopped smiling. *There*, Starrett thought, *that's much more the real Maggie*. Her high cheekbones, pert nose and full lips—along with the eyes—painted a potent picture of sadness. In his numerous and troublesome dreams, Starrett had never done justice to her classic beauty. Her black hair was long, kind of curly, mostly unruly, and it always looked as if she'd started off her day with her hair properly groomed and clasped up in some grand style, but as the day wore on, wisps had escaped from here, there and just about everywhere. On most other women, Starrett thought, the hair would have looked an absolute mess, but on Maggie Keane, it just looked incredible and, if anything, added to her sad vulnerability.

"Bejeepers, Maggie, you're on your rounds a bit early today," Starrett said as soon as he could catch his breath.

"Yeah, I was hoping to steal the milkman's business, Starrett," she said in her cheeky Donegal accent. "Can I put you down for a pint a day and two on Saturday and Sunday?"

"Only if they're pints of Guinness and you promise to deliver yourself," Starrett said. "Won't you come on in, Maggie?"

"Jeez, I thought you'd never ask," she said waltzing past him and into the living room.

She stopped in the middle of the room and looked around.

"It's very you, Starrett, but at the same time, more tidy and classy than I'd been expecting."

"I'm not sure whether to take that as a compliment or a criticism," Starrett replied.

"Oh, it's a compliment; believe you me, it's a compliment," she said, walking back towards him. She was slightly taller than he was, and wearing a long, black, summer dress, with little purple flowers peppered over it. She wore a brown suede, waisted jacket and sensible Camper walking shoes. None of her clothes were figure-betraying, but she had the air of someone who was slim and very fit.

But the striking thing about Maggie Keane, as far as Starrett was concerned, was that she didn't look as if she was a day over twenty, and yet Starrett knew her date of birth by heart: 14–06–65. Over the years he had often used those exact digits as combination numbers for locks, hotel safe codes, anything really where he needed six numbers he could trust himself to remember.

"Coffee?" Starrett asked.

"OJ?" she countered.

"You're on," Starrett replied, leaving her in the living room and heading towards the kitchen.

"I was intrigued when I heard you'd started to work on this place," she called out after him. "I'd never have put you down as Mr DIY, but a spy tells me you did most of it yourself. The overall effect is so American. I really do love the feel of it."

Starrett was happy, maybe even ecstatic, that she had known what he had been doing. Furthermore, she'd known that he'd done it himself, and on top of that, she said she'd *loved* what he had done with it. He was so lost in this thought and so preoccupied with getting six oranges into the blasted juicer that he didn't notice her follow him into the kitchen.

"Goodness, Starrett," she praised. "Fresh orange juice *and* a modern functional kitchen."

He knew that she was now sending him up.

"How's your mother?" he asked.

"She's fine, thanks to you."

Surely that was yet another compliment? Starrett steadied himself in preparation for the crash he was sure was imminent.

"And your kids?" Starrett asked, working on the theory that all mothers were so proud of their children, they could often be distracted from other courses by the mere mention of their offspring.

"Joe is great; he's nineteen now. He's brilliant at maths, and he looks just like Paul Newman as Butch Cassidy. I think he's going to be a heartbreaker. Moya and Katie are nine and ten respectively and, well . . . they're all so lovely it's humbling, to be honest. And you, Starrett, how are you and your English doctor getting along?"

There it was: the sting in the tail.

Even though he'd been on his guard, it still took him by surprise. It was not so much that Maggie Keane was so up to date on his current romantic social standing that surprised him as that she'd just made him feel like he'd been caught cheating.

Starrett switched off the juicer, feeling Maggie's eyes glaring into the back of his neck. He reached up to the cupboard to his left and pulled down two tall glasses, into which he poured the orange juice. He turned to Maggie and handed her one. As he looked into her eyes, he knew that he could never lie to her again.

"What can I tell you, Maggie?" he started, watching as she took a long drink, draining her OJ in one swig. "I've known her for a while professionally, but for some reason unbeknownst to me, it's evolved into something over the last couple of days."

"This time it's serious though, isn't it, Starrett?" Maggie Keane said, as much an admission to herself as a question for the detective.

"Oh, Maggie," Starrett sighed. "I haven't seen you in—what?—in nearly two decades, and then I receive a call about your mam's bogus gas suppliers, and here you are making me feel like I'm visiting the confessional for the very first time. Tell you what, how's about I make us both a bite of brecky?"

"Oh my goodness," she said. "He cooks now as well. Haven't you become the modern man?"

"Necessity is the mother—"

"—of the frying pan," she interrupted. "You can count me in, though. I don't usually do breakfast, but then I don't normally do dawn visits either."

Feeling self-conscious with Maggie scrutinising his every move, Starrett set about preparing breakfast. It wasn't a totally unpleasant experience. Yes, there was something of an atmosphere between them, but then, at the same time, there was a kind of bond.

"Look, hi . . ." Starrett started somewhat hesitantly. "Maggie, I was very sorry to hear about Niall."

"Yes, I got your wreath, Starrett," she said in a gentle voice. "I was very touched by that."

She paused, stoking up her energy and breath, and saying in a much louder voice, "Starrett, if Niall hadn't died, I wouldn't be here today."

Starrett wasn't exactly sure what she meant, but he didn't feel it appropriate to ask her.

"Niall was a great husband and a loving father, and he saved me from myself at a time when I quite simply needed saving. In the end, he knew what was happening to him. The doctors had given him eighteen months, and I didn't know anything at all about it. He kept it from the kids and me. He didn't tell me about the cancer until the last four weeks. He'd set everything up; we're well taken care of. You know, he never spoke to me about you until he was dying. I think he was really trying to find a way of . . ." She paused and wandered over to the cooker, peeking over his shoulder. "Oh, that smells good. I think I'm going to have to revise my opinion of breakfasts."

She helped herself to what remained of the OJ in the juicer and carried it over to the high-backed stool by the window. As she looked out way past the horizon, she said, "You've got a great view here, Starrett."

Yes, I know, I'm looking at her now, he thought.

"An ideal vantage point for you to spy on the girls who drive up to see you."

Starrett sighed good-humouredly.

"Tell me, Starrett, what is it with you and women? If it's not an obsession, then it's definitely a preoccupation. Don't get me wrong, it's not what you would call unhealthy. And yet," she said, "there's never ever been one of them who've had anything bad to say about you."

The smell wafting around the kitchen was enough to turn a vegetarian on to bacon and pork sausages. Starrett was doing the knives, forks, plates, cups and saucers thing as he said, "Well, Maggie, I will admit, yes, I am very interested in women . . ."

She cocked her head and raised her eyebrows.

". . . professionally speaking, of course. Ninety-five per cent of all crime in Donegal is relationship-related. I need to understand women. I mean, if I'm to have any chance at all of doing my job properly, I need to have some understanding of what's going on in your minds."

"And what have you learned so far, Inspector Starrett, from all this first-hand research?"

"Nothing," Starrett admitted immediately. "*Absolutely* nothing. That is, apart from the fact that women are from . . ."

"O sweet Jesus, Starrett, please don't say 'Venus'."

"Actually, I was going to say, 'Women are from women and men are from women *and* men.'"

"Aye, well, but it wouldn't have looked as good on the auld dust jacket," she said, breaking into another of her awkward smiles.

Starrett wondered just how difficult Maggie was finding all of this. And just why was she here? Was it because Maggie had decided that her husband had been dead long enough—three years and one month? Or was she scared that Starrett was getting too close to Samantha Aljoe?

Starrett placed the six rashers of bacon on to a strip of kitchen-roll, using a second piece to dab away any excess fat from the surface.

"Nice trick, Starrett," she said, coming up behind him to study his technique. She was right beside him and, probably unconsciously, she lifted up her left hand and rubbed his back in a circular motion.

Starrett was suddenly aware that her hand had frozen mid-motion. She raised her offending hand to cover the "Oh" her blood-red lips were making.

"Look, Starrett," she said, just as he was about to turn towards her with the two plates of breakfast, "I'm so, so sorry, but I just can't do this yet."

Without another word, she whooshed, ghostlike, across the kitchen, her dress rustling in her wake. He heard the front door close behind her.

"Should I keep your breakfast warm or what?" Starrett asked himself quietly.

Chapter Twenty-Nine

THAT PUT A kind of dampener on Starrett's Sunday. Instead of moping around, thinking of what might have been, he decided to go into Tower House, review the case and write up his crime book.

When he'd finished, he jotted down on a notepad some thoughts about several areas that warranted further investigation.

1. Amanda Morrison: she must surely have more information.

2. Ivan Morrison: no matter how unlikely it may seem, the churchman must be high up the list of potential suspects because of potential motive and opportunity.

3. Owen Bonner: by virtue of his reputation, he is worth a closer look.

4. Daniel McGuinness: I've read and reread the interview between Gibson and Garvey, and something makes me uneasy about it. I'm not exactly sure what it is, but I'll need to interview McGuinness myself ASAP.

5. Betsy Bell: who else has Betsy told about Amanda & Moore's affair? Who else has Amanda had an affair with?

6. Colm Donovan: as Moore's long-term friend, he

told Garvey & Gibson remarkably little about
him.

7.

Once Starrett had written down the number 7, he couldn't think of
anything to put there. Yes, he intended to speak to Nora Moore again
when she was in a fit state to do so. On top of that, he'd like to have
had more evidence to work with. Remarkably little had been turned up
so far.

Starrett could hear keys jangling in the distance, then doors slamming and two sets of feet marching up a corridor. He assumed it was
the sound of one of the previous night's inebriated guests being
released, about to face the real rough justice of his wife.

The garda station was, of course, open on Sundays, but operated
on a skeletal staff. Sundays, unlike Saturdays, were bad days for police
business. Well, Starrett corrected himself, they were good days, in that
people in his neck of the woods rarely broke the law on the Sabbath,
since the men of the cloth ruled the parish with a bigger stick than An
Garda Síochána did. Now they'd be entertaining and rejuvenating their
flocks. In the good old days, they would also have been publicly berat-
ing and shaming the congregations from the pulpit.

Starrett decided that he would break the habit of his adult life and
follow the masses to church on that particular crisp early-summer
morning.

"I'll need a tie," he said to himself as he hoaked about in his desk
drawer until he found one that a) wasn't too wrinkled and b) matched
his light blue shirt.

As he walked up the steep incline of Bridge Street, Starrett realised,
with a certain degree of humour, that he hadn't actually been to a
church service since he'd left Ireland for England all those years ago.
Well, to the odd wedding, christening and funeral, but he'd never voluntarily visited a house of worship to celebrate his faith or to claim the
apparent abundant forgiveness the clergy were keen to dish out. He
wondered how much sinning would continue if the various churches
did not continue to offer large helpings of absolution. Why wouldn't
anyone be encouraged to enjoy the odd sin or two when all they had
to do to achieve absolution was to troop into their respective house of
worship and throw a few cents on to the collection plate?

Today Starrett fancied checking out the quality of forgiveness that the Second Federation Church dished out.

o-O-o

As Starrett quietly chose a pew at the back of the church, he was happy, extremely happy, that he'd worn a shirt and tie. The congregation of the Second Federation Church was by far the best-dressed congregation he had ever beheld.

All the men and boys were dressed in jackets and pressed trousers or suits, shirts and ties. No female wore trousers, and every woman wore a hat. He recognised several people amongst the fine rosewood pews whom he'd never have dreamed would have been members of anything quite as liberal as this 'godless church'.

There was Tom, Harriet and their son Dick, who owned the garage out on the Milford Road. Starrett had always filed them as a mixed marriage and therefore a family who sang under no spire, but here they were singing their hearts out under the Second Federation Church's hammer and pen emblem. Starrett thought it looked slightly communistic. There was Declan and Diane McCluskey, famously big fans of the Bachelors singing group, because they'd named their four girls Charmaine, Ramona, Marie and Marta. Starrett had always figured them to be lapsed Catholics: lapsed because Declan had been married before and he'd had to go to Manchester to secure his divorce decree. And then there was the new family in town from Sligo: Ivor Gallagher, his wife Patricia and their children Paddy, Jack, Roisín and Dolores. It certainly hadn't taken them long to find room in the Inn of the Beginning. But what surprised him most was the presence of a couple of gardaí and their wives and families, all of them singing their hearts out.

The first minister was playing to a packed house. Starrett wondered if this was a common occurrence or if there were extra bodies on board because of the church's recent notoriety. There, in the expensive seats, proud as punch and shining like a new pin, was Betsy Bell, leading the choir in both voice and fashion. She was singing loudly enough for nearby rival churches to take their tuning from her perfect pitch.

Starrett thought he recognised the tune. Bejeepers, he did. The organ was filling in the brass riffs: *Da Ta Dat Ta Da* followed by Betsy leading her fellow worshipers into the chorus of "Sweet Caroline", a flipping Neil Diamond song! What would they be singing next? "I'm A Believer", Starrett shouldn't wonder.

At the end of "Sweet Caroline", there was a great deal of hustling and bustling and rumbling and rustling of clothes as the congregation sat down as one.

Ivan Morrison rose from his grand, engraved wooden chair and, slowly and deliberately, climbed the nine steps up into the pulpit, the tail of his cassock arriving a second or two later.

"Greetings, brothers and sisters," he began in his fine baritone voice, which boomed into every corner of the church. "*All* we have is each other. But that's not *all*, because that's *enough*! More and more, brothers and sisters, we seem to be having a hard time accepting this, because some of us start to look for additional pleasures to fill our lives. Some of us start to seek out other distractions to help us along. What we have to realise is that by breaking the rules of life, all we do is bring unhappiness to ourselves and, consequently, to those close to us. Subsequently this disharmony prevents our community from functioning properly."

After several minutes along the same theme, Starrett's mind wandered. As an orator, the first minister was hardly JFK.

"So, what we need to do," Morrison was saying, sounding like he might be winding up, "is to be there for each other, to help pull each other from the wreckage of life." He paused, hands outstretched at a ten-to-two angle, looking down towards the floor. *Perhaps he's checking if his shoes are shiny enough*, Starrett thought, *always assuming he can see his shoes*. The first minister looked back to his adoring flock and said, "I vow to be there for my fellow men."

"We vow to be there for our fellow men," the congregation said in a singsong reply.

"Now, we'd like you all to join in with this wonderful choir of ours and help them sing 'Don't Think Twice, It's All Right'."

Starrett didn't recognise the song. If he'd known that the Second Federation Church's themed lyrics had come from the pen of none other than Bob Dylan, he might have been extremely shocked. They sang two other songs Starrett wasn't familiar with. In the first, Ray Davies' "Days", the sentiment "I thank you for the days" was right there in the middle of the Second Federation's park. During, "Have I Told You Lately That I Love You?" Starrett overheard someone close to him whisper, "Rod Stewart does an excellent version of this one."

After the singing, Ivan Morrison read out a summary of the week's events, during which he publicly welcomed the Sligo family into their midst. Morrison used the pulpit to plug Ivor Gallagher's trade, and said he hoped "all of us will be able to find some work for his very capable hands".

Starrett wondered if there was a chance Morrison had personally recruited Mr Gallagher to their community as a replacement for James Moore and if his work for his uncle had dried up already to warrant Morrison's plug from the pulpit.

At the conclusion of the public announcements, everyone closed their eyes and bowed their heads in prayer.

"We thank each other for our family and friends," Morrison said solemnly.

"Thanks you, brothers and sisters, for our families and friends," the congregation replied.

"We thank each other for our food," Morrison continued.

"Thank you, brothers and sisters, for our food," the flock replied.

"We thank each other for our clothes."

"Thank you, brothers and sisters, for our clothes."

"We thank each other for our homes," Morrison concluded.

"Thank you, brothers and sisters, for our homes," his flock finished.

The choir then led them in a gospel-music style version of "Teach Your Children". Starrett felt it was a beautiful song to finish the service with. It was one of those songs which, because of its perfect melody, made you feel you already knew it well enough to risk attempting to join in. He certainly had no problems with the sentiment of the lyrics—that it's the parents' responsibility to teach their children well. At the conclusion of the song, as if on cue, the sun outside broke through the clouds and shone its bright light through the stained-glass window behind Morrison and the choir. It was quite spectacular and, if you were so inclined, could well be deemed a spiritual moment.

Starrett reflected on the differences in the atmosphere in the Second Federation Church between the joyous service he'd just enjoyed and the last time he'd attended the church just two days earlier.

Then the service was over and that was it. The choir gently sang the repeated refrain, "Take good care of each other", as the congregation filed orderly out of their pews in twos and threes and blinked on the doorstep to accustom their eyes to the bright sunlight.

As religious services went, it was certainly one of the best Starrett had attended, due in no small part to the joyousness of the music. He was surprised by the feel-good factor he experienced through sharing this music with a couple of hundred people.

"Ah, Inspector Starrett," Morrison said, when it was Starrett's turn to blink his way out into the sunshine. "I thought I recognised your face in there, although I must admit I couldn't quite make out your voice amongst the others singing."

"I believe I enjoy a register which can be picked up only by dogs and bats, First Minister Morrison," Starrett said, shaking the offered hand. "Look, I know this may not be a good time, but I do need to have another chat with you."

Morrison kept on shaking the detective's hand and smiling at him. Starrett supposed it was for the benefit of the other parishioners.

"I'll tell you what, Starrett," Morrison said. "Have you any plans for lunch?"

"Actually, no."

"Splendid," the first minister replied, the creases of his smile unshifting. "Why don't you join me at the Manse in, say, twenty minutes, and we can break bread and enjoy some wine together."

"You're on," Starrett said, just before Morrison was distracted by another parishioner in search of his clammy hand.

Chapter Thirty

STARRETT DECIDED TO go for a walk by the side of the Swilly to fill the twenty minutes.

For the first part of his journey, there were several modern houses blocking his view of the water, but soon he'd left them behind, and the single-lane road snaked its way between the water on the left and the rolling hills opposite. There was only one more house on the road, at the very end on the right, and that had recently been refurbished in keeping with its hundred or so years' history. Houses, particularly old houses and the stories they could tell, fascinated Starrett. Donegal could still boast numerous old country houses, many of which were falling into ruin because the owners had died without heirs, or else new generations couldn't agree on how to proceed with their legacies. Family life and family pride often seemed to follow a troubled pathway.

Starrett wondered about Dr Sam Aljoe's family life.

He thought about the coincidences of fate. He knew that she could quite easily have gone back with him to his house the previous evening. There was a moment in his car, just after midnight, when he believed she would have offered him a reprieve for his final four months if he'd asked for it. But he hadn't. They'd cooled down and kissed each other goodnight, both believing that they were happy to hold out so that they would eventually make great love together.

Or maybe, Starrett wondered, was there a something, or a someone, holding him back from taking the final step?

More distressing was the thought of what would have happened at

6.20 that morning had Dr Aljoe actually accompanied him back to his house the previous evening. But Samantha Aljoe had returned home alone.

And what had Maggie meant when she'd said, "I'm so, so sorry, but I just can't do this yet"?

Can't do *what* exactly?

Can't make love because she wasn't ready?

Can't become friends again, because she'd left a roast in the oven back at home?

He wondered if she'd actually meant, "Let's just leave this a while longer." And if that was what she did mean, what was the "while longer"? Hours, weeks, months or years?

Maggie Keane had certainly been out of his life for a long, long time, but—as she'd proved that very morning—the length of time had not weakened her power over him. In fact, if anything, it was even stronger than it had been.

Thinking of the two women made him feel hungry. Then he remembered that he had a lunch date in approximately three minutes, at a location at least five minutes' walk away.

o-O-o

On reaching the Manse, Starrett was greeted by Agga, the maid, who showed him straight into the dining room, where Morrison was already seated at the table, looking keen as Colman's to get stuck in. As soon as Starrett was seated, the first minister asked Agga to serve the soup.

"Any news from your wife yet?" Starrett asked, unfolding his blue napkin.

Morrison addressed himself to the maid: "Agga, is there any word from Mrs Morrison?"

"No, First Minister," she replied.

"No news from my wife, Inspector," Morrison said, tearing into his soup before the ripples had a chance to calm.

"If you don't mind me saying so, First Minister, you don't seem at all concerned," Starrett said, the scent of potatoes and leeks floating up from the steaming hot soup.

"Look, Inspector, in this life, man should not waste his time trying to bring about changes to things outside his control. I can't just magic her up out of the air, now, can I? I mean, she was here and then she was gone, and either she is going to come back or she's not."

"But surely she could be in danger, First Minister."

"If you really thought she was in danger, you would have asked about her the minute we met on the steps of the church this morning."

"But she's your wife," Starrett said, trying another approach. He was beginning to wonder if the first minister and Betsy Bell were in each other's confidence.

"You've never been married, have you, Inspector?"

"No, I never have," Starrett admitted. "I mean, I think marriage is a great invention, but then again, so is a bicycle pump."

Morrison merely grunted, and Starrett continued: "The way I've always looked at it—and no offence, First Minister—but unless both lives are going to benefit greatly from the marriage, then one quite simply just shouldn't bother."

"Well, of course, there are many reasons why two people get married: for companionship, convenience, or for financial motives. In my particular case, we both felt we'd achieve something from the marriage that we couldn't get elsewhere."

"Yes, yes, I understand all of that, I really do, and I hate to labour the point about your particular marriage, but here are the facts as I see them: your wife was having an affair with James Moore; James Moore was murdered—"

"Excuse me, but James Moore was *crucified*, Inspector," Morrison broke in. "Crucified in my church."

"Technically he was murdered, First Minister; the method of murder was crucifixion."

"People never say that Jesus Christ was murdered. They always talk about him being crucified. It wouldn't have been enough merely to murder Him. No, he had to be publicly humiliated and destroyed."

"Are you saying that whoever killed James Moore felt the need, not just to kill him, but also to humiliate and destroy him in public?" Starrett asked.

"I'm saying that you'd be wrong not to consider that point of view at least. We are no longer—at least not on the face of it—the barbaric race we were at the time of Jesus' death. So James Moore was crucified in private, and his remains were displayed in public."

"Can I just backtrack a wee bit?" Starrett said, ignoring his ever-cooling soup. He found it very difficult to eat and talk simultaneously.

Morrison, experiencing no such difficultly, slurped away as Starrett continued, "I just wanted to pick up on the reason why James Moore was crucified, and why he wasn't just murdered in some other way."

"Well, think about it, Inspector," Morrison said. "Wouldn't it have just been so much easier to have shot him, stabbed him or poisoned him, and disposed of the body in the Swilly with a concrete block chained to his feet? So, you have to ask yourself, why would his assassin need to crucify him?"

"OK, I'll bite."

"My belief is that the assassin felt Moore was a fornicator, and he was crucified so that he could have his soul saved, and—maybe more importantly—have the soul of his partner rescued. Simple as that," Morrison grunted, before returning his attention to his soup. "Now, Inspector, you tell me why you think he was crucified and not just murdered by lead, steel, air or water."

"I don't know. Perhaps the assassin felt that by staging the murder as a crucifixion, they had a better chance of avoiding detection."

"So you genuinely think that the whole thing was a charade to misdirect you?"

"That is a distinct possibility, First Minister."

"If you really believe that, then I think there is a danger you may be overlooking a vital clue."

"I'm intrigued," Starrett replied, finally tasting his soup, which was indeed as delicious as the aroma had promised. "But look, I hope you don't mind me saying this, but you'd be the person with the most obvious motive, and so you would have to become our chief suspect when the body was found in your church."

"Oh, I'm a suspect, am I?" Morrison laughed, soaking up the remains of the creamy soup with a piece of wheaten bread, and using his fingers to stuff the bread into his mouth. "Well, if I were a suspect, do you think I'd be offering you this insight into the case? I'm very comfortable with the fact that I know I didn't do it."

Starrett laughed. "Rarely do murderers ever admit, 'I did it, I'm your man, Garda.' Besides, you could be trying to dodge me off your trail."

Morrison shrugged his shoulders in a noncommittal manner.

Once the chicken and vegetables had been served, Starrett continued. "I need to ask you a more delicate question. We now know that your wife was conducting an affair with Mr James Moore . . ."

"You now know," Morrison snapped at Starrett, completely ignoring his food. "What? You mean, you shared a bed with them?"

"No, but . . ."

"You mean that you personally witnessed them making love?"

"No, but . . ."

"For heaven's sake, it's a small town. Amanda is a beautiful woman. Idle tongues and empty vessels make the most noise and cause the most hurt."

"OK, well, let me ask you another question. Was your wife having a relationship with anyone else?"

"*Another* relationship," Morrison barked, spitting out the majority of his mouthful of chicken, broccoli and new potatoes. "What on earth has poor Amanda done to deserve all of this?"

"I'm sorry, First Minister, but I really do need to find out if she was cheating on you."

"For someone to cheat on you, they would first have to deceive you. In my marriage with Amanda, she has never ever cheated on me. We both live our lives, and we both get on with them. All I require from Amanda is discretion. The relationship, as you refer to it, with Moore, if one existed, would have been unique in that it would have been the first time she betrayed me."

"I was asking if you were aware of any extra-marital affairs she may have been involved in besides the one with Mr Moore—if such a one existed in the first place. I am not making any judgements on your marriage here, just trying to uncover as much about the dead man as I can. James Moore is dead, he was mur . . . sorry, he was *crucified* in your church and, around the same time, your wife disappeared, so . . ."

"So, you figure that if it wasn't me as a jealous husband, then it might have been a jealous ex-lover?"

"Well, yes," Starrett admitted.

"I'm afraid I really can't help you there. It isn't a case of my having my head buried in the sand; it's more a case of what I don't know won't hurt me."

"But that's a bit different from what you were claiming a moment or two ago, when you suggested that your marriage was open."

"Yes," Morrison sighed. "But I also pointed out that I need discretion. No one wants to have his face rubbed in the dirt, particularly, as I say, the dirt of *this* town."

"OK, fair point," Starrett replied. "Would you please tell me this, then: when exactly did you find out that there may have been something going on between Amanda and James Moore?"

"On Friday morning," First Minister Morrison replied, as a forkful of green beans disappeared into his mouth.

"The morning the body was discovered?"

"Yes."

"And how did you find out?" Starrett pushed.

"My caretaker, Thomas Black, discovered the body. Of course, he immediately told me. He's a very loyal servant, and he felt that because of what had happened to Moore, I would be better equipped to deal with things if I knew about the rumours that were circulating."

"Better equipped for what?"

"Better equipped to deal with the fact that there was a possibility that the relationship was a reality and possibly about to become common knowledge."

"And that was really the first time you heard about it?" Starrett asked.

"And that really was the first time I heard about it."

"Let's go back to the point about your wife going missing. Does that happen much?"

"It's not so much that she goes missing as that she goes away, doing her own thing. We update our diaries weekly, and Amanda is always available to attend our agreed functions and events, but aside from that, we're both totally free to tend to our own social preferences."

"But with Mr Moore being murdered on the same day Amanda went missing, and taking into consideration the information Mr Thomas Black gave you, were you not worried that there might have been some kind of connection?"

"Not at all, Inspector. I was convinced it was nothing more than another shopping trip. I've got loftier things to worry about than the stress my wife is causing her credit card!"

After that, the lunch proceeded in near silence, and Starrett walked away from the Manse having listened to a lot of blathering but not having collected much information. He'd also been served up plenty of food.

He dropped in briefly to Tower House, brought the crime book up to date and added Thomas Black's name into the vacant number seven slot on his notepad.

He went home and watched Donegal beat Armagh, and as predicted in the Bridge Bar the previous evening, Packie Garvey was indeed the man of the match.

Chapter Thirty-One

THEN IT WAS Monday, a new day, a new week, a new month, and Starrett was at his desk at 06.45.

Nuala Gibson and Francis Casey added further fuel to Starrett's suspicions of a budding relationship by arriving together. Unfortunately for them, Starrett was hanging around the reception area of Tower House, checking the overnight bulletins from headquarters, as they arrived. They signed in at a very respectable 07.22.

"Nuala and Francis," Starrett said. "I'm very impressed. Members of the gardaí clocking in before eight o'clock is as rare a sight as chicken lips."

"Rare, and they're probably just as dangerous to kiss, I would imagine," Gibson replied. Casey shot her a recriminating glance.

"Francis, do us an auld favour would you?" Starrett said. "Wait around for Packie, give him my congratulations on yesterday's result, and then you and he hightail it up to have a wee chat with Thomas Black, the caretaker at the Second Federation Church."

"Not a bother," Casey replied.

"Fair play to you," Starrett continued, sprightly. "I'm going to commandeer Bean Gharda Gibson here, and we're going to scoot out and revisit the mountain."

"Would that be Muckish or Dan the Man McGuinness you'd be referring to, Inspector?" Gibson asked.

"Listen to her, would you," Starrett said, nodding at Casey. "We'll have to try and get her on the *Late, Late Show*, won't we?"

Casey beamed in pride, betraying to Starrett how smitten the novice garda was.

Ten minutes later, Gibson and Starrett, with Starrett at the wheel, had reached Milford and turned off on to the R245 towards Carrigart. It really was a beautiful drive, and Starrett was relieved that Gibson was confident enough not to need to fill the empty air with conversation. The narrow road wound its way though a stretch of dramatic woodland before delivering them to the broad water of Mulroy Bay at Cranford. They could see a small flotilla of bobbing fishing boats guarding the fish farms. It was somewhere around this neck of the woods that two assassins of yesteryear had set out in a small boat to sail to the other side of the bay to dish out some rough justice to the third Earl of Leitrim. Starrett and Gibson drove through more trees and on into the hills generously peppered with houses. To Starrett, the buildings seemed to follow a certain kind of (barely) logical plan. Every now and then, you'd have a truly grand Georgian house, which would be surrounded by several neo-South Fork dormer bungalows. Obviously this Donegal-favoured style was the local way to get around the planning office's preoccupation with single-storey dwellings. On and on they drove, under a cloudless and deep-blue sky, passing an occasional herd of black and white cows grazing dangerously close to the water to their right.

In Carrigart most of the shops had set public seats outside.

"That's probably why Dan McGuinness likes it around here," Gibson observed. "Just so he can have a wee breather outside each and every shop he visits."

Again the McGuinness children managed to convince the gardaí that their father most definitely wasn't in. This time they swore it was true.

So Starrett and Gibson returned to Starrett's BMW and continued on down the Atlantic Drive, along the grassy sand dunes, past the legendary Rosapenna Hotel, which had been around for well over a hundred years but still hadn't discovered the recipe for lunchtime scrambled eggs, and down into Downings, as you do.

There was certainly far more activity around the Moore household than there had been when Starrett had first visited the previous Friday.

A couple of middle-aged men were standing in the doorway,

smoking and chatting, switching from foot to foot as if the pavement were too hot for their feet. Neither Starrett nor Gibson recognised either man.

"Aye, how's it going and all?" the elder of the two said by way of greeting to the gardaí.

"Aye, fine," Starrett replied.

"Youse catch the rat, yet?" the other asked. They were both northerners.

"We're still working on it," Nuala Gibson replied.

The conversation seemed to dry up, and the four of them stood in silence for a moment.

"It's a wild habit," the elder man observed, raising his cigarette butt, not so much in conversation about their doorstep activity but more in explanation as to why they weren't inside.

"Aye, indeed it is," Starrett replied, remembering the eight cigarettes he had left in Packie's top pocket.

The older man stood down from the step and swung open the front door of James Moore's house for them.

"How's the missus of the house?" Starrett asked, just before they walked in.

"Aye now, the form's not great," the older one replied.

"Ah, but sure then, how would it be?" the other added as Starrett and Gibson disappeared into the house.

In fact, when Starrett and Gibson went into the front room, they found Nora Moore in reasonably good spirits. The distraction of busying herself with fussing over her guests was helping. There were seven people in the front room, still known in some households as the "good room", because it was used only on Sundays, or when visitors came calling, or when the children were courting or, as was currently the case, for a wake. Nora was there with her "good teapot", doing the rounds and refreshing everyone's brew. Following behind was her son, Chris, with a plate of biscuits. A woman dressed to the nines in a purple suit, whose hair—a brittle-looking spider trap—had obviously spent too many hours under her hairdresser's dryer, was perched on the very edge of her chair, looking as if she feared she might catch something from it. She was the only one in the room using a cup with a saucer, which had to be balanced precariously on her lap every time she took a sip.

Despite this, she looked as if she'd been the centre of attention and conversation before the gardaí had arrived, and she didn't look best pleased that she'd been interrupted mid-flow.

Without any preamble, she turned to Starrett and said, "And when will the family be receiving the remains?"

Nora stopped pouring the tea and looked around.

"Well, we're hoping to do that as soon as possible," Starrett replied solemnly.

"And can you not give us a clue as to when 'as soon as possible' might be? My sister can't reconcile her grieving until she has the remains to bury."

"Inspector Starrett," Chris Moore said, "this is my aunt Peggy. Aunty Peggy, this is Inspector Starrett and, ehm . . ."

"Garda Nuala Gibson," Starrett said.

"Yes," the conscientious son continued. "Inspector Starrett here is leading the investigation into my father's death."

"Oh, if that's the case, Inspector," Aunty Peggy said, "perhaps I might have a word with you out in the garden?"

Before Starrett had a chance to reply, Chris Moore continued the introductions. To Aunty Peggy's left was another woman, smaller and wearing less showy clothing. "This is Mrs Artery, our next-door neighbour," Chris said. "And this is Mr David Brigham and Mr David Brown—the two Davids. They own the hotel next door."

Then, pointing to a very niftily dressed elderly man, "And this is Mr Gerry McGinley from the St Vincent de Paul. He's been very kind to us. This . . ."—he pointed to the corner of the room, which had been hidden behind the door Starrett and Gibson were blocking—". . . is Mr Daniel McGuinness."

Starrett had to admit that McGuinness didn't look anywhere near as big as Packie and Nuala had described him. Nonetheless, he was still grossly overweight, and obviously a regular visitor because he seemed to be sitting on his own specially reinforced stool, which looked to Starrett more like a slightly undersized, if necessarily sturdy, table. As on his last meeting with the gardaí, he was dressed in black and was resting both his arms on a walking stick held out in front of himself.

"I'll be out of your hair now, Nora," the discreet Gerry McGinley said as he stood up and put his empty teacup down on the table. Then he went over to Chris and put his arm around the boy's shoulders and whispered, "But don't forget, Chris, if you or your mother need anything else, you've got my number. Just give me a call, no matter about the time."

"He's a very nice man," Nora said to Starrett as Chris showed the St Vincent de Paul volunteer to the door.

"Yes," the Inspector replied. "I'm sure." He then turned his attention to Aunt Peggy: "Sorry, Mrs Cowan."

"Everyone around here calls me Aunty Peggy; you can call me Aunty Peggy, too."

"You said you wanted a word . . ." Starrett looked pointedly towards the door that led into the garden. Aunt Peggy rose to her feet, brushed the crumbs off her purple skirt and, handing her cup and saucer to Chris, led the way outside.

Before they could reach the door, Nora rolled her eyes and said to Starrett, "Thank you for coming out, Inspector. I'm sorry I was in such a state on Friday; we'll have a chat when Aunty Peggy is finished with you."

Once she'd got Starrett out into the garden, Aunty Peggy Cowan had no time for niceties. "Right, Inspector, we're all adults around here. We all know what's going on. Jimmy had strayed, and I will admit to you, Inspector, he is the last man in this town I would have accused of having roving eyes. But there you are, and here we all are as a result of it. I did mention to Nora on more than one occasion that it would serve her better to remember that it was Jimmy she was married to and not that fat lump McGuinness."

Starrett's face obviously reflected his surprise.

"Oh, and don't go looking at me like that, Inspector; of course, nothing was going on. I mean, just look at him; the very thought could bring on one of my migraines. But they were behaving like two schoolkids, always stealing off here, there and everywhere for their cappuccinos and croissants. There are *two* more things the French have to answer for! You see, Daniel and Nora had a thing all those years ago, and then Nora ran off with your man from the Rosapenna Hotel. Well, she didn't really run off with him anywhere other than to the sand dunes. Anyway, Daniel either wasn't there or else didn't care to pick up the pieces; and that was where poor Jimmy stepped in. They got married; Daniel got himself hitched to someone else. Both had families; both marriages turned into disasters. Then they decided that it was each other that they had really, *really* loved in the first place. It truly makes me sick; all this revisiting unresolved childhood romance stuff that's going on these days. You know, you want to give them a good shaking, bang their heads together and say, 'The reason it didn't work out all those years ago was simply because you just weren't meant for each other!'"

Aunty Peggy's voice rose to such a volume during the last part of her speech that Starrett was convinced that all those back in the house—not to mention the entire population of Downings—were party to her feelings.

"Well, that certainly throws a new light on things," Starrett said, as much to himself as to Aunty Peggy.

"Oh, my goodness," Peggy said, looking like a diva estranged from her stage. "You mean to tell me that you didn't know Daniel and Nora used to be an item?"

"I believe he did mention it to one of my officers," Starrett replied. "But I think we were all thinking in terms of two love-sick teenagers."

"Look, Inspector, my sister, well . . . truth be told, she's not really very interested in s-e-x, if you know what I mean?" Aunty Peggy paused and looked around her to make sure no one was listening in. She was speaking in a voice not much above a whisper, using her lips to make mouth-wide gestures in order to emphasise and make sure her point was hitting home. "I think that she latched on to someone who would not distress her with any untoward s-e-x-u-a-l demands. Daniel McGuinness . . . do you see what I mean? Yes, she was as unhappy with her lot as Jimmy was with his, but, unlike him, she wasn't about to do anything about it. However, if by rekindling some sort of connection with Daniel, she was able to be involved in an illicit relationship—and I'm talking platonically illicit now—well, then, that really was all she needed."

"And what about him?" Starrett asked. "What would he have gained from the relationship?"

"Maybe even the same thing. For instance, if he'd tried to strike up a relationship with anyone else, heaven forbid, perhaps they would have put s-e-x-u-a-l demands on him. No . . ." she said, shaking her head furiously from left to right. "I don't believe that there was anything like that going on between them."

"OK, Mrs Cowan . . ."

"Aunty Peggy, please, Inspector. Everyone calls me Aunty Peggy."

"OK, Aunty Peggy," Starrett continued, feeling uncomfortable addressing a woman he'd never met before in such intimate terms. "I'd like to ask if you thought James was aware of Dan's attentions to his wife."

"Ehm," Aunty Peggy said, drawing the word out into three syllables. "Not exactly in *that* way, if you know what I mean. Daniel McGuinness is a professional visitor. He has been for five or so years now, ever since his accident. He has a circuit, and he'll drop in on the people he favours, I'd say, at least three times a week. People welcome him. He's a bit of a character, and to be fair to the poor soul, he's had a hard life. The wife upped and left him for a bodhrán player, for heaven's sake; but, anyway, then Daniel had his accident so he couldn't work any longer."

"Did his wife leave him and then he had the accident, or was it the other way round?"

"I don't properly remember. It seemed to happen around the same time. Nora went to visit him when he was laid up. I think Jimmy might even have encouraged her to. So did Jimmy know about his Nora and Daniel? Daniel and Jimmy were good mates, and Daniel was always dropping into the house. Jimmy would arrive home from work and as he came in the back door, Nora would say, 'There's an extra one for supper tonight, Jimmy,' and as Jimmy was taking off his boots at the back door, he'd shout through, 'Oh, hi, Dan, how's it going?' It wasn't that he was ever going to catch them in bed or anything."

Here Aunty Peggy broke into a fit of the giggles.

"Oh my goodness, can you just imagine those two in bed, Inspector? Oh, forgive me, Jimmy, and God bless your children and my sister. I'm not being disrespectful of you, honest I'm not."

She spent a few moments regaining her composure before continuing. "I suppose it made it easier for him that Nora had some kind of company. Everyone could see Daniel was just about the only one who could pull her out of herself. What a mess, Inspector, what an absolute mess. How will it all end?"

Starrett ignored her question and clicked his teeth a couple of times before saying, "Aunty Peggy, tell me about Jimmy. What kind of a man was he? How did you get on with him?"

"He was a very nice man, maybe too nice, if you really want to know the truth. Jimmy would literally give you the shirt off his back. He wouldn't let a bad word be said about anyone under his roof. Nora didn't really know what she had. I think she figured that, after all she'd been through, getting a decent man would be enough. But I told her that you don't marry a man because he lets you walk on the inside of the footpath. As a couple, they really just didn't compliment each other. It was fine for Jimmy to be a hippie, but he really needed to be with a stronger woman, you know, someone who was organised, maybe even ambitious enough for both of them. And our Nora, well, she needed a dominant man. She really needed another version of our father, that's the truth of it, and it was like she knew she was never ever going to meet as great a man as him, so she just gave up. Take my Dolphie, for instance. He's his own man. He and my father treated each other as equals, and that's the way it needed to be. Going back to Jimmy, he and I always got on great, but then I didn't have to live with him. But, Inspector, as a father, he really came into his own. He loved his children, and he had the patience of a saint"

"Did you and he talk a lot?"

"You mean more than, 'How's work?' or, 'How's Uncle Dolphie?' or, 'Can you believe this weather?' "

"Yeah."

"Erm, the thing about Jimmy was that he loved to investigate things and think things through. Uncle Dolphie and I have travelled the world quite a bit, so Jimmy was always intrigued to learn about our travels, but we'd never tell each other our darkest secrets the way I'm sure Nora and Daniel did. For instance, I'd never tell him that Uncle Dolphie snores like a ship's foghorn, and he'd never tell me what Mandy Morrison had on her bedside table."

"So, you knew about that?"

"Yes, Inspector, I knew about that."

"And what did you think about it?"

"What did I think about it? Well, Inspector, I'll tell you exactly what I thought about it. I thought, 'Maybe Nora's not fulfilling her bedroom duties, and if this woman is helping on that score, perhaps

Jimmy will get it out of his system before he settles into middle age, and my sister and her family can grow old peacefully.' I thought Mandy would be off to someone else before long, and if poor Jimmy didn't end up with a broken heart, it could have been the best thing all round. But, as Uncle Dolphie always says, 'One way or another, we all end up paying for our sins.'"

"Look, Aunty Peggy," Starrett said, the Aunty Peggy part still sticking in his throat like a fishing hook, "thanks for that, I've got one more thing I'd like to ask you. How well did you know Mrs Amanda Morrison?"

"Oh, I'd say we're both part of the same social circle. I met her through Betsy Bell. We're not best friends or anything like that, but we do frequently bump into each other at various functions. I know her husband Ivan much better."

o-O-o

Starrett didn't have time to fill Gibson in on the outline of his chat with the very enlightening Aunty Peggy. Every detective deserves an Aunty Peggy, he thought. Someone at the core of a family who's not scared of having an opinion, and even less scared of voicing it. He wondered if Aunty Peggy was really that straightforward, telling the story as she knew it. Or could she be putting her own spin on facts, spurred on by some unknown motive? Maybe she didn't want her sister to assume saint-like status in everyone's eyes. Maybe she had some kind of score to settle with Dan McGuinness and she knew exactly how deep she was dropping him in the smelly stuff.

But Starrett was leaning more towards the theory that Aunty Peggy considered herself the family matriarch and was as keen as he was to have this crime solved and the sordid events of the last few days put behind them all, as soon as possible.

Starrett suggested that he and Nora adjourn to James's workshop to have a chat. Chris Moore—who was within earshot—offered to accompany his mother. She very gently stroked the side of his face with her full hand and said that she would be OK and that she needed him in the house to look after the non-stop flow of visitors.

"Chris told me you were very kind to him on the beach the morning you came to see us," Nora said as they entered the workshop.

Today the workshop looked darker than it had on Starrett's last visit, which was peculiar, because it was a much brighter day. The pulpit still stood on its side; it probably couldn't be upended until it was taken out of the workshop.

"Chris is a good lad, a credit to you and your husband. He'll be OK, believe me."

"I do hope so," Nora replied. "He's the man of the house now."

"Do you know who James was making this pulpit for?"

"I've no idea," she said, walking over to it and tracing her fingers along the intricate carving of the front ridge. "I seldom knew what Jimmy was up to. It was very weird just now. I was totally distracted when you said, 'James'. No one called him James; it was always Jimmy. He even called himself Jimmy. I remember the first time I met him. He'd gate-crashed a party, my sister's party in fact, and I'd just gone through a troubled teenage romance and was off boys. He was *so* laidback it was comforting. Not only was he not the kind of boy who'd chat up girls, but if I'd tried to chat him up, he would have run a mile. His mate introduced him grandly as 'James', and Jimmy said something about how we were in Coleraine and not Stormont Castle. At least it was a change from my last boyfriend, who would have demanded that he be introduced as Master James. So, in a way, it was not as much who he was as who he wasn't that attracted me to him, which, as Aunty Peggy kept pointing out to me, is not really a very good reason to be attracted to someone."

"Ah," Starrett said with a grunt. "Hindsight's only for backward people."

"Well, I know what you mean, but Daniel is always saying that we need to learn from our mistakes."

If Aunty Peggy's information is correct, I'll bet he does, Starrett thought but out loud he said, "Yes, Aunty Peggy was telling me that he's a very good friend of yours."

Nora Moore looked at Starrett with her head turned slightly at an angle. She tightened her mouth so that her lips disappeared into her jaw. It was not a particularly pretty sight, especially on a woman like Nora, who wasn't very feminine-looking to start with. She reminded Starrett of a farmer's wife who had been unconcerned about her looks for so long that her beauty, her poise and all of her feminine qualities had now permanently left her. Nora walked like she was in bare feet on cobblestones. On their walk down the garden, her movement had fascinated Starrett, but gradually he had started to feel uncomfortable on her behalf. Her hair was stringy, lank and lifeless. She was make-up free, and the skin on her hands was clean, but patchy and red, giving the impression of someone who had scrubbed herself clean. Her eyes were not bloodshot, but incredibly white and clear. Starrett knew that nothing could really be read into this, because in all the grief he'd been party to, he had yet to see two people react in the same way.

Her single concession to the devastating situation she had found herself in was a shapeless, knee-length, black dress and an unbuttoned black cardigan. It wasn't exactly new: the third button from the bottom was missing.

"Yes, my sister is not the most discreet of people, is she?" Nora said. "Look, Inspector, Daniel and I have been friends on and off for years, and I will admit that we've become friends again over the last couple of years, but that's all either of us needs or wants, and neither of us feels it's a second-best type of relationship, because it's not. It's the kind of relationship that any person can have at the same time as being married. Jimmy worked all the hours God sent, and I know he was happy as Larry Cunningham out here working away, thinking great thoughts, but I'm in there working away, and it drives me crazy if I haven't got someone to talk to. Daniel's the same, so I suppose that's why we drifted back towards each other."

"Was Jimmy aware of this friendship?"

"Ach, sure Daniel was a great friend to Jimmy as well."

"Nora, in my investigation, I've discovered that Jimmy had another good friend . . ."

"Oh, that sounds ominous."

"Well . . ."

"You can be totally frank with me, Inspector."

"It appears that he was having a relationship with a married woman."

"Who?" she demanded in an unemotional voice.

"Mrs Amanda Morrison."

"I've never heard of her. She's not from around here, is she?" Nora said. She wasn't acting the wronged woman; she was calm, perfectly calm, with no edge to her at all.

"Not originally, no. Mrs Morrison moved to Ramelton a few years ago, when she married the first minister."

"You mean the minister of the church Jimmy was found in?"

"Yes."

"You, you . . ." she said, shaking her head vigorously. "You don't mean to tell me that Jimmy was murdered in the church of a man whose wife he was having an affair with?"

Starrett, replied, "Yes, well, we're not sure that he was actually murdered there, but . . ."

"So are that woman and her husband in jail, then?"

"No, we're not holding anyone at this point."

"What?" she said. "Jealous husband, wronged lover . . . isn't that enough? There's absolutely no one else who would have had any reason to take Jimmy's life."

"Well, Nora, we don't know that for sure, do we?"

"I was married to him for fourteen years. I can tell you that for sure. Surely our marriage should be worth something?"

"The thing is, a person doesn't necessarily do something that provides grounds for murder."

"You really don't think it was them, do you?"

"The truth is, I don't know."

"So it *could* have been them?"

"It could have been them, but by the same token, it could have been anyone."

"OK, I get it. You mean anyone like Daniel, for instance?"

"Again, Nora, I just don't know."

Then she mumbled something like, "Men, you're all the same; you're never there when you're needed."

"Sorry?" Starrett said.

"Nothing," Nora said in a draught of frustration. "Look, for my children's sake I really need you to make sure the person responsible is caught. It will be hard for my children to face what's already going to be a very hard life, if some rich folks get away with this, just because they're rich and we're poor. Do you know what I mean?"

Starrett didn't know if she was philosophising, or asking a down-to-earth, everyday question.

"The thing that is important here," he said, conscious of lecturing a grieving widow, "is that you've got to be there for your children. It's your strength that will get them through this."

"I know, I know," she sighed. "It's just that I keep waiting for my turn to be happy, and it just never seems to arrive. If anything, it always seems to drift further and further away from me."

Chapter Thirty-Two

THOMAS BLACK, THE caretaker and "faithful servant" of First Minister Ivan Morrison, lived at the bottom of Mortimer's Lane, across the road from the Manse's expansive gardens, in a wee cottage. Although he'd been up and out since six o'clock, Garvey and Casey had come calling when he'd nipped back to his cottage for the first of his numerous daily cups of tea.

Thomas' cottage was pokey and clean, and his furniture was old and functional but certainly not decorative. He did make a cracking cup of tea, though, and it nearly blew Packie's eyebrows off.

The two gardaí spend the first five minutes of their visit talking to Black across the kitchen table as he prepared the tea. The table and three wooden chairs were handy enough, Garvey thought. The plain, dark-green wallpaper, which had started to peel in a couple of places, looked like top of the range and might have originally been intended for somewhere as grand as the Manse. The black stove, which had been in the cottage since it was built in the late 1800s, looked old enough to have undertaken a similar stint of duty in another cottage before that. The shiny brass mantelpiece was packed to overflowing with letters, cards and bric-a-brac. This included three tin canisters containing (so it transpired) loose-leaf tea, sugar and biscuits; three ancient photographs, including one of JFK; a battered silver transistor radio; and a Whoriskey's fold-over calendar frozen at May 2001—presumably Black liked the photograph of the month, the beach beneath Smuggler's Creek over at Rossnowlagh. Three coat hooks behind the door supported what looked like half a lifetime's worth of coats, jackets, cardigans and flat cloth caps. Finally, on a wee wooden stool close to the stove, sat a pair of slippers and a copy of the *Donegal News*.

"How long have you lived here, Thomas?" Packie asked.

Black sucked in about a bushel of air as he considered this question. "Aye, last September, I'd say it was thirty years since."

"That is a long time," Packie replied. "Well, you've got it nice and cosy."

"It suits me 'right."

"But, erm," Francis said, "that's longer than the Second Federation Church and First Minister Morrison have been here."

"Oh aye, and I've seen a few before that," Black replied.

"But I thought Morrison was the first minister?"

"Inaugural," Black offered. "He's always saying that he's the inaugural first minister of the Second Federation Church. Now, is that a mouthful or what?" Black broke into a wide grin which betrayed a mouthful of imperfect, tobacco-stained teeth.

He was a small man, wiry-framed, but he looked strong, very strong. Packie would have pegged him as sixty to sixty-five years old. He had a full head of hair, which was so black that Garvey was tempted to ask if Black was really his family name or a school nickname. His unkempt hair popped out in unsymmetrical tufts and curls from under a checked flat cloth cap, which seemed to be glued to his head. He wore a pair of blue dungarees over a black shirt, with scuffed black work shoes.

"Don't you see?" he continued. "The Manse across the road was originally built as the manse for the church beside it, which was a Presbyterian church. There were originally two Presbyterian churches in the town, and when they amalgamated, they sold off the Manse, the Second Federation Church bought it, and here they are."

"So, you're not a member of the Second Federation Church then?"

"I don't have time for any religion; I'm too busy working for First Minister Morrison. He likes what he likes, and he likes it when he likes it, and if you see to that, he treats you fine. Aye, after all these years, I'm happy enough working there and living here for free. I know my place. I'll just keep my mouth shut, and with a bit of luck I'll be here long after he's gone. Ach no, lads, besides which I do all my worshipping down in Conway's Pub. They do a grand pint of Guinness in there."

"That was a sorry state of affairs at your church on Friday morning last."

"Whoa, tell me about it," Black said, shaking his head.

"You're too far away down here to have seen or heard anything going on up there on Thursday night, I suppose?" Casey asked.

"Oh, aye, sure there's rarely a car goes by here. I'm surprised nothing was heard up on the hill though. I mean, your man must have been hollering louder than a hyena with all that torturing going on. And you'd also think there would have been a bit of noise going on as he was brought into the building."

"You haven't picked up any information from any of your mates over the weekend?" Packie asked.

"Not a sausage," Black replied. "Must be a local, though."

"Really?" Packie said, his head jolting back in surprise. "Why do you say that, Thomas?"

"Well, it must have been someone who knew their way around the church, someone who knew they weren't going to be disturbed. If you were a stranger, you'd never risk being trapped inside a church doing your evil deed, now, would you? You'd need to feel somewhat comfortable in your surroundings, wouldn't you?"

Casey was about to respond when Packie shot him a glare.

"Interesting, Thomas," Packie said, encouragingly. "Has anyone around town been behaving suspiciously or anything?"

"Not that I've seen on my travels, no," Thomas said, firmly closing that particular door.

Thomas Black, like the majority of the local residents the gardaí had interviewed following the discovery of Jimmy Moore's body, was happy to speculate in general, but reluctant either to name names or to point a finger.

"What about James Moore, Thomas?" Francis asked. "How well did you know him?"

"He did a lot of work for First Minister Morrison and his wife in the Manse's library."

"Yes, we know that," Francis replied.

"I'd see him about back then quite a bit. I'd never met him before that, although I believe he was a friend of Colm Donovan who also did a bit of work around the Manse from time to time. James Moore was a quiet man, kept himself to himself, was extremely neat and tidy. I'll tell you, I've seen some carpenters in my life, but never any who had the gifted hands that man had. His work was just A1. Everything he touched turned out absolutely A1."

"Did you see him and Mrs Morrison together much?" Packie asked.

Thomas Black looked from Garda Garvey to Garda Casey, trying hard to read the situation.

"Well, Mrs Morrison was obviously around the Manse . . ."

"Thomas, it's only fair that we should tell you . . . First Minister Morrison told Inspector Starrett that you had notified him that Mrs Morrison and Mr Moore were having an affair."

"Well," Thomas said, "I suppose if you couldn't find out about that, there was little or no hope you'd ever solve any crime at all."

"So," Garvey continued, drawing the word out, "how did you know they were having an affair?"

"I will admit that she was more discreet than usual, but ach, sure, it's none of my business, really. Look, I don't want to be quoted on this, but Mrs Morrison is a fine woman, always very nice to me. She treats me well, makes sure I'm invited to Sunday lunch every now and again. They always have someone for Sunday lunch; it's their big social meal of their week. But I speak as I find. You'd have to say that she was liberal with her favours, and the first minister was down in Belfast a lot, and my house is only just across the road from the Manse. I couldn't help seeing who was coming and going. Listen, lads, she's still a young woman, she's a beautiful woman, and as I say, what I saw was really none of my business."

"Thomas," Packie said, his Galway accent sweet and gentle, "what you tell us is not gossip; it's valuable information. Of course, we'd never jeopardise your job, but we really do need to know who else Amanda Morrison had been seeing."

"Look, lads, you don't need me to tell you that; you'll pick that up easily enough. But what I can tell you is that this time it was serious. The thing with Jimmy Moore wasn't a quick roll in the hay. No, I'd say they both knew that this was the real thing."

"What makes you say that?" Garvey asked, intrigued that Black would be so perceptive.

"It was very easy to see that they cared about each other and about the people around them. With an affair, people are just taking advantage of each other, which is why affairs usually burn out without developing into anything."

"Jeez, Thomas, that's very profound," Garvey said, without thinking.

"And beyond me?" the caretaker replied.

"No, Thomas, sorry. Look, please . . ."

"It's no bother, Packie," Thomas said graciously. "Yes, I've never married and I'll tell you why I never married. You see, my mother and father, God rest their souls, met when my mam was sixteen and my father was seventeen. They got hitched on my mam's twenty-first birthday and were happily married and loved each other each and every day of their lives. My dad died first, when he was eighty-three, and my mother died the night after she buried him. When I was growing up and out courting, I'd always ask myself if the girl I was with and I could ever enjoy even a fraction of the love my mam and dad enjoyed. Sadly, the answer was always 'no', and that's why I never bothered. Ach, sure, it wasn't a great loss to anyone, I know, but I suppose I did it out of respect for my parents."

"That's a great story, Thomas, that really is."

"Aye, I know it is." Thomas Black sighed. "And you know what? I thought I saw something similar in the love Mrs Morrison and Mr Moore had for each other."

"Early on Friday morning, you told First Minister Morrison that you believed his wife and Mr Moore where having a relationship," Garvey said.

"Yes, I told him that. I believe he needed to know."

"Do you think there was any chance First Minister Morrison already knew about the relationship?"

"I couldn't say for sure if he did or if he didn't," Thomas Black replied, "but he reacted the same way he did when I told him that the roof of the garden shed needed repairing. He just said, 'OK, Thomas, thanks for that, I'll deal with it.'"

o-O-o

Casey and Garvey left Black on his high doorstep and walked slowly back up Mortimer's Lane. When they levelled with the gateway of the Manse, Garvey broke off and walked through it. Then he turned and looked back down towards Black's cottage. He studied the location of both buildings from every angle, and, try though he might, he could see no way in which Black would have been able to see the comings and goings at the Manse from inside his cottage, or even from his front doorstep.

"So," Garvey said to his colleague as they resumed their journey up the last few yards of Mortimer's Lane, "it would seem that Thomas Black would have had to go out of his way to see who was or wasn't visiting Mrs Morrison when her husband was out of town."

"You mean he would have had to have been spying on her?" Garda Casey asked, as the two of them took a right into Church Street.

"Yes, that's exactly what I mean," Garda Garvey confirmed.

Chapter Thirty-Three

AS STARRETT AND Nuala drove into Daniel McGuinness' yard, an enormous Irish wolfhound ran straight across the front of their bow, and Starrett had to slam on the brakes, unceremoniously bringing them to a sharp halt. Fortune had once again sided with the inspector, because around the bend was a three-year-old boy, sitting in the middle of the driveway, playing with a dog's bone and a Fairy Liquid container. Every time the little boy beat the container with the bone, a few more green bubbles would float out of it, and he was giggling himself pink.

"O Jesus, Mary and Joseph!" Nuala said, seeing how close their car was to the child.

"The devil's children enjoy the devil's luck," Starrett said, as much to himself as to her.

"Oh, he's a wee dote, isn't he?" she said, rushing out of the car to pick him up.

They knocked on the door and were admitted by another of the big man's extensive brood.

"You left Nora's before we had a chance to chat," Starrett said by way of introduction.

There he was, perched on his throne, hands resting on his walking stick.

"Oh, you know, Starrett, you pay your respects and then you have to leave them to it," he grunted, looking at Nuala with the child in her arms. "You look good like that; you should get your man to give you one."

Nuala blushed and handed the baby to his mother, who appeared to be Dan's hired help. A quick nod of the head to the left, from McGuinness, was all it took for the girl and baby to get out of there in a flash, leaving the trio in privacy.

"Nora was telling me that thee and she are great friends," Starrett said, and despite having no invitation to sit, found a chair for Gibson and then one for himself.

"Well, Nora and myself go way back, and I have to admit that she was particularly supportive in my own time of crisis."

"Yes, I heard about the accident, Dan," Starrett said. "It was a bad fall, wasn't it?"

"The doctors thought so, aye."

"But no doubt broken by that soft mattress of euros, eh?" Starrett added, smiling. "What was it they said you were awarded? Three quarters of a million?"

"Jeez, man! Keep your voice down for heaven's sake or I'll have relatives I never knew existed turning up on the doorstep," Dan said with a hiss. "It wasn't anything near that."

"Ah well, sorry about that," Starrett said. "But you were telling us about Nora?"

"Yes, she's a good friend. We can talk, I mean really talk, and as Jimmy was also a good mate of mine, there was never any chance of anyone misreading the situation vis-à-vis any jiggy-pokery carry-on."

"I believe you told my colleagues that you knew Jimmy was seeing Amanda Morrison," Starrett said, matter-of-factly.

"Yes, indeed I did."

"But you never told Nora about it?" Starrett said, speeding up slightly from his usual drawl.

"Nope."

"You're sure about that?"

"Positive."

"You see, from where I'm sitting, Dan, I have to admit that I'm having a problem with that."

"Oh, and why's that?"

"Well, I just remember a great chatting-up technique from my school days, which was doing the dirty on the current boyfriend by telling the object of your affections who else the boyfriend had expressed an interest in."

"Aye, and now you're running the gardaí? That says something, Starrett; that says something."

"Now from what I can make out, you probably had a hard time getting over everything that happened with Nora when you were young. Then, many years pass, and one of your best friends also happens to be married to your childhood sweetheart, your wife leaves you, you discover your childhood sweetheart's husband is involved with another woman. So would you drop your best mate in it? It's a simple question. Surely there's no need to phone a friend?"

"Well, Starrett, erm, all I can tell you is all I know, and all I know is that I didn't tell Nora about the relationship. Don't you see, I'd no need to. There was nothing I felt was missing in my relationship with her."

"Have the two of you discussed Jimmy's relationship with Amanda since his death?"

"When I went to pay my respects on Friday, she was in a bad way. She accused me of knowing, I said I had, and she said, 'Thank you for not telling me.' And that's as much as we've discussed it."

"Do Betsy Bell and Aunty Peggy Cowan know each other?" Starrett asked.

"Yes, I believe so."

"So, at some point, Betsy might have told Peggy about Amanda and Jimmy."

Dan lifted his right hand from the cane and wobbled it open-palm in an "I think we're talking 50/50 chance here" gesture.

"So, in short, Nora's best friend knew that her husband was cheating on her. Nora's sister knew that her husband was cheating on her, and you're expecting me to believe that neither of them would have thought enough of her to tell her what was going on?"

Dan merely shrugged his shoulders, which resulted in a tidal wave of ripples across his body.

"OK, Dan, have you any idea how Aunty Peggy and Amanda knew each other?"

"Maybe university, but that's a guess."

"And finally, Dan, since my colleagues originally questioned you, have you thought of anyone who might have wanted to hurt Jimmy?"

"I've thought of little else," Dan the Man wheezed, "and I keep coming back to First Minister Morrison. I think the more you investigate Jimmy's past, the more you'll discover that he was a good man, a great father and, apart from his affair with Amanda Morrison, he really did keep his nose clean. I can't for the life of me think of anyone else he might have wronged.

Chapter Thirty-Four

ONCE THEY'D LEFT the big man's house, Starrett turned to Gibson and said, "Look, let's run straight on out the Letterkenny road and pay another visit to Colm Donovan. Hopefully he'll know the name of the gaffer on the Fast Trout job up in Creestown."

"You're on," she replied. "And just in case you hadn't noticed, I think I should point out that you're the one driving the car."

"So I am, so I am," Starrett said, thinking that Gibson was fun to be with. "What did you make of that little moment we shared with Dan McGuinness?"

"I suppose it all depends on whether you feel he's lying or not about the extent of his relationship with Nora. I mean, Pitt and Jolie, they are not . . ."

"Sorry, who?"

"OK, let's see, yep, they're not exactly Romeo and Juliet."

"Good, OK, I'm with you now."

"I don't know, but they say that for some people, the cheating itself is an added attraction."

"If not the only one," Starrett said. "And no matter what anyone says, the Donegal nights are cold and wet and long, and necessity is the mother of invention. Still, the notion of Dan the Man on top of Nora . . ."

"I'm having great difficulty imagining it too," Gibson said. "By the way, the last time Packie and I interviewed Colm Donovan, he and the sergeant mentioned something about the House of Love. They said it was somewhere on the Milford to Kerrykeel road."

"Yes, I know it well," Starrett replied.

"What is it?"

"Ach, sure, there was this couple, very much in love. The lad was very ambitious, and he wanted them to have a grand house in time for their wedding. He got a beautiful plot of land with a great view of the water, and he spent every minute God sent him working on their dream house. If he wasn't working on the house, he was working on the two other jobs he was holding down in order to pay for the materials for their grand house. In the meantime . . ."

"He was totally ignoring his girlfriend?"

"You've got it."

"And so she started cheating on him?"

"Sadly, you're spot on again," Starrett said as they passed the Silver Tassie Hotel.

"And?"

"Do you want fact or legend?"

"Oh, both, please."

"Well, the locals said he did away with her. Drowned her in the water their grand house overlooked. They also say he was very clever because he ensured that her body could never be found, and as there were no witnesses to the actual murder, he got away with it scot-free."

"And the facts were?" Nuala asked.

"She moved to England with her new boyfriend. There was a problem with some missing money, and we tracked her down to Stockport, where they were both holed up in a single-room bedsit without a view. The boy stopped work on his "dream house", and the unfinished shell stands as a testament to their lost love. He lives nearby with his parents and has dropped out of life."

"A bit of a Syd Barrett?" Nuala asked.

"Sorry?"

"Oops, please forgive me. He was the original guitarist in Pink Floyd, but I thought I might have been on safe ground because they predated Neil Diamond by three or four years."

"Tell me this, Nuala Gibson," Starrett enquired, as they pulled into the tidy yard of Colm Donovan's bungalow. "How do you know all of this music stuff?"

"Oh, that's easy. My father's a big music fan."

Starrett was considering an answer when a large, white husky-type dog attacked their car. Ignoring the almighty racket and the saliva drooling down from the dog's ever-widening jaws, Starrett confidently opened the car door and stepped out. The dog ran up to him, barking furiously and loudly. Starrett, using three straight fingers, one bent finger and one thumb, reached out to the dog and started to tickle it behind the ears. The dog stopped barking and started whimpering in delight, playing like a puppy with the detective.

"Fine guard dog you've turned out to be, Digger," Donovan said, emerging from the house. Then to Starrett: "I've never seen him do that before."

Donovan looked into Starrett's car and recognised Gibson. Starrett walked up to him and introduced himself. Donovan looked slightly taken aback.

"We've come to trouble you again about Jimmy Moore," Starrett said, as Gibson got out of the car, all the time with her eyes glued to Digger.

"Aye, you're lucky, you just caught me in," Donovan volunteered. "I just nipped back to pick up some more scaffolding frames."

"Sorry, Colm, it's just a quickie really. Jimmy worked on a job at the Fast Trout . . ."

"Aye, I know it, up in Creestown."

"And I was wondering if you would know the name of the gaffer he worked for up there."

"It was a Bonner Construction job, wasn't it? It was tor . . . well, it burnt down overnight."

"Yeah, that's the one," Gibson said.

"Aye, that would have been . . . now, let me see," Donovan said, removing a packet of Camels from his T-shirt sleeve and offering Starrett and Gibson a ciggy before lighting up solo. "Pat Duffy was the ramrod on that job."

"Do you know him?" Starrett asked.

"Not really, no, but I know *of* him. I run around with a crowd he used to run around with."

"He knew Jimmy?" Starrett asked.

"Indeed he did," Donovan confirmed. "He would have been a big supporter of Jimmy's."

"Would you know how I could contact him?"

"He and the family moved back to Sligo a few months back. Pat's mother-in-law took bad, and his missus wanted to be nearby."

"Are you sure he moved to Sligo and not to Cork?"

"No, no, Pat's definitely a Sligo man, and that's where he went. Why would you have thought that?" Donovan asked, appearing surprised.

"I think it was Owen Bonner who told us his gaffer went to Cork."

Donovan clicked his teeth.

"Would Jimmy have known Bonner?" Starrett asked.

Donovan thought for a few moments before he replied, "I don't know, to be honest. I think he would have known what he looked like."

"From the newspapers?' Gibson asked.

"No, I think Jimmy told me that he'd spotted Bonner and some of his cronies at the Fast Trout. They'd made him a bit nervous, and that's why he left without his tools."

"Right then," Starrett said. "You wouldn't have a number, would you?"

"Nah, but I could get you one."

Donovan promised to ring in Duffy's number to Tower House. Sitting in the BMW, Starrett studied the scene in his rear-view mirror as the youthful Colm Donovan climbed into his souped-up VW Golf, screeched out of the courtyard and zoomed off into the distance without any of the scaffolding frames he had claimed he had come back to pick up.

Chapter Thirty-Five

THE MORNING HAD been one of the most brilliant June mornings a garda inspector could ever have wished for, but just as Starrett and Gibson reached the noisy manhole covers on the Ramelton–Rathmullan road, the heavens opened up as if God had turned all of His taps on full. There was thunder and lightning, rainbow on top of rainbow, raindrops as big as elephant's teardrops, and there were hailstones as large as golf balls. It got to a point where they could barely see six feet in front of the bonnet of their car.

The unmarked garda car Starrett had ordered to be parked in the lay-by opposite Betsy Bell's house was still there. This was a near-perfect surveillance spot: not only was it perfectly positioned to view the front entrance of Mrs Bell's house, but because it was also a natural place for sightseers and courting couples in cars to stop, a parked car attracted little attention from drivers passing by.

Betsy came out her front door almost the moment they pulled into her driveway, pulling on fashionable, multi-coloured, head-to-toe waterproofs. Obviously she had already been on her way out.

"I need to get out for a breath of fresh air," she said, opening the car door for Starrett. "I was just building up to an attack of room fatigue."

"How's Amanda?"

"She not the best just now, Starrett. She seemed to brighten up a little after your last visit. Then I heard her on her mobile, and now she's withdrawn into herself again, and I'm quite worried."

Starrett remained seated in the car. He had no intention of getting drenched.

"Hop in the back there and we'll take you for a wee spin," he suggested.

"Okey-dokey, you're on," she said, but then added, "What about Amanda?"

"I can go and sit with her, if you like," Gibson offered.

"That would be nice. She's sleeping at the moment," Betsy said, closing Starrett's door and running around to open the passenger side for Gibson.

As she was circling their car, Starrett said to Gibson, "We may be here for a while. Get hold of Casey and tell him what we learned from Donovan about the Fast Trout gaffer. He can start the wheels turning on that score."

"Right."

Just then, Betsy Bell opened her door, and they exchanged places. Gibson scampered across the yard, with Betsy shouting, "Toodaloo!" after her. She then turned to Starrett and said, "You don't know how big a treat it is to get out of the house, even though it is bucketing down."

They both sat watching Gibson swerve from side to side as nimbly as George Best at his peak, deftly picking her way through the puddles.

They drove to Rathmullan, the noise of the rain lashing against the outside of the car, drowning out the sound of the engine. Rathmullan, like all seaside towns, needs sun to show off its full charm. Needs sun to draw the people on to the streets and, more importantly, needs sun and the accompanying blue skies to bring out its picture-postcard perfection.

Eventually Betsy said, "There's a nice little coffee shop up here, second on the left just before the old church ruins. It's run by Sandra, a fun lady from Dublin. She does a lifesaving cappuccino and even better crepes."

"Seems just what the doctor would have ordered for himself on this miserable day," Starrett said, taking the directed left and pulling up in front of the tastefully refurbished old Methodist Hall.

The rain had fairly packed Sandra's, but Starrett and Betsy Bell managed to squeeze into a small table in a quiet corner.

"Betsy, can you remember who else you might have told about Amanda and Jimmy?" Starrett asked, as soon as they were seated,

"I suppose we didn't really come out to discuss the weather," Betsy offered with a strained smile. "But would you mind if we get our order in first?"

Starrett remained silent for a while after the waitress disappeared.

"I would have been very careful," Betsy said, without further prompting.

"Did you tell Nora Moore's sister?"

"Aunty Peggy?" Betsy asked and Starrett nodded. "You say that as though you know for a fact I did."

Starrett did not reply.

A few more moments of silence followed, during which they could hear scattered fragments of other people's conversations.

"Yes, Starrett, I did tell Aunty Peggy," Betsy Bell said eventually.

"Right, I figured," Starrett admitted.

"But listen to me, Starrett, I know Aunty Peggy well enough that I could make her promise never to tell Nora, and I knew it was a promise she would keep."

"You're absolutely sure about that?"

"I'm a hundred per cent convinced," Betsy Bell replied confidently. "And the reason I told her was that I wanted someone on Nora's side to know. It was starting to look like Mandy and Jimmy were going to try and make a go of it together. I know Mandy is my best friend and all that, but equally I was worried. Ivan is capable of looking after himself. In fact, he probably wouldn't notice the difference, provided he could find another bright young thing to hang from his arm at his precious functions. Nora, on the other hand, was extremely fragile at the best of times, according to Peggy. So I figured that Peggy should be ready to help pick up the pieces."

From the distance came the rattle of more thunder. The general coffee house chit-chat fell to silence for a few seconds before, conversation by conversation, it slowly regained its previous momentum.

"How did Peggy react?" Starrett asked, when the chatter was loud enough to afford them privacy.

Betsy paused as the waitress delivered their drinks and crepes. Once she'd gone, Betsy stuck her finger through the froth and chocolate on the top of the cappuccino and licked it off. "I'm sorry about that. I can never resist. Sorry, where was I?"

Starrett broke into a wide grin. He wiped his right hand up over his forehead, over his head and down to the back of his neck, before saying, "You were about to tell me how Peggy reacted."

"I thought she wasn't surprised," Betsy replied, a fork full of crepe, banana and maple syrup hovering close to her mouth. "She said that if you didn't love your husband, it's never enough just to stay with him."

"Is there any chance Peggy might have told anyone?"

"I made her swear on her husband's life that that she wouldn't even tell Uncle Dolphie."

"And *you* didn't tell anyone else?"

"No," Betsy replied firmly, before the first mouthful of crepe disappeared. "Oh my goodness," she purred, "This is absolutely divine. Who needs men when you can have Sandra's crepes?"

Starrett smiled as he asked, "OK, do you know anyone else who knew about James and Amanda?"

"Colm Donovan knew. Jimmy told him."

"I didn't know you knew Colm."

"Yes, he knew my late husband, Billy. Colm was always around doing some manner of work or other on the house. When Billy died, God bless his soul, I kept using Colm; he knew how everything worked. It was Colm, in fact, who first suggested that I use Jimmy to do my kitchen."

"Right," Starrett said, "and did Colm Donovan have any observation or comment to make to you about the relationship?"

"I think he was very concerned about how it was all going to end. He said Amanda was well capable of looking after herself, but he felt Jimmy was new to it all, and that he was most probably in way over his head."

"Tell me this, Betsy, did Amanda Morrison tell you anything else about Jimmy? Anything at all?"

"No," Betsy said in a whisper, appearing very distracted.

"Are you worried about Amanda?"

"Yes, I am. Starrett, you got to see her for yourself. She's definitely gone downhill and she's rambling a lot. Last night she was saying that Jimmy was crucified as a punishment from God."

"Is she sleeping much?"

"Most of the time she does nothing but sleep. In fact, I think if she doesn't snap out of it soon, we might need to consider getting her professional help," Betsy said, preparing for her final mouthful of crepe.

"If she's really that bad, we should maybe get back there immediately and assess whether or not we do need to get someone in to see her," Starrett said, as he too finished his crepe.

Seven minutes later, during which time the rain stopped, they were in Betsy Bell's home, with Nuala Gibson reporting that she'd not heard a single sound from upstairs.

Betsy went upstairs to check on Amanda.

Starrett and Gibson could hear her gentle footsteps padding across the carpet upstairs. Suddenly the same feet were running to what appeared to be the landing, and they heard Betsy calling, "Mandy! Mandy!" repeatedly with rising panic.

Betsy ran downstairs shouting, "She's not there! She's not there!"

They searched every room in the house, followed by the outhouses, but they couldn't find Amanda Morrison anywhere.

Amanda Morrison and the rain had disappeared together.

o-O-o

Starrett looked at his watch; it was 13.48.

"When was the last time you saw her?" Starrett asked Betsy as he made her a strong cup of tea.

"It would have been just after nine o'clock this morning. We had breakfast together. She was very depressed that she couldn't go out for a walk in the garden because of the heavy rain, so she went back to bed."

Gibson had checked with the gardaí in the unmarked car. According to them both, the only comings and goings so far that day had been Starrett and Gibson arriving, Starrett and Betsy Bell departing and Starrett and Betsy Bell returning. No one else had entered the driveway.

"That's *all* we need," Starrett said, as much to himself as to Gibson and Bell. "Maybe someone found out she was here. Did she ever answer the phone?"

"As I mentioned, she took one call on her mobile, but apart from that she was terrified of the sound of it ringing, which was unusual for her, because she used to live on the phone. I got the feeling she was terrified picking it up in case Ivan was on the other end."

"And you didn't tell anyone she was staying here, Betsy?"

"No, I promise you, I didn't, Starrett."

"Had she been out for a walk since she came to stay here?"

"Mandy wasn't a great walker. A wee dander around the garden every now and then to clear her head, but that was it."

"Then we can rule out that she's just gone for a stroll. I have to consider the possibility that she didn't leave of her own free will. Someone may have taken her."

"But surely either myself or Garda Gibson would have heard something, some kind of disturbance or other?"

"Not necessarily, no," Starrett replied. "Firstly, she might have gone voluntarily; and, secondly, that auld thunderstorm we've just been through has been creating quite a bit of a racket all morning long."

Starrett and Gibson returned to Tower House in Ramelton, leaving the two gardaí from the unmarked car with Betsy Bell, who was still hoping that Amanda would return to the sanctuary and safety of her cosy home.

Chapter Thirty-Six

THE MOMENT STARRETT returned to Tower House, he put out an all-ports bulletin on Amanda Morrison and made the telephone call he'd been dreading ever since Maggie Keane's visit.

"Could I speak with Dr Aljoe, please?" he said into the mouthpiece, once he had been connected.

"She's over in Donegal Town at the minute, Inspector," a female voice announced. "A body was found first thing this morning in a hotel room. Suspicious circumstances, you know."

Which was emergency-services-speak for someone had suffered what appeared to be a non-accidental death. Starrett hadn't heard of any such incident, but then he had been out on the Moore case all morning.

"Right so," he said, surprised he wasn't relieved at not having to address the imminent issue with the doctor. "Could you please have her ring me as soon as possible?"

"Of course I will, Inspector," the voice replied.

Starrett thought he heard a tad too much familiarity on the other end of the line, as if he were speaking to someone who was aware of recent developments between the doctor and the inspector.

The remainder of the afternoon passed quietly for Starrett. Garda Francis Casey was the only member of the squad to make a discovery of any significance on the James Moore case. He tracked down Pat Duffy in Sligo. From Duffy, Casey discovered that it looked as if Owen Bonner had been telling the truth. Moore's toolbox had indeed been accidentally removed by the men taking away pieces of the dismantled bar. Pat Duffy himself had returned the toolbox to his mate, Moore. He said he might have joked to Moore when he first arrived with the tools that they'd all been destroyed in the fire, and that was probably where the confusion over the facts had arisen. Duffy further advised Casey that both he and the fire brigade had agreed that the fire had been accidental, most likely caused by a cigarette butt not being stubbed out properly.

Starrett raised his eyebrows at this piece of information.

Casey had checked with the fire brigade, and their records corroborated Duffy's account. He apologised to Starrett for uncovering such bad news.

"Bejeepers," Starrett said immediately. "We can remove the name Owen Bonner from our list of suspects. I wasn't comfortable with it. I thought it was probably unlikely he'd torch that particular pub; it was his dad's, and I'm sure that if he had been going to torch it he wouldn't have been seen on the premises the night before it went up."

"Could Moore have witnessed something, though, that put his life in danger?"

"I doubt Bonner is in the frame in this one, Francis. We can concentrate our energies and resources on the rest of the investigation."

Starrett then had a chat with the major, bringing him up to date on the investigation. Major Newton Cunningham wasn't best pleased about Amanda Morrison's disappearance.

The next time Starrett looked at his watch it was 20.50. The majority of his team had gone home and he was just about to call it a day when the telephone rang.

"Starrett," he answered.

His face went ashen as the colour drained from his cheeks. He returned the handset to its cradle, his hand remaining glued to it as he sat staring into the distance.

Starrett didn't know how long he'd been sitting there when Gibson and Casey came into his office to wish him goodnight.

"What's happened?" Gibson exclaimed the moment she saw Starrett's face.

"It's Amanda Morrison," Starrett replied in a whisper. "Her body's just been found down on Rathmullan Pier."

Chapter Thirty-Seven

BY THE TIME Starrett and Garvey arrived at Rathmullan Pier, the Scene of Crime Unit—including pathologist Dr Samantha Aljoe—was already there.

An eerie scene confronted Starrett as he walked down the wooden planks. The unfolding drama was floodlit, like a large bubble of white light attached to the end of the pier. Slightly to the right, and creating a grand silhouette, was a Killybegs fishing boat, the *Father Anthony*, bobbing up and down furiously in the water as the wind raged and pulled at its every extremity. The torrential rain of earlier in the day had been replaced by intermittent showers. Just now the rain was holding off, though the powerful wind was threatening to pull Starrett's head off of his shoulders. As he approached the end of the pier, he saw that the beams of the arc lights were strong enough to draw up condensation from the rain-soaked surface. Outside the bubble of light, it was dark, very dark, especially coming off the back of the previous week's full moon.

The walk to the end of the pier seemed to take Starrett for ever. He spotted Dr Aljoe immediately because of her signature one-piece, semi-transparent, light blue plastic suit, while the remainder of the gardaí scene of crime officers were in standard-issue opaque white outfits. The trousers and white blouse he could glimpse beneath her work suit couldn't have been very efficient in keeping this terrible cold at bay, but that didn't seem to be troubling the doctor, who was working away as efficiently as ever.

As Starrett walked the final few yards along the narrowest part of the pier, he wondered if there was anything more he could have done to protect Amanda Morrison. He recalled thinking that he was being overly protective by isolating her in the first place. How had someone managed to steal her from right under their eyes? He thought it unlikely that she would have chosen to make the journey herself, alone and on foot, in torrential rain. So just who would have wanted to harm her?

Could it have been First Minister Ivan Morrison? Or maybe even Daniel McGuinness, either by himself or with Nora Moore as an accomplice? Or maybe some person, or persons, as yet unknown. What information had Amanda Morrison taken to her death? Perhaps knowledge that someone needed to keep hidden. If so, what could it have been?

When he finally arrived at the crime scene, Dr Aljoe merely nodded at Starrett to acknowledge his arrival. She was bent over the water-soaked body of Amanda Morrison. As ever, Starrett had to look twice at the body to convince himself that he was looking at the corpse of a person.

Her hair was matted with water and seaweed. Her unsymmetrical eyes, small nose and large mouth mocked her in her death, as they never had during her life. The counterbalance to these less than beautiful features—her vitality and her swagger—were now absent for eternity. A combination of the chaos of her soggy clothes and the sombreness of death in these circumstances was what convinced Starrett that there really was such a thing as a human spirit, if only because it was now so noticeably absent.

Starrett wondered who would cry for Amanda Morrison.

For her final journey, she had been dressed in light-blue Wellingtons, a calf-length, dark-blue, pleated skirt and a black hooded plastic mackintosh. One of her Wellingtons was missing, and Starrett studied her bare ankle. He was a great believer in the theory that people show their true ages through their ankles and their necks. Necks can be covered and ankles can be hidden, but they rarely are, unless they need to be. Amanda's toenails were painted a vital red, a matching shade to the lipstick once pained on her now blue lips. Starrett studied the toenails. They were long, very long. The Inspector marked the passing of time by how quickly his own toenails grew. He had come to the conclusion that toenails didn't grow at a consistent speed. They grew fast when your life was hurtling by and they grew slower when your life was passing at a more reasonable pace. He now focused his attention on the exposed ankle. It was wrinkle-free and vein-free, which Starrett found baffling. If she'd been in the water for some hours, surely she should be showing more signs of her submersion.

Starrett could see a rope burn around this same ankle. It was a severe burn, with the blacks, blues and purples making a mockery of her otherwise flawless skin. The colours looked as if they'd be more at home in a Derek Hill painting than on the snow-white skin of the first minister's dead wife.

Surely Ivan Morrison couldn't be responsible for this slaying? But then again, perhaps fuelled by a need for vengeance, it was possible that he'd sought and obtained retribution on James Moore. Surely, however, there could be no reasonable explanation or justification for wreaking this kind of havoc against his own wife.

Dr Aljoe said something to him. He could see her lips moving and he could see her looking at him, but, between his own distraction and the noise of the wind, he didn't hear her words.

"Sorry?" he said.

"It looks like she committed suicide," Dr Aljoe repeated.

The look he returned to her must have said, "Suicide! Are you crazy?" because that was exactly what he was thinking.

"She came down here in the rain with a heavy heart and stones in her pockets. From what I can tell, she must have lost her nerve to jump, because it appears she started to climb down the ladder towards the water. She lost her footing, fell towards the water, but caught her foot in the mooring rope and tumbled headlong downwards. She was found off the end of the pier, dangling by her leg, with her head just under the water. Her skirt had fallen over her head. She was spotted only when the fishing boat came in. If she hadn't become entangled in the rope, well, goodness knows when, if ever, the body would have been washed up."

"You're absolutely sure there is no way someone could have done this to her?"

"I don't see any unexplained marks about her body," the doctor said, a little defensively. "If she was brought here forcibly to be thrown into the water, there's no way she wouldn't have struggled."

"But the rope around her ankle, the skirt up over the head, showing off her womanhood, you know: could it be another publicly humiliating display like the crucifixion?"

Dr Aljoe softened her stare into a gentle and caring look, as if she understood what was going through his mind. She looked as if she wanted to spare him the embarrassment of being contradicted in public. He loved her for what he saw in her heart.

"You're most probably right," he eventually said. "It's *too* public a place to carry out an evil deed; it's not a public *enough* place to leave a body expecting it to be seen. She would have been under water at high tide."

Starrett gave permission to bag the remains. It had started to rain again. The inspector watched as some of crime scene people diligently continued their work, minutely searching the deck of the pier, though he suspected that any evidence had long since been washed away. However, on top of one of the wooden supports, which disappeared into what was reputedly some of the deepest end-of-pier waters in Europe, he spied a pink handbag, just sitting there, resisting the wind and the rain. It was fixed to the joist with a piece of wire, no thicker than that of a coat hanger. He borrowed a pair of white gloves from one of the team and carefully released the bag. He gingerly opened it, Dr Aljoe at his side. The bag was empty, apart from a piece of paper. Starrett sheltered the handbag with his body as he placed the piece of paper in a see-through evidence bag and then held it up to the light.

The writing was neat, circularly formed and feminine.

Dr Aljoe quietly read out the words:

Sorry,

I'm tired of being in love and being all alone,
When you're so far away from me.
I leave myself,
My friends
And all,
For Love.

Amanda

Starrett read and then reread the note several times.

"Mark Knopfler and William Shakespeare, in that order," Aljoe offered.

"Sorry?"

"Her first two lines are from Mark Knopfler's song 'So Far Away', and the final four are a quote from Shakespeare's *Two Gentlemen of Verona*," she said, both of them still looking at the note.

"You can't help but think she was one of those poor unfortunates who feel that taking one's life by drowning is a pleasant way to die. Let me tell you something, Samantha, drowning never ever happens in graceful slow motion. It's a quick, brutal and violent way to end one's life. It's certainly never the thing of beauty it's made out to be."

"You won't get any arguments from me, Starrett."

"But I suppose when you're in a hurry to leave . . ." Starrett said, feeling a need to lighten the situation, "you never stop to check what's on the other side of the door."

"Look," she went on, gently touching his arm, "I've got to get back to Letterkenny General."

"Sam, I . . . ah," he started.

But he stopped.

He stopped because he'd just seen the remains of a person who had been destroyed by this thing called love. He stopped because he knew how close he and the doctor were to falling into some kind of love of their own. He stopped because he couldn't find the words to express how he wanted to try to preserve the higher love that might have blossomed again between himself and Maggie Keane. He stopped because he didn't want to sully that love, even though it was intangible and probably never ever attainable.

Then he thought about James Moore and Nora Moore; about Dan McGuinness and his absent wife; about Nora and Dan McGuinness; about Ivan Morrison and Amanda Morrison; and then he completed the circle by thinking about James Moore and Amanda Morrison. In that moment, he thought he knew that chasing the unobtainable was not just a waste of everyone's time; it was a pure unforgivable waste of life.

Perhaps love really was just where you found it.

Samantha Aljoe, in her silly plastic suit, with her magnificent hair bunched and crunched up in some elasticated plastic cap, looked at him as if she understood all of the above. What's more, she looked as if she were aware of the decision he was reaching.

"I'll ring you later," she said, with the familiarity of a lover.

She left him standing on the end of Rathmullan Pier looking after her. He kept looking after her until she reached the land end of the pier, hopped into her car and drove off.

Chapter Thirty-Eight

STARRETT AND GARVEY were tempted to stop off for a drink in the White Hart, but all the police activity on the end of the pier had produced quite a crowd of onlookers, and Starrett could just see the headline in the following week's *Donegal News*: "Garda Officers Down Pints Midway Through Murder Investigation". What with all the recent, albeit self-inflicted, hammering that the Donegal gardaí had received, sensitivity was at the top of the agenda, so they agreed they would nip into the Bridge Bar for a pint of Bríd's finest in Ramelton.

On the way back, they stopped off at Betsy Bell's. It seemed to Starrett she'd been expecting the worst, because she had Eileen McLaughlin keeping her company. The two gardaí who were still parked in the driveway showed Starrett how Amanda had escaped their guard through a gap in the hedge at the foot of the garden, their powerful torch beam illuminating where one person had trudged through the long grass of an adjoining field. Because the road bent around sharply to the left just after Betsy Bell's house, the two gardaí sitting in their car wouldn't have seen her go out through the field gate and down the road. It would have taken Amanda roughly forty-five minutes to walk into Rathmullan, taking into account the thunderstorm and torrential rain.

Betsy Bell was brave and philosophical about her friend's death.

"You know," she said, "Amanda was never ever going to have another happy day in her life. She might have had mediocre days, but she would most definitely have spent the rest of her life regretting what might have been."

"Just to think, this time last week she was ecstatic, truly happy for the first time in her life," Eileen offered, the way people do on solemn occasions, feeling the need to add something, anything, to the proceedings, if only to comfort themselves.

"And you're saying she wasn't murdered?" Betsy asked Starrett.

"We obviously have to see what the autopsy has to tell us, but off the record, we're convinced she took her own life."

"Well, at least that's something; I couldn't bear it if both Mandy and Jimmy had been murdered," Betsy said. "That would have been just too sad a story."

Starrett sighed and said, "Betsy, I'm afraid there's no such thing as a happy story. A happy story is just one that hasn't yet ended."

"Oh, Starrett, I need cheering up, not depressing," Betsy Bell said as Eileen made similar tuttings.

Starrett grimaced, stretching back his mouth to reveal his fine set of molars. He couldn't find anything uplifting to say, so he said nothing.

"At least she made her own decision," Betsy said a few seconds later. "Starrett, have you any idea yet who killed Jimmy?"

"No, Betsy, not yet. But tell me, when Amanda was talking into her mobile, did she take a call or make the call?'

"I'm sorry, I don't know."

"OK" Starrett replied, "if you're OK here with Miss McLaughlin, then Packie and myself had better get back into Ramelton and see what's what."

"We'll be fine," Eileen said, coming over all mother hen.

"Yes, thanks for asking, Starrett, but we'll both be dandy. I dare say we'll crack open a bottle of claret or two to celebrate Mandy's life."

o-O-o

On a typical Monday night, the Bridge Bar is relatively quiet. On the Monday Starrett and Garvey went for their drink, punters were as rare as albino crows, so they managed to find a table easily and were left in peace to enjoy their pints and discuss the case.

"Bejeepers, what an absolute mess this is turning out to be," Starrett said, once they'd settled in.

"What if someone wants us to think it was a suicide because they don't want us to investigate Mrs Morrison's life?" Packie asked, wiping off his Guinness moustache.

"Well, there was only one set of tracks through the field, besides which Dr Aljoe was pretty sure Amanda committed suicide."

"But why take the coward's way out?"

"Oh, steady on," Starrett said, breaking into a long whistle. "Tell me this, Packie, do you remember back to your school days when you'd take a wild fancy to a girl? I'm sure that you eventually made a connection, and I'm equally sure that eventually you were dumped—maybe she shot you down for someone else, maybe even your best mate. Can you remember how devastated you felt when that happened?

"Yes, I certainly can," Packie replied, with feeling.

"Well, just remember how desperately and absolutely alone you felt, right? Now multiply that feeling of loss and emptiness by at least a thousand times, and you'll understand a little of what Amanda Morrison was feeling. Packie, Amanda Morrison really felt that there was nothing else she could do but end her life because, to her, her life had already ended, four days before she gave up her final breath to the sea."

They sat in silence for a few minutes, sipping their Guinness and allowing their thoughts to buzz around.

"How does this change things?" Packie asked

"Well," Starrett replied, "I feel it's got nothing to tell us about Moore's death."

"But?"

"But whoever crucified James Moore was indirectly responsible for Amanda's death."

"Which means that if it was Ivan Morrison who killed Moore, then he's also destroyed the thing he cherished most?" Packie offered.

"Not to mention saved himself a heck of a lot of embarrassment," Starrett replied, somewhat uncharitably.

"Are you going up to the Manse to inform Morrison?" Packie asked.

"Too late. When I radioed in the details to the Tower Houser, the major felt that it was only right that First Minister Morrison be informed immediately. I believe he's already been told. I would have liked to have done it myself to see how he reacted to the news. But fair play to the major, there are no flies on him; he'll have him well and truly sussed. He said to stop in at his house on the way home tonight for an update. So, Packie me boy, I'm afraid that's me for the night. I'm off."

o-O-o

But the night wasn't quite over for Starrett. He was in for two more surprises.

The first occurred immediately he arrived at the major's house.

"I think our friend Ivan Morrison is involved in the Moore murder some way or other," the major said, before taking a small sip of his throat-stripping poteen. "Either that or he's the most anal-retentive man I've ever met. I'd love to see what kind of relationship he had with his mother."

Starrett had an inkling that this was the same potato-brewed poteen that the gardaí had confiscated from a farm up on Gortahork, after a woman reported that her husband had gone blind while drinking the mountain brew. On further investigation, it transpired that the man's sight was miraculously restored the moment the woman had put her clothes back on again. Starrett had only to wet his lips with the stuff to realise he'd much prefer to drink razor blades.

The major's house was safely hidden away in the centre of a budding forest on the water's side of the Ramelton–Rathmullan road, about a mile and a half before the latter. From the outside, it was a bit of a dog's dinner, thanks to the various extensions and rooms which had been added on over the years. The interior was a different matter entirely, with antique wood panelling, a smattering of oil paintings, World War II memorabilia, antique furniture and a sweeping wooden staircase that took the breath away. The major's study, his pride and joy, overlooked the Swilly. Three walls were floor-to-ceiling bookcases, centred around the sturdy wooden door. The fourth had been knocked through to make a huge window. Starrett and the major had positioned themselves in grand leather chairs close to the glass wall and were contemplating the far side of the lough, as they focused on the poteen.

"Oh, bejeepers, Major, how on earth do you drink this stuff?" Starrett asked, shaking his head violently from side to side.

"After a time the warm flush that rises inside you starts to grow very darn pleasant."

"Yes, I believe paint stripper has a similar effect, but I'm not sure you'd want to subject your body to it."

"I'll tell you this and I'll tell you no more, Starrett. It's the one medicine, the only medicine, with the power to make me forget how bad my back hurts sometimes," the major said with a sigh, as he helped himself to another generous sip. "Anyway, our friend Morrison . . . I visited him, as you do, to inform him of his bereavement. And I will admit, Starrett, that even after all these years, it's not something I'm terribly good at. I always feel, especially as I seldom know the deceased, I'm not being as visibly regretful as I feel I should be. But anyway, I go to see the first minister. He opens the door. I tell him I have some grave news for him. He invites me in. He is more preoccupied with entertaining me than he is to discover the nature of the grave news I have come to deliver. He pours me a large whiskey. I sit him down and tell him what I've needed to tell—that Amanda took her own life. I spare him some of the gory details, as you do; all the time I'm watching him like a hawk. He blows some air through his lips. He looks at me. He appears to me as if he's trying to work out from me how he should be reacting, but the look on his face is saying, 'Oh, what a stupid girl!' It's a look usually reserved for one's servants. He certainly doesn't break down. He doesn't even shed a tear, for goodness sake. But then, Starrett, I bet you'll never guess what he says to me?"

Starrett grimaces in preparation.

"He said, 'Well, it's good luck she's not a Catholic. At least we'll be able to bury her in our graveyard.' Can you believe that?"

"Some people do behave strangely; it's a way of delaying their grief."

"I know, I know, but this was something different. I mean *entirely* different!"

"Did he make any reference to James Moore?"

"Not at all," the major barked, sipping a little too deeply and paying dearly for it. Starrett had to thump him several times on the back.

When his coughing stopped, the major, in a slightly higher register, asked, "Is your money on the first minister, Starrett?"

"Does that mean yours is?"

"He's a cold fish that one, I'll tell you. Something in his personality doesn't quite add up. You know, if you told me tomorrow that he'd murdered James Moore and his wife, I wouldn't be shocked."

Starrett set his glass of poteen down on the major's coffee table. Ninety-five per cent of Starrett's potent poteen remained in the glass. The inspector had given up when even the vapours of the drink had made his eyes water. He said, "I'd better be heading home. Dr Aljoe was hoping to give me the autopsy report tonight."

Major Newton Cunningham took a long considered look at Starrett before saying, "Ah, yes, the beautiful doctor. If I were a younger man and the current Mrs Newton Cunningham weren't around, aye well, there's a woman who'd certainly tempt me. Mind you, the thing with these classically beautiful women is that they don't tend to remain on the open market for very long, if you know what I mean. I'll tell you this and then you can be on your way . . . If I were you, I'd be over there in person to pick up those autopsy results."

Starrett left the major with his bloodshot eyes staring deep into his rapidly disappearing glass of poteen.

o-O-o

Starrett wasn't Major Newton Cunningham, and so he immediately returned to his own house. There were already three messages on his answering machine that had come from the aforementioned Dr Sam Aljoe. He rang her back straight away.

"Oh, it's you, I've been expecting your call," she said in a sleepy voice.

"Sorry it's so late," Starrett replied, lighting up his first ciggy of the day, a ciggy he'd stolen earlier from the ever-diminishing stash Packie Garvey was carrying for him.

"I'm afraid I've more sad news for you, Starrett," Aljoe began.

"Oh?" Starrett said, taking a long and rewarding drag of the cigarette.

"Starrett, are you smoking?" asked the doctor.

"Yes."

"I hate to kiss men who smoke, Starrett."

Now there's a deterrent, if ever there was one, Starrett thought, immediately stubbing out the barely smoked cigarette.

"There, it's gone," he said.

As the thought of kissing crossed Starrett's mind, Maggie Keane's image flashed in there as well, vying for attention.

"Amanda Morrison was pregnant when she took her life," Dr Aljoe said after a pause.

"Ah, Jeez, Sam," Starrett said.

"And Starrett, I'm afraid there's more."

"No?"

"I'm pretty sure that James Moore wasn't the father of the baby."

Chapter Thirty-Nine

"RIGHT," STARRETT ANNOUNCED, raising his voice a decibel or two. It was the following morning, Tuesday, four days since the body of James Moore had been discovered, and Starrett and his team were gathered in the incident room on the first floor of Tower House. "Let's see what we've got here, and let's see if we can make any sense of this."

He strolled over to the notice board, which pretty much replicated the information he'd just been writing up in his crime book that very morning.

"We've basically ruled Mr Owen Bonner out of this one, have we?" Major Newton Cunningham asked. The major was resting against a radiator between two floor-to-ceiling windows that overlooked Gamble Square. His eyes were totally clear, the poteen-induced bloodshot gone, maybe not long gone, but gone nonetheless.

"Well, we've ruled out a possible motive on his part," Starrett replied. He realised that he was behaving like a mother, treating his suspects as children and not really wanting them to go.

"So, who have we in the frame now, then?" the major asked, shifting around to find a more comfortable position on the radiator.

"Well, we're checking out Daniel McGuinness, with or without Nora Moore, and we're checking out First Minister Ivan Morrison. That's really it for the moment, I'm sorry to say."

"Last night's news must put Morrison at the top of the list, though." Nuala Gibson said. "His trophy wife was pregnant with his trophy-baby, and here was a mere carpenter in the process of running off with mother and baby. How far along was the pregnancy?"

"Three months," Starrett replied.

"Are we sure Ivan Morrison was the father?" the major enquired. "He doesn't seem the type to me."

"No," Starrett replied. "All we know for certain is that Amanda was pregnant and that James Moore was not the father. I think the first thing we need to do is ascertain if Ivan Morrison was."

"Well, who else could it be?" Nuala Gibson offered, sounding shocked. "Surely Amanda Morrison wasn't having an affair with James Moore *and* sleeping with someone else at the same time?"

"I would doubt it," Starrett said, "but let's not speculate. Let's first check out if Ivan is the man. Also, let's not forget that Ivan claims he didn't know about his wife's affair until after James Moore's body was discovered, which, if true, would also wipe out his motive. All of which takes us back to the unlikely pair of Dan McGuinness and Nora Moore, which I'm not entirely convinced of."

"Starrett, let's not throw away the only crumbs left on our plate. At least not until the next meal arrives," the major said, looking worried.

"True, true," Starrett replied, searching around for some notes he'd brought in with him. "I've been thinking about the crucifixion. I think we're missing something here. I've been trying to discover if there is anything we could learn about James Moore's death from what the Gospels tell us about Jesus Christ's crucifixion and from various reference books."

Starrett could see he'd captured everyone's attention, including his own. He ran through the facts, as he knew them:

Jesus Christ had been arrested in the early hours of the morning.

His first punishment was from a soldier, who beat Jesus across the face for not answering the high priest Caiphus' questions.

The palace guards then blindfolded Jesus and asked him to identify them as they paraded past him.

Each soldier, in turn, spat on Jesus and hit him across the face.

Early the following morning, Jesus, battered, bruised, dehydrated and exhausted from a sleepless night, was taken to the court in the Fortress Antonia, which was the seat of government of Judea, to face Pontius Pilate.

Procurator Pilate really wanted nothing to do with the whole affair.

He sent Jesus across to Herod Antipas, the Governor of Judea.

Jesus suffered no further mistreatment at the hands of Herod, who immediately returned Jesus to Pontius Pilate.

Pilate had misread the mob and thought that they would have been satisfied with the beatings and humiliation Jesus had received thus far, but the ugly mob protested that Pilate was not doing his job properly by defending Caesar against the pretender who, some say, was claiming to be the King of the Jews.

Pilate could resist the mob no longer, and eventually, some say reluctantly, he gave Jesus up to be whipped and sentenced him to death by crucifixion, literally washing his hands of the whole matter

Jesus was stripped of his clothes, his hands tied to a post above his head and he was then whipped by a Roman Legionnaire using a flagrum—a short whip consisting of several leather thongs with two small balls of lead attached near the end of each.

Jesus was whipped about the shoulders, back and legs. The flagrum would at first cut the skin only, but soon the lead balls would cut deeper, drawing blood. Eventually blood would start to spurt wildly when some arteries would be severed.

The centurion in charge would have ensured that the whipping stopped before Jesus was in fatal danger.

Jesus was untied. His back would have been an absolute mess of skin and blood, but before He had a chance to pass out, the Romans put a robe across His shoulders, placed a stick in His hands and pressed down on His head a crown woven of long thorns. Again there was copious bleeding.

When the Romans tired of mocking and repeatedly striking Jesus, the robe was torn from His back, the stick removed from His hand, and He was beaten across the head, gouging the thorn crown even deeper into his scalp. And then he was whipped again.

Then, to comply with Jewish customs, He was allowed to dress in his own clothes.

The cross was tied across His shoulders, and He and two thieves and the Roman crucifixion procession, headed by a centurion, made their way slowly to his place of execution.

By this time, Jesus was obviously much too weak to carry his cross, and He fell under the weight of it. The rough wood of the cross crushed into His body, causing further damage. The Romans, now tiring of their sport and growing impatient, selected a strong-looking North African, Simon of Cyrene, to carry the cross, with Jesus barely stumbling along behind.

It was a 650-yard journey from Pilate's Fortress Antonia to Golgotha.

Jesus was offered, and refused, wine mixed with myrrh, which would have acted as a painkiller of sorts.

Simon was ordered to place the cross on the ground, and Jesus was thrown on top of it.

The legionnaire hammered a nail through each of Jesus' wrists and deep into the wood.

The cross was next raised, then both feet were nailed together, again the nail going deep into the wood.

The legionnaire would have been careful neither to stretch the hands to the extreme nor to nail the feet to the cross with the legs fully stretched. He would have left some "give" in both sets of limbs.

Jesus Christ was now crucified.

His body weight would slowly have pulled him down, and this would have caused excruciating pain. He would have reacted to this, His brain totally overloaded because of the unbearable pain, by involuntarily pushing himself up with His feet.

All this would have done would have been to cause Him even greater pain.

Then cramp would have set in, and He would have been unable to push himself upwards. He could breathe in air, but He could not exhale. He would have fought with himself to steal one last breath. The carbon dioxide building up in the lungs and bloodstream would have caused the cramp to subside somewhat.

In spasms He would have been able to push himself upwards to steal a quick life-saving breath and exhale.

It was during this period that He uttered His seven final recorded sentences:

The first He said as he looked down and saw Roman soldiers throw dice for His garments: "Father, forgive them, for they know not what they do."

The second was to the thief, crucified beside him, who sought forgiveness: "Today thou shalt be with me in Paradise."

He then addressed his beloved apostle, John: "Behold thy mother." And then to John's mother: "Behold thy son."

For this fourth cry, He quoted the start of the 22nd Psalm: "My God, My God, why hast thou forsaken me?"

All the hours of pain he had endured thus far, all the twisting and turning on the cross and the continued damage this had done to his system eventually gave way to another, even greater, agony. He would have felt a crushing pain deep in His chest, as the membrane that surrounded His heart slowly filled with serum, which started to crush His heart.

Jesus was nearly dead. He had lost a critical amount of tissue. His heart was losing its struggle, and the tortured lungs were so desperate for gulps of air.

The drying tissues sent their flood of stimuli to the brain.

His fifth cry was, "I thirst."

A sponge soaked in cheap wine was raised on a lance to His lips. He didn't, or couldn't, take any.

"It is finished," He said, as the end neared.

After hours of agony He had one final surge; he tried to raise himself up using His feet, tearing them even more on the nail. He steadied himself, took a last breath and cried, "Father! Into Thy hands I commend my spirit."

"Just to make sure Jesus was dead," Starrett said in conclusion, "a legionnaire drove his lance up through His ribs and into His heart."

"Right barbaric lot, the Romans, weren't they?" the major said at the end of Starrett's summary. "Here we are 2,000 years later and people are still getting crucified. It's heartening to know how well civilisation is progressing."

"Just to think," Garda Casey said, "if there had been a different crowd there that day, perhaps he'd have got off with just the beating Pilate wanted to inflict."

"No," Gibson said in disagreement. "You can bet your bottom euro that even back in those days, there were spin doctors who had their plants in the crowd, ready for the appropriate moment."

"I saw a documentary about it a few months back," Packie Garvey said, "and they went back to Golgotha. People were scattered around the hill in twos and threes, outside their little tents, sitting around eating or what-have-you, and the commentator said that there were always people around the hill keeping vigil. I just wondered if there have been people sitting around on that same hill keeping vigil since the day Jesus was crucified."

"Maybe our murderer saw the same documentary," Starrett said. "How much detail did they show?"

"None of the gruesome stuff," Garvey replied. "It was more of a religious experience—like a pilgrimage. But they did say that the hill and all the surrounding hills would have been packed with people. It was apparently like some bizarre tourist attraction."

"But why would people be attracted to that?" Starrett asked, addressing himself as much as Garvey. "I mean, what's the attraction in looking at a human who has been reduced to nothing more than a chunk of meat. You don't see people queuing up outside Gormley's. Unless . . ."

Everyone was staring at Starrett now, as he stared out the window up towards the butcher's shop close to the bridge over the River Lennon.

"Maybe that's it . . ." Starrett continued quietly.

"Maybe what's it?" Major Newton Cunningham asked.

"It just might be nothing," Starrett said, starting to pack his papers away. "We're missing something here. Can you please go over all of the information we have again and then go over it one more time after that? There must be some name or maybe something else. Garda Gibson, you and I will pay another visit up to Babylon."

"Anything I can do?" the major asked, as people began to wander away.

"Well, maybe you could try Betsy Bell again. You had great success with her the first time."

"Splendid suggestion, Starrett. I can't think of a more pleasant way to spend my morning," the major said, rubbing his hands with enthusiasm.

Chapter Forty

ON THE WAY out of town, Starrett pulled into the drive of the Manse of the Second Federation Church.

Agga answered the door and advised the gardaí that First Minister Morrison had just finished breakfast and was out on his rounds.

"I do believe I left my hat in the dining room the last time I was here," Starrett said, drawing a puzzled look from Nuala Gibson. "Do you mind if I go and look for it?"

Agga and Nuala followed Starrett as he quickly nipped into the house and the dining room. He looked high and low and everywhere in between as Agga and Gibson looked on, Starrett entertaining them with a tale about how the Queen of Sheba was so beautiful that kings and princes came from all over the land just to try to win her heart. The Queen of Sheba loved many but stayed with none, and all of those who fell for her charms were tricked out of their treasures and wealth.

"It wasn't that any of them shouldn't have seen it coming. I mean, if only they'd managed to avert their eyes from her beautiful face for the briefest of seconds, they would surely have noticed her hairy legs and cloven hooves."

Agga raised her hand to cover her open mouth and then crossed herself, all the time staring at the inspector.

A few seconds later, Starrett and Gibson left the Manse, but minus Starrett's alleged lost hat. When they got back in the car, this time with

Nuala behind the wheel, Starrett produced a glass from inside his jacket. He held the glass gingerly between his thumb and forefinger before placing a clear evidence bag around it. In the bottom of the glass were the precious remains of Ivan Morrison's breakfast orange juice.

As Starrett and Gibson negotiated the tricky road into Letterkenny Starrett noted, with a degree of pride, that yesterday's rain had added to the richness of the green hills, valleys and waterways.

"Tell me this," Starrett said from his vantage point in the passenger seat. "Do you by any chance know Maggie Keane?" At the same time he held on to the glass inside the evidence bag.

If Gibson was surprised by this question, she didn't show it. "Yes, I know Maggie," she said, without the proverbial batting of an eyelid. "She went to school with my mam."

"What's your mother's maiden name?"

"McGann; her Christian name is . . ."

". . . Phyllis. Of course, Phyllis McGann," Starrett said, his voice betraying the fact that if he'd been the one driving, they'd probably have ended up in the schuck. "So, you're Phyllis' daughter? Unbelievable. I went to the same school as them both."

"I know," Nuala Gibson said, her tone very matter of fact.

"How the devil is Phyllis?" Starrett said, wanting to close this conversation but needing to find a subtle way to do so.

"Yeah, she's good, she's got her health . . ."

"And a daughter who's showing great promise in the gardaí. Who'd have thought? Has Phyllis met young Francis Casey yet?" Starrett asked, inching away from his troubled waters, but happily leaving Nuala out there swimming in the middle of them.

"Not yet, but Francis met Maggie, though."

This shut Starrett up good and proper.

Luckily enough, a few minutes later they arrived at Letterkenny General Hospital. This time Starrett walked straight through to Sam Aljoe's office.

"Ah, Starrett, it's yourself, as the local nurses in the hospital have a habit of saying. Do you always walk around with a glass of OJ, or should I feel privileged?"

"Ah, this," Starrett replied, nodding in the direction of the glass he was raising to shoulder height. "Tell me this, Doctor, how long will it take you to tell me if the person who was using this glass is the father of Amanda's unborn child?"

"Shouldn't take too long," she said, slipping on a surgical glove and taking the bag from Starrett. "Tell you what," she continued. "Why don't I take Garda Gibson here through to the lab and introduce her to young Adhemar McIvor. She can stay with him and monitor him conducting the necessary tests. He's a bit of a whizz-kid."

"Good," Starrett said, "because I've got some rather unpleasant business about Moore's remains to discuss with you."

Starrett waited in Aljoe's shoebox-sized office.

When she returned, Starrett wasn't entirely sure, but he had a hunch that the doctor had enjoyed a freshening-up visit somewhere or other on her return journey. He had to admit that she did look stunning, really stunning, as in "pretty as a picture". Starrett couldn't work out if he was just being pernickety, but he suddenly had a thought that Maggie Keane looked the way she looked, whereas Samantha Aljoe was made up to look the way she looked. Was he merely rising above his station by thinking he had a choice of these two amazing women?

Dr Aljoe sat down at her desk and swung her chair around to face him. They were so close, their knees were in danger of touching. No wonder she'd suggested they met in the Coffee Dock the first day.

"OK," Starrett said. "I think I've found a possible reason why James Moore was crucified."

"What?"

"My problem was that I was getting too preoccupied with the religious implications of the crucifixion. I started to fear that two thieves were also going to turn up nailed to a tree somewhere. I even considered looking at James Moore's father's life. I was trying to figure out if Moore had been crucified to save Amanda Morrison's soul."

"Because Jesus was crucified so that all the world could be saved?"

"Something like that, yeah," Starrett replied, trying not to get too bogged down in the details now that he was trying to leave that theory behind. "You see, when you're young, you're taught that Jesus Christ was crucified on a cross with two thieves so that all mankind could be saved, so we could all go to heaven. Right?"

"Right."

"And the pictures that accompany the scriptures are of this man on

a cross, usually with a crown of thorns on his head and a few droplets
of blood, but always with a look of compassion on his face. It's like he's
saying, 'OK, Father, if you must, I don't mind, just as long as you're
sure that we'll save mankind.' There's a nail through each palm, and
another through both his feet and, again, there's but a few drops of
blood been spilt. He's usually backlit with this powerful beam of light,
which acts as some kind of halo around his head. And the reason for
all of this is so that we don't frighten the children when we're retelling
the story. But the reality is somewhat different. I realised, when I was
discussing the facts of a real crucifixion with my team, that the scene
was more likely to be the totally brutal annihilation of a human
being . . ."

"Just like we discovered at the Second Federation Church with
James Moore," Dr Aljoe offered.

"Exactly." Starrett agreed and continued, "Jesus, following his time
of punishment on the cross, would have been totally unrecognisable.
He would have looked more like a carcass in a butcher's shop than the
bearded gentleman he'd been forty-eight hours previously."

"So, you're saying that the person who crucified James Moore was
trying to make sure we wouldn't recognise him?"

"No," Starrett replied, but paused for a second to consider this as
a possibility. "What I'm saying is that perhaps we should consider that
this murder wasn't part of a master plan. What if someone with an axe
to grind met up with James in the early hours of the morning, just as
he was leaving Amanda Morrison's bed? This person started fighting
with James, and the fight got out of control. Maybe it ended when
James just didn't get up, following one of the punches. The boyo in
question, following some time of panic, calmed down, started to think
this through, and realised that his evidence was all over James, so he
orchestrated the crucifixion, complete with side-show, purely and
simply to hide the signs of the original fight."

"OK, that makes sense to me," Aljoe said. "So what you want to
know from me is: did any of this show up in the autopsy?"

"That's the sixty-four million dollar question."

"Well, if that was the plan, Starrett, it certainly was very effective."

"Meaning?"

"Meaning that James Moore was in such a sad state it would be impossible to tell which of his injuries killed him. I can tell you this, though: with the amount of blood spilt on the floor up around the pulpit of the Second Federation Church, James Moore was still alive when he was nailed to the cross. I don't know how strong his heart would have been, but it was still pumping blood."

"Which kind of blows my theory right out of the water?"

"Well, perhaps and perhaps not. Perhaps it started out as a fight and escalated into something else. Tell me this, Starrett, are you saying this because you've discovered someone with bruising around their fists which would suggest that such a fight took place."

Starrett took a moment to consider his five suspects.

"Actually, no." He sighed. "Which kind of shoots my theory down in an even larger pile of flames?"

At which point, Nuala Gibson and Adhemar McIvor turned up at Dr Aljoe's door.

Gibson offered Starrett a resigned smile and said, "Well, it would appear that First Minister Ivan Morrison is not the father of his wife's child, either."

"Then who could it be?" Dr Aljoe asked, studying Adhemar's findings.

"Ask me one on Mary from Dunloe," Starrett said.

"Who's Mary from Dunloe?" Aljoe asked.

"Now that is a good question," Starrett said. "Let me get back to you on that one as well."

Chapter Forty-One

"LET'S HEAD STRAIGHT on over to Nora Moore's," Starrett said, as soon as he and Gibson were back in the car. This time he sat behind the wheel and they bypassed Ramelton by taking the N56 to Kilmacrenan, over the remote Loughsalt Mountains, past Glen Lough, skirting Carrigart, and down into Downings.

They drove pretty much in silence. Following his return from London, Starrett had sworn to himself that he would never ever take the Donegal countryside for granted again, so he tended to prefer to drive in silence, savouring his journeys through the spectacularly dramatic surroundings. He also liked to use his time to run through the facts of his cases. The James Moore case was proving to be one of those cases where the more he learned, the greater the mystery became.

As they drove into Downings, he chose to distract himself from the case in hand by viewing some of the beautiful young ladies they passed.

"Tell me this, Nuala, and tell me no more," he said, breaking his silence. "You see that girl there?"

"What, the one with the tight jeans and the ponytail?"

"That's the one. Now, you see the way she's walking, like swaggering?"

"Yeah?" Gibson replied hesitantly.

"Hopefully this isn't a question which will have me up in front of the auld tribunal," Starrett said, "but can you tell me if she's walking with that particular swagger because she has a ponytail, or if she has a ponytail because she walks with that swagger in the first place?"

"Well, it's easy," Gibson replied. "She walks with that swagger so the cars will stop and she can get to the other side of the road."

"Fair play to you, Nuala," Starrett chuckled, as they pulled up at the Moore house. "Right, here we are."

Nora Moore seemed to be maintaining better spirits. She took Starrett and Gibson through to the kitchen and instructed Chris to make tea and sandwiches for the two detectives.

"When you were here last, I seemed to forget that you're actually on our side," Nora said, sidling up to her son. "It took my first-born here to point out to me the error of my ways." She briefly hugged her son, who gave her an "Oh, mam" kind of shrug. "Have you made any further progress?"

"Well, did you hear . . . ?"

"You mean about poor Mrs Morrison? Oh, my goodness, it's all people are talking about, even if they go all quiet when I come around them. Did she really kill herself?"

"Yes," Starrett sighed. "It seems pretty cut and dried."

"Very sad; God will never bless her soul now. She must have been at her wits' end."

"Nora, can we talk to you about the last time you saw Jimmy?" Starrett asked suddenly.

"Yes, of course," she replied immediately.

There was something about Nora Moore that Starrett couldn't quite put his finger on. It wasn't that she was exactly blossoming in the wake of her husband's untimely death; far from it, in fact. It was more that there was an inner resolve and strength Starrett hadn't expected following their first meeting. Starrett noticed that Chris followed her every move. Perhaps he was the power behind her strength.

"We all sat down to dinner, didn't we, Chris?"

"Yes, we did, Mam," he dutifully replied, bringing Nuala Gibson over a cup of tea. He then offered her milk and sugar before repeating the same process with Starrett, who asked, "Do you know where he went after dinner?"

"He just went out," Nora replied. "Didn't he, Chris?"

"Yes, Mam," Chris replied, adding, "I mean, there wasn't an atmosphere or anything. Mam and Dad weren't arguing or anything like that."

"No, no, we weren't fighting," Nora said, picking up her son's thread. "Jimmy and I had gone beyond that. Well, we never really argued, to be honest. Confrontation wasn't really Jimmy's thing. He had his own opinion, he knew mine was possibly different, but he'd never try and persuade me to his way of thinking. He believed in live and let live. You know, Chris and I were talking about this last night. Jimmy was a good man and a great father, and I know you're meant to react in a certain way when your husband is cheating. You know, string him up by his short-and-curlies. But, with hindsight, it would have been good if Jimmy could have found some peace and contentment in his life, and if Mrs Morrison was the woman he could have enjoyed that with . . . Goodness, maybe I'd have been able to find some peace for myself. Jimmy and I really were just the wrong people for each other. It's as simple as that. We'd never have married in today's society. We'd have had our fling and gone our separate ways. Mind you, we did bring three wonderful children into the world, and I'll respect Jimmy's memory until the day I die, if only for that."

"OK," Starrett said. "When you told me your husband just went out, did you think he was going out to his workshop, or to the pub, or around the corner to a mate?"

"No," it was Chris who was to reply. "I remember hearing his van door close and hearing him drive off."

"Where's the van now?"

"I don't know. You know, that's weird," the wife and mother replied. "I haven't even thought about that van for a second since . . ."

"Chris, what kind of vehicle was it?" Starrett asked quickly.

"It was an old, light-green VW van," Chris replied.

"And the number?" Gibson asked.

"GE 580 T," both Moores recited.

"So," Starrett continued, as Gibson took a note of the registration number, "did you think he was going out on a job?"

"The thing about my father, Inspector, was that he didn't really consider carpentry to be work, so it wouldn't have been unusual for him to get up from the dinner table and go back to a job. He wasn't a great drinker; he wasn't big on the telly. We wouldn't have thought much about it."

"And did you manage to think of anyone he might have been making the pulpit out in his workshop for?" Starrett asked.

"Well, now, funny you should ask, but I was searching through my father's papers, and I came across this order form. It was actually commissioned by L'Opera."

"The new disco in Letterkenny?"

"Apparently," Chris replied.

"OK, we're nearly done," Starrett said. "I've just got one more question: Mrs Moore, did your husband have a habit of leaving his ring off when he was out working? I understand some builders and carpenters do, you know. Apparently rings can get caught in nails or splinters and be quite dangerous."

"No, Jimmy never took the ring off from the day we were married. It was quite tight."

"Could you describe it to me, please?" Starrett asked, proving that a garda's final question is rarely the last.

"Yes, of course," Nora replied. "It was made of silver, with a small Celtic shield on it; you know, the one with the three interlocking eternal circles of life?"

o-O-o

"How come we've not come across the VW van?" Nuala asked, as they headed back towards Ramelton.

"You'd have to say that was poor work on our part," Starrett admitted, "Particularly with the distinctive Northern Irish registration plate."

"Shall we pop in and see Dan the Man again?"

"I do need to," Starrett admitted, "but I haven't learned enough since the last time to be in a position to ask him any more meaningful questions, so let's leave it for now and head straight back to Tower House.

Twenty minutes later, they were back in Ramelton.

"Just in time to catch a quick brecky in Steve's before the school crowd," Starrett said.

"I think I'll pass on that one," Nuala said, hopping out of the car.

"What, another morning of mineral water and an apple or orange for you and Francis?"

She stopped in her tracks and slowly sat back into the car again, leaving the door open.

"I'd been meaning to have a quick work with you about that, Inspector."

"Oh dear, this sounds official," Starrett said, putting the gear stick into the neutral position.

"Hopefully not tribunal official," Nuala Gibson said, testing her words the way one might test ice. "If Garda Casey and myself were to have . . . you know, a relationship, would you be OK with it?"

"Would I be OK with it or would the Garda Síochána be OK with it, do you mean?"

"I'd settle for it being OK with you, as my senior."

"I'm totally fine with it, Nuala. I believe the official point would be that they don't encourage internal relationships in case it might ever compromise you in the line of duty."

"I know. I've been thinking about that, and I think we can avoid putting ourselves in that position."

"So you're convinced about Francis then, Nuala?"

"I think so. It's just that he doesn't say a lot."

"As a law-enforcement officer, you don't really need to say a lot more than Clint Eastwood ever did. Aye, and he proved to be quite effective, didn't he?" Starrett said.

Gibson caught a fit of the giggles. "Hardly the first comparison that would have come to my mind, but you know, Dirty Frankie, I could probably learn to live with it."

"Aye, and then as Francis often proves," Starrett went on, "just because he's not saying a lot doesn't mean he's not thinking. I'll tell you this, Nuala: I'll take a thinker over a talker in my team any day of the week."

Starrett just wished someone would grant *him* absolution when it came to his own affairs of the heart.

Chapter Forty-Two

STARRETT WAS ENJOYING his breakfast when by happy coincidence who should walk into Steve's Café but Sergeant Packie Garvey.

As you're done with your slim pickings there," Starrett said, nodding at Garvey's tea-mug, "I fancy another wee visit to our man Colm Donovan. Just to see if anything else has sprung to his mind."

When they arrived at Donovan's yard, there was no sign of Digger, the albino dog. A woman on a ladder was cleaning the outside of the kitchen window.

"Is Colm around?" Starrett asked, walking across the yard.

"No, he's not."

"I'm Inspector Starrett and this is Sergeant Garvey."

"Look, sorry about that," she said, stepping down from the ladder and drying her hands on her apron. "It's just plain stupid trying to clean windows with J-Cloths. It's a total waste of time. I've sent Colm down to Whoriskey's to get me some chamois. He's always helping himself to my stuff. Ah, here he comes," she said as a finely tuned engine could be heard zooming up the road. "Watch out, he's like a bear with a sore paw at the minute."

He hopped out of the car without seeing Starrett and Garvey, glanced at the woman and flung a pack of fawn-coloured material at her. The lightweight pack decelerated so quickly that it was barely moving when it hit her on the arm and dropped to the ground.

"Don't be getting shirty with me. You took my last couple," she said good-naturedly, then swung around in the direction of the gardaí. "Gentlemen, have you met my bad-tempered husband?"

Donovan's head swung around at twice the speed of the rest of his body.

"Jeez, Inspector, I didn't see you there. Sorry about that," Colm said, forcing a smile across his stony face. "Women, they'd have you fecking demented, wouldn't they?"

Garvey opted for words of solidarity, while Starrett held his own council.

"So, have you locked up yer man yet?" Donovan asked, leading the two gardaí in the direction of the sheds at the opposite end of the yard, and out of his wife's hearing.

"And who would 'yer man' be?" Starrett asked.

"The first minister himself."

"And why would we be locking him up?" Starrett continued.

"Well, how's about you start off charging him with the murder of his wife?

"We now know Mrs Morrison committed suicide, Colm," Starrett replied quietly.

"Or she was murdered in a way that made it look like she committed suicide," Donovan suggested. "But if not that, then how's about for crucifying Jimmy Moore?"

"Give us an excuse," Starrett replied, keeping up the pace of the exchange.

"Jimmy was sleeping with the minister's wife."

"That's not an excuse; that's a possible motive," Starrett explained. "But he claims he wasn't aware of the affair until after Jimmy's body was found."

"Oh he does, does he?" Donovan mocked. "Is *that* what he claims?"

"It is," Packie confirmed.

"Well then, I can prove to you that he knew different," Donovan said. Opening a door of a corrugated-iron hut and using a dustbin incinerator to jam the door open, Donovan showed them in out of the sunlight.

The hut was a mess. It was obviously used to store things Donovan would most likely never ever need or use again in his entire life, but stuff that seemed too valuable to throw away: the shiny drum of a tumble dryer, for instance; a video machine; a television set with a screen coated with dust.

"Really, Colm," Starrett said, keeping his voice neutral. "And how can you prove that?"

"Simple one that," Colm said, removing the pack of Camels from the sleeve of his shirt. Starrett and Garvey waited while Donovan offered them each a cigarette, which they refused, lit his own, and took a deep drag. They watched him relax a little as the nicotine worked its way into his bloodstream.

Then he finally spoke: "You know how the first minister likes to think he's a bit of a whizz on the keyboards, and how he loves to compose?"

"Yeah," Starrett agreed. "I seem to remember someone telling us about that."

"Well, on the pretext of wanting to be able to record music from anywhere in the house, he had the entire house wired for sound."

"Right," Starrett replied, with an image in his head of Morrison on the toilet playing a keyboard and singing "Raindrops Keep Falling on My Head."

"A mate of mine who used to work for RTÉ did the work for him, and one of the rooms he wired for sound was the spare room upstairs."

Donovan looked first to Starrett, then to Garvey, and then back to Starrett, hoping the penny would drop.

"The spare room upstairs eventually became Mrs Amanda Morrison's room . . ."

"Right," Starrett replied. "And do you know if the system is still operative?"

"Still operative, and let's just say the first minister had been recording a different sort of music being played recently in his wife's bedroom."

"And where is all of this controlled from?" Starrett asked.

"From the first minister's office," Donovan replied, a bit of a sneer on his face. "There's a door in the wall just by his desk. It's not full height, which, of course, he doesn't need, does he now?" Donovan said, pausing for a laugh. "It looks more like the door to a cupboard, but the space is big enough for a piano, an organ, speakers and his recording set-up, which consists of a mixing-desk, tape recorders and what have you."

"Have you actually heard any of these recordings?" Starrett asked.

Donovan looked as if he were going to reply but thought better of it. Eventually he said, "Don't just take my word for it. Go and check it out for yourselves."

Chapter Forty-Three

THE FIRST MINISTER'S only apparent concession to his recent bereavement was that, when the gardaí came calling, he was dressed in a cassock.

Agga must have been off duty, because Morrison opened the Manse door himself.

"Ah, Inspector Starrett and . . ."

". . . Sergeant Packie Garvey," Starrett added.

"Come in, why don't you?" Morrison said, holding the door open wider, but still Starrett and Garvey had to do some serious breathing-in to squeeze past the first minister.

"Yes, I'd been hoping you'd call around again. Why don't you go on though to the living room?"

Starrett led the way, but instead of turning left after the grand wooden staircase, he turned right into Morrison's study, where he immediately took a seat and nodded to Garvey to do likewise.

"No, no, I meant the living room with the bay window, next to the study."

"This is fine for us, very cosy, First Minister. I love the way you've done it out, very creative," Starrett offered, speaking nineteen to the dozen. "Tell me, which artist painted this?"

Clearly Morrison was undecided about whether to insist on moving to the other room. Eventually he spoke: "It's by Charles McAuley. Have you ever heard of him?" He slipped into his swivel seat and spun around to face the painting.

"Never, no," Starrett replied. "Now, you said you'd been hoping to see me?"

"I was quite upset, Inspector, to discover that you knew the whereabouts of my wife, even though I didn't. In fact, it now becomes apparent that all the time you were asking me where she was, you already knew."

"Yes, but if *you'd* asked *me* if I knew where she was, I would have had to tell you; but as you didn't, I was under no obligation to do so. And, of course, we mustn't forget that your wife was quite keen to keep a low profile."

"Yes, that's all very well, Inspector, but something happened during her couple of days' isolation which drove her to take her own life, and I'd hate to think that it was your harassment of her."

"I can assure you, sir, that no such pressure was applied or implied, and that Mrs Betsy Bell was never too far away from your wife's side during any of our exchanges."

"Nonetheless, Amanda took her life," Morrison said, looking like a dog who'd fought hard for a bone and, having won it, wasn't going to let it go easily. "I'd like to ask you if she told you anything during your several exchanges that I should be aware of?"

"For instance?" Starrett asked.

"Oh, you know, anything of a personal nature," said Morrison.

"About you?"

"Yes, about me," the first minister replied, moving his tummy into a more comfortable position.

"Well, she did say a few things," Starrett began, noticing Morrison shoot Garvey a quick look. "But, I . . . erm, feel that I need to check out a few more details before I discuss them with you."

From the look on Morrison's face, Starrett realised in that split second what it must feel like to be a darts player who has just thrown three triple-twenties. Since his problem was that he'd thrown his darts totally blindfolded and hadn't a clue what target he'd hit, he hadn't a clue about which direction his questions should now take. Starrett rose out of his chair and walked across the study, pretending to want to take a closer look at the McAuley. At the last possible moment, he turned quickly to his left and turned the handle of the small door, at the same time remarking, "Oh, what have we here, then?"

By the time Morrison had realised what was happening, Starrett was in the studio area and had managed to find a light switch.

"Sorry, sorry, those are my private rooms. You must come out of there immediately," Morrison demanded from outside the door.

"What's this, all this studio stuff?" Starrett asked, ignoring his demand.

Morrison rushed in on Starrett and looked as if he were about to grab the inspector and physically remove him from the secret room. Garvey jumped up to restrain the first minister, who brushed the sergeant, who was no weakling, aside as if he were a piece of driftwood. Garvey went flying across the room and landed against a shelf beside Morrison's desk. The contents of the shelf—books, files, a container of pencils and pens, and a saucer containing loose change, a watch and some rings—went flying across the floor.

"*Get the feck out of here!*" First Minister Ivan Morrison roared, his baritone voice echoing back out into, and around, the hallway. "I'm warning you!"

Starrett ignored the warning and continued to search the names on the spines on the rows upon rows of white boxes crammed on to the shelves that lined the wall behind the mixing desk.

Out of the corner of his eye, Starrett could see Morrison commence a mad-bull rush at him. Morrison was going at such a speed that there was no way he was going to be able to stop until he ran into something. At the last possible moment, Starrett side-stepped to his left, and a split second after the displaced air whooshed past Starrett's face, Morrison crashed into the mixing desk, rolled over the top of it and landed on his head on the other side. His bulk and padding ensured that he was not badly injured, but equally his generous girth meant that he was stuck upside down between the desk and the rear wall. His little legs were still pedalling and he was grunting, heaving, huffing and puffing, but he just couldn't free himself.

"First Minister, is it OK if the sergeant and I have a look around this recording studio of yours?"

There was a lot of noise but nothing coherent coming from the other side of the desk.

"We'll take that as a yes, then," said Starrett.

"What exactly are we looking for?" Garvey asked.

"A tape box with an interesting title. Something like 'spare room recordings', 'Amanda', 'JM', or something similar, dated some time over the last three months," Starrett whispered.

Eventually they found three boxes with the legend "Dot & JM Late Night" and the dates varying from April to May of that year.

"Do you mind if we play these?" Starrett asked the mass of wobbling blubber.

"Sounds a bit like swearing to me, but as I know for a fact that a minister would never swear, I'll take it that you're complying with our request," Starrett said.

There was a lot more huffing and puffing from Morrison.

"Thanks for confirming that for us," Starrett said, and then, addressing his sergeant, "Packie, are you any good at working these tape recorders? I'm terrible with this sort of stuff."

"Yep," Packie replied, taking the spool from the first box and threading it into a small tape-machine built into the wall. "Hopefully we can play it on its own speaker, because with the minister here, I'm not going to be able to get at the controls properly."

Packie did manage to play the tape-recorder through its own tinny-sounding speaker. The tape hiss gave way to the sound of a door opening and closing quietly. The recording system must be sound activated, Starrett figured.

What the three of them heard was not the sound of two people hopping between the sheets and cheating on their spouses, but rather the sound of two people who obviously cared for each other deeply, physically expressing their feelings for each other. Once Starrett ascertained that the two participants were Mrs Amanda Morrison and Mr James Moore, he turned off the tape.

Starrett and Packie waited until Ivan Morrison's huffing and puffing stopped and he'd calmed down. In the meantime, they tidied up as best they could. Starrett replaced the fallen shelf Garvey had overturned. He picked up the books and repacked them on the shelf. He replaced the files on the end of the bookshelf near enough to where they'd been gathering dust several minutes previously. They picked up the numerous pencils and pens from the four corners of the floor and finally replaced the loose change and other items back on the saucer. These other bits included paper clips; cufflinks in the shape of a question mark (obviously for when Morrison was in an agnostic mood) a watch that had long since stopped, and three rings. One of the rings stopped Starrett in his tracks. It was silver, with a wee shield with a Celtic design of three circles engraved on it. Starrett checked the drawers in Morrison's desk until he found a brown 10x8-inch envelope. He placed the saucer and its entire contents in the envelope, sealed it, signed and dated the flap and then had Packie witness the signature and date.

"OK, First Minister, we'll help you up out of there if you promise to calm down."

"OK, OK, just get me out of here," came the muffled reply.

Starrett and his sergeant set about the monumental task.

After a few failed attempts, Starrett said, "There's as much chance of getting him out of there as there would be getting Quasimodo to stand up straight."

Morrison had hit the recording machine with such force that it had moved towards the wall as he tumbled over it. The simple solution to the problem was to move the recording equipment (and the minister), back from the wall, but at first it wouldn't budge. Finally Garvey figured out that the wheels had been locked in a stationary position. As soon as he'd established how to release the lock, the machine came away from the wall easily, and First Minister Morrison tumbled unceremoniously over the wall side of the recording equipment and fell in a heap on the floor.

Starrett helped him up and dusted down the now surprisingly meek and mild-mannered minister.

"Are you arresting me?" were his first coherent words for several minutes.

"If necessary I am, but in the meantime, I'm inviting you to accompany us to the garda station to help us with our enquiries," Starrett replied quietly.

"Can I go in my own car?"

"No," the Inspector replied firmly.

"Forgive them, Father, for they know not what they do," Morrison said, as he led the two gardaí out of the Manse.

Morrison insisted on sitting in the front of the car with Starrett on the short journey down to Gamble Square. He also insisted on following Garvey and Starrett into Tower House. As there were only a few people in the square at the time to witness the short procession— a few housewives out for the day's messages, and Colm Donovan on yet another run to Whoriskey's—there really wasn't much point to Morrison's visual statement. Yet everything Morrison did, he did for show, Starrett thought. But surely that couldn't have been his motivation for murdering his wife's lover?

Chapter Forty-Four

"DO I NEED my solicitor?"

The three men were seated in the interview room, a long, cold, purple-painted room, half of which was underground. The barred windows that overlooked Gamble Square were at ground level. Although the bars were mainly to keep out the local villains who seemed to think that there were always vast quantities of confiscated drugs on the premises at Tower House, they did serve to bring a certain degree of seriousness to most of the interviews that took place in there.

Garvey turned on the tape-recorder and announced, for the record, the names of those present.

"Well, First Minister Morrison, it's entirely your call if you would like your solicitor present," Starrett said, once the preliminaries had been taken care of. He was sitting at one end of the table, fingers laced behind his head. His feet were up on it, and he was using his legs to push his chair back to a precarious angle. "At this point, we're not charging you with anything. We just need to ask you a few questions."

"OK, let's proceed," Morrison replied, in a voice usually reserved for the pulpit. "However, I wish to advise you that I reserve my right to ask for my solicitor at any time I deem necessary." He was sitting directly across the table from Garvey, with Starrett to his right. Garvey had removed a notebook from the breast pocket of his uniform and was preparing to make notes.

"OK, First Minister," Starrett began, "do you remember when we first interviewed you, you told us that the first time you were aware of your wife's relationship with Mr James Moore was on the morning Mr Moore's body was found crucified in your church?"

"I do remember that, and I accept that's what I said," Morrison replied.

"Right, so," Starrett continued. "Would you now concede that the tape-recording we just listened to in your study in the Manse, the tape-recording you made of your wife and Mr James Moore in your wife's bedroom, proves that you were aware of your wife's relationship as early as April this year?"

"I accept that as well, Inspector."

"Do you accept that this now means you had a motive for murdering your wife's lover?" Starrett said.

Garvey made a fuss of finding a clean page in his notebook and had his pen poised at the ready for the first minister's answer.

"I accept that to be so," Morrison replied curtly.

"And do you realise that, in 1879, street lighting using electricity was used for the first time anywhere in the world, on a street in Newcastle, England, in fact?" Starrett asked.

"Sorry?" Morrison asked, looking totally confused.

"Well, I just wanted to be sure you were still with us," Starrett explained. "It's just that I'm not sure you realise the seriousness of the situation. Perhaps you do need your solicitor, Ivan."

"Inspector, I'm answering your questions truthfully," Morrison replied, looking a little flustered.

"Yes, but can you see where this is leading?"

"I can see where you might think it's leading, Inspector," Morrison replied. "Yes, I did lie to you when I told you I found out about my wife's indiscretions only on the morning of Moore's murder. I realise that, in your mind, the fact that I had prior knowledge that my wife was cheating on me gave me a motive for murdering Moore, and some men might have reacted in such a way. Quite simply, I am not one of those men. When Thomas Black, my loyal servant, came to me on Friday morning last, he felt he was doing me a favour by tipping me off as to what was happening. Of course, I pretended that it was the first I'd known of it. I am the first minister of the Second Federation Church, for heaven's sake. I have a status to maintain in the community; I have a responsibility to my flock. Of course, I knew what my wife was up to, and I knew about all of her other lovers as well. My wife and I had an agreement, and the agreement was that she would be discreet. And she was discreet. But then she fell for our carpenter. The rest, as they say, is history."

"OK, earlier this morning," Starrett started, "we removed several items we found in your study."

Morrison looked worried.

"We are now opening an evidence bag containing these items," Starrett said, making a noisy fuss of tearing open a brown envelope and taking particular care to keep the tear away from his and Garvey's signatures. He removed the white china saucer with its contents from the bag it which it had been placed after being fingerprinted. "Do you recognise this?"

"Yes, of course, it's from my study. I hate to have loose change in my pockets, so I always dump it on that saucer. When it fills up, I put it in one of the several charity boxes in our church."

"Is loose change all that's kept in the saucer?" Starrett asked.

"Of course not. You can see for yourself. There's a watch I've been meaning to have fixed, and there are my cuff-links and a couple of rings," Morrison replied in the voice of an intolerant parent.

"I'd ask you to confirm to me that all of these items are yours?" Starrett pushed.

"I've already acknowledged they are," Morrison said.

"Would you just humour me and put this ring on your finger, please?" Starrett said, handing him the ring with the Celtic shield on it. Testing for fingerprints had revealed it to be wiped cleaner than a nun's conscience.

Morrison took the ring and then dropped it back on to the saucer as if it had burnt him.

"That's not mine," Morrison snapped. "It's obviously too small for my hand. Look, I said a couple of rings, and here are the couple I was referring to."

Morrison took the other two rings and showed that they fitted on to his finger.

"So who does the other ring belong to?" Starrett asked.

"I don't know. It's certainly not mine!"

"I know that because I suspect that this ring belonged to Mr James Moore," Starrett said.

Morrison recoiled into his chair with such a force that it appeared he'd been smacked across the face.

"It can't be! It can't possibly be. What was it doing in my study?"

"That's *exactly* what we'd like to know, First Minister," Starrett replied.

"You planted it in my study; that's what happened. You're trying to plant evidence on me!" Morrison shouted, now totally losing control.

"Well, you've already admitted to us that you've lied about having prior knowledge of your wife's affair. What's to say that you are not lying to us about this?"

"You think I'm going to leave anything as incriminating as that lying about my house for all to see?"

"Well, let's be fair here, Ivan, you didn't exactly leave it in full public view. In fact, one could say that you went out of your way to hide it. You hid it in your secret den, the same secret place you used to spy on your wife," Starrett said.

This time Morrison didn't reply.

"Did you lie to us about anything else?" Starrett asked.

"Perhaps 'lie' is too strong a word, Inspector. Shall we just say that I was less than forthcoming with information when you enquired if I knew of any other men Amanda was having an affair with."

"OK, Ivan, how about you be a wee bit more forthcoming with us now?" Starrett asked.

"Oh, you know, there was a lecturer from Queen's University who she went out with for a time; a television presenter for the BBC in Belfast; then a TD from Dublin. She seemed to concentrate on professionals, people who had as much to lose as she did if the affair were discovered. That was perfect for me really; as I say, discretion was all I was asking for. Then she seemed to develop a taste for a bit of rough and, what was worse, a bit of rough that lived on our doorstep."

"You mean James Moore."

"Well, Moore wasn't her first bit of local rough," Morrison said, seeming more comfortable with this line of questioning.

"Oh, and who was the first?" Starrett asked, wondering if even an obvious snob like Morrison could be referring to Owen Bonner as a bit of rough.

"That would have been a local builder called Colm Donovan."

"You're sure about that, First Minister?" Starrett asked. The wind had totally departed from his sails.

"Sure about it?" Morrison snapped. "I've got hours of tapes to prove it, and they make the tapes you just eavesdropped on sound like kindergarten tea-parties by comparison, which incidentally is why you didn't find them on your recent raid of the Manse."

Chapter Forty-Five

S TARRETT LEFT THE basement and went straight out for a breath of fresh air. He wasn't surprised to see the very same Colm Donovan sitting across the square in his car, making a production out of reading the *Donegal News*. Starrett started walking towards the opposite pavement in a direction that would take him right past Donovan's car. He passed Eamonn Friel's, the mobile barber's, on the way, and just as he was about to pass Donovan he made a fuss over spotting him.

"Ah, Colm, didn't expect to see you again so soon."

"Aye, just in for a bit of a trim and a read of the auld paper. Anything to get a bit of a break from the wife; you know what it's like," Donovan said, starting to fold up the paper noisily.

Starrett leaned over the car, his left arm resting on the roof.

"Thanks a million for that tip-off on First Minister Morrison, by the way," Starrett said. "We found the recording equipment just where you said we would. You'll be happy to hear that we also found a few other bits of incriminating evidence as well. Packie's in there right now, questioning the first minister."

"Aye, no bother, no bother at all," Donovan said. "Er, has he pleaded guilty yet?"

"Not as yet, but with all the circumstantial evidence we've collected, I'm not sure we're going to need the auld confession. He can save that for his maker, can't he?"

"Aye, you're right there, but it's a sorry auld mess though, isn't it?" Donovan said.

Just then, a proud housewife with her recently scalped and severely embarrassed son walked out of the back of the mobile barber's van.

"Right, I'm up next," Donovan said, as he finished folding the paper into four and throwing it on to the seat beside him.

Starrett opened Donovan's car door for him and walked him over to the barber's. Starrett followed him up the steps, but stayed leaning against the doorframe as Donovan strolled over to take a seat.

"Aye, just a little bit off the back and sides," Donovan instructed. "Leave the top as it is."

"Right, we're to leave the piebald bit for the experts, are we, Colm?"

"Ach, aye," Donovan said submissively as the barber wrapped a towel around his neck, covered the towel with a Royal Blue cape and began to clip away.

"Right then, Colm, I'm off. I'll leave you with one bit of advice," Starrett said, removing a pen from his top pocket. "Never criticise your barber's football team."

They all had a good chuckle at that, and Starrett finished writing something on a piece of paper he'd unearthed from one of his pockets. Walking towards Donovan and the barber, he said, "Colm, here's the number of my direct line over in the station, just in case anything else comes to you on our boyo indoors. You'll give us a shout, won't you?"

Starrett fumbled with the pen as he was trying to reposition it in his top pocket. The pen dropped to the floor behind Donovan's back and close to the barber's feet. As he hunkered down to retrieve it, he discreetly grabbed as much of Donovan's freshly cut hair—some with the roots still intact, proving that the comb is mightier than the scissors—between thumb and bent forefinger as he could.

In a matter of a minute, Starrett was racing up the steps of Tower House. He blagged an envelope from the desk sergeant and placed the valuable hair inside. Then he rushed upstairs and, within another three minutes, he was in his car and speeding along the Letterkenny Road with Sergeant Garvey and Garda Casey not too far behind in a garda van.

They tore along the road just inside the 10 per cent over the official speed limit they were legally allowed. Just past the Silver Tassie, they hung a quick right, pulled into Donovan's yard and drove straight across to the corrugated-iron shed. Starrett hopped out and pointed to the dustbin-shaped domestic incinerator.

At this point, Mrs Donovan came running out the back door to see what all the fuss was about.

"What's the problem, Packie?" Mrs Donovan shouted. "What's going on here?"

"Mrs Donovan, I'm afraid we have to confiscate the auld incinerator," Starrett said. "Sure, you know it's illegal to burn any domestic stuff in your garden these days."

"Aye, well, take it then; it's no loss to me. The soot plays havoc with the clothes on the line when I does me washing."

"Right then," Starrett replied quickly. "Thanks for the permission."

As the garda convoy pulled out of Donovan's yard, the van hung a left into Ramelton and Starrett took a right towards Letterkenny.

Chapter Forty-Six

"IT's YOU AGAIN," Dr Aljoe said, welcoming Starrett into her tiny office. "People will be starting to talk. My only problem is that we're not really giving them anything to talk about *yet*."

"I've got a deal to offer you," Starrett said, taking the envelope from out of his inside pocket. "Could you please have your boy genius Adhemar check and see if the owner of this hair is the father of Amanda Morrison's unborn child?"

"Another potential father, you mean? That's three, Starrett. Unbelievable! That means Amanda was the recipient of four times the average sexual activity of this teddy-bear-shaped country of yours."

"Four eh? Which means that one in four . . ."

"Exactly! Starrett, I can do the mathematics as well. One in four never knows the pleasure."

"And the other side of the deal is, while Adhemar is busy on that, I'll take you to lunch."

"Well now, how could a girl refuse such an offer? Just give me a minute to deliver this to the lab. I'll freshen up, and then I'll be right with you."

When she returned ten minutes later, she'd freshened up and *how*. Starrett knew at that very moment that he would probably come to regret the conversation he was determined to have with Samantha Aljoe over lunch.

Five minutes later, they were in a busy Yellow Pepper. The main room of the friendly restaurant was packed, so they had to take a table for two in the back annexe, which was kind of OK because it was more private in there.

"We seem to have taken a step backwards, some time between our second date and you visiting me in the lab with that half-drunk glass of orange juice you wanted me to examine," she said, her usual smile disappearing from her face.

Starrett was relieved, very relieved, not only that the subject had been brought to the table, but also at the forthright way she had chosen to do so.

"The thing is," Starrett said, after the waitress had taken their order, "during that time someone came back into my life."

"Ah," Dr Aljoe said. "Right, that figures. Has anything happened between the pair of you yet?"

"No. Nothing at all. In fact, far from it," Starrett protested. "She walked out on a meal I prepared for her."

"But there's a chance that in the future . . ."

"Well, if I'm being *very* honest here, because of my previous behaviour, nothing is likely to happen."

"I see," Aljoe said, a faint hint of a smile washing over her face. "Mysterious *and* honourable. I do like a man with a past, you know. Most women do. Most mothers, on the other hand, don't. Unless of course they're involved with the man with a past themselves."

"Agreed."

"So, you're reluctant to let anything further happen between us for fear she might come back to you?"

Their food arrived and the question was left hanging in the air between them.

"Yes," was all he said once the waitress had left them to their food, although when she'd asked the question, he had planned to offer a fuller explanation.

"Don't you see all of this is making you even more attractive?" Aljoe said, enthusiastically starting on her food. She seemed to Starrett to be a woman who was enthusiastic about everything. "You know, you could have let things reach their natural predicted conclusion between you and me, and then just disappeared from the scene?"

"Ach, sure," Starrett said, in effect saying nothing.

"I suppose part of me wishes that's what you had done."

"But only until such a time as I would have behaved like the cad you're describing. Then you would have felt totally different about me and about my taking advantage of you," Starrett said, playing with his food. "Besides which, there are two other mitigating circumstances."

"Two, Starrett?"

"You and I will continue to come into professional contact, and I have to try to behave properly, for once."

"Yes, I see. Equally, from what you're telling me, it seems there is a chance that this other woman won't come running to you. In fact, I suppose we could speculate that there's an equal chance that she might even meet someone else and go off and marry him. Then you could come knocking on my door again."

"Yes, but with my luck there'd be an equally good chance that you'd also have met and married someone else as well."

"True, very true," she said, appearing to enjoy that scenario. "But maybe you should still promise me that if plan A doesn't work out, you'll still, at the very least, come knocking on my door, if only to check on my marital status. You've got to promise at least to give me the pleasure of shooting you down, Starrett."

"I promise," Starrett said, wondering why she had to look so beautiful during such a conversation.

"In the meantime, Starrett, I'd still like to be your friend. I enjoy your company and," she said, placing her fork in the middle of her curry and rubbing her hand affectionately on the back of Starrett's hand, "I do genuinely . . . like you . . . and, besides which, if I hang out with you, people will think I'm a lot younger than I am."

Her mobile phone rang a subtle tone and saved Starrett any further embarrassment. She bent her head low, finger in her free ear, and stared at the table as she listened intently.

"Yes . . . OK . . . understood. Thank you, Adhemar, good work. I'm nearly done here. I'll see you soon."

"Well, it's third time lucky for you, Starrett. The man with the piebald hair was indeed the father of Amanda Morrison's unborn child."

Chapter Forty-Seven

INSTEAD OF TAKING the main road back to Ramelton, Starrett veered off to the right just before the Silver Tassie, nearly opposite Colm Donovan's yard, and headed down towards the water. Although he'd made a bit of a show with Dr Aljoe of having to get back to Ramelton as quickly as possible, he really was in no real hurry now. Two important things had been resolved in the last half hour.

Firstly, he now knew who had murdered James Moore, and he wanted to spend time reflecting on Moore's life and his family and his strange bunch of friends. He needed to work out exactly how he could bring the case to a successful conclusion. It was one thing to know who the murderer was; it was quite another to prove that fact beyond all reasonable doubt.

Secondly, he wanted to consider what he'd just resolved with Dr Sam Aljoe. All things considered, that had gone quite well. Number one, she'd introduced the subject, and number two, she seemed to have taken it well. Heck, maybe she realised she'd be better off without him anyway. At least she'd made a bit of a show about being upset about it, and at their farewell on the steps of Letterkenny General Hospital, she'd given him a warm hug and kissed him fully on the lips. It would be just his luck if Maggie Keane's mysterious source of information had been observing them and rushed off to spill the beans.

Would he and Dr Aljoe remain friends? Hopefully, he thought. After all, at the very least, they were going to be working together, and there was still something about her that intrigued him.

He wondered how his relationship with Samantha Aljoe would have developed if it hadn't been for Maggie Keane's albeit brief reappearance. Was their relationship over just because he said it was? Was it really as easy as that? Had people total control over who they had relationships with?

He thought back to an instance other than his own, when he had asked Garvey about a budding relationship he had been having. When asked if he thought it was going to work out, Garvey had replied, "No, I don't think so." Did that mean that the relationship was doomed to failure? he asked himself, as he pulled up by the graveyard at Killydonnell Friary. Starrett's big question to himself as he looked out over the Swilly back towards Scalp Mountains was, "Is a relationship bigger than the two people involved in it?"

Starrett repeated his question to himself: Was his relationship with Aljoe over just because he said it was? That certainly hadn't been a kiss of friendship she'd given him as a goodbye kiss on the steps outside the Letterkenny General Hospital. Perhaps she just wanted to let him know what he was going to be missing.

Where in relationships does it start to go horribly wrong?

Take James Moore and Amanda Morrison, for instance. Amanda married someone for money, status and security. James married someone because he was too weak to say no. Both marriages were doomed to failure. Amanda, young, beautiful and frisky, started to take lovers. She kept her extramarital relationships discreet and far away from her husband's parish. Then, in a moment of weakness, she became involved with a local builder, Colm Donovan. On a sidebar, Starrett wondered what exactly First Minister Ivan Morrison had meant when he'd said that the tape-recording of Amanda and Colm making love made the one of Amanda and James Moore sound like a kindergarten tea-party? What exactly had been captured on tape? Whatever had happened, they'd certainly been lovers and she'd fallen pregnant with Donovan's child. James Moore, on the other hand, had remained faithful in a loveless marriage with Nora.

Then both their worlds meet. A seemingly mild-mannered man is drawn towards a serial adulteress and sex-siren, and they experience, by all accounts, genuine love.

They start to deal with it, but are powerless to prevent the fallout they are creating around them. The wronged husband, Ivan Morrison, becomes aware of the relationship and realises that this time it *is* different. If the wronged wife, Nora Moore, already a bit of a casualty herself, doesn't find fulfilment in the bulky arms of her childhood sweetheart, she certainly finds the comfort there that she needs. Then there is the discarded lover, Colm Donovan. Donovan quite simply can't deal with the fact that he's lost his sexual partner. Given another six months, their relationship would probably have just fizzled out when they grew bored of each other sexually, but that hadn't been allowed to happen. Now, as a result, two people are dead, and the lives of several others will never be the same again. And it could all be traced back to the moment James Moore went into Betsy Bell's house to rebuild her kitchen.

As Starrett walked back to his car, he wondered if all the players in the drama had been powerless to change the events and their outcome. Then he thought about Maggie Keane, Samantha Aljoe and himself; how would that one resolve itself?

He wondered how quietly Colm Donovan would come in the end.

Chapter Forty-Eight

STARRETT FELT AS if he'd nearly reached the last chapter of a book, but unless he fully understood everything that had occurred before, the ending would be meaningless.

Fortunately, by the time he returned to Tower House, Sergeant Packie Garvey, Bean Gharda Nuala Gibson and Garda Francis Casey were already making great progress on the contents of the incinerator.

They discovered a belt buckle, a US Marshal's one, just like the type Chris Moore said his father wore. They discovered several metal buttons with the Levi lettering, just like the ones that had been stitched on to the denim shirts Chris and his brother and sister had bought their father two Christmases before, and which, at the time of his death, had been part of the carpenter's daily uniform. They discovered two metal toecaps exactly like the ones used on Timberland boots; moreover, one of them had a severe dint in it, a dint which could have been caused by a scaffolding pole falling directly on to it, a scaffolding pole like the one that had fallen on James Moore's foot the day he rescued his friend Dan McGuinness.

Starrett went to his office and wrote up his crime book. That done, he returned to the interview room to visit a very subdued Ivan Morrison. Starrett explained to him that he had to detain the first minister for his own safety and that he was no longer under suspicion. Morrison asked only that Starrett inform Betsy Bell of his whereabouts: he felt that she might be concerned about him.

Next, Starrett visited Major Newton Cunningham and presented the details of his case.

The inspector was in no hurry to pick up Colm Donovan. He knew that as long as Donovan thought Ivan Morrison was in the frame and under the spotlight, the builder would feel comfortable. He picked up the pieces of evidence Garvey and the team had recovered from Donovan's incinerator, cleaned them up and placed them in plastic evidence bags.

Starrett and Garvey then drove down to the Moore household in Downings. Most of the journey passed in silence, save for Garvey saying, "I still find it hard to believe that Colm Donovan could crucify a fellow human being."

"Does that mean you accept that he could *murder* another man? It's just that you don't think he could have crucified him?"

"But jeez, Inspector, nailing a man to a cross—good God, what's that all about?"

Starrett didn't reply; he was preparing himself for meeting the Moores.

Dan McGuinness was installed in the Moore kitchen, as were Nora and Chris, who, after the initial greetings, said, "You've solved the case, haven't you? You know who killed my father?"

"We've a little way to go yet."

"But you have someone in mind?"

"Yes, we do," Starrett replied.

"But you won't tell me who he is yet, will you?"

"No, Chris. We need to be 100 per cent sure," Starrett replied. "We need you to look at these thing, please, and see if you can identify them."

Garvey placed the plastic evidence bags on the centre of the kitchen table.

"Ah, no . . . it's my dad's belt buckle," Chris Moore said, slumping down on the chair in front of the table. Tears streamed down his face, and then he started to sob.

The boy searched though the remainder of the evidence bags, the crinkling of the bags and his sobbing the only sounds in the kitchen. Dan McGuinness waddled over towards Chris. His large hand dwarfed the boy as he touched his shoulder in comfort. Nora did the same on the other shoulder. Chris was biting hard on his lips as he turned to face his mam, holding an evidence bag up towards her. "Mam . . ." he started.

"I know, Chris," Nora said, letting go of her son's shoulder and walking over to the airing cupboard beside the fireplace. From inside it she produced a freshly pressed denim shirt, which she handed to Starrett.

"Could I possibly borrow it for a few days?" Starrett asked.

"Yes, if it helps, but could you please look after it for us?"

"Right, yes, of course," Starrett said, walking back to the table and sitting down beside the boy. "Chris, I need you to know how important the information you gave me when we had our chat down on the beach, and out in your father's shed, was. All the stuff you remembered was invaluable to us."

Dan McGuinness stood fast with his hand on the boy's shoulder. Starrett rose, and Nora took his place at the table.

As he and Garvey were about to pull out of the drive, Chris came rushing out of the house, furiously wiping his eyes. He ran over to Starrett's side of the car, the passenger side. Starrett wound down the window, and Chris put his hand through it in order to shake his hand.

"I just wanted to say thank you, thank you both," Chris said, stooping slightly so he was addressing Garvey as well. "Thank you both for working so hard on my father's case."

"Fair play to you, Chris," Starrett said from his heart. "As I said, we couldn't have done it without you."

Chris Moore, now the man of the Moore household, stood back from the car. He waved them goodbye with one hand and dried his eyes with the other.

Chapter Forty-Nine

COLM DONOVAN WAS picked up without fuss at his house. Garvey told Starrett that Donovan seemed more amused than concerned.

By the time Donovan was led into the interview room, Starrett had laid the evidence bags carefully out on the table before him. Starrett had also placed Moore's freshly pressed denim shirt in a large evidence bag.

Donovan clocked the belt buckle immediately, but didn't say a word.

"How can I help you?" Donovan asked Starrett before he'd even sat down.

The inspector nodded to Garvey to commence proceedings officially by turning on the recorder and announcing the date, Tuesday 7 June; the time, 16.45; and those present: Colm Donovan, Sergeant Packie Garvey and Inspector Starrett.

"Colm, would you like your solicitor present?" Garvey asked immediately.

"Sure, what would I need a solicitor for?" he replied through an awkward smile.

Starrett found it hard to believe that people still insisted on refusing a solicitor in the hope that such an action might send out an "I don't need a solicitor therefore I've got nothing to hide" message.

Starrett decided to avoid the dance of trying to trap Donovan in a game of words.

"Colm, we know you had an affair with Mrs Morrison," he stated for the record.

"Aye, me and Jimmy both."

"And, of course, you know that Mrs Morrison was pregnant?"

Colm moved around in his chair, not exactly looking uncomfortable. He was leaning back in it, with Starrett stretched over the table that separated them. The detective was so tight up to the table, he was barely sitting on his chair.

"We know that you were the father of her child, Colm," Starrett said.

This statement hit the intended button.

Donovan tightened his jaw. He pushed his chair further back from the table with his feet and removed the pack of Camels from his sleeve, offering them to Garvey.

"I'm sorry," said Garvey, directing his words as much at Starrett as at Donovan, "but there's no smoking allowed."

Starrett said, "Colm, can you tell me what you were doing between the hours of 22.00 on Thursday 2 June and 02.00 on Friday 3 June, just gone?"

Donovan looked at Garvey, and at Starrett; then he turned his attention to the evidence bags spread out on the table in front of him. He looked at the tape-recorder, before looking back at Starrett. The inspector had very non-judgemental, compassionate eyes and a way of looking at people that made them feel that he completely understood them. Starrett and Donovan remained locked in a stare, as the clock on the wall ticked loudly.

Finally Donovan spoke: "I was crucifying Jimmy Moore."

Chapter Fifty

"OK," STARRETT SIGHED. "Let's stop for a moment here and get you a solicitor."

"And my priest, please," Donovan added immediately.

As Starrett awaited the solicitor and the priest, he kept his crooked and lucky fingers crossed and prayed that Donovan would need such an absolution that he would provide the details on tape.

Twenty minutes later, local solicitor Russell Leslie and Donovan's parish priest, Father Paul Flynn, joined the original trio.

Garvey made a fresh announcement for the benefit of the recorder, and Starrett said, "OK, Colm, where did you first see James Moore on the evening of Thursday last?"

"I saw him when he entered the Manse," Donovan replied.

"What time would that have been?"

"I'd say somewhere between eight-fifteen and eight-thirty."

"Where were you exactly when you spotted James Moore entering the Manse?"

"I was parked in St Mary's Terrace, across from Mortimer's Lane."

"Did he see you at that time?"

"No. He came up from the bottom of Mortimer's Lane. He always parked down outside Conway's pub."

"Were you hanging around on the off chance he might show up?"

"No, I'd just been in to see Amanda."

"Oh?" Starrett said in genuine surprise.

"I'd been in to see her to try and talk some sense into her,"

Donovan said. "Aye, she was a beautiful woman and all, but she could be shirty enough when she wanted to be. She was scared I was going to ruin her romantic candlelight dinner with Jimmy, so she was keen to get me out of the way. Jimmy was my replacement, you see, but I never for one moment believed that they would ever get it together."

At this point, Father's Flynn's eyebrows reached towards the faraway heavens.

"How did you and she meet?"

"When I was working for Betsy Bell's husband, Billy. After we chatted a few times, she made no bones about the fact that she wanted me and . . ." Donovan paused to steal a brief glance at Father Flynn before continuing, ". . . she asked me to come up to the Manse and unblock one of her drains."

Russell Leslie rolled his eyes, as Father Flynn crossed himself.

"How long ago would this have been?"

"Oh, maybe as much as a year ago."

"And when did it finish?" Starrett asked

"About three months ago."

"But when I first interviewed you," Garvey said, "you told us Jimmy was having an affair with Amanda at that point."

"Yes, well, I wasn't exactly going to admit to you that I was having an affair with Amanda, was I? There was an overlap where I was still riding her, even though she was growing interested in Jimmy. They hadn't done anything at that stage, of course. But then, when they started, didn't he only come and blabber to me about it?"

"So, even when we questioned you first, you were trying to put First Minister Morrison in the frame for James' murder?" Starrett suggested.

"Trying," Donovan admitted. "Anyway, she told me to get out. She told me Jimmy was coming around for dinner. She told me if I didn't leave her alone, she would make sure Betsy and some of her other friends would never use me to do work for them again. It all got a bit ugly. Don't get me wrong, I'd never hit a woman, but we were shouting and screaming at each other. I told her she was going to seed and that she'd better watch out or she'd lose her man. She patted her stomach and said, "This is not fat: this is a child, Jimmy's child." She told me they were going off together and that was it and to get out. I knew it wasn't Jimmy's child; it was my child. Aye, Starrett, I knew it was my child."

"How did you know that?" Starrett asked.

"I knew," said Donovan, "because Jimmy had had the snip. He'd said he quite simply didn't want to have any more children with Nora, so he'd taken the best precaution."

Father Flynn crossed himself again.

"When she told me she was pregnant," Donovan continued through his now permanent pained expression, "it really took the wind out of my sails. I didn't have the stomach for an argument any more. I let her throw me out, and then I saw Jimmy go into the Manse about twenty minutes later. I sat in my car fuming, and I waited until Jimmy came out."

"What time would that have been?" Starrett asked.

"Just before eleven o'clock."

"And then?" Starrett prompted.

"Then I steamed down Mortimer's Lane after him in my car. I pulled up beside him, opened the passenger door and offered him a lift. I was so fecking mad I was barely able to contain myself."

"Aren't you meant to caution your client about saying anything incriminating?" Father Flynn interrupted, addressing Russell Leslie.

"No, I'm just meant to ensure that there are no legal irregularities or improprieties taking place during the interview. So far, everything has been done by the book," the well-dressed solicitor replied.

Donovan ignored the interruption and carried on: "I told him that he had to stop seeing Amanda or else I was going to tell Nora. He told me that he and Amanda had decided to give their relationship a proper go and that he was about to tell Nora himself. And I lost it. I stopped the van just outside the library, and I hit him so *fecking* hard with a base-ball bat I kept beside me in the seat that he was knocked out. I sat there for a while. I don't know how long I waited for him to come around, but he didn't, though he still had a pulse. So I drove back up towards the house, and I started to worry that as he'd been out for so long, I'd probably done him brain damage. I was worried he was going to die on me and that I'd go away for ever. Then I had a thought: if Jimmy was dying or dead, maybe I'd be able to win Amanda back. I only needed to prove to her that I was the father of her child. Then my brain just went off on one. I had an idea of how I could get rid of that pompous idiot, the blasted first minister, at the same time. I'd crucify Jimmy in Morrison's church. At the same time, I felt that I was making an example of Jimmy *and* I'd be able to remove any evidence connecting myself. A double-whammy, you could say. So, I drove back to my yard—"

"Any idea what time this would have been?" Starrett interrupted.

"I'd say we're well after midnight by this time."

"And Jimmy still hadn't come around?"

"No. He was out cold, but still showing a pulse. I picked up some wood, rope, barbed-wire, nails, as well as the tools I figured I'd need. I drove back into Ramelton and, as usual, the Second Federation Church's doors were unlocked. I carried Jimmy and my stuff into the church and laid him out in front of the pulpit. Then I locked the door from the inside."

Father Flynn crossed himself again.

"Then I said to myself, 'What the feck do you think you're doing here?' I said, 'Cop yourself on, Colm.' And I gave up on the idea of killing him. And then, maybe because I'd moved him, he started to come around, to make gurgling sounds. Then blood started to come out of his mouth. I started to panic. I though he was going to die, so I went back to my original plan. He was still making gurgling noises, so I tore off all of his clothes. I tied a couple of my wife's chamois about him as a loincloth. I got a lot of gip from the wife over nicking her chamois. She missed them immediately when she next went to clean our windows."

"Aye, right," Starrett said.

"I turned him over and I used his belt to lash him about the back. Honestly, Starrett, it was like I was watching someone else whip him. I fell in a right old rage at him. My heart wasn't really in the first few strokes of the belt. Then I started to grow angrier at Amanda and what they'd been doing together, and it was like a frenzy just took me over."

"Ah God, Colm son. What's to become of you?" Father Flynn said.

Donovan didn't so much as glance at the priest, before carrying on, "When he was lying on the floor, I got one of the bits of wood and whacked him across both legs to break them. I nailed two pieces of wood together to make a cross, and I nailed Jimmy to it. God forgive me, but that's what I did. I remember thinking at the time that I was behaving too calmly for what I was doing. I can remember being surprised by how easily the nails sank into him. I wrapped the barbed wire around in a circle and put it on his head and I drove it deep down into his scalp. I'm not proud of it now, but I whipped him again. I kept thinking that the closer I could make it appear to Jesus' crucifixion, the more likely it was that Ivan Morrison would be suspected. Jimmy was still out cold, and there was fecking blood everywhere. I struggled to put the cross up, and then, once I'd finally got it in position, I had to take it down again because it was too unsteady. I had to nip out to the van and get some rope to fix the cross to the pulpit." Donovan stopped talking as if he was just realising for the first time what he'd done.

He continued in a whisper: "Then I took one of my long wood chisels and I stabbed him through the heart to put him out of his misery."

Starrett knew that Donovan had battered the body of James Moore a lot more than he was admitting.

"Aye, I thought I'd looked after it all. I rang her on her mobile, after you found the body. She was up at Betsy's. I wanted her back. I told her she was having my child. I explained to her how I knew that Jimmy couldn't father children any more. But then," Donovan said, "I obviously drove her over the edge. She had to go and jump in the water and kill herself and the babby too. I'll never forgive myself for that." He stopped and seemed to be searching his mind for some kind of reason, something that would explain it all. All he was able to come up with was, "If only she'd left it alone and stayed with me, none of this would have happened."

"If only you'd stayed with your wife," Father Flynn said.

Chapter Fifty-One

DONOVAN WAS LED away by Garvey to be processed and charged. His solicitor tagged along, presumably to make sure everything was done by the book.

Starrett noted how everyone in Tower House looked at and treated Donovan differently now from how they'd looked at and treated him a mere hour and ten minutes earlier, when he'd first entered the building. Then he'd been just a local builder. Now he was a self-confessed murderer, and a murderer who'd crucified his victim. Gardaí young and old, men and women alike, were stealing second looks at him now, trying to figure out how an ordinary builder from the townland of Ramelton had nailed a fellow human being to a cross.

Starrett supposed that even murderers had to come from somewhere. They had to be born into some family; someone had to be their father, their mother, brother, sister, wife, son and daughter. In the coming months, all of these people and all of Donovan's life would be put under the spotlight, as each in turn tried to reach some understanding as to why human beings are driven to murder.

Starrett's take was that murderers are largely frightening because there is no logical understanding as to why they do what they do. Even Donovan, in a cool, calm and collected way, had described to his priest, his solicitor, and arresting members of the Garda Síochána how he'd watched a detached version of himself whipping and—eventually—killing his former friend, James Moore.

Starrett walked Father Flynn up to the front door.

"How did you know it was him?" Flynn asked, once they'd reached the high steps of Tower House.

"Oh, lots of things," Starrett said with a sigh. "Well, there were his wife's missing chamois, and we found Moore's wedding ring in Morrison's study, but only after Donovan had tipped us off to go looking for something else in the same room."

"Planted?"

"Yes," Starrett agreed. "You see, Donovan had also done some work in the Manse and would most certainly have known his way around the place. Maybe he was even able to copy a key." Starrett stopped there. He and the priest watched as a dog waddled across Gamble Square, totally unperturbed as two cars swerved and braked hard to avoid it.

Village disasters averted, Starrett continued, "Anyway, there was one thing that kept niggling away at me. I kept coming back to the point that if the first minister had murdered James Moore and if he'd wanted to make it look like the crucifixion of Jesus Christ, then he most certainly wouldn't have broken James Moore's legs."

"Good point, Starrett," Flynn said. "First Minister Morrison, for all his earthly faults, is well-read in the scriptures, as you appear to be yourself."

Starrett ignored the compliment. He was thinking that pretty soon James Moore and Colm Donovan would achieve a degree of notoriety. Maybe there'd even be documentaries; maybe the ex-lovers, husbands and wives of all the principals in the drama would be selling their stories to the tabloids.

As if reading his mind, Father Flynn said, "I'd better head back home and change into my good suit, ready for the interviews."

Chapter Fifty-Two

ON THE SATURDAY night, two and a half weeks later, Starrett was having a quiet early drink in the Bridge Bar. Newspaper articles concerning the crucifixion of James Moore had largely run their course. The last of the big media wagons had pulled out of Ramelton, and things were returning . . . well, not so much to normal, as to how they'd been before the crucifixion.

Starrett was enjoying a drink with two mates, John McIvor and James McDaid, when he noticed a couple he recognised. He went over to them.

"Mr and Mrs Gallagher," he said, shaking their hands.

"Please call us Ivor and Patricia."

"I will, indeed I will," Starrett smiled, using his pint of Guinness to point around the bar. "I see you're settling well into village life. How's it going?"

"Aye, well," Ivor said, "I've got as much work as I can handle."

"And more than that," his wife said. "I haven't seen him an awful lot since we arrived here."

"Oh, Ivor, be careful about that," Starrett cautioned. "It's not a village to leave a beautiful wife unattended in."

"Oh, we're OK now," she said, snuggling up close to her husband and embarrassing him slightly. "We've got him all to ourselves for this entire weekend."

"Good," Starrett said. "I'll leave youse to it."

On the way back to his traditional back corner of the bar, Starrett spotted Nuala Gibson and Francis Casey enjoying a wee drink over by the stage area. He stood them a round and exchanged pleasantries with them. As he walked away he thought he heard Nuala say something about, "a friend of yours", but the noise of the bar drowned her voice out. He just rejoined his mates, and they picked up their conversation about classic cars, Formula One, Eddie Irvine and American West Coast contemporary music.

About thirty minutes later, they were interrupted by a quiet, almost apologetic, "Excuse me?"

McIvor said, "Not a bother, what can we do for you?" and he rubbed his hands together grocer style.

Starrett was looking at McDaid and McIvor, and the intruder was standing to his right, but out of his line of vision.

"Excuse me," the gentle voice said again, this time adding, "Starrett."

Then he recognised the sound, the scent and the presence beside him: it was Maggie Keane.

"Ah, Maggie," Starrett said, turning, and she leaned her cheek to him to receive his kiss.

"It's good to see you again."

"It's good to see you too," Starrett replied.

She was dressed in a black, figure-hugging trouser suit and white shirt. With her long, dark hair and her eyes of blue, she looked simply beautiful. She tried a smile, but it didn't work too well, so she reverted to her usual serious look.

"Ah, sorry, forgive me," Starrett said, taking his hand from the small of her back where it had been resting since he had kissed her on the cheek. "These boyos are two members of the James gang, John and James."

"Our big brother Jesse is at home tonight washing his nylons," McDaid said, and offered hands were duly shaken.

"This is Maggie Keane," Starrett said.

"Pleased to meet you," Maggie said, shaking McDaid's hand more enthusiastically. "Goodness, you must be very old if you know what nylons are, I believe they went out with de Valera."

"Aye, gone but never forgotten," McDaid said wistfully, as McIvor and Starrett cracked up.

"What can I get you to drink, Maggie?" Starrett asked, using the opportunity of the question to put his hand back on the small of her back.

She answered so quietly that Starrett had to say, "Sorry," and lean his ear in very close to her mouth.

She blew gently into his ear, and the thrill it sent from the tip of his toes to the crown of his black-haired head nearly buckled his legs from under him. When he turned to look at her, she winked wickedly and mouthed the words "red wine".

Bríd, the owner of the Bridge Bar, passed by the four of them and looked twice before saying, "My goodness, Maggie Keane. How are you doing? It's certainly been a long, long while since we've seen youse two in here together."

At which point McIvor and McDaid looked at each other in a Laurel and Hardy moment, then turned back towards the bar and, in a display of synchronised drinking, took generous sips of their Guinness.

Maggie wasn't a great shouter, so Starrett suggested they go outside on to the pavement, where they could at least hear themselves think. The pavement was, as usual, packed with smokers, and as Starrett stole a glance at Maggie's perfectly formed, Ferrari-red lips, he regretted the last Player he'd smoked. Coincidentally, it was also the final cigarette in the stash Garvey had been holding for him. He resolved, as never before, to quit smoking. They crossed the road, away from the smokers, and sat on the low wall, which bordered the road from the steep drop down to the River Lennon.

Starrett was dressed in his regular outfit of black leather shoes and tailored trousers, topped off with a pink shirt and dark blue American-style windbreaker.

"I'm sorry about the other morning," she said once they'd settled.

"Ach, not a bother," Starrett replied, sipping at his Guinness. "It was great to see you again, no matter how brief the visit."

"I just found myself slipping back into that couples thing with you again, and I had this flash of betraying my husband."

"But sure it was only a bite of breakfast."

"But I was very comfortable with you in your house, Starrett, and that scared me, that's all," she said, and took a good gulp of her wine.

"Maggie, it was really great to see you again and spend a little time with you. I dreamt for so long about seeing you again and what we'd do and what we'd say . . ." Starrett paused, picking his next words carefully. "I don't want to scare you away again or anything, but I really would like us to be . . ."

"To be something again?" she prompted.

"To be something again," he agreed. "*I'm* not even sure what, but I'll take a wee bit of seeing you, over not seeing you at all, every time."

Maggie Keane was sitting so close to him that he could feel her ribs against him; he could smell her. She was looking down to the ground. Her jet-black hair fell about her shoulders, obscuring her face and eyes from him. As far as he could tell, she was comfortable sitting there beside him.

If the truth be told, she wasn't entirely relaxed, maybe even a little ill-at-ease, but inside her heart, there was basically contentment. She looked as if she'd returned home. She might not be staying long, but at least for now, she was home.

"I hear you and the good doctor have stopped stepping out," she said.

He decided to say nothing and hid the space with another sip of Guinness. *God bless the Guinness*, he thought, *the saviour in millions of such tricky moments.*

Starrett was using his left hand to hold his glass. Maggie shifted her wine to her left hand and then lifted her other hand briefly, touching the back of his, as she turned slowly to look at him. He sensed the movement and moved slowly in her direction. She caught his eye and winked.

It was classic Maggie Keane: always her way of telling him that it was OK.

"You've still got kind hands, Starrett," she said, lifting his hand in her own. "I see your crooked finger . . ."

"Is still crooked?"

"Well, yes," she agreed.

They sat for a while like that, content in each other's company and not needing to say anything, maybe even a little scared of saying the wrong thing.

Eventually Maggie spoke: "Starrett, you know I didn't bump into you by accident tonight. There was something I wanted to ask you."

"Oh?"

"Yes, I wanted to know if you would come to a party?"

"Bejeepers, aye, you can count me in," Starrett said enthusiastically. "What are we celebrating?"

"It's Joe's twentieth birthday, and he's humouring me by having a 'do' for the family at the house before he goes off with his mates somewhere for a proper party."

She seemed to sense his unease. Resting her hands back on his knees, she said, "Joe, Moya and Katie have all heard about you, Starrett. Niall was a big fan of your detective work, so you're a bit of a legend with the kids in our house. They still follow your career."

"Bejeepers," was all Starrett could say.

"I told them I was going to invite you to Joe's party, as my date, and they're all very excited about the chance to meet you."

"As your date, eh?"

"Yes, Starrett, my date."

"I'll need to check my diary," he replied.

"I'll take that as a yes, then? Listen, Starrett, I'll let you get back to your mates. I'm off with Nuala and Francis for dinner at An Bonnán Buí down in Rathmullan."

"Great food," he said.

"Right," Maggie said, walking back across the road. "I'll say goodbye here."

As she started to give him an awkward hug, Starrett took her in his arms and pulled her towards him. She came willingly, and the two of them stood there amongst the smokers for a few seconds, happily hugging each other.

Starrett had the feeling that she would have stayed in his arms for ever. As they pulled away from each other, she looked him straight in the eye and winked.

PAUL CHARLES
Sweetwater
"Almost like an Inspector Morse without the irascibility and lovelorn aspirations...The puzzle slowly fits together, exposing a rich pageant of human relationships. An exemplary case for the quiet sleuth of British crime fiction." Maxim Jakubowski, *Guardian*
ISBN 978-0-86322-367-9

JACK BARRY
Miss Katie Regrets
From Dublin's criminal underbelly comes a gripping story of guns, drugs, prostitution and corruption. At the centre of a spider's web of intrigue sits the enigmatic figure of Miss Katie, a crabby transvestite who will, under pressure, kiss and tell. And, perhaps, kill.
ISBN 978-0-86322-354-9

SAM MILLAR
The Redemption Factory
"While most writers sit in their study and make it up, Sam Millar has lived it and every sentence... evokes a searing truth about men, their dark past, and the code by which they live. Great title, great read. Disturbingly brutal. I enjoyed it immensely."
Cyrus Nowrasteh
ISBN 978-0-86322-339-6

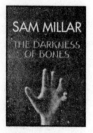

SAM MILLAR
The Darkness of Bones
In a derelict orphanage, a tramp discovers the mutilated and decapitated corpse of its former head warden. Millar's second crime novel is a tense tale of murder, betrayal, sexual abuse and revenge, and the corruption at the heart of the respectable establishment.
ISBN 978-0-86322-350-1

KEN BRUEN
WINNER OF THE SHAMUS AND MACAVITY AWARDS FOR BEST NOVEL, WINNER OF THE CRIME WRITERS ASSOCIATION OF AMERICA BEST SERIES AWARD FOR THE JACK TAYLOR NOVELS

The Guards "Bleak, amoral and disturbing, *The Guards* breaks new ground in the Irish thriller genre, replacing furious fantasy action with acute observation of human frailty." *Irish Independent* "With Jack Taylor, Bruen has created a true original." *Sunday Tribune*
ISBN 978-0-86322-323-5

The Killing of the Tinkers
"Jack Taylor is back in town, weighed down with wisecracks and cocaine ... Somebody is murdering young male travellers and Taylor, with his reputation as an outsider, is the man they want to get to the root of things ... Compulsive ... rapid fire ... entertaining." *Sunday Tribune*
ISBN 978-0-86322-294-8

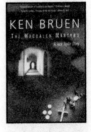

The Magdalen Martyrs
"Exhibits Ken Bruen's all-encompassing ability to depict the underbelly of the criminal world and still imbue it with a torrid fascination... carrying an adrenalin charge for those who like their thrillers rough, tough, mean and dirty." *The Irish Times*
ISBN 978-0-86322-302-0

The Dramatist
"Collectively, the Jack Taylor novels are Bruen's masterwork, and *The Dramatist* is the darkest and most profound installment of the series to date... Readers who dare the journey will be days shaking this most haunting book out of their heads."
This Week
ISBN 978-0-86322-319-8

KEN BRUEN (ED)
Dublin Noir

Brand new stories by Ray Banks, James O. Born, Ken Bruen, Reed Farrell Coleman, Eoin Colfer, Jim Fusilli, Patrick J. Lambe, Laura Lippman, Craig McDonald, Pat Mullan, Gary Phillips, John Rickards, Peter Spiegelman, Jason Starr, Olen Steinhauer, Charlie Stella, Duane Swierczynski, Sarah Weinman and Kevin Wignall.
ISBN 978-0-86322-353-2

KITTY FITZGERALD
Small Acts of Treachery

"Mystery and politics, a forbidden sexual attraction that turns into romance; Kitty Fitzgerald takes the reader on a gripping roller coaster through the recent past. This is a story you can't stop reading, with an undertow which will give you cause to reflect." Sheila Rowbotham
ISBN 978-0-86322-297-9

J.S. COOK
A Cold-Blooded Scoundrel
An Inspector Devlin Mystery

In London, at a time when Jack the Ripper is still fresh in the memory, a well-known male prostitute is brutally murdered, the head neatly severed, and the body set on fire.
ISBN 978-0-86322-336-5

EVELYN CONLON
Skin of Dreams

"A courageous, intensely imagined and tightly focused book that asks powerful questions of authority... this is the kind of Irish novel that is all too rare." Joseph O'Connor
ISBN 978-0-86322-306-8